An inconvenient engagement turns a marriage of convenience into so much more in this sparkling new series from award-winning author Sara Portman . . .

Lady Emmaline Shaw's reputation was irreparably damaged when her fiancé, John Brantwood, disappeared immediately after their engagement four years ago. Since then, she's grown from a shy, uncertain girl to a woman who knows her own mind. And what she knows is that London society holds nothing for her.

Rumor has it that John ran off to war and died in battle. Now, as the new Duke of Worley, his shocking resurrection throws the *ton* into a tizzy and makes him one of England's most sought after bachelors—except that he's already engaged.

John needs a wife capable of smoothing his beloved sister's introduction into society. But though Emma happily grants him his freedom, her fiery beauty and resilient spirit hold him captive. In fact, John has no intention of letting her go. Her fate is now in his hands, but will her heart be safe there as well?

The Reunion

The Brides of Beadwell

Sara Portman

LYRICAL PRESS
Kensington Publishing Corp.
www.kensingtonbooks.com

LYRICAL PRESS BOOKS are published by

Kensington Publishing Corp.
119 West 40th Street
New York, NY 10018

All Kensington titles, imprints, and distributed lines are available at special quantity discounts for bulk purchases for sales promotion, premiums, fundraising, educational, or institutional use.

Special book excerpts or customized printings can also be created to fit specific needs. For details, write or phone the office of the Kensington Sales Manager: Kensington Publishing Corp., 119 West 40th Street, New York, NY 10018. Attn. Sales Department. Phone: 1-800-221-2647.

Lyrical Press and Lyrical Press logo Reg. U.S. Pat. & TM Off.

First Electronic Edition: September 2017
eISBN-13: 978-1-5161-0049-1
eISBN-10: 1-5161-0049-2

First Print Edition: September 2017
ISBN-13: 978-1-5161-0052-1
ISBN-10: 1-5161-0052-2

Printed in the United States of America

For Millie, because I was genetically predisposed to do this.

Chapter One

Resurrections can be dreadfully disconcerting.

London society had weathered all manner of scandals and while each new transgression never failed to result in heads bent in hushed whispers and even the occasional matronly gasp, few incidents inspired waves of true shock among the *ton*. It appeared, however, that a duke's return from the dead was among these few scenarios able to truly discompose the titled elite.

With frustratingly little information available in the four weeks since the miraculous return of the Duke of Worley, rumors abounded regarding his whereabouts for the four years of his absence. Theories existed of such variety and outlandish improbability, it was impossible to determine which, if any, might hold a thread of truth.

Discussion of the duke's mysterious return dominated all society events, second only, of course, to conjecture on his marital state and physical appearance.

"I have heard he is only half a man," whispered Lady Grantham at one such event, "and had to be *carried* into his ancestral home because his legs were severed."

"That cannot be," insisted Lady Wolfe. "I have heard he is quite well, but has shamed his family by marrying an American actress and living abroad with her these past four years."

"You are both incorrect, I'm afraid," interjected their hostess, the Duchess of Fairhaven. "My son informed me just this morning that Worley has been gravely ill and is still now recovering. He hopes to be well enough before the end of the season to assume his responsibilities. My son attended Eton with him, you'll remember."

The other ladies nodded, neither one inclined to contradict the duchess, who outranked them by a significant margin. All three women understood without clarification that Worley's assumption of his responsibilities referred to the necessity to choose a bride. With four years wasted and his father now deceased, it was imperative he begin a family and continue the line. This was likely of particular interest to Lady Wolfe, whose daughter, Georgiana, was currently enjoying her *second* season in London, much to her mother's dismay and her father's expense.

It was not of particular interest, however, to Lady Emmaline Shaw. She'd had the unfortunate luck to step out onto the terrace for a spot of privacy and fresh air mere moments before the gaggle of clucking matrons proceeded to congregate just inside the only set of French doors that would allow her to return to the ballroom. She didn't want to hear another word about the elusive Duke of Worley, amazingly returned from the dead after four years missing. She cursed the unfortunate timing that placed her in London on the occasion of his reappearance. She was only in the city for one month out of the year, and only then to appease her aunt. Couldn't the man have selected any of the other eleven months for his triumphant return, when she would be safely ensconced at her cottage? She rubbed her bare arms against the evening breeze and prayed for the gossiping ladies to move their conversation elsewhere. She considered simply excusing herself and walking through.

"You realize, of course," Lady Wolfe whispered conspiratorially, "what a tangle this creates for the unfortunate Lady Emmaline Shaw."

Emma stepped deeper into the shadow and tossed out the idea of charging through their conversation.

"I would hardly call the girl unfortunate," the duchess said sharply. "Her conduct over the past four years is the reason for her present lack of prospects. She's been naught but a burden to her aunt and uncle."

From the terrace, Emma's brow lifted.

"Not that I'll harbor any pity for that woman either," the duchess added. "To my mind, Lady Ridgley has failed in her responsibility by allowing her niece to behave as she has."

Emma pressed herself against the cold stone wall and fumed at the voices filtering out to her. She would accept their judgment as a predictable consequence of her choices, but she was incensed at their attack on her aunt, who had been a pillar of love and support after the death of her parents. These women had no intimate knowledge of Emma or her beloved aunt. They were certainly not in any position to pass judgment.

"One cannot question her decision to withdraw from society, really, for that first season," Lady Grantham ventured. "Grief can be so damaging, after all."

Well, thank you. Emma resolved to extend her kindness to Lady Grantham when next they met.

"It is only during the following *three* seasons, by my estimation," Lady Grantham continued, "that her behavior became truly insupportable."

Emma's fists clenched. *Humph. Insupportable, indeed.* It was not as though she'd spent the past three years gadding about society, engaging in flirtations and clandestine rendezvous. She'd simply chosen not to parade herself through an endless stream of social events to shop for a husband.

She'd done that once. And frankly, the experience left her with little desire to repeat it.

Emma mentally retracted her vow to make a friendly overture to Lady Grantham.

"Either way, the betrothal will have to be dealt with," the duchess concluded.

Lady Wolfe gasped. "You don't believe...they would still consider themselves...*engaged*?" The excitement of that delicious tidbit added a hint of tremor to her voice.

No! Stifling a gasp of her own, Emma reached a hand out and gripped the stone balustrade for support. It wasn't possible, was it?

"There's no question of him actually marrying the girl. Not now, anyway. But she'll have to be dealt with in some manner." The duchess sniffed importantly. "I expect she'll be difficult."

Well. That was just unfair. Emma stood in the shadowed corner of the terrace and glared in the direction of the unseen duchess. The Duchess of Fairhaven couldn't have any idea whether Emma would prove cooperative or difficult in regard to the issue of her prior betrothal.

How could the duchess know if *Emma* didn't know? Biting her lip, she cursed herself for not recognizing the complication on her own. Naively, she'd never even thought of it. Certainly, if anything ended a betrothal as neatly as a death, it was a presumed death, wasn't it? Of course they were not still engaged. It violated common sense. Why, she could very easily have been married to someone else. It had been *four years*, after all.

Admittedly, she'd been uncooperative that first season. She was only seventeen, and being forced to spend the summer attending parties in London rather than back home riding her horse had seemed more punishment than privilege. She'd never expected her father to take it upon himself to select a husband for her after only one season—particularly not one who so openly disliked her.

Then he disappeared. Presumed dead, they were told—killed in battle—when no one had even known he'd run off to the war. He was only Viscount Brantwood at that time, but his father's ill health was common knowledge. The shock at his running off to fight when the responsibilities of the dukedom loomed was eclipsed only by the shock of his death. All society mourned with the Duke of Worley who'd lost his wife and young daughter years before and had now lost his only son to the war.

Emma became infamous among the *ton* as the subject of the most notorious and dramatic rejection in recent memory, yet she was still expected to mourn the loss of her betrothed. In place of grief, she had felt…relief. The relief was accompanied by a horrendous guilt. She had dreaded marrying him, but she would never have wished for his death.

Then, in the year that followed, she'd lost her parents and her life had completely changed. Emma herself had changed over the past four years, but the girl she had been and the woman she had become had one important trait in common.

Neither one wanted to marry the Duke of Worley.

"Of course she'll be difficult," the duchess continued mercilessly. "She's no prospects, I'm sure."

"I believe there is someone actually." Lady Grantham's voice rose with the honor of holding information the duchess had not yet learned. "I have heard she is being courted by a widower—a Mr. Greystoke, I believe."

"Ah, yes, Mr. Greystoke," came Lady Wolfe's contribution. Emma would have wagered her dress that Lady Wolfe had never heard Mr. Greystoke's name before that very moment.

"So you can see my point," the duchess said, her tone ripe with disdain. "Her only suitor is an aging nobody. She will humiliate herself clinging to the chance to become a duchess."

"Will she refuse to break the engagement?" Lady Grantham asked.

"Of course," the duchess answered. "*He* cannot break the engagement. He is entirely reliant upon her to do the decent thing."

"He can't possibly consider her a desirable match."

Emma wasn't sure which of the ladies had spoken last, but the words spread relief through her body. Of course the matter of the betrothal contract would not be a problem. Wanting to thank the viper-tongued duchess and her cohorts, she realized her choice to shun society and become a veritable pariah over the past four years would be her salvation. The duke would seek her out and demand an immediate release from the contract, which she would grant.

Emma was no longer disturbed by the comments filtering to her through the open terrace doors. The very social unacceptability that fed their gossip would ensure her freedom. Determined to contribute to it, she stepped out of the shadow. Reaching up to smooth her twist of chestnut hair, Emma straightened her shoulders, lifted her chin, and charged into the room—straight through the gossiping matrons without nod or recognition to any of them.

The initial silence she inspired was quickly replaced with a chorus of gasps, disapproving clucks, and even one "Oh, my," as she walked away. Her back to the ladies, she felt her lips turn upward.

It was deliciously freeing, that short walk. It was unforgivably rude, which had been exactly the point. She'd failed to acknowledge any of the ladies, regardless of rank, and it was quite clear she'd been in a position to overhear their conversation. Such blatant disregard for propriety was out of character for Emma and she enjoyed it.

Exhilarated by the minor rebellion, she scanned the sea of faces and feathers to locate her aunt. She would discuss the issue with Aunt Agatha. *Disgrace, indeed.* Aunt Agatha had the kindest heart of anyone Emma had ever known. Her aunt's opinion on this matter would be reasonable and her advice judicious. She would certainly know the best way to handle the dissolution of the engagement. Perhaps a well-drafted letter would suffice.

"Oh, Emma," Aunt Agatha said as Emma approached. "You've saved me coming to find you. We were just discussing you, dear." Her tone was carefully calm, but Emma observed the way one of her hands anxiously gripped the fingers of her other.

"Oh, not you too." Had everyone abandoned reasonable thinking? Emma brought her hand to her brow and wondered if the growing ache in her head was real or simply the result of her great desire for an excuse to remove herself from this event and this city.

"What do you mean, dear?"

"Please tell me you were not discussing my surely *long-expired* betrothal to the duke."

Aunt Agatha's pale eyes shifted to meet those of the other ladies.

Emma sighed. They *were* discussing it.

"I worried this might happen." Aunt Agatha's lips formed a grim line as she regarded her niece.

Lady Hawthorne stepped forward. "Memories can be inconveniently long among our society, I'm afraid."

Emma looked into the caring eyes of a woman who had been her mother's friend as well as her aunt's. Her kind regard was mirrored in Lady Blythe's expression, and Lady Markwood's. If these women had been discussing her, she trusted it was not for the sake of heartless gossip. It was rooted in genuine concern.

"But it has been four years. I...I could have married in that time. *He* could have married in that time."

Agatha laid her gloved hands gently over Emma's. "But you didn't, dear. I'm afraid you are betrothed regardless of your feelings or the duke's."

Emma straightened her shoulders. "Then it will have to be dealt with as soon as possible. We will have to sever the arrangement by mutual agreement. I'm certain he will find me as unacceptable as I find him."

Again, the ladies exchanged glances. This time Emma could not guess their thoughts.

Aunt Agatha spoke softly. "Are you entirely sure you will find him unacceptable?"

"Aunt Agatha!" Emma lurched back from her aunt as though she could distance herself from the very suggestion. She could not fathom marriage to such a hateful, arrogant man. She remembered every cutting word as he'd stared at her with disgust, asking if she was even out of the schoolroom, demanding to know if she was old enough to speak, and accusing her of being old enough to know she wanted to be a duchess. Having just learned of the betrothal, she'd been mute with shock and betrayal. That day and many days since, she'd regretted not gathering her wits to give the answer he deserved.

Her outburst drew looks from people nearby and she lowered her voice. "I am certain. Four years ago, he found the prospect of marriage to me so abhorrent he fled the country, completely disregarding the shame to both families. You could not love me so little that you would want me to marry such a man."

A pained look crossed her aunt's delicate features and Emma felt a stab of guilt at the harshness of her words. Aunt Agatha was simply concerned for her future, but she was not without alternatives. She'd given serious consideration of late to the suit of Mr. Greystoke. He was a widower at least fifteen years her senior, but he was kind and seemed to share her preference for the peace of life outside London. Even if she never married, she had the cottage she'd inherited—the only unentailed portion of her father's estate. The house was little more than a hunting box and her existence would probably be considered genteel poverty by most in attendance here, but the cottage held a special place in her heart.

"Perhaps you shouldn't be too hasty to sever your arrangement, at least until you've had a chance to become reacquainted with the duke," suggested

Lady Blythe, a fair-haired, petite woman who managed to assert a good deal of authority when she so chose.

"Reacquainted? I was never *acquainted* with him in the first place." Emma exhaled slowly and reminded herself of the ladies' good intentions. "Please, I know you are only concerned for my happiness," she began, but she was interrupted by...

Silence.

The music stopped, but that phenomenon alone would not have been sufficient to give her pause. No, the *entire ballroom* stopped. The crowded room was startlingly silent, conversations and dances utterly frozen. It was as though the candlelight stopped twinkling and the potted ferns stopped growing.

Everyone looked.

She followed their eyes and released a small gasp before she could prevent it.

He strode into the room with nothing more than a sweeping glance for its occupants and still the silence reigned.

Emma watched with the others. He was there—all in one piece, looking every bit the duke.

Chapter Two

John Brantwood, Seventh Duke of Worley, walked directly into the crush at the Fairhaven ball and scanned the room, pointedly ignoring how the entire populace stared at him as though he were about to give a speech. He had some notion he'd become the favored subject of gossip, but the lack of subtlety unnerved him. He would be more comfortable once the gawking stares reverted to surreptitious glances made over shoulders and peeks from over top of lemonade glasses. Four years away now seemed like twenty. His life in Boston had been a modest one and it felt deuced awkward to be strolling into the ballroom as though he were the duke. *Christ. He was the duke.* And his damned valet had him tied up so tight in his clothes, he thought he might start pulling at his cravat and fidgeting like a child in church.

He didn't, of course. Nothing that occurred in his time away could undo the years of training and experience that preceded it. He adopted the bored mien expected for his position and sauntered into the room because he belonged there—even though he didn't quite feel that he did.

He had a higher purpose for appearing at one of the most heavily attended events of the season. He needed a wife—as quickly as he could arrange it. He could rely on his rank and fortune to ensure his suit was well received; it was simply a matter of selection. He'd been back in England for more than a month and he could no longer afford to delay.

Where is that damned Brydges?

He'd recruited his long-time friend Hugh Brydges as a reluctant co-conspirator to aid in his plan, and he scanned the faces to find him. The whole room seemed to be waiting and watching, but he finally noticed an irreverent smirk that differentiated itself from the crowd.

The smirk and its owner sauntered over without any regard for the rapt attention of the gathered revelers.

"You've cleaned up well, *Your Grace*," Hugh said with an exaggerated examination of John's appearance. "Death agrees with you, it would seem." John watched Brydges drop his chin to acknowledge a couple who'd maneuvered themselves near enough to overhear. Brydges didn't engage them in conversation and they moved reluctantly past. He turned back.

"You know I'll never get used to calling you Worley instead of Brantwood."

"Call me whatever you like. You always have." The last thing John needed was his oldest friend your-gracing him all the time.

Brydges nodded.

Hugh Brydges was one of the first people John contacted upon his return to England. He was the only friend in England who knew the truth of John's whereabouts during the past four years, and he diligently kept John informed of the duke's lies, his declining health, and eventually, his death. Brydges was the only man John counted as a truly loyal friend. Most thought him a shallow, unserious person, but John knew better. At school, Brydges had been popular company for his biting wit and rebellious spirit. Few other than John had noticed the quiet determination with which Brydges had addressed his studies.

As such, John was not surprised when Brydges's teasing demeanor abruptly sobered and his friend faced him with a dissecting look, mouth drawn in a grim line and eyes probing. "You're as determined as ever, then?" Brydges asked.

"I am."

"Does this sister of yours understand you're falling on your sword for her? Are you certain she deserves it?"

John's chin rose. Deserve it? Did Charlotte deserve to be robbed of her father, of her home, of her place? No, she did not. If John could do something—anything—to return even a fraction of what had been taken from Charlotte, how could he possibly consider inaction?

"It is the very least she deserves," he said quietly, but with all the strength of his resolve. His determination alone wouldn't accomplish it, though. Charlotte had lived in America for most of her life. He would need every social advantage to quell the inevitable rumors and questions regarding her legitimacy. Selecting a duchess—the right duchess—to aid in this cause was imperative. "You'll not change my mind, so register your complaints and be done, Brydges. I'll expect you to be in top form this evening."

Brydges's grave expression disappeared as quickly as it had come, and he looked out over the sea of revelers with an amused smile. "On the contrary, I have no complaints."

John took in the same view of dark jackets and pastel gowns and released a burdened sigh before casting a doubtful glance at his companion. "You're amenable then to an evening among eligible young ladies and their mothers? Even a third son might find himself snared if he is not careful."

Brydges was the son of an earl, but with two older brothers and nephews aplenty, he had no obligation to produce heirs. And while other third sons lamented the unlucky fortune of their birth order and sought to woo heiresses, Brydges had convinced his father to use the funds that would have purchased a military commission as capital to begin a stud operation instead. It was flourishing nicely, providing Brydges the happy freedom of bachelorhood for as long as he so chose.

Still, he grinned at John as though he were perfectly content to be plunk in the middle of one of the biggest marriage mart events of the season. "I wasn't looking forward to the job, but since I've been freed of the burden, I've no complaints now."

John cast his friend a quizzical look. "How so? Have you assigned your duties to another?" He planned to rely on Brydges to make introductions and discretely remind him of those acquaintances he should recall. He'd forgotten much and the great number of marriages and deaths among the gentry made his remaining memories unreliable.

Brydges faced the crush as he spoke, doling out nods and waves to those who openly stared in their direction. "I've been recruited to find you a fiancée. Since you already have one, I find I am without employment after all."

Already had one? "What do you mean?"

"Don't scowl. They're curious enough already."

"Explain yourself," John demanded.

Brydges finally showed mercy for John and faced him. "You're engaged." He stood back to take in the reaction to this revelation.

"What?" Of course he was not engaged. He was also not in the mood for games.

"You have a fiancée."

John shook his head as if that could somehow un-muddle his brain. "You're getting ahead of yourself, Brydges. I am in London to *acquire* a fiancée."

Brydges affected a superior pose. "I was a bit surprised myself, you'll understand, but I have been here no more than half an hour and have been duly informed by four separate individuals that you are already engaged."

The gossips were just as rampant—and as poorly informed—as he remembered. "It's a ridiculous rumor. I've been in virtual isolation at Brantmoor this entire month. I've been in London for less than six hours. How the hell could I have gotten myself engaged?"

"I didn't say you are *newly* engaged. Rather, you are *still engaged.* To Lady Emmaline Shaw, apparently."

"What the devil?"

"It would seem she never married. And you, according to gossip, are not dead. Your betrothal is intact." Even as Brydges teased him with this revelation and grinned broadly for their curious audience, his sharp eyes watched for John's reaction.

It was not a happy one.

"Preposterous." Even dead, his father was imposing his irrational will. John had plans to mend what his father had broken and those plans required a wife, but not the awkward, mumbling child his father had chosen. She'd been unsettlingly quiet, just staring at him with owlish eyes and clinging to her mother's side. Regrettably, he'd taken his anger at his father out on the girl, which was unfair. All in all, it had been an unpleasant encounter.

"How is it possible she remains unmarried after four years? And how is it possible you didn't know this?"

Brydges shrugged. "I didn't investigate the girl. But I understand she isn't out in society much. It seems everyone forgot about her."

John looked askance at his companion. "If everyone forgot about her, why have they chosen to remember her now?"

Brydges's brows arched mockingly. "I should think the answer to that question quite obvious."

John found little humor in his friend's antics while the weight of this new complication settled coldly and tightly around his shoulders. The thought of marrying a girl who was scared to death of him was unappealing, but more importantly, he hadn't the luxury of marrying a frightened mouse even if he wished it. To accomplish what he wanted for Charlotte, the next Duchess of Worley would need the kind of strength Lady Emmaline Shaw simply did not possess.

He carefully blanked his expression so others would not see the extent of his frustration. "She won't do. The contract will have to be dissolved—quickly. I won't waste time."

He needed someone who could perform as a hostess and make social connections—one who would not shrink from hurtful gossip or social slights but could, instead, rise above the petty cruelties society could levy.

Charlotte needed a champion—but not *her.* The Prince Regent himself would suffer from such a champion.

John spied their hostess charging toward them. He turned his frustration on Hugh. "Why didn't you warn me of this before?"

"How the hell should I have known? I don't make a habit of frequenting parties full of hopeful young ladies and scheming mothers." He said it even as he offered a charming smile to the swiftly approaching Duchess of Fairhaven and the husband she dragged behind her.

John's brow arched. "No?"

"Unlike you, I am not on a bride hunt," Brydges muttered through his false grin. "Don't think I'll be reformed, either, simply because I'm willing to aid you in your ill-advised quest."

John lowered his own voice as he responded. "It never occurred to me you would. *I* have no other choice."

Brydges cast John a droll look. "There's always another choice," he whispered vehemently before turning the full force of his charm on their hostess.

* * *

Barely an hour passed before John felt suffocated by the crowd, clothing, and inane conversations. Having fled outdoors, he stood on the patio and breathed deeply.

He grimaced, belatedly remembering fresh air was no more available *out* of doors in London than indoors. He was impatient to be done with his task and remove himself to Brantmoor, but he feared his plans may have been a bit ambitious. The effort it had required to play the duke as expected—to somehow be charming *and* superior—exhausted him. How had he not noticed before how extensive and trivial the rules of behavior were? If he, who had been brought up to the life, found it unfamiliar and stifling after only four years away, how would Charlotte find it?

Damn. He must go back in there. She must have a mentor.

The past betrothal was an unexpected obstacle. Several of the mothers with whom he'd conversed had subtly probed as to the status of any prior commitments. The few who'd been impertinent enough to mention the lady directly had taken pleasure in informing him of her present status as a near-hermit. Frustratingly, he was entirely at the mercy of Lady Emmaline Shaw. If he had only himself to consider, he would break the engagement and damn the consequences, but he had to think of Charlotte and her smooth introduction into society.

Even if his fiancée were to cooperate and withdraw from the engagement herself, could he even find a woman meeting his requirements in the fortnight he'd allowed? If the ladies he'd met over the past hour were the most intelligent among this year's crop of marriageable beauties, this year's crop was a sad lot indeed. True, several among them were remarkably lovely, but not one seemed able to speak about anything more complex than the last party she attended and whether or not Miss So-and-so played the pianoforte pleasingly. One girl had simply stared mutely at him in an encounter uncomfortably similar to one he'd had four years earlier.

Allowing himself just a few more moments of respite before returning to his tiresome project, John lifted his gaze to the night sky, seeking a glimpse of the stars. Often over the past four years, he and Charlotte had looked up into the night, finding a comforting sense of order and inevitability in the vastness of the sky and the clarity of the stars.

Tonight there was only darkness, the stars hidden by the veil of the city's polluted air.

* * *

Emma smiled politely at Lady Hawthorne, completely unaware of what the woman had just said. Her mind, it seemed, was as determined as her eyes to involuntarily chase the duke as he made a circuit of the room and seemed bent on gaining an introduction to every attractive young miss in attendance. Not that it mattered to Emma, of course, but it was cuttingly rude for him to have ignored her all evening when the matter of their unresolved engagement was the current topic of conversation among no less than half of the assembled revelers.

Emma's frustration with him grew. And the more it grew, the more she found herself searching the room to discover whose company was so important that it kept him from showing her what she deemed basic consideration.

The frustration his behavior triggered was truly irrational. She should be relieved to know her briefly held fears regarding their prior engagement were baseless. He clearly considered himself uncommitted, which was precisely what she'd hoped.

Emma shook her head. His social agenda was no concern of hers. She excused herself from the present conversation, of which she recalled little, and headed off to find her aunt. Surely she had stayed long enough at this miserable event to appease Aunt Agatha and could be allowed to leave. As she moved among the crowd, she kept her head down and refused to seek out the location of the duke. She was feeling quite proud of herself until she collided with another person and realized perhaps she should have at least been looking in front of her.

Which she did immediately, only to wish she had not.

She squared her shoulders, refusing to be intimidated by the Duke of Worley, or her recently renewed status as his rejected fiancée. "My apologies, Your Grace," she managed with some confidence. "I was distracted."

For a brief moment, his blue eyes studied her. Then he fell easily into the careless charm he'd no doubt been applying to all the ladies that evening. "How unkind of you," he chastised with a grin, "to imply someone else could have been so much more distracting to your attention."

Four years away may have improved his disposition, but clearly not his opinion of her.

"How unkind of *you*, Your Grace, to assume my own thoughts could not be interesting enough to distract my attention." She tilted her head to the side as she looked up at him. "Of course, I must allow that you know me very little. And if your opinion of me has been at all predicated on the average intellect of the company you've kept this evening, your assumption, though flawed, is at least understandable. I'm sure you've been apprised of the current rage in bonnets and the relative abilities of several young ladies on the pianoforte, have you not?"

His startled laugh drew the attention of those in the room who weren't already watching him. To his credit, he did not bother denying it. His eyes danced with laughter as he smiled warmly at her. He leaned closer in the manner of old friends sharing a confidence. "Even dukes feel the weight of their responsibilities, you know. You might say we feel it more keenly than others."

His time away had *not* improved his manners. What gall to speak so callously of his intentions without even acknowledging to her the need to resolve their prior commitment. She could scarcely believe it.

She seethed with it, but managed to control her tone. "How admirable of you then to attack them with such voracity, Your Grace. You mustn't allow me to keep you from your noble crusade. My aunt will be looking for me."

"I'll take you to her," he offered, reaching for her arm. "It is the least I can do after nearly injuring you in a collision."

"Nonsense," she insisted, evading his reach. "The collision was my fault. And I can see my aunt from here. I am perfectly able to reach her without an escort."

His smile was contrite, though the mirth still shone in his eyes. "I've complete trust in your capabilities, madam. Could I perhaps have the *pleasure* of escorting you to your aunt?" With a glance to note the audience they'd collected, Emma acquiesced. He was hours late in acknowledging her presence, but she supposed she was better served in cooperation. She allowed him to take her arm and lifted her chin in battered dignity as they walked in the direction of her aunt.

Emma glanced up at the duke, her mind calculating. If she could suggest a few moments of private discussion chaperoned by Aunt Agatha, they could conceivably have this whole mess resolved before everyone retired for the evening. She was formulating the words to propose just such a thing when he spoke first.

"I am ashamed to admit you have the advantage of me, madam. If I am to lead you to your aunt, I must learn who you are to ascertain which of these good ladies she might be."

Aunt Agatha's arrival at Emma's side was timely, for she was able to grip the woman's arm for support as she drew back and stared up at the duke. "You mean to say you do not know who I am?"

He looked uncertainly at her aunt and then back again. "I am sincerely sorry that I do not. Please don't take offense at my poor memory. Four years is a long absence and I'm afraid I've found much to be unfamiliar."

Of course. He had not decided to be solicitous after all. He had no intention of paying his respects to his betrothed. He hadn't even taken the time to have her pointed out. Well, if he was still in the dark, he could rot there.

She turned to her aunt. "I believe we should go." She didn't wait for confirmation, but turned and walked directly away.

"Emmaline, wait."

She did not pause at her aunt's words, but kept her course for the door until she felt a strong grip close around her arm, halting her progress. She wrenched her arm from the duke's grasp and spun to face him.

He loomed large above her, his blue eyes peering. "What is your *full* name, Emmaline?"

She hated that she could feel her cheeks flush. Of what had *she* to be ashamed? "My name is Lady Emmaline Shaw, and I was just leaving. Good evening, Your Grace."

Once again, the strength of his grip prevented her departure. She turned again to give him the full measure of her dissatisfaction, but his look was one of such sheer bafflement, she almost pitied him.

She exhaled impatiently. "Oh, for heaven's sake. Let's have this out, shall we?" She turned to Aunt Agatha, who seemed as lost as the duke. "Perhaps the three of us could seek out some privacy in which to discuss matters."

Aunt Agatha looked from Emma to the duke and back to Emma. "I think that would be wise."

Emma stalked toward the center staircase with her aunt following closely. She didn't turn to determine whether or not the insufferable duke trailed them.

Chapter Three

John walked into what he assumed to be the Duke of Fairhaven's study and stared in disbelief at the woman who'd strode confidently into the room ahead of him.

"Your Grace." Her sharp tone had softened only slightly to one of condescension and she looked directly, challengingly, at him with golden brown eyes. Her almost imperceptible curtsy matched her haughty demeanor. "How thoughtful of you to remember me after so many years. We were engaged, of course, but we only met the once, didn't we?"

John was momentarily speechless. How the hell had this happened? Over the past few hours, he'd learned his betrothed had lost her parents, all but withdrawn from society, and had no suitors but an aging widower with a brood of children. Yet no one felt compelled to share the most pertinent piece of information—that she'd been in attendance all evening?

Could this sharp-tongued woman be his fiancée? He examined her face and tried to recognize some trait of the younger girl, but his memory of her features was not sharp enough from the one brief meeting. She seemed taller than her younger self, though her erect posture might have been the difference. More dramatically, she no longer carried the childlike plumpness he recalled—just the curves of a woman.

He shook his head. "Lady Emmaline, may I say in my defense, you've changed much since I last saw you."

"That's to be expected, is it not, over the course of four years?" she asked tightly. She selected a small chair near the center of the room and primly lowered herself into it.

"I suppose it is." He somewhat recovered his wits and took a chair as well. The years had been inordinately kind to his former fiancée. The lank brown hair he recalled was now silky chestnut. Tendrils of it strayed from her twist and danced against creamy skin that descended into the full bosom of her rust-colored gown. He was more confused than ever as to why she had not chosen to marry after his announced death. Could she possibly have imagined herself too grief-stricken at his death to have married another?

"I must tell you, Lady Emmaline, how it pains me to know that you suffered, believing me dead, and what a shock my return must be for you. If I could have spared you the experience, I would have done so."

She regarded him coolly. "Were you unconscious, then, for the better part of four years?"

"I was not," he conceded, resisting the upward tug of his lips.

"You lost your memory, perhaps?"

"Ah...no."

"I didn't expect so." She pressed her lips together.

"Emmaline..." The aunt stepped forward, but lost her nerve. She took a seat near the door.

John turned back to his fiancée. "I understand it was difficult for you, to lose your parents and prospective bridegroom all at once."

"Save your contrition," she snapped, "for those who would be inclined to accept it. A society full of marriage-minded parents may be too overcome with joy at your homecoming to notice the dubiousness of your absence. I have no such distraction."

He smiled because he couldn't help himself. She was just so different from all the hopeful, naïve, and frankly silly girls he'd been showing his attention to all evening. She bore absolutely no resemblance to her prior self. He had either entirely misjudged her or she was completely transformed. "I see you've developed quite an assertive nature in the meantime."

"I don't see how you could possibly be in a position to make a comparison of my nature, Your Grace, given that you do not know me now and you certainly did not know me then."

"I believe I may be gaining a bit of insight today," he told her with a wry half smile. He was more awake now than he'd been all evening. What sort of strange glutton for punishment was he that this sharp-tongued set-down was the first bit of this event he'd found genuinely entertaining?

"Your gaining insight into my nature is completely unnecessary," she said, her chin lifting. "Allow me to rescue you from an awkward conversation, Your Grace. You are released. I formally acknowledge your consideration in recognizing the prior contract between our parents, but as both parties to that contract are now deceased, I do not consider you bound to honor it. *I* will break the engagement, allowing you to keep your gentleman's reputation unblemished." His amused grin collapsed into a mien of pure confusion. "*You are releasing me?*" "I am." She folded her hands complacently in her lap and continued to regard him in an infuriatingly calm manner. She released a resigned sigh as though the entire situation were an inconvenience she'd as soon be done with.

"Your Grace," she continued, "I'm sure you expected your altered intentions to shatter the hopes of a desperate, unmarried spinster. It's obviously been a blow to your ego to discover that I am perfectly content with the dissolution of our arrangement." She paused as though she expected he needed a moment to catch up.

Which he supposed he did. He couldn't believe it. Surely her pride was not so injured she would choose an elderly widower over the opportunity to be a duchess? He had expected her to accept her fate out of an inability to object, but this woman was not frightened in the least. Would she be so irresponsible as to decline the offer of a secure and comfortable future? He wasn't sure how to react, what to say. She, however, seemed to have no shortage of words.

"I apologize for preventing you from delivering what I'm sure was to be a heartfelt and carefully worded speech," she told him matter-of-factly. "Had I understood your sensitive pride, I should have allowed you to speak first, of course." Her smile brimmed with sweet innocence, but the flecks of amber fire in her eyes belied the serenity of her expression.

"How considerate," he mocked. Why did he continue to prick her ire? But he knew why. He wished he possessed a fraction of her fervency. When all he felt was his customary cold, steady resolve, engaging her felt like warming himself at a fire.

"I always endeavor to be." She smoothed a nonexistent wrinkle in her skirt and looked expectantly up at him.

John wasn't certain whether to laugh or applaud. Far from the shy mouse of his memory, the Lady Emmaline that sat across from him today was an admirable opponent. She'd successfully reduced him to stunned silence and, as his sister could attest, he was rarely silent. Yet he surprised even himself when he told her, "Madam, I appreciate your...flexibility...as it pertains to our marriage contract. I, however, do not find myself to be quite so flexible."

Her golden eyes flew to his. He watched a gratifying flash of fear and annoyance cross them.

"I don't understand," she told him, yet he could tell by her wary expression she understood quite clearly.

"Lady Emmaline," he explained, lest there be any confusion, "I do not release you."

Chapter Four

Emma stared. What could he be thinking? Of course he didn't want to follow through on their ridiculous betrothal.

"I don't believe you," she said.

His look was dubious. "I'm not asking you to accept an unknown on faith. I'm telling you, you are not released. What is there to disbelieve?"

"I do not believe you have any desire or intent to marry me any more than I do you. What I *do* believe is that you expected a desperate girl who would be disconsolate at your rejection. I believe you feel robbed of your authority as the one who grants and takes away." She gripped the wooden arms of her chair and peered at him. "Is your ego really so bruised you would punish me by threatening to push forward with this ridiculous engagement? You would bat me around like a cat's toy just to remind me of your superiority?"

Truly, how cruel could he possibly be? The arrogance. Never mind that he was a duke; he was a man. Like a child in the throes of a tantrum, he was too focused on imposing his will to be concerned with the actual outcome of preference.

The duke leaned back and crossed his arms. "I have no wish to punish you, Lady Emmaline. Only to marry you."

She looked around the room, wishing some rational person might pop out from behind the curtains or under Fairhaven's desk to serve as witness to this ridiculousness. Aunt Agatha said nothing and no other was forthcoming. She glared at him again. "You lie."

He let his arms drop and met her gaze directly. "On the contrary, I could not be more genuine. I am in need of a wife and came to London for that purpose. As it happens, I am already engaged to a perfectly acceptable lady, saving me considerable time and effort in searching one out. The solution is really quite simple."

She leaned forward in her chair and lanced him with her severest look. "Do you deny you arrived here today for the express purpose of selecting a bride from among the new debutantes?"

He leaned forward as well and met her look without guile. "No. I don't deny it."

She sat back in her chair. "Well, then. We are in agreement. I appreciate your..."

"I came here for that purpose," he interjected, "but I find I have changed my mind."

"Changed your mind?"

"Indeed." He looked a bit nonplussed himself by the revelation.

"Ridiculous." She spoke the word aloud, but to her aunt rather than to him. Clearly, explaining to *him* the ridiculousness of his position would be futile. "Could you please help me explain, Aunt Agatha, the absolute absurdity of this notion?"

Aunt Agatha bore the look of a trapped animal. She gave a delicate cough before responding. "Perhaps we should at least listen to his explanations, dear." She turned her attention to the duke. "You do, I hope, have explanations, Your Grace?"

"Certainly." He smiled at Aunt Agatha as though pegging her an ally then faced Emma again. "Don't you want to know why I have changed my mind?" His impenetrable confidence set her fingers itching.

"Very well, Your Grace," she ground out. "Pray tell me, why have you changed your mind?" She couldn't imagine what sort of excuse he could possibly fabricate.

"The situation is this: I find I require a wife with specific...attributes. When I learned of our continued engagement, I was convinced from our prior encounter that you did not possess those attributes. Our conversation has proven otherwise."

"I see." She did not see at all. He was baiting her still, she was certain of it. "And what would those attributes be that I have demonstrated so well in our brief meeting? Could it be that you simply require a wife with all her limbs and teeth, Your Grace?" She crossed her arms. "Or perhaps you require a wife who is not deaf or mute? I suppose I have aptly demonstrated my ability in those areas."

Absurdly, he smiled at her then, as though she had said the most charming thing imaginable. "You have just demonstrated it—perfectly so. I seek a wife with a spine—one who will not shrink from adversity. When most women would have acquiesced to rank, parental authority, and contractual obligation, you've proven instead you have backbone to spare. I not only admire that, Lady Emmaline, I'm counting on it." He nodded as though she should feel congratulated by his words.

The arrogance. Did he honestly believe she expected or would accept his compliments? This game had gone on long enough. She rose from her seat.

"I will not be treated in this manner, and your rank, Your Grace, does not excuse you. As you refuse to participate in a rational conversation, I will just have to rely upon your earlier representation that you did, in fact, intend to dissolve our contract. Please consider it dissolved. Now, if you'll excuse me, I am tired and would like to return home with my aunt and uncle."

"Lady Emmaline..." He rose also and stepped closer.

Her instinct as he advanced was to step back, but she would not grant him that power. She stood her ground.

"*Lady* Emmaline, I find I must prove my intentions to be genuine. Since you require proof, I will call on you tomorrow with a ring of my grandmother's. You may consider it a betrothal ring."

Could he be serious? That he would tease her with the betrothal made her angry, but could he actually intend to go through with it? She could scarcely breathe at the thought. She gaped at him. "You're truly serious, aren't you? You actually intend to marry me."

"Yes. I truly, actually intend to marry you. And when you consider all of the circumstances, I don't think you will find the prospect so abhorrent."

The last restraints on her anger fell away. "Are you daft? Do you honestly not understand why I wouldn't want to marry you—the man who once found the prospect of marriage to *me* so abhorrent he chose possible death on the battlefield as a preferable fate?

"You arrive four years late," she continued, "with no explanation or apologies and have the unmitigated gall to wonder why I am not brimming with gratitude for your consideration. Have you no conscience? You allowed everyone to believe you were dead. Your own father went to his grave believing he had no remaining heir, that his entire family had been lost to him."

The duke stepped back and adopted a sober expression. "I am greatly sorry, Lady Emmaline, that you were harmed by my actions. I can assure you, the timing of my departure in relation to our engagement was purely coincidental. There were matters of pressing importance to be handled abroad and I left without notice or preparation. I can also assure you I was not personally involved in the dissemination of inaccuracies pertaining to my death."

"Matters of pressing importance? This is the explanation I'm to receive? You expect me to believe it was a matter of pressing importance for you to flee to Spain to join the fight against Napoleon?"

"I have only been to Spain once, Lady Emmaline, and that visit was not made in the past four years."

"You're talking in riddles."

He stepped forward and met her gaze with an earnest expression. "You've asked for an explanation. That's a fair and reasonable request." His gaze moved among both ladies as he continued. "As I've explained, I find myself in urgent need of a wife."

Emma's glare intensified.

"I understand your duty as duke, Your Grace," Aunt Agatha asked. "But is there some *other* reason for this urgency?"

"I have a sister, Charlotte,"—his expression softened as he spoke her name—"who is of an age to make her debut in society. There will be... challenges...because her upbringing has been unorthodox. I seek a wife who will not shrink from those challenges. I was under the mistaken impression my current betrothed was too meek to serve the purpose." He waved a hand toward her form as though presenting her for inspection. "My judgments have proven inaccurate. I would in fact wager, Lady Ridgley, that your niece possesses more backbone than any other lady of the *ton*."

Aunt Agatha squinted at the man as though she could make his words come better into focus. "I thought you had but one sister," she said.

"Correct."

Emma spoke up then. "Pardon my directness, Your Grace, but I understood your sister to have died as a young child."

The duke turned back to Emma and addressed her with no trace of humor. "I assure you she is alive and well and will arrive in England shortly."

Somehow, his clarifications managed to provide no clarity whatsoever. "Goodness," she said tartly, well aware of her tone. "How many resurrections can one family possibly produce? Perhaps I should not be so confident in the validity of your title, Your Grace, when your departed father could turn up at any moment."

"Emma," Aunt Agatha warned, but her tone lacked conviction.

The duke paused, as though measuring his words carefully before he continued. "Just as you were falsely informed of my death four years ago, reports of my mother and sister's deaths several years before were also inaccurate."

"But that information came directly from your father," Aunt Agatha pointed out.

"It did, but it was false," he said grimly, his expression tightening at the mention of his father. "My mother and sister were alive and residing in Boston for many years. I only learned the truth when I gained my majority and my mother wrote to me through a solicitor to request my aid."

Emma sat again. The story was a bit fantastic. "That is why you left the country?"

"It is. Within days of meeting you, I received word that my mother had taken gravely ill. I felt I had no choice but to go. I learned from a friend the story he circulated about my death." He recovered his teasing smile as he glanced at Emma. "I assure you, I have never been the patriotic sort."

The lightness of his teasing after the shock of his story took Emma off guard because she caught herself almost responding with an easy laugh of her own. She coughed instead.

"I must say," Aunt Agatha interjected. "That's an astonishing story. I gather you plan to bring your mother and sister back to England, now that you've inherited?"

His voice was small when he answered. "My mother passed away last year. It is only Charlotte who will be returning to England. She is my sister and the daughter of a duke. She deserves to take her place here."

Emma wasn't quite sure what to make of all this. She supposed she would have to rethink at least some portion of her resentments toward the Duke of Worley. She could see how he might owe a greater loyalty to his mother and sister than to the fiancée he barely knew and never wanted in the first place. Still, he'd been incredibly hateful when they were introduced. He'd handled the situation poorly, by her estimation, and one could not forget her reputation *had* been irreparably damaged. Most importantly, she still didn't want to marry him.

"I suppose I understand, Your Grace, why you felt you had to disregard our engagement at the time. I don't see, however, what this has to do with me currently."

He turned to her with a pleading expression. "Charlotte needs a champion, Lady Emmaline. Her background is unorthodox. Her true identity will be questioned and vicious rumors will be circulated. She needs more than me to take on the gossips. She needs you as well."

Emma glanced at her aunt to gauge *her* reaction to this nonsense. What could he be thinking?

"That's the most backward idea I've ever heard." She adjusted herself in her seat. "If you require a fiancée with social clout, I assure you, I wield absolutely none. Thanks in no small part to you, if I may speak plainly."

"You'll be a duchess. You'll have all the clout in the world, provided you've the strength to demand it."

"I will *not* be a duchess." She said it to the duke, but her eyes implored her aunt for just a bit more help. "It's insupportable that you would want to marry me, Your Grace. I believe the total amount of time you've spent in my company is only now approaching an hour."

"You make a strong impression." He laughed when her brow lifted. "Oh, come now, Lady Emmaline. It's not as though I've claimed to fall in love with you in the span of an hour."

Aunt Agatha rose from her seat and looked about the room. "Emma, I expect your uncle must be wondering where we've gotten off to."

"Certainly not," Emma said to the duke, ignoring her aunt. "You should know, however, that I am not without *genuine* suitors." She couldn't meet his eyes as she made the claim.

She could feel his stare boring into her profile. "Is that really what you want?" he asked. "Living in relative poverty with an old man, caring for someone else's children?"

Emma and her aunt both gasped at once.

"What do you know of it?" Emma demanded.

"You can't possibly claim to be in love with this Greystoke character," he said, practically spitting the name as he spoke it, "and I don't accept it as a valid objection."

She pivoted in her seat to face him, too offended to find his proximity intimidating. "Very well, then. What *will* you accept as a valid objection?"

"Please, both of you," Aunt Agatha interrupted. "Let's not be too hasty in deciding what's best for everyone."

Her aunt's suspiciously neutral comment garnered Emma's full attention.

"Perhaps we should continue this conversation after we've had some opportunity to think things through and Emma has had a chance to confer with her uncle," Aunt Agatha proposed.

The duke nodded. "I believe your counsel to be wise, Lady Ridgley. It is clear to me that your niece doubts the sincerity of my intentions. As I promised earlier, I will call upon you tomorrow to present her with a betrothal ring that was once my grandmother's."

He stepped to where Emma sat and took hold of her hand. "I look forward to more demonstrations of your attributes tomorrow afternoon,

Lady Emmaline." With a nod to her aunt, he released her hand and was out the door before she could object.

Silence hovered between the ladies for a time. Emma spoke first. "He is the most arrogant man. He just assumes I'll be happy to marry him." She plunked her hand into her lap, frustrated with herself that she hadn't gathered her wits quickly enough to snatch it away from him. "You'll notice he offered no apology for the way *I've* been treated throughout this situation."

"Oh, Emma." When Aunt Agatha faced her niece, her pale eyes were brimming with unshed tears.

"Aunt Agatha." Emma rose and rushed to her aunt's side. "I didn't mean to upset you. I'm only annoyed at his arrogance. I know he'll see reason eventually. Everything will be fine."

"My dear," Aunt Agatha said, brushing at the tears that leaked. "I didn't plan to be a countess. I knew I was marrying a second son when I married your uncle and he wasn't supposed to inherit. I never needed any of this." She waved her hand as though indicating the Fairhaven's study, but Emma knew her meaning to include her own home and the life of a peer in general. "When he did inherit the earldom, the most precious part of that estate was you. God never saw fit to give us children, but you've been like a daughter to me."

Emma reached for one of her aunt's hands and squeezed it. "You've been like a mother to me."

Aunt Agatha reached up to brush a hand along Emma's cheek. Her voice trembled as she spoke. "Having you with us has been wonderful for me. I've been in no rush to send you off to someone else's household." Her hand fell and her gaze followed. She shook her head softly. "I think perhaps I've been selfish and shortsighted."

"But you haven't, I…"

"Hush now, Emma, and let me finish." There was a quiet strength behind her aunt's words, and more assertiveness than Emma was accustomed to seeing from her.

Emma nodded and did as she was told.

"Your uncle will not live forever. This cousin from Yorkshire, whom we've never even met, will inherit and what will that leave you? Nothing but that lonely cottage and an old maid's existence? I should have worked harder to secure a good marriage for you. In that one respect, I fear I've failed to meet my obligation to your parents."

Emma was overcome by the extent of her aunt's affection—and troubled by the guilt she'd never meant to inspire. "Aunt Agatha, you mustn't speak this way. You haven't failed at all. I love my cottage and I'm so very grateful for all that you and my uncle have done for me—grateful that you stood by me, when I fear I've been an embarrassment to you."

"Do not even think it. Of course you've never been an embarrassment. I only want what's truly best for you—to see your future secured as your parents tried to do when they lived. Now the duke has returned." Aunt Agatha's grip on her hand grew tighter. "The very man your father chose for you. I can't help feeling this is my second chance, Emma. I owe your parents to see this marriage through."

Emma was at a loss. *See the marriage through?*

She sat. The movement wasn't studied or graceful. She just plopped onto the settee as though one moment she had a pair of useful, sturdy legs and then she didn't. Everyone, it seemed, wanted her to marry the Duke of Worley. How could she possibly fight them all?

Chapter Five

"I don't believe you."

John leveled Brydges with a beleaguered glance from across the breakfast table. "Then it appears you are in agreement with my betrothed," he said, listening to how his words echoed in a room far too cavernous to be simply a breakfast room. Worley House had seemed...smaller...before.

"Why the devil would you want to marry a woman who despises you?" Brydges asked, allowing his silver to clang to his plate.

Why did everyone fail to understand? "I've given myself very little time to marry an appropriate woman. I am currently affianced to one. It is the most expedient solution." He placed his own fork gently. "She is still smarting from my abandonment, but I am sure that will pass once she has time to consider my reasons. After all, I am here to make good on the commitment, am I not?"

Brydges sat back in his chair and considered his friend. "It is clear you have not spent the past four years in London ballrooms. You underestimate the capability of a scorned woman to hold a grudge."

"I'm sure she will she see reason. I am only expecting that she be amicable, not that she fall madly in love with me. Lord, no one wants that."

John certainly didn't want that. In truth, he couldn't even risk it.

"I think you are one who will not see reason," Brydges claimed, crossing his arms in front of his chest. "Currently, she hates you. If she comes round now anytime soon, it will most likely be to grasp at the chance to become a duchess."

"She is hardly a social climber," John pointed out. "She is the daughter of an earl." He shook his head. He was not asking Brydges to marry the girl.

"Yes, but you very nearly ruined her. Don't forget her most likely prospect before you arrived was hardly a peer of the realm." Clearly recovered from the initial shock of John's revelation, Brydges turned back to the table and recovered his fork. "She may very likely choose to become a duchess over becoming nursemaid to a brood of someone else's children, but that does not necessarily mean she will be an ally to you or your sister." He leaned in more closely and leveled John with one of his rare, serious gazes. "If she is the sort to allow a title to sway her, then she is the sort to be offended by your sister's common life in Boston."

John considered this logic. He picked up his tea cup and swirled the liquid in it before drinking it and setting it with deliberately finality on the table. The man's point was valid. Hell, even Brydges didn't fully understand just how common Charlotte's life had been in Boston. But Charlotte would arrive soon. There was no time for second guessing.

"If Lady Emmaline is the type to be concerned about titles and such," he said, "then she is the type to be concerned with protecting family reputations and avoiding scandal. Regardless of her purpose, our desired outcomes shall be the same."

"Your desired outcome for Lady Charlotte?" Brydges asked.

"Yes."

"And what of yourself? Marriage is a long business."

John hesitated. He and Brydges had been friends for years and discussed a great many things, but love and marriage were not typically among them.

"I prefer a wife with whom I will be amicable. Any man would. I do not expect—or even desire—a grand love affair."

To what positive end would that take him? Ceding common sense to passion had proven disastrous for his father's family. It had turned his father into a fool.

No. Not a fool. Fools were ridiculous but benign. His father had become something else entirely. Hateful. Destructive. Obsessive. Unseeing.

Loving a woman beyond sense had ruined his father and, in turn, ruined the woman and her children. No. John had no desire for a passionate affair of the heart. His purpose was to make recompense for this father's failings, not repeat them.

"I can't help but feel you are making too great a sacrifice. Surely Lady Charlotte, the daughter of a duke, can make her entrée into society without your marital martyrdom."

"You will not sway me, Brydges."

"What does Lady Charlotte think of all this? Is she truly that concerned with her 'place' as you say? She should know better than anyone that titles are no way to identify worthy men. Your father wasn't worthy of any of you." "The debt owed to Charlotte has nothing to do with titles. It has everything to do with the life she should have led-- a life of ease and abundance, with parties and dresses and the petty cares of young girls who have never known true hunger or toil. Instead she..." John pushed his chair abruptly back from the table and stood, feeling every inch of his resolve as though it were an iron frame over which his body was formed. "The success of Charlotte's debut and acceptance in society will begin the restoration of years of neglect and it will impact her far longer than this first season. There will never be a question again of Charlotte's legitimacy. She will be launched into society by her own family—by none other than my own wife. And that shall be Lady Emmaline Shaw."

* * *

The afternoon following the Fairhaven ball, Emma sat in the drawing room reading a book while Aunt Agatha embroidered a cushion. It was a quiet, domestic scene and, quite possibly, the first truly awkward moment Emma had ever shared with her aunt. Their respective occupational ruses aside, there was no doubt as to the true purpose for finding themselves in the drawing room at that time of day. Nor was there any doubt as to the reason why Aunt Agatha had clearly taken extra effort with her appearance since the morning.

Even Emma could not deny there had been care behind the selection of her dress and the arrangement of her hair. Her aim had been to appear appropriately—but not enthusiastically—dressed. She felt she had achieved the desired effect, though she had in a moment of vanity chosen the most flattering from among the appropriate options.

They were, of course, awaiting the arrival of a caller. Emma found herself unable to focus on her book, anticipating instead the inevitable confrontation when the Duke of Worley arrived with his grandmother's ring. No doubt he would arrogantly expect her to slide it right onto her hand and bless her good luck for having gotten it.

She was almost relieved when the expectant silence was interrupted by the entrance of the butler. With measured calm, she closed her book and laid it aside while Jenkins presented her aunt with a calling card.

At Aunt Agatha's nod, Jenkins left the room.

Smoothing her skirt and straightening her posture, Emma took a deep breath to counteract the involuntary quickening of her pulse. She lifted her chin and faced the door with a careful mask of serenity as Jenkins returned.

"Lady Blythe and Lady Markwood."

The tension drained from Emma's shoulders. She chided herself for her anxiety. She had no reason to be anxious over the arrival of the duke anyway. He would come when he came and she would see the matter resolved.

Aunt Agatha's friends were shown into the drawing room, with Lady Markwood sweeping in first to greet Agatha and then Emma. She gripped Emma's hands and peered into her face. "How are you managing, my dear?"

"I'm fine, truly. Thank you for your concern." She knew the ladies' interest was rooted in kindness, but she felt no obligation to provide details.

Lady Blythe was much more direct in her approach. "Well, has he spoken to you?" she asked after taking one of Emma's hands in hers for a brief squeeze.

"He has, actually."

When Emma said nothing further, Lady Blythe looked to Aunt Agatha who in turn looked to Emma to expound, but Emma remained silent.

Lady Blythe's expression darkened. "Well, then."

Both she and Lady Markwood shared the look of uncomfortable gravity one expects to witness at a funeral. Emma felt as though she were attending the theatrical final moments of her reputation and future prospects.

Still, she was not of a mind to clear up any misconceptions despite the look she intercepted from Aunt Agatha. Doing so would only result in further debate, as the opinions of Lady Blythe and Lady Markwood would most assuredly mirror her aunt's.

"Please, be seated, ladies." Emma certainly needed to sit.

Lady Markwood perched at the edge of a chair. "I feel I should warn you, Emma, that you have garnered some interest among the gossips."

Emma graced her aunt's well-meaning friends with a reassuring smile. "I appreciate your concern, but I believe that was perfectly clear to me last evening. I find it interesting, though," Emma added, with only moderate success in keeping the sharp edge from her tone, "that the duke's return has reminded everyone of my existence. It's as though I only truly exist in relation to him. I am not Lady Emmaline Shaw, but rather the Duke of Worley's infamously rejected fiancée."

Emma's outspoken comment garnered no initial response beyond silence and awkwardness from the three elder ladies.

"Nonetheless," Lady Markwood continued eventually. "The vultures are circling."

Aunt Agatha rested a hand on Emma's arm. "Perhaps, since we are among friends, you could share more of your visit with the duke, Emma." Emma was saved from responding by another intrusion from Jenkins. "Lady Bosworth and Mrs. Woodley, my lady."

An almost imperceptible flash of annoyance crossed Jenkins habitually placid features as the two women pushed past him into the room. Jenkins had been a fixture in this house all of Emma's life and she could guess the depths of his disdain for these two ladies who must have rudely insisted upon being immediately announced.

A series of meaningful glances were exchanged among the ladies already present. Emma was acquainted with Lady Bosworth and Mrs. Woodley but, by design, she was not well acquainted. One as tall as the other round, the equally ill-mannered pair were usually found together and were notorious gossips. They had never, to Emma's recollection, called upon either the present or prior Countess of Ridgley before today.

Aunt Agatha rose to greet the newcomers. "How kind of you to call." She said it through an expression of such sincerity, Emma wondered if perhaps her aunt could have been called to the stage under different circumstances.

"We've been meaning to for so long," Lady Bosworth insisted, "but you know…things." She gave a limp wave of her hand as though to say, *I've no intention of providing the rest of my thought, so go find it over there.*

"Yes, it has been an age, hasn't it," Mrs. Woodley added, her brow furrowed as though she strained to recall their last visit.

"I suppose."

Aunt Agatha was more kind than Emma would have been in her place. Of course it had been an age. It had been the ridiculous woman's *entire* age.

"But we were fortuitously nearby this afternoon, so naturally I *insisted* we call," explained Lady Bosworth.

Aunt Agatha patted Lady Bosworth's hand. "A happy fortune, indeed."

Truly, Aunt Agatha was a saint.

False excuses thus disbursed, the new arrivals turned to study Emma with unveiled curiosity. So intense was their examination, if Emma's manners had been only slightly lower, she would have made a face at the peering matrons.

"And how are you, dear?" Lady Bosworth asked.

"I am well. Thank you for inquiring."

Lady Bosworth pursed her lips skeptically.

It appeared the vultures were not only circling, but had flown in for a closer inspection. Everyone wanted to know if she'd been jilted yet and, if so, how she was tolerating it. They wanted the honor of relaying the final destruction of her reputation—in all its gruesome detail—to their circle of acquaintances. How would the women react if she claimed to be perfectly grand, awaiting the duke's return with her betrothal ring? The thought only occurred out of pettiness and she tamped it down.

All eyes turned collectively as Jenkins once more entered the room. He had recovered his dignified expression as he once more handed Aunt Agatha a pair of calling cards.

After a brief glance at the cards, Aunt Agatha responded with a bemused nod. "Perhaps you could bring extra chairs from the earl's study once you've shown the ladies in. Thank you, Jenkins."

More ladies? At this point, it seemed the only distraction saving Emma from answering to the amassed spectators was the arrival of more spectators. She almost—*almost*—would have preferred the arrival of the duke.

Emma stiffened when Jenkins announced the additions to their party. She was tempted to glare when Lady Grantham and Lady Wolfe strolled into the room as though they were welcome and wanted, the latter dragging her reluctant daughter. Georgiana Wolfe appeared so uncomfortable when introduced that Emma decided the girl may actually possess some common sense. She could not say the same for the elder ladies, considering the complete lack of pride it must have taken for them to visit and feign cordiality. They knew full well Emma had overheard every hurtful, gossiping word the previous evening.

While the newly arrived ladies eyed Emma and were eyed in turn by Lady Bosworth and Mrs. Woodley for poaching on their gossip-hunting ground, Jenkins and a footman carried in first one and then another high-backed chair from the earl's study, arranging them to create a conversational circle. Though muted with age, the scarlet brocade upholstery still looked garishly out of place against the delicate gold and sage of the drawing room.

Others must have agreed, for as soon as Jenkins and the footman departed, a shuffling commenced. All the ladies sought to find a seat, studiously avoiding the red chairs as though they might themselves appear garish sitting upon them. The matter was finally resolved with some tactful direction from Aunt Agatha.

Emma, who had remained seated throughout the debacle in what was likely an unforgivable lack of manners, found herself joined on the settee by the Ladies Markwood and Blythe. Lady Bosworth and Lady Grantham occupied the room's two sedately colored armchairs, while Lady Wolfe and her daughter sat upon two wooden-backed chairs pulled from the card table in the corner. Mrs. Woodley, as the lowest ranking woman in the room, and Aunt Agatha, as the gracious hostess, were relegated to the boldly colored transplanted chairs. Thus arranged, the ladies conversed on trivial subjects. There was a discussion of the fine selection of food at the Fairhaven ball and the wonderful music at a prior event hosted by Lord and Lady Gilchrest. Several polite questions were directed to Georgiana, who responded with equal politeness and the appropriate deference of a well-trained daughter.

Emma participated very little, noting with detached interest that an uninformed outsider would have seen nothing more than a group of ladies engaged in a pleasant afternoon visit. He would likely have failed to notice the large number of curious peeks at Emma and would have had no reason to be suspicious of subtly probing questions regarding her plans for staying in London or attending certain events.

Emma provided direct answers when she could and did not elaborate, frustrating them all in their quest for information. As an unfortunate consequence, everyone seemed loath to leave, lingering long past the brief stay dictated by etiquette.

As Emma had no intention of sharing the status of her engagement—which was, frankly, uncertain—she could only take comfort in the knowledge that polite topics of conversation would eventually become sparse.

When Jenkins entered the room with yet another card, Emma considered feigning an ailment. Only loyalty to her aunt kept her in her seat while he left to show the caller up.

"The Duke of Worley."

That man would appear at *this* moment. Could he not detect from the number of carriages lingering nearby that she and her aunt were occupied hosting a meeting of the Gossiping Ladies' Society?

As every head turned toward the door, he sauntered past Jenkins and into the fray, hesitating only a moment to digest the numbers in attendance.

He greeted Aunt Agatha first then worked his way around the circle, greeting each woman with the same charming attention he'd displayed the past evening. In return, the ladies fawned over him as though he bore no responsibility at all for the scandalous abandonment of his young fiancée or for failing to appear at his father's sickbed. He was, after all, a young, unmarried duke of significant fortune. Thus, he could be forgiven any transgression. Emma sat rigidly in her chair while he finished the circuit with a murmured remark that managed to inspire a blush in both Wolfe ladies.

Then he faced Emma. His azure eyes twinkled with amusement as he addressed her. "Here I was worried you might be without company. It appears you have no shortage of social connections."

He was calling her a liar for claiming she lacked social clout, yet he knew as well as she, most of these women were not visiting out of friendship. Aware of her audience, she regarded him with a polite smile. "We *are* particularly well attended today, Your Grace. I was only just wondering to myself what the cause may be."

"Have you no theories?" he asked.

"None that occur to me."

All the ladies listened unashamedly with the exception of Georgiana Wolfe, who listened but had the decency to squirm. Was it too much to hope that he would leave and return when they would not be performing for an audience?

"I would invite you to sit," Emma said, "but I'm afraid I have no seat to offer."

"A problem easily solved," he said. "Shall we have our walk as we planned?"

A clever maneuver on his part. They had not planned a walk, but he had to know she wasn't likely to argue the point. She *would* need a more private moment with the duke to reiterate her earlier position on their engagement, but a walk in the park at the most crowded time of the afternoon would not afford much privacy.

"Thank you, Your Grace, but as you can see, my aunt has visitors. As she is not available to accompany us, I fear we shall have to delay our walk to some other time."

"Nonsense," Lady Wolfe interjected, practically leaping from her chair as she shoved her daughter forward. "Georgiana would love to take some fresh air. She'd be happy to round out your numbers for a walk in the park."

Emma judged by Georgiana's appalled look that her earlier assessment had been correct, and the girl was indeed a rare jewel of rationality despite her mother's best efforts.

As chaperones went, a young, unmarried girl to protect the virtue of another was not ideal, but no one could really suggest to Lady Wolfe's face that her daughter may not be a fit chaperone—a fact which Lady Wolfe surely realized. She looked quite pleased with herself and her coup. Not only would she have every reason to stay and observe the aftermath of the outing, but she had also created an opportunity to place her very unmarried daughter in the immediate company of a duke who, in everyone's expectation, would be equally unspoken for by the time the outing was done.

As a triumphant Duke of Worley led two scowling ladies from the drawing room, Emma wondered how many of the gathered spectators would have the gumption to remain until they returned.

* * *

John had maneuvered the walk in order to escape Lady Ridgely's overpopulated drawing room, but once they arrived, he realized the inadvertent brilliance of the decision. It seemed the whole of fashionable society had come out that afternoon in a carriage, on a horse, or on foot. It was the perfect day for it—warm, but not uncomfortably so—yet John suspected the determined crowd would have reliably appeared even if the weather had not been quite so favorable. They came for the choreographed dance of nods and greetings, the purpose of which was to notice and to be noticed and, above all, with and by whom one was noticed.

John tilted his face up to the sun and breathed deeply of the flower-scented air. He didn't generally enjoy crowds, but a stroll with his fiancée would certainly quell the current expectation that the betrothal had ended. She was quite becoming, after all, in a pale green day dress.

Why hadn't she gotten married to someone else in all this time? Where had the suitors been in four years? John supposed poor judgment on the part of other gentlemen wasn't entirely surprising and, as it benefitted him now, he could not object to it.

"Shall we walk toward the Serpentine?" he proposed

Lady Emmaline stared at him as though he had suggested they stand in the middle of Rotten Row and flag down carriages. Miss Georgiana Wolfe, who seemed determined to walk several paces behind in the manner of a lady's maid or governess, did not respond.

"It may be crowded near the lake," Lady Emmaline said.

"For good reason. It's the most scenic spot."

Lady Emmaline's lips pursed. Her amber eyes regarded him coolly for another moment. Just when John felt certain she would voice her objection and insist upon hiding in some out-of-the-way locale, she gave an acquiescent dip of her chin. With no opinion contributed by Miss Wolfe, their group walked in the direction of the Serpentine.

"How have you enjoyed the season, Miss Wolfe?" Lady Emmaline asked over her shoulder in an unveiled attempt to coax the girl forward. "Have you had an opportunity to attend the theater?"

"I like London very much. And I particularly enjoy the theater." Her answer was polite, but she did not yield the buffer of her position.

When silence followed, John gave Lady Emmaline a cheerful smile. "It is remarkably warm today, wouldn't you say?"

"Yes, but it is not unpleasant," she responded. "I rather enjoy the outdoors." She turned to call over her shoulder again. "Do you enjoy the outdoors, Miss Wolfe?" She paused in her stride, a maneuver that forced the girl to step alongside her. John halted as well, lest he find himself well ahead of the ladies.

"I enjoy taking some air occasionally." Miss Wolfe glanced nervously at John before she admitted, "I'm not much of a horsewoman, though."

"Not all can be." Lady Emmaline said kindly, with a reassuring hand upon the girl's arm. "You're fortunate enough to be lovely and will, I'm sure, be forgiven almost any other failing."

Miss Wolfe's cheeks took on a soft blush at Emma's compliment. She shot another uncertain glance at John.

Lady Emmaline saw to it that conversation continued between the two women, posing questions to Miss Wolfe with enough frequency that the young lady could not possibly withdraw again. The inquiries became impossibly mundane, but John admired Lady Emmaline's fortitude in continuing to generate them. She asked where Miss Wolfe had acquired the ribbon that adorned her bonnet and conducted a complete survey of which instruments the girl might have learned to play. When she inquired as to the list of any novels Miss Wolfe may have recently enjoyed, John knew without question the woman would go to any length to prevent him from addressing the true purpose of his visit. Clearly, she was no more favorably disposed to the situation after a night to think on it. His fingers closed around the small ring that weighted his pocket. She would exhaust herself of idle conversation eventually. He suspected she already found the conversation as painful as he did.

John was saved from concocting an interruption by feminine calls of "Georgiana! Georgiana!"

"Oh, it's Elena Westbrook. And Caroline Dunford," Miss Wolfe said as they approached a group of young ladies waving animatedly.

John did not recognize the girls, of course, but he easily recognized the desperate relief in Miss Wolfe's expression as she spotted her saviors. The girl hurried away at such a pace, John suspected she would have grasped at any passing acquaintance for whom she could remember a name.

"You should consider Georgiana Wolfe," Lady Emmaline said, turning back to John after watching the girl join her friends.

He eyed her and could not help the upward tug at the corners of his mouth. "Do you mean to suggest I propose marriage to the girl who just fled from my company as though she happened upon an escape route from inside Newgate?"

Lady Emmaline's eyes rolled skyward at his dramatics but, in all fairness, the girl had *run* away.

She crossed her arms in front of her chest. "She only did so because she has enough sensitivity to understand the present awkward situation—one she knows full well was engineered by her mother, not by you. She seems a reasonable, intelligent girl."

"And you're not?"

"I am perfectly reasonable. I am simply uninterested in becoming your duchess."

John cocked his head to one side and studied her. "And why is that precisely?" he asked. "Why would a perfectly reasonable young lady choose to be the wife of an aging widower with little income and a brood of children when she might be a duchess instead?"

She cast an assessing glance around them before stepping forward to John and lifting her gaze unflinchingly to his. "Why should I supply an explanation for my actions when you've failed to provide a satisfactory one for yours?"

It was not an informative response. "Have you developed an affection for this Greystoke fellow?" he pressed.

Lady Emmaline's eyes fell to her hands. "He is a perfectly amiable gentleman," She said. Her voice was gentle but firm.

"So you have not."

She looked up sharply and was no longer gentle in responding. "My feelings toward Mr. Greystoke are none of your concern."

"Particularly as we've already established you have none." He watched her, daring her to dispute it.

She remained silent, and they both knew she was unwilling to voice the lie.

"Which leaves us the question," he continued, "of why you object to marrying me when it is the best course for us both."

"The best course for me?" She hissed, her widening eyes taking in the sun like amber flashes of lightening. "How can you know the best course for *me*?"

"You've already conceded your consideration of a match predicated on security rather than a deep affection," he explained in a cautious tone, lest he further stoke her ire. "If you are seeking to secure your future—as we all must do, Lady Emmaline—surely marriage to me can provide greater comfort and security than that which may be offered by almost any other."

She did not respond with an immediate objection and John was hopeful she had seen the sense in his rationale. As she continued to study his face in silence, an unreadable expression upon her face, his confidence waned.

She turned away to view the lake and presented her profile before responding. "You presume too much in knowing the sort of life in which I might take comfort." The slight breeze caused her skirts to ripple, a fluid motion at odds with the erectness of her posture as she gazed out onto the idyllic beauty of the park reflected in the water of the Serpentine. She was quite lovely and, though the strength of her resolve was in conflict with his present agenda, he admired her for it.

"It may be that we get on well together," he suggested. "We could be... friends. Even affectionate friends."

She turned then to peer incredulously at him. "Friends?" she echoed, her voice elevating nearly an octave. "*Affectionate* friends? You cannot be serious. Before our engagement, I was virtually unknown. *You* put my name on everyone's lips as the most infamously rejected fiancée in living memory. My family were humiliated." She paused in her tirade to notice passersby looking their way and lowered her voice to an angry hiss. "Did you truly believe I would leap at the chance to marry you now?"

"I understand the offense I have given to you and your family, Lady Emmaline, and I am sorry for it. I urge you not to allow injured pride, no matter how justified, to overrule good sense."

She lifted her chin. "A certain amount of pride is necessary to maintain one's dignity."

John sighed. It seemed he was hurting his case rather than helping it. "What of the fact that the gossip was untrue?" he tried.

She squared her shoulders but the strength of her posture did not extend to her expression. She did not meet his eyes when she responded, "As you and I well know, society rarely bothers with anything so trivial as the truth."

In that moment, it occurred to John that the woman he had offended, the woman who had been harmed by his abrupt and mysterious departure was not the person who stood before him now exhibiting quiet determination. She had been a young girl, barely grown, and though he had known her even less at seventeen than he knew her now, he could guess she had not yet had this woman's strength. Perhaps the iron of her will had been forged from the very predicament in which he had placed her. He reached out to take her gloved hands in his.

"I am very sorry, Emmaline, to have been the cause of suffering for you and your family."

Wide, golden eyes looked up at him in what he could only count as alarm. Because he had addressed her too familiarly? Because he held her hands? He could not know, because though she opened her mouth to raise what he could only assume was an objection, she never gave voice to it. Instead, her attention fell to where her hands sat limply in his and she stared a moment as though assimilating this contact before finally pulling them away.

After a pause, she said, "I still think you'd do better to consider Miss Wolfe. Her connections are very good and you'd gain an ally among the most determined gossips." She had recovered her matter-of-fact tone, but he believed the color on her cheeks was a bit brighter than it had been a few minutes before.

"You refer to her mother. You are proposing that dragon of the drawing room as a social champion for my sister."

"Georgiana is a steady, pleasant girl. You would not be unhappy with her, I think."

He was not chiefly concerned with his own happiness.

Or was he?

Brydges was correct on one point. Marriage was a long business. Miss Georgiana Wolfe seemed to be a quiet, sweet girl who would take interest in whatever she had been instructed. John had no plans for love, but he'd prefer the companionship of a woman who knew her own mind.

He looked at Lady Emmaline. "The picture of Lady Wolfe is not a high recommendation for Miss Wolfe herself," he pointed out.

She gave a slight shrug. "If you wish respectability and social clout for your sister, she's better able to provide it than I am, as your scandalously rejected fiancée."

"Ah, but if we married, you wouldn't be rejected. Your reputation would be restored when I honor the engagement and reveal that my intentions to do so never wavered."

She released an exasperated huff. "No one will believe that."

"People will choose to believe it—because you'll be a duchess."

She did not dispute his prediction. "I still don't understand why you don't simply choose another. If not Miss Wolfe, then someone else."

"Even if I disregard my increasing conviction that you are better suited than any other, seeking out and courting another fiancée would require precious time I cannot afford. Consider, Lady Emmaline, that I seek respectability for my sister. If I must marry, the most respectable choice is to marry the woman to whom I am already affianced."

She leaned her head back and stared directly up at him. "Should I be gratified then that you finally find me convenient?"

She was determined to take exception with him, even when he applied the most reasonable logic to their circumstance. "You make it sound as though I have been guilty of reckless whim. I assure you, that is not the case. My decision to marry has been carefully considered and you cannot deny that we shall each achieve our purpose from the arrangement. You do have to marry someday, Lady Emmaline. In choosing to honor this betrothal you can secure not only your future, but the future of a girl who would otherwise be robbed of hers."

"If this arrangement is so mutually beneficial, Your Grace, then why do I feel such a pawn in your stratagems? Perhaps I desire a marriage that is not so mercenary."

John nearly groaned in frustration. She was debating in circles. She had already as good as conceded she was considering marriage to an old man for whom she harbored no great affection. How was that arrangement any less mercenary than this? He stepped closer and clasped both of her arms below the shoulder as though in the next breath he might pull her into an embrace. "Would you believe me if I declared a great passion for you and insisted I would have no other?"

He watched the brilliant spots of color take residence on her cheeks, but she was not cowed. She glared bravely back at him. "No. I would not. I, for one, am fully aware you have not been pining for me these past four years."

He lowered his hands but did not retreat. "It's true. I've not been pining for you all these years. I think you would not have me flatter you with false declarations."

She did not answer, but her chin rose defiantly and he was oddly tempted to trace a finger along that firmly set jaw. "I do like you, Emmaline," he said, keeping his hands firmly at his sides. "I very much like what I have come to know of you so far. I admire your inability to be cowed by society. By me. Your strength is rarer than you realize." He met her gaze with honesty in his own. "And appealing."

They stood mere inches apart for an expectant breath of a moment while John waited to see how she would respond.

For some reason he could not name, he was disappointed when she simply stepped away, gave him the briefest of polite smiles, and suggested, "Shall we continue our walk?"

John glanced to where Miss Wolfe still stood chatting with her friends. "We have lost our chaperone, but perhaps that matters not, as we are engaged to be married."

Her hand was limp as he reached out to take it and lay it on his arm, but her response was not so compliant. "I don't even recall agreeing to a walk in the park. I am quite sure I haven't agreed to this engagement."

"We are already betrothed. It's already been agreed to." He tilted his head toward hers and spoke softly. "*Contractually* agreed to."

Her expression was a warning and he smiled at the vehemence of it. "Rest assured, I do not abduct and enslave women, Lady Emmaline. I am convinced we should be married, but I well understand my challenge is to convince you of the wisdom of it. You will not accept my ring today, but I am determined to prevail."

Her expression shifted to wary suspicion.

"I give you fair warning," he said cheerfully. "My will is as strong as yours."

Chapter Six

Emma wanted nothing more that evening than a few quiet hours reading alone in her room. There were several reasons she longed for that unattainable isolation, not the least of which was the rain that buffeted her uncle's carriage as it rocked and bounced through the slick and puddled streets of London on its way to the residence of Lord and Lady Spitzer for their famed end-of-season ball. The carriage provided a cocoon of relative shelter, but the dampness penetrated and the sounds of the storm cut off any attempts at conversation.

It was just as well.

Emma had done all the talking she could tolerate over the past several days. Her disturbing conversation with the duke had been followed by a probing conversation with Lady Wolfe. She'd since had more than one troubling discussion with her aunt. The interactions had each been equally frustrating, as Emma had failed to make her point in any of them. The duke still considered himself engaged; Lady Wolfe still considered herself an authority on the subject of Emma's future prospects; and Aunt Agatha still believed seeing this betrothal through to fruition meant the difference between success and failure in her duty to Emma's parents.

In all honesty, her failures influencing Aunt Agatha and Lady Wolfe were minor annoyances compared to her apprehensions about the duke. He was too sure of himself. He had called her by her given name. Twice. He had called her Emmaline—not Emma, as her family did, but stripped of her courtesy title and spoken in his deep baritone, it was too familiar, too intimate. She didn't like it.

She didn't like that he had touched her either. She like even less that his touch had elicited an unexpected response. To her mind, his ability to interfere with her rational thinking justified a new level of wariness where he was concerned. When he'd clasped her shoulders and threatened to declare a great passion, he'd done so only to make his point. Stupidly, she'd been affected anyway.

She attributed the magnitude of its effect to the foreign nature of the sensation. Surely, if she'd invested the time most other young ladies did in chasing after gentlemen, she'd have encountered countless men she found appealing in appearance. Unfortunately, she was not accustomed to having the direct attention of a man such as the duke, or to the feelings that attention aroused. She was disappointed to think the first real hints of attraction she'd experienced were inspired by *him*. And now her curiosity had been piqued, which she saw as a personal failing.

In order to avoid Worley altogether, she had proposed declining the invitation to the Spitzer event, but her aunt insisted a late withdrawal would cause more speculation than an appearance. Beyond that, Mr. Greystoke was to be in attendance and she owed him some explanation or apology for her present predicament. Though he'd never directly addressed her with a proposal of marriage, his purpose in London was clear and his particular attention to Emma had been unmistakable.

The fact was, whether she wanted to marry Worley or not, she was currently engaged to the overbearing duke and, therefore, an ineligible match for Mr. Greystoke.

In truth, she didn't know if she ever could have married him, kind and admirable though he was. She'd never been fully resigned to the idea. Neither did she want to marry the duke, but the feelings he had inspired with a simple touch on her arm and a whisper of breath on her neck left her thinking of attraction and desire—thoughts that had no business occupying the mind of an almost spinster with no prospects other than a fatherly old man.

Emma stared out the window at unfocused scenes of London while her thoughts settled on an important consideration.

In considering Mr. Greystoke, even halfheartedly, hadn't Emma accepted she could no longer hope for a match built upon a great shared affection? Common sense had dictated she consider Mr. Greystoke and now common sense probably required she consider the duke as well. It vexed her that the duke was correct in that point.

Still, she couldn't quite bring herself to truly consider either alternative. She wanted to live at the cottage. She'd healed there. She felt whole there. Perhaps she could have given up life at the cottage for the opportunity for true affection and a family of her own—but not to raise another woman's children with a man she didn't love. And not to become the duchess of a man she barely knew.

She could not marry Mr. Greystoke and so she must speak with him. She would not marry the duke and so she vowed to stay well clear of him. She knew what she had to do, but still her mood was black. She rather thought the heavens agreed with her, for they'd done everything in their power to create an ill night for going out.

* * *

Emma's first thought upon entering Lord and Lady Spitzer's London residence was that it was not as grand as the Fairhaven's and, if they refused to limit their guest list, they should have considered renting the assembly rooms rather than attempting to squeeze so many into the rooms of their town house. The event was already a crush. The din was assaulting, contributed to in no small part by the shouted greetings of Lord Spitzer's nearly deaf mother as she stood with her son and his wife to greet arriving guests.

"So nice of you to come, my dear." The diminutive woman shouted up from underneath a feather-adorned turban, making Emma feel particularly tall. "I was very fond of your mother, you know. Tragic, what happened."

"Yes, it was. Thank you for your kind words."

"I beg your pardon, dear?" The lady rose on her toes toward Emma, nearly skewering her with the feather.

"Yes, it was," Emma shouted back. "Thank you for your kindness."

The elderly woman nodded and turned to bark at the next newcomer.

Relieved to move on, Emma followed her aunt and uncle in greeting Lord and Lady Spitzer. Her relief was short-lived, however, when the first party they encountered upon entering the main salon was a group of ladies over which Lady Wolfe held court.

"Lady Ridgely." She greeted Aunt Agatha with a simpering nod. "Why I was just commenting to some of the ladies what a lovely time my Georgiana had walking with the duke in the park while I visited you this week. She was so delighted to have received his particular attention."

"I'm pleased she enjoyed it." Aunt Agatha would never have pointed out Lady Wolfe's poor memory of recent events, but Emma was tempted.

"How do you do, Lady Emmaline?" Lady Wolfe finally addressed her, though she didn't appear to enjoy it and did not wait for a response. "It may interest you that I noted Mr. Greystoke's attendance this evening."

Emma was not surprised by Lady Wolfe's less-than-subtle implication that girls such as her daughter were meant for men like the duke while

Emma, whose social standing had been so reduced by her scandalous rejection and disinterest in society, should be grateful for the attention of Mr. Greystoke.

Because she could not disagree, she took offense not for herself but for Mr. Greystoke, who was an honorable gentleman. "I shall be happy to share his company, thank you."

It was a well-timed reminder of the need to seek the gentleman out.

In the end, however, there proved no need, for Mr. Greystoke found Emma and her aunt soon after their quick departure from the company of the unpleasant Lady Wolfe. He strode purposefully toward them, his smile open and genuine, and Emma was assaulted by waves of guilt for what she had come to do.

He was slight in stature, by no stretch an intimidating man. Still, the streaks of gray in his hair and his reserved manner lent him an elegant dignity that defied the inexpensive cut of his clothing. Emma thought of the sum he must have invested in even modest clothing and accommodations to participate in a London season. Now the season was nearly over and he'd wasted most of it courting a woman who could not marry him.

He gave a slight bow upon reaching the ladies. "Lady Ridgley. Lady Emmaline. You are both lovely, as always."

Aunt Agatha's smile was genuine. "And you are as gracious as always. It is a pleasure to see you, Mr. Greystoke."

He turned to Emma.

"Good evening, Mr. Greystoke," she said, oddly glad the moment had come and would soon be done. "We are always glad for your company, as you must be aware."

He appeared pleased at her comment and her guilt swelled.

If only she knew how to begin. How *does* one break an understanding that was never explicitly discussed?

Emma glanced at her aunt, who nodded encouragingly. Unfortunately, Emma did not need encouragement—she needed words. She turned an overly bright smile toward Mr. Greystoke. "I was hoping, actually, that we might have an opportunity to speak together. You may know…that is, you may have heard…"

She realized she was wringing her hands and slowly placed them at her sides. Her eyes fell to address him somewhere in the vicinity of his chest. "You see, four years ago I was engaged. To the Duke of Worley. Well, he wasn't the duke then, but he is now. And we all believed he had died, but he clearly didn't. And so now you see…well, I thought because you and I had become particular friends I should be the one to inform you that, well…."

Mr. Greystoke reached out and laid his hand on Emma's arm to halt her speech.

She obeyed, relieved to adopt silence and await his reaction.

"There is no need to explain, Lady Emmaline. I understand the situation completely."

At his words, a good portion of the tension lodged between Emma's neck and shoulders fell away.

"Your betrothed, the duke, called on me this afternoon."

"He what?" All of the tension in her shoulders returned anew. She gave her head a slight shake. "He called on you? Today?"

"Yes." Mr. Greystoke nodded as though the news should be welcome.

Of all the arrogant things for that man to do. He had warned her, hadn't he? She should have guessed he would not limit his attempts at persuasion to direct conversation. Mr. Greystoke had slowly and respectfully courted her for weeks. He did not deserve to be rudely warned off his course merely because it conflicted with the grand plans of a duke. She exhaled in an unsuccessful attempt to release her frustration and retain her composure.

"Mr. Greystoke," she began, speaking in a slow and measured tone meant to calm her own rising ire as much as his, "please allow me to sincerely apologize for the high-handed manner in which I'm sure His Grace chose to inform you of our prior betrothal. It was entirely arranged by our parents. Everyone believed he'd died, otherwise I never—"

"There is no need for an apology, I assure you," Mr. Greystoke interjected, a benign curve bending his lips. She could not find the merest hint of indignation in his manner, despite its clear provocation. "You could not have foreseen this," he said reassuringly, "and the duke was quite gracious. I rather felt as though he were asking my permission."

"Your permission?" She couldn't seem to stop herself from repeating his words.

"Yes, in a way he did. He explained about the prior contract between your parents, but said he also knew that you and I…well, that I had courted you." He cleared his throat. "He insisted that if I truly believed in your strong affection toward me, he would step aside and graciously allow you to withdraw from the engagement so that we could marry."

Emma swallowed. The duke had offered to step aside? To allow her to marry Mr. Greystoke? She stared at Mr. Greystoke, his contented smile and purposeful approach taking on new meaning. Could one's breath halt even as one's pulse quickened? She swallowed heavily. Had the duke stepped aside? Had this man actually asked it of him? Had she just moved from one trap to another without any awareness that her future was being arranged without her consent or consultation?

"I told him, of course, that we got on amicably, but I did not imagine you were, well...in love...with me." He coughed again. Then he grinned as though he found the entire thing amusing. "Can you imagine a man such as myself competing with a wealthy duke for a lady's affections?"

Sweet air filled her lungs again. Of course a humble, unassuming man such as Mr. Greystoke would not have asked the duke to step aside. Emma decided she was not entirely comfortable with the magnitude of her panic, nor the significance of her relief upon hearing that the duke had not yielded her hand to Mr. Greystoke.

Aunt Agatha filled the hole left by Emma's long silence. "You have been very gracious to accept that my niece and her betrothed must honor the commitment made by their parents."

"Of course they must." He gave a befuddled chuckle. "I never expected to be called upon by a duke, I can tell you—definitely not one who would treat me with the respect and deference I received from your fiancé, Lady Emmaline. He truly seemed willing to walk away at my word, though I would not have asked it of him." Bemused, he shook his head.

Emma felt as though she were clinging to a wild horse that moved to everyone's commands except her own. When had she become no more than a spectator in her own life? She had to regain some measure of authority over her own future. She had to speak on her own behalf. "I feel I should fully explain." The words came about a bit louder and more frantic than she had intended. She released a quick breath. "It appears I am, in fact, betrothed to the duke," she said carefully, "but I have not yet decided if I wish to remain so."

"What's this?" His brow furrowed—with concern or confusion, Emma couldn't tell. "You don't want to marry him?"

She wasn't quite sure how to articulate it anymore. She didn't want to marry him—at least she didn't believe she did—yet somehow she was more certain now, following the duke's return, that she did not wish to marry Mr. Greystoke either. And somehow all of his reasoning managed to make her objections feel more like childish obstinacy as opposed to common sense.

She struggled to give a sensible response. "It's just that so much time has passed and I don't really *know* him at all. The duke has openly confirmed our engagement, so if I withdraw now...well, you can imagine how my actions would be viewed. I would not really be a desirable match for anyone I suppose, given everything taken all together." She punctuated her ramblings with a weak smile.

Mr. Greystoke addressed Emma earnestly. "I am not your father, Lady Emmaline, though I am nearly old enough to be," he said with a brief, self-deprecating smile. "And it would seem I am not to be your husband, so I can claim no right to offer any opinion on your future. But allow me to say, as your friend, that I was much impressed by the Duke of Worley—not by his status or finery, but by the manner in which he treated me. Not many men of his ilk possess sufficient humility to show concern for a man with barely a fraction of his consequence."

Emma swallowed. Humility? Perhaps he treated Mr. Greystoke respectfully, but what of her? He had trod upon her toes without any thought for it.

She stood a little straighter as she regarded Mr. Greystoke. "I do accept your advice, as my friend, and I am grateful for your concern. I have been feeling sorry for myself these past few days, wishing I were not in this difficult situation. Please, let me be sorry as well for the trouble I have caused you."

"On the contrary, Lady Emmaline. I could never consider time spent in the company of a lovely young lady to be troublesome."

His graciousness only added to her guilt. The guilt then fueled her anger at the duke. Of all the arrogant, high-handed, presumptuous... Oh, she could not think of enough words to describe how utterly unfair it was. To think the duke had very nearly ended their engagement by trapping her in another!

She had pledged to avoid the man for the evening, but could no longer do so. Instead, she felt compelled to seek him out immediately and tell him exactly what she thought of his interference.

* * *

The duke was maddeningly easy to locate. He had drawn a predictable crowd of admirers. Even Emma had to admit he was pleasant to look upon... from a distance, of course. If one did not linger close enough to be aware of his arrogance and insincerity, one could find him dashingly handsome. She had only moments before observed that Mr. Greystoke carried a quiet elegance, but there was no comparison between the two men. The duke was so much more.

More what?

More everything.

Broad-shouldered and tall with an easy posture, he had the bearing of a man who didn't need to claim a title to be consequential. Yet he possessed a very impressive title—one to match every other impressive thing about him, from his impossibly blue eyes to his richly dark hair. It was annoying, that.

Emma maneuvered herself intentionally into the duke's line of sight. After lingering there just long enough to be sure he was aware of her presence, she turned her back to him, smiling and nodding in another direction. She knew he would approach her before long, and he did.

"Good evening, my dear."

The quietly spoken words traveled the entire length of her body before she slowly turned and faced him.

"Your Grace." She focused on her effort to remain placid in his presence. Why was she so discomfited by his proximity?

"Each time I see you, I am more satisfied with our betrothal, Lady Emmaline. You are especially fetching this evening."

She eyed him warily, displeased with the involuntary pleasure she experienced at his compliment. "What I *am*, Your Grace, is a few years older and a good deal taller than is quite fashionable for unmarried ladies."

He laughed at her rebuke. It wasn't a cold, brittle laugh, but warm and lustful. She was unwillingly enveloped by it and stepped back.

"What you *are*," he said, "is unable to graciously accept a compliment. I did not, you'll recall, declare you to be fashionable. I have no need for 'fashionable.' I am just a man, however, and find I do desire 'fetching.'"

His eyes raked over her as he said it, and she was momentarily without the sharp retort she would so have liked to deliver.

"Tell me," he continued at her silence. "If it is unfashionable to be tall when one is unmarried, but perfectly acceptable to be tall once one is wed, how do the wedded tall women ever become so, I wonder?"

She released a breath of laughter before she could prevent it. The thought was nonsensical, but exactly the sort of irrationality that thrived among society. "Very well, Your Grace. I concede every woman can be fashionable if she will simply wait until her particular attributes into vogue. Perhaps next year, tall brunette spinsters shall be all the rage."

His grin was inviting. Too inviting. "Unfortunately for you, you will not be one. You shall be a tall, brunette duchess instead. Also quite popular, I am told."

There it was. The reminder she needed. She had a purpose here if she could just manage to stay attentive to it. She squared her shoulders. "I thought perhaps we might find an opportunity to speak more privately, Your Grace."

He nodded and in a few moments had orchestrated their separate but simultaneous exit from the ballroom followed shortly by a reunion on the garden path. It was startlingly easy. Emma wondered how any naïve young girl remained virtuous when propriety was so easily circumvented. If some young swain had pursued her with any persistence during her debut season, would she have been savvy enough to resist? She wasn't certain. The involuntary sensations she experienced in the duke's company had her wondering if she would be savvy enough even now.

"May I take your interest in a private word as a sign you're becoming amenable to our engagement?"

Emma waited to respond to the duke's question until they reached the privacy of a secluded corner of the small garden attached to the Spitzer residence. The evening was warm and the garden fragrant, but she could not enjoy it. Steeling herself against any silly, girlish fluttering she might be experiencing, she held herself erect as she addressed him.

"You may not."

Her terse words triggered an abrupt collapse of his pleased expression. His brow arched. "Should I be concerned for my safety? We are without witnesses, I realize."

Her eyes narrowed. "You may find your own humor diverting, just as you find your own intentions noble, but I do not." She stepped toward him and glared. "How dare you speak with Mr. Greystoke on my behalf? You have no right to meddle in my personal affairs or in my future."

"Many would disagree with you, you know, and insist your future husband is, in fact, obligated to be concerned with your personal affairs and, most certainly, your future. Mr. Greystoke didn't seem offended by my calling on him."

"*I* am offended. You are not my future husband. I am firmly decided. You may consider the engagement broken as of this moment."

"You've decided, have you? You will marry Greystoke?" He shook his head. "Ridiculous."

Emma took a step backward and crossed her arms over her chest. "I…I don't plan to marry Mr. Greystoke either."

He threw up his hands in frustration. "Well, if you're not going to marry him and you're not going to marry me, what the hell *are* you planning to do?"

Her chin jutted forward. "I have a cottage."

He stopped, stared. "A cottage?"

"Yes. It's mine. It was the only portion of my father's estate that was not entailed. I inherited it when my parents died." She did not reveal that the cottage was very near his home at Brantmoor.

"I see. And how do you plan to sustain yourself in this cottage. Have you an income?"

"A modest one, from funds set aside by my father." She straightened her shoulders, bristling under the mocking tone of his question. "I assure you, I will not be a pauper." She would not be wealthy by any means, but what need had one of carriages and gowns when one lived in the countryside anyway? "You're allowing yourself to be ruled by pride. The daughter of an earl would never be content in a country cottage, with no wealth or diversion." She stepped forward. Her finger poked his chest, intentionally disregarding its unyielding expanse. "That insulting statement only proves you know nothing of me or what I require to be content. The cottage is my home and has been for three full years. I reside there except when I am visiting my aunt and uncle." Her hands landed on her hips. "If I had only had the good sense to remain there, I wouldn't be in this predicament."

She expected him to rant more, to tell her how ridiculous she was to choose life in a cottage when she might live with her aunt and uncle, or with him if they married, yet he said nothing. He stepped to the small stone bench nearby and waved his hand, inviting her to sit. She did, taking care to leave the few inches of unoccupied seat between them.

His brow furrowed, he studied her as one might a specimen of some academic interest. "You and I know very little about each other."

Emma exhaled, relieved to know her words had somehow penetrated. "Virtually nothing, Your Grace."

His shoulders slumped slightly and she thought she heard him release a sigh before he looked up at her. "You may dispense with 'Your Grace,' if you'd like. The formality seems a bit odd in the context of such frank conversation, wouldn't you say? My name is John. There were no titles in Boston."

John. She knew she would think of him as John from now on, though she had no intention of speaking it. Emma's eyes fell to her hands as she held them in her lap. "Perhaps the formality is more appropriate, Your Grace, since we are not to be married after all."

She looked up to find him gazing intently at her, his blue eyes seeming shadowed by more than the moonlit darkness. She was acutely aware of the narrow stretch of stone that separated them.

"I'm going to tell you a story that I've shared with very few people. Once I do, I'll feel damned foolish addressing you formally all the time."

She bravely held his gaze, though her instinct was to hide from it. "What sort of story?"

His tone was grave as he continued. "My father was not a good man. He was irrationally jealous of my mother, convinced she was engaging in all sorts of affairs. I'll tell you I was young and had no way of knowing, but my mother denied all of it until her death and I'm inclined to believe her."

He paused as though awaiting her acceptance of that fact, so Emma nodded, encouraging him to continue.

"When his rages became intolerable and he began insisting Charlotte was another man's daughter, my mother feared for Charlotte's safety and fled. My father told everyone they were visiting distant relatives in America. A few months later he reported learning they'd caught fever and died. I spent my entire childhood believing my mother and sister were dead."

He seemed ready to share more, so Emma probed softly. "How did you learn otherwise?"

"After I finished my schooling. My mother contacted me through a solicitor to tell me that she and my sister were alive and in need of help. My father knew this and refused to aid them—his own daughter. I sent everything I could spare and some I could not, but it was not enough. My father thought my debts had grown from a dissolute lifestyle and agreed to pay them if I fulfilled my duty and got married."

"Hence our engagement," Emma concluded softly.

"Yes. And when I learned that my mother had taken ill and the two of them were left quite alone and unprotected...I had no choice but to go to them. Charlotte has endured hardships she should not have." He stared into the evening darkness. "I want to begin to make things right for her, to restore even a piece of what she has lost. No—*all* of what she has lost."

He had so much conviction as he spoke of his sister. She found it startling—and inspiring. How could she not be moved by such an impassioned speech? "Emma," she said after a silent moment. "My family call me Emma."

John turned and smiled. She was glad her small gesture had restored it and at the same time, apprehensive for the quickening it caused in her heartbeat.

"Emma." He reached over and pulled her hand into his lap, where he held it. "I've been so intent on my purpose, I've been very inconsiderate of your feelings."

Emma struggled to characterize her feelings at just that moment. He held her hand, nothing more, yet she felt anticipation as though she stood on the precipice of something far greater.

"Emma, I *am* sorry for the trouble I've caused you, both then and now."

"Thank you." She swallowed. Could he have any way of knowing how this simple contact was affecting her? Would she be less affected if she had more experience with courting and flirtation?

"You've surprised me, you know. So much about you is...unexpected. How could I have foreseen such a clever, headstrong, and beautiful woman who'd rather live alone in a cottage than among the whirl of high society?" His hand reached up, and she froze as he allowed his fingers to graze her face. "Perhaps if I'd realized," he teased, "I'd have taken you with me four years ago."

What an odd sensation, Emma thought, to feel as though one were both rigid with anxiety melting into liquid all at the same time. John's gaze dropped to her lips and she felt, perhaps even wished, that he might kiss her. Did she truly want him to kiss her? She'd chosen the life of an old maid. Could there be much harm if she allowed herself a kiss before she did? She felt herself leaning forward, felt her eyelids fall just as his lips brushed hers. Her body had never seemed so interconnected before, with the touch to her lips wreaking such havoc elsewhere on her form. She felt a weightlessness low in her middle that grew as his mouth lingered on hers. Then it was over and he pulled away as gently as he had come.

"Now I'm certain I should have taken you with me," he whispered. His smile was wry, but the intensity that lingered in his eyes matched the sensations that still coursed through Emma's body.

She gazed up at him, unsure what to say, aware of the heat in her cheeks, aware of her chest as it rose and fell.

He closed the distance between them again. "May I have your permission, Emma," he implored her, "to kiss you again?"

Her brief nod was barely executed when his lips met hers again. This touch was not soft or teasing, but met the urgency she hadn't realized she harbored as he crushed his mouth to hers. She felt his hands settle on her waist and pull her closer. Her arms roped around his neck.

She hesitated only an instant when she felt his tongue gently probe her lips apart. When she opened for him, and the kiss deepened, the only thought still finding purchase in her mind was what a shame it would be to live out her life never having experienced this, never having fulfilled—even just once—the promise of where this could lead.

His lips separated from hers and trailed kisses across her jaw and onto her neck as her head lolled back, cradled by his arm. Whenever had she become such a wanton and why didn't she seem to care? She *should* care. This was more than a simple kiss. Yet she clung to him.

Voices nearby penetrated her awareness, suddenly confirming that she *did* care. She was draped across the duke's lap for heaven's sake!

"Damn." John's muttered curse confirmed he'd heard them as well.

Emma pushed against John's chest, trying awkwardly to rise until his hands closed around her waist. In one swift movement, he rose from the bench, lifting her with him, and set her neatly with her feet on the ground. He pushed her in the direction of the house and whispered an urgent, "Go!"

She went, darting into the cover of the garden path and hurrying toward the house, all the while reaching up to gauge the condition of her hair and assure her dress was straight. She stopped just beyond the door that led to the rear hall and took several deep breaths to collect herself.

My God, what had she been thinking? She'd nearly trapped herself into the very marriage she'd been trying to avoid!

Wait...

No. She discounted the thought as soon as it materialized. John could not have planned to force her hand by compromising her. He'd been more useful than she had in helping her flee before she was seen.

She should go inside, but she couldn't yet. She crossed her arms over her stomach and took two more deep breaths.

As quickly as her brain ceased reeling from John's kisses, it was tumbling again over the story he'd shared about his family. Emma could scarce believe it. She no longer wondered at his malevolence upon their first meeting. Would she have reacted differently in his place. What a monster the old duke was! Imagine abandoning one's daughter at just fourteen years of age to fend for herself without protection? She could hardly comprehend it.

His son had done the opposite. John had sacrificed everything to rush to his family's aid. His father might have lived for decades, leaving him in exile indefinitely with no title or wealth or advantage of birth. If the old duke had been a monster, what did that mean for the new duke? She was not entirely comfortable declaring him the hero of this melodrama, but she suspected he may be. He had put the fortunes of his mother and sister ahead of his own.

Emma wondered who else knew how low the old duke had sunk in abandoning his family. Why, if she had children of her own, she would protect them at any cost.

Silly thoughts, really. Old maids living in country cottages did not have children. For that matter, neither did they engage in the kind of activity in which *she* had been an enthusiastic participant only minutes before.

Emma leaned against the wall and touched her fingers to her lips—where he'd kissed her. She knew why she'd allowed him to kiss her. No rationale her mind could conjure would have been strong enough to fight her body's will while his lips had hovered near hers. But why had he kissed her? She'd broken the engagement. It was over. They were not to be man and wife.

He should not have kissed her. He would have no reason or occasion to kiss her again.

She had no sound reason to feel disappointment.

Chapter Seven

Four bawdily laughing gentlemen strolled through the arbor, crossing the very path toward which John had unceremoniously shoved Emma just seconds before. He'd managed to strike a casual pose on the bench before they spotted him, but not a single muscle in his body was relaxed. Every bit of him was tense, every sense still very much alive.

"Is that you, Worley?" one of them asked.

He couldn't name any of them, but recognized the lot as a group of young pups Brydges had pointed out at the Fairhavens', bragging of besting one or two of them in cards.

"Thought I'd take some air," John answered, gratified that his voice came out as its normal baritone. "It's a mad crush in there."

The shortest one stepped forward with a saucy grin. "Can't blame you for needing an escape. I'd vow the ladies are three to one with gents this evening. Fellow can't find a moment to himself."

"That's a lot of hogwash coming from you," one of the others chimed in. "You've been chasing Miss Denton around the floor all evening."

"Ah, but I wonder," another one questioned. "Is he chasing her full bodice or her father's full pockets?"

"Both, I suppose," the first one admitted, not at all ashamed of himself.

John rose and gave a curt nod. "I'll leave you gentlemen to your amorous strategies." He had neither the mood nor the composure at that moment for inane chatter, though he considered as he walked away that he was grateful for the interruption. In all truth, he doubted he'd have had the presence of mind to stop before things had gotten further out of hand if not for their near discovery.

It was poorly done of him. Wouldn't be the first time an engaged couple had been caught in a premature embrace, but he'd specifically set out to overcome, not increase, the scandal attached to his family. He'd have enough explaining to do when he presented Charlotte to society. He didn't need to cultivate a reputation as a seducer of innocents.

He just couldn't seem to deny himself the kiss, not when she'd given it so sweetly.

He was committed to marrying for Charlotte's sake, but he never expected to be so happily reconciled to his choice. He was attracted to her. Very much. Not surprising, he supposed, given she was a very appealing woman. He also genuinely liked her. Very much. That bit was more surprising. He had not expected her to *understand*. Most women would have considered Charlotte's fate unrecoverable and would have considered him more the fool for voluntarily following after her. But he had seen her indignation on his sister's behalf. He was sure of it.

Yes, Emma would be a better wife than he had hoped to find and a better, more understanding champion than he could have hoped for Charlotte. He could not possibly allow her to end the engagement now.

* * *

After a brief visit to the ladies' withdrawing room to confirm the acceptability of her appearance, Emma returned to the ballroom. She stood in the corner, sipping lemonade and watching the dancing, as she was still a bit too disordered to socialize. She felt someone step up beside her and her pulse quickened.

Annoyed though she was with her reaction, she looked up anyway, only to discover it was not John, but the man she had seen with him before. The gentleman's golden looks and manly physique made him handsome despite his less than crisp appearance, but the mockery in his eyes put Emma off from the start.

"Excuse my impropriety, but I don't believe I've had the pleasure of making your acquaintance, madam, and I was too impatient to await an introduction. I am Hugh Brydges." He gave a slight bow that was barely more than a nod and yet managed to be debonair all the same.

His charm seemed a bit too affected. She eyed him warily. "It's a pleasure to meet you, Mr. Brydges, though I suspect you already know who I am."

He nodded in concession. "Will you fault me for my concern for a friend, Lady Emmaline? I consider the duke a great friend and wished to become acquainted with his fiancée."

Emma chose neither to confirm nor deny the title of fiancée to the duke. She merely kept her expression guarded and sipped her lemonade. "Have you known the duke long?" she asked eventually.

"All my life." His answer was a bit more vehement than she expected. "Have you?"

"If you are truly his great friend, you know the answer to that question."

His laugh was brittle. "I suppose I do, but I could not help asking it."

She turned to face him full on. "Was there something in particular you wanted to know about me, Mr. Brydges?"

He looked out among the dancers as he answered her, as though the conversation were not important enough to warrant his undivided attention. "Merely a general curiosity, I assure you. But I suppose I already know all that is pertinent."

"If you know so much about me, you must know I am not among society much. I'm afraid I am inexperienced with such sophisticated customs as veiled insults, Mr. Brydges, and prefer to hear mine directly. What, in particular, do you feel compelled to say to me?"

He gave up all pretense of civility and sneered in disgust. "Already the haughty duchess. This is all very convenient for you, isn't it?"

"Convenient for me? Are you under the impression that I have forced the duke to honor the engagement against his will—that *I* am the one who will not sever the betrothal?"

"I only observe how cooperative you are in marrying a man you do not know, and that in doing so you will, gratifyingly, become a duchess."

"It seems you *observe* very little, Mr. Brydges. You can know nothing of me and my reasons for doing anything."

"I am well aware of Worley's purpose for marrying. Determining yours does not require much in the way of deductive reasoning."

"If you know his purpose for honoring this betrothal, you know it is for his convenience and not mine."

"His convenience?"

"Certainly. I was inconvenient four years ago for your friend the duke, but have apparently now become the opposite. It seems I serve at his pleasure."

"Ah yes, this has all been at his pleasure." His eyes flashed with anger. "I'm sure his exile in Boston was rather like a holiday. I'm certain a lowly shipping clerk lives nearly as comfortably as an English duke."

That gave Emma pause. "Are you saying he took a post as a clerk in Boston?"

He smirked at Emma's reaction to his revelation. "I'm afraid those with no access to family wealth must fall back on employment to survive. It's a very American attitude, apparently."

Emma was silent, ignoring the man's sarcasm. Why had the thought not occurred to her before? John had no support from his father or access to any funds of his own. Many of his peers would not have possessed the resourcefulness to find appropriate employment. In truth, most of his peers would not have gone in the first place.

Her lack of response only fueled Mr. Brydges's tirade. "I see you are suitably shocked to discover your gallant duke was employed in trade during his absence. I wonder, do you consider that a fate worse than death for a gentleman? Perhaps marriage to Worley will not be so elevating after all."

Emma had heard enough of this man's ridiculous spouting. "You, sir, claim to be a great friend to the duke, but do him a disservice. How dare you imply his efforts to protect his family were less than honorable? Any woman should consider a marriage to the duke elevating, not because of his title but because of the noble sacrifice he made for his family. I wonder if you, sir, could make the same choice if called upon to do so."

"A noble sacrifice, is it? I gather you've already been practicing your speech of explanation for the gossips. Very well done, really, with just the right note of passion. If you fail in your quest to become a duchess, you might give Drury Lane a try."

Emma's fists balled at her sides. What had she done to earn this man's venom? She had no earthly idea where it originated, but she refused to hear another word. "You are insufferable. How dare you insult me in such a manner, particularly if you do believe I am your friend's betrothed? I'll have you know we've broken our engagement only moments ago upon *my* insistence. What have you to say of my quest now, I wonder?"

Emma charged off without any sense of direction, but not before she registered his shock at her revelation. Perhaps she'd been unwise to reveal it to him. She had no way of knowing the true nature of his friendship with John. Perhaps they *were* close and he would tell John of her impassioned defense. She cringed. Why *had* she defended him so vehemently?

Did she regret breaking the engagement?

No. No she did not.

Marrying for convenience—particularly the convenience of the other party—could not possibly be the path to happiness. The kiss in the garden had been a mistake. It changed nothing. It was merely an attempt by a determined man to bring her around to his will, by fair means or foul. What she had felt was simply wonder at a new experience—nothing more.

She looked behind her. That man, Mr. Brydges, was following. Why couldn't he simply leave her be? She would have asked him as much had her attention not been distracted by a disturbance to her left. She stopped and moved closer to the crowd gathering there. At first she heard only the muffled laughter of the group of onlookers, but eventually she heard voices rising above the twittering and snickering. Voices she recognized.

"You're that duke who disappeared for a few years, aren't you?" she heard the elder Lady Spitzer shout.

Oh, heavens. She was shouting at John.

"Yes, but I mean to stay now," Emma heard John say, raising his voice so that it, too, carried a fair distance, "I'll not disappear again."

Emma wove her way through the gathered eavesdroppers until she spotted John and Lady Spitzer. John's back was to her so she could not see his face. She could, however, see Lady Spitzer's as she peered up at the duke. If Emma had felt tall next to the tiny old woman, John must feel a giant.

"How fortunate for you that you are not dead," the lady hollered, inspiring more snickers from the crowd.

Emma heard John chuckle as well. "Fortunate, indeed."

"What was that?" Lady Spitzer tipped toward him.

"I said, it is fortunate indeed," John repeated, shouting this time.

"Not so for your uncle, I imagine. Poor man thought he'd inherited, I suppose."

"Great uncle, actually," John called back to her, though she stood less than a foot from him. "And I understand he was relieved, though I've never met him."

"What was that?" She squinted as she asked it, as though she couldn't quite see him either.

"I've never met him."

"You'll have to put your house in order now," Lady Spitzer stated loudly. "You'll need a wife and an heir."

"Certainly."

Several onlookers noticed Emma's presence behind John and her cheeks blazed under their scrutiny.

"You had best have a short engagement," the old woman counseled loudly. She gave a decisive nod as though her word settled the matter.

Emma did not turn, but she was keenly aware of Mr. Brydges, standing a few yards away, also taking in the spectacle. She lifted her chin and waited for John to confirm to the rest of the party what she had already revealed to his friend.

Sara Portman

"On the contrary, Lady Spitzer," she heard him say. "I have been engaged these four long years. But I assure you," he called out, "we will now be married with all due haste."

Emma's eyes flashed to Mr. Brydges in time to witness the triumph he displayed before he gave a mocking bow and, stepping back, was enveloped by the crowd.

Chapter Eight

"I am convinced he is the most arrogant, high-handed, insensitive man in the whole of England."

Emma marched through the front door of her uncle's town house with such ferocity, she nearly overturned a porcelain urn standing on one side of the entryway.

Her uncle smiled blandly as he watched one of the footmen rush to steady the rocking object. "My dear, don't be so sure. I'd say the House of Lords is packed to overflowing with arrogant and high-handed men from all corners of the British Isles."

"Perhaps, Uncle, but I do not take exception with those men, as they have not chosen to practice their arrogance upon me." Emma untied the green ribbons of her bonnet and pulled it from her head. "Even considering the rampant arrogance you claim runs through the peerage, I defy you to name one other lady among the congregation at St. George's today whose first knowledge of her pending nuptials occurred when she heard her own name during the reading of the banns in church."

Emma still seethed from it. She had been so angry upon hearing it, she had nearly called out her objection. She should not have been surprised, not after his shouted announcement to Lady Spitzer on the prior evening. Every time she began to believe there was decency in him—that he might be capable of some consideration for *her*—he proved otherwise by taking some high-handed action that rendered her powerless in her own life.

"You can hardly claim ignorance of the betrothal, Emma." Aunt Agatha removed her own bonnet as she stepped into the hall. "That very subject has occupied your thoughts and everyone else's for much of the past several days."

"Still, he knew very well I was not resigned to the marriage. Calling for the banns to be read was premature."

To think, the insufferable Mr. Brydges had suggested *she* might possess the talents for Drury Lane. He should look to his friend the duke instead. All his apologies for disregarding her feelings were clearly a grand performance. How very smug he must feel, thinking he had her well and trapped after shouting his intentions last evening and ordering the banns the next day. "How very efficient he is. Well, I'm not trapped yet. I can still maneuver out of this."

"Are you quite sure you want to, dear?" her uncle asked.

"Have I ever given you any reason to doubt it?"

"Have you thought of the poor girl whose debut he's orchestrating?" Aunt Agatha asked. "Think of what she'll face—navigating London society when she's known nothing but a simple life in Boston. Only think how difficult that will be for her."

"I'm sure you are correct, but I could not imagine a less suitable person to ensure Lady Charlotte a successful debut. Mine, as you'll recall, was a dismal failure."

"Perhaps." Aunt Agatha studied the flower arrangement on the hall table rather than her niece. She plucked several stems from the vase and placed them to better advantage. "I suppose Marion Gilchrest, or perhaps Lady Wolfe would be better equipped to take the girl through her paces. Their daughters are quite accomplished."

Emma's guilt swelled at the thought of the inexperienced Charlotte under the tutelage of a hawk such as Lady Wolfe. She shook her head. "I know your game, Aunt, and it will not succeed. I do sympathize with young Charlotte, but that is not sufficient reason to marry her brother."

Aunt Agatha dropped her ruse of flower-arranging and faced her niece. "Perhaps it is not sufficient reason on its own, dear, but when all the other, perfectly sufficient reasons have failed to sway you, I thought it might tip the scales." Her wan smile was barely apologetic. "The duke's sister will need considerable help in preparing herself to face the *ton*. I expect she could also use a kind and sympathetic friend, don't you agree?"

Much as she tried, Emma could not find an objection to refute her aunt's logic that didn't sound entirely selfish and unkind. She released a weary sigh.

"I do not begrudge the duke his plans for his sister. I believe his intentions are noble and wish him great success in his endeavor. I simply don't understand why *I* must be caught up in it. You heard the gossip at the Fairhaven ball," Emma insisted. "All the *ton* would consider him a fool to actually marry me."

"But he has publicly confirmed his intention to do so. If you do not marry him, they will consider *you* the fool."

"Aunt Agatha!" Emma couldn't dispute the claim, but she hadn't expected such plain speaking from her aunt.

"I mean no insult, my dear—only to share the truth of it. You know by now my wishes for this marriage have nothing to do with the opinions of society. I have no sons or daughters of my own to see married. If the Ridgley name bears some tarnish for a broken engagement, your uncle and I should be affected very little, if at all." She stepped forward to take Emma's hands. "I seek only your security and happiness, my dear. Do you truly believe you'll be happiest living alone in your cottage, with no husband or children to care for? I know your memories of your mother are deepest there, but that can only lead to melancholy."

Emma sighed heavily. In truth, the counsel of her aunt and uncle was not lost upon her, and, righteous indignation aside, this decision bore so many facets, her mind was befuddled by them. "I wish I had never been affianced to him," she said wistfully.

"But that is already done, my dear, and cannot be undone." The earl lifted a folded letter from a salver on the hall table. "You have a letter from your friend Miss Betancourt. Why don't you take some time to yourself, Emma? Your aunt and I will leave you to your letter and your thoughts."

* * *

Emma took the letter to her room. It sat unread on her bureau as she lay back, fully dressed, across her bed and considered the case of the duke's sister. She could not help but sympathize with Charlotte. Emma's debut at seventeen had been disastrous in all respects. She'd masked her insecurities with resistance and lack of effort. When her father took matters into his own hands to secure her future, he'd named that very lack of cooperation as the reason, insisting she'd have no prospects at all if he left the matter to her for another season.

And Emma at least had the advantage of being brought up knowing what to expect. Moving about in society was a carefully choreographed dance and poor Charlotte Brantwood would not even recognize the tune. How awful to think of the unwitting, frightened child subjected to the harsh treatment of Lady Wolfe. Emma simply couldn't see Georgiana Wolfe having the strength of will to manage John or protect Charlotte.

Not John.

The duke.

She really must stop thinking of him as John if she did not intend to marry him.

If she did not intend to marry him? Was she considering it?

She supposed she was.

She recalled the brief moment in her conversation with Mr. Greystoke in which she believed *he* may have established a claim to her hand. Somehow, she didn't feel the same sense of alarm in considering marriage to John.

She could admit he was not the villain she'd imagined him to be all these years. She could respect, even admire, the choices he'd made for his family. She was embarrassed to think of how passionately she'd defended him to Mr. Brydges. Did she truly believe any woman should consider herself fortunate to marry him? Was she becoming resigned to the rationality of marrying her fiancé, or was she allowing herself to be influenced by what she'd experienced in his arms? She could not be certain that it was common sense rather than girlish, romantic feelings urging her to consider the marriage, and that conflict was very troubling to her peace of mind.

She would be very naïve, after all, to imagine his interest in her was anything more than a means to an end. He'd told her as much.

John himself seemed to be at the root of her indecision, for though she knew he did not harbor great affection for her, she could not bring herself to decide for certain whether he truly possessed the nobility of character she had begun to suspect. Still, he had refused throughout the period of their re-acquaintance to honor her wishes, despite the clarity and repetition with which she'd conveyed them. Would he be a fair husband? Would he be domineering and high-handed? Would he sell her cottage once she married and it was no longer hers, but his? Could she be happy married to a man like him? Would her happiness count for anything?

She could not know. And therein lay the crux of her final resistance.

With no further answers to be derived from her self-analysis on the subject of marriage, Emma sighed and turned to the distraction presented by her letter from home.

Although the greatest share of Emma's life thus far had been spent at either the family estate in Lancashire, or the house in town that had been her father's and then her uncle's, she would always feel that *home* was a cottage in the small, insignificant village of Beadwell. And Lucy Betancourt, the local vicar's daughter, would forever be her closest and dearest friend.

Emma broke the seal on Lucy's letter, anticipating a long narrative full of the details of life in Beadwell since Emma had been away.

Dearest Emma,

I have alarming news from home. The detestable Mr. Craw-ford has declared a crime committed against him in which the perpetrator has destroyed his fence and killed his chickens. He has named none other than the sweet boy Simon as the guilty party. The entire village is concerned for what will become of poor Simon if Mr. Crawford takes his charges to the magistrate, as he has threatened. I'm afraid it shall become a matter of each man's word against the other, and what persuasion shall a poor smithy's son have against the word of a gentleman? Dear Mrs. Brown is beside herself with concern. If you are able at all to return to Beadwell, I fear you may be the only person with connections enough to be of some benefit to poor Simon.

Your dear friend,
Lucy

Preposterous.

Emma threw the letter onto her table. Simon would never do such a thing; she was sure of it.

Guilt filled her. Simon had been Mr. Crawford's target solely because Emma was far away. The odious man had been harassing her from the moment her parents were gone. Now he was threatening Simon because of her personal interest in the boy.

How frightened Simon must be.

Rage filled Emma. How could a man do this to a boy? All for a piece of property. It was unspeakable.

Once again, she cursed the timing of her presence in London. She should be home, where she was needed.

Emma put her head in her hands and let the guilt enrobe her. If only there were not the matter of the unresolved betrothal—she would rush to Simon's aid immediately.

What was she thinking?

She could not allow Simon to face false charges when she was personally responsible. He was only thirteen—a child. She had to do something, and she would continue to manage her own affairs. The Duke of Worley did not control her. His announcements and grand plans could not prevent her from being where she was needed most. Banns or no, he could not have a wedding without a bride.

Chapter Nine

Mr. Crawford lived in a stone house not much larger than Emma's cottage, set back from the road and covered on one side with creeping ivy. She always thought it seemed a bit too picturesque to house such a ruthless man. Emma's present anger with Mr. Crawford had been left to grow, unchecked, all through a very long journey from London in her uncle's carriage. It was probably greater, still, for her current state of hunger and thirst, but she was too concerned for Simon's welfare to be distracted by the need for rest or a meal. She was determined to have the matter done. This nonsensical feud could not continue.

Once Emma was handed down from the carriage by the coachman, she charged up the path to the weathered front door and knocked.

The door was opened—not fully, but enough for Emma to see Juliana Crawford. Mr. Crawford's daughter looked as she always did, painfully thin, pale, and as worn as the house around her. She and Emma were near in age, or so Emma believed, but Juliana had resisted all overtures of friendship over the years. Emma always suspected Juliana's father would not allow it and considered that yet another reason to dislike the man.

Because it was not appropriate in the present circumstances to extend her condolences to Miss Crawford for the unlucky fate of her birth, Emma simply said," Good afternoon, Miss Crawford. Is your father home?"

Juliana swallowed and glanced behind her before answering. "Wait here," she instructed, and shut the door, leaving Emma still standing at the threshold.

Finally, the door swung wide and Mr. Crawford himself appeared. Oddly fastidious when compared with his barely maintained home, Mr. Crawford's shave was clean, his diminishing hair neatly clipped, and his clothing, if simple in style, neatly tailored and unrumpled. None of this attention to grooming, however, softened the effect of his sharp, angular features, which seemed to always point accusingly at the person to whom he directed his attention. If he was startled to find his neighbor on his doorstep or to see the earl's carriage in the middle of their sleepy village, he disguised it well.

There were no greetings dispensed.

"You're here to discuss Simon's mischief, I imagine," Mr. Crawford said, as though he felt it were about time someone did.

"I am. Perhaps you could invite me in?"

He stepped aside and waved for her to enter. Once inside, he led her to a tidy parlor filled with well-worn furniture and threadbare upholstery, where he found enough manners to invite her to sit.

"Well?" he asked sharply. "What is it you've come to say about the boy?"

"Simon has been in my employ for nearly three years, as you well know, Mr. Crawford. I know he is a good boy."

Mr. Crawford eyed her shrewdly. "He's a motherless troublemaker who's caused no end of vexation for the village."

Emma nearly rose from her seat. "That's a lie." She glared at him.

He glared back.

Emma inhaled and exhaled slowly. "Mr. Crawford, surely we can discuss this reasonably as long-standing neighbors."

The older man shrugged, then graced her with a very unappealing grin. "I'm nothing if not reasonable."

"I understand you've accused Simon of killing your chickens?"

"Not just that," Mr. Crawford insisted. "He broke in at night, ruined my fence, killed my chickens, *and* stole the pig."

This was the first Emma had heard of the pig.

"All that?" Emma asked, now watching Mr. Crawford with a sharper eye. He had added quite a bit to Simon's supposed crime. He knew as well as she if Simon were found guilty, no one would consider his age. This list of concocted crimes would ensure he would hang, or be transported on a convict ship. Either would be a death sentence.

The man nodded.

"I wonder...what does a thirteen-year-old boy want with a pig?" she asked.

"Why, to eat it, I imagine."

"Yes, but this boy is fed by Mrs. Brown. It's not as though he needs to steal food to eat. We both know Mrs. Brown. It's more likely he is overfed, is it not?"

He grunted in response.

"And how do you know he's killed chickens? Are all your chickens gone?"

"No. Just some of the chickens."

"How do you know he killed them?"

"Because I found the dead ones. I knew he'd done it."

"How do you know it was him?"

"Because he's full of mischief, that one. Everyone knows he did it."

Mr. Crawford shifted his weight and looked up at her with narrowed eyes. "But," he drawled, "if you're concerned about the boy's fate, I might be willing to accept a settlement to abandon the prosecution."

"What sort of settlement did you have in mind?"

"Don't play coy, girl. You know full well what sort of settlement."

Of course she did. He wanted what he had always wanted—her property, the parcel of land that stretched between the back of her cottage and the back of his house. He'd been harassing her for it, claiming it to be rightfully his, since the day her parents died and she inherited it. Well it was not his. It was hers.

"No," she said, squaring her shoulders. "The answer will always be no."

"I wouldn't be so quick to answer, were I in your position," he said with arid smugness. "You said yourself you wanted to see what could be done about the boy. I suppose if you returned that property to me, I could find it in my heart to forget the boy's mischief."

She did not yield, but said simply, "That seems an uneven exchange for the loss of a pig."

Mr. Crawford smirked. "Maybe it's a large price compared with a pig, but it's not so large compared to the life of the boy, I'd think—if he's as important as he seems to be."

How very clever he was. Yes, Simon was important to her. He was not just a local boy she happened to employ. He had been under the particular care of Emma and the Browns since his mother had passed away. Mr. Crawford knew this. The whole village knew this.

Just as the whole village knew Simon was innocent.

Emma stood. She would not listen to this any further. "It seems to me your only proof is a few dead chickens and a theory no one else believes, Mr. Crawford. You will not be successful. And I *will not* give you my land."

Mr. Crawford rose as well. His confidence had not wavered despite her adamant refusal. "I didn't suppose you would be willing to just give me the land, Lady Emmaline. I would be happy to offer you a fair price for the property if you were willing to consider selling it," he said. "Fair, considering the circumstances."

Oh, she could well imagine his idea of "fair, considering the circumstances" and it was nowhere near a reasonable sum. But the sum was of no consequence. She would never, for any price, sell the land that included her garden.

"No."

"You'll be sorry for your quick answer once I've had my discussion with the magistrate," he spat. The he straightened, his eyes gloating. "Who do you think will have more sway—a respected country gentleman, or the orphaned son of a blacksmith?"

Simon was not an orphan, but Emma did not bother to argue that point.

"What of the daughter of an earl?" she asked. "You discount *my* sway with the magistrate."

He snorted. "You are the daughter of a *dead* earl. He has little consequence now. And you are a woman. Besides, of what import is the word of anyone who was miles away in London when the theft occurred?"

He looked so pleased with himself at this point, Emma could have easily lost control of her temper, but she did not. "You overestimate your case, Mr. Crawford. No one, not even you, believes your accusations. Simon may not be the son of a gentleman, but he has more friends than you realize. Perhaps you would have done better to cultivate some of your own."

With those words, she spun on her heel and departed the Crawford residence. She did so with her head high, conveying all the assurance of her words. She only wished she felt as confident as she pretended to be.

* * *

Emma had sent the coachman ahead when she arrived in Beadwell, planning to return to the cottage on foot after speaking with Mr. Crawford, and she was glad for the walk. She found herself seeking another direction, however, another place that was as much home as her cottage. Her mind rambled desperately. As hated as Mr. Crawford was in the village, he was a gentleman. There was a baron or knight or something somewhere in the line of Crawford's he could claim as relations. Those connections wouldn't measure a bit in London, but here in the countryside it certainly elevated his status to well above the local blacksmith. Simon's fate hinged on the magistrate and whether or not the man could be convinced to believe Mr. Crawford's fictitious version of events. Frustratingly, Emma *had* been in London when the supposed chickens had been killed.

Chickens! For heaven's sake. Of all the ridiculous things. Of course she would be dealing with dead chickens on top of everything else. Why could she not have had a pleasant and restful summer? Between Mr. Crawford and the Duke of Worley, Emma had just about all she could stomach of overbearing, manipulative men. She groaned aloud as she walked and realized she had been nearly stomping her way to her friend's doorstep.

The parsonage house was a small dwelling of crumbling stone with a wide, arched entryway and carved wooden door that had always seemed to Emma to be oddly out of place on the otherwise modest residence. It sat in the shadow of the church steeple that towered above the village and was, at times, the only sign of Beadwell's existence not hidden from view by the surrounding hills. Emma's rap on the door to the house had barely struck when the portal was flung wide revealing the bright and welcome grin of her dearest friend.

"Emma, you've come!" Lucy said, gathering Emma into her warm embrace. "I was certain you would."

"Of course," Emma said, as Lucy stepped back to examine her. "I left London as soon as I read your letter. How could I not?"

"I've been expecting you since word reached us that your uncle's carriage had been spied in the village," Lucy said. "I've already told my mother I'm leaving. Let's walk to the cottage."

Emma laughed at Lucy's exuberance and allowed her friend to take her by the arm as they set off toward her home.

"Were your aunt and uncle very disappointed," Lucy asked, "to have your visit interrupted?"

"They were very understanding. There was no question that I must come." Her initial hesitation had been irrational, after all, and couldn't possibly signify.

Lucy nodded.

Emma's smile was wistful. "My uncle might have come himself, once he saw my concern, but with parliament in session, he felt he must stay in town."

"I'm sure you were sad to leave their company," Lucy noted.

Emma made a face. "Their company, yes, but I was not sad to rid myself of the company of others in London."

"Oh my. It sounds as though you have a good deal to tell."

"I do," Emma confirmed, "but all of that can wait until we have discussed Mr. Crawford. I fear our problems there may be more difficult to resolve than I anticipated, and perhaps I was shortsighted in not asking my uncle to come."

"Have you spoken with Mr. Crawford?" Lucy asked.

"I have. It was not a hopeful conversation."

Emma explained in detail her conversation with Mr. Crawford and his attempt at blackmail.

Lucy gasped. "Your mother's garden? But you couldn't!"

"Rest assured," Emma said fervently, "I will not. I will find some other way to protect Simon."

"We shall find a way together, I promise," Lucy said, with a reassuring squeeze of Emma's hand.

"Now, I am intrigued to hear tales of London," she said. "I must know whose presence was so unpleasant as to require escape."

"Perhaps you are aware that the Duke of Worley's son, or rather, the new duke, has miraculously returned to England?" Emma asked.

"I am," Lucy confirmed. "Was it difficult for you, Emma?" Lucy asked, her delicately pale features marred with concern. "It had to be strange, hearing the news, knowing you were once engaged to him."

Emma released her breath in an anxious huff. "It appears 'once' may not be as accurate as 'still,'" she said. Just giving voice to the situation caused her shoulders to slump in defeat.

Lucy stopped walking. "Still? As in, *still* engaged?"

"Apparently society has long memories for these kinds of things," Emma said, with a sideways glance at her friend. "We are both living and both unmarried and neither of us has ever formally broken the engagement."

"But the man ran off to the war!" came Lucy's incredulous reply. Her usually placidly blue eyes shone bright with indignation on Emma's behalf. "Pardon my saying so, but isn't that a fairly eloquent method of breaking off an engagement? It's not as though he ever corresponded with you, did he?"

"You would know if he had," Emma said.

"How very trying for you. Have you spoken to the duke? Has he finally broken the engagement?"

"Therein lies the trouble," Emma said, as the women turned onto the narrow lane that led to her cottage. "I have spoken to the duke and he does not desire to break the engagement."

"But, why ever not?" Lucy's porcelain cheeks pinked brightly. "I don't mean to say that any man wouldn't be incredibly fortunate to marry you, certainly. But why this man? He didn't want to honor the engagement four years ago. Why now?"

Emma sighed and looked ahead. "He has provided his rationale, I suppose, some of which I am inclined to believe. In the end, he has decided he must marry and, as it happens, he is already engaged to me, much to my misfortune."

"What do your aunt and uncle say?" Lucy asked.

Emma made no effort to hide her pitiful deflation from Lucy. "My aunt believes I should marry the duke. She fears that she failed my parents by not seeing me married off before now."

"Hmmm," was Lucy's only reply. It was not quite the rejection of Aunt Agatha's reasoning for which Emma had hoped.

The ladies walked around a bend in the road and the weathered stones and intersecting gables of Emma's tidy, cheerful cottage came into view. She was struck by how glad she was to be home. She was weary—weary of traveling and of problems with unclear solutions, and desperately in need of several moments of restorative calm surrounded by the beauty and fragrance of her mother's garden.

Her pace quickened.

As she opened the door and stepped inside, the serenity she had eagerly anticipated was snatched from her grasp like a forbidden treat.

"Ah, Lady Emmaline," the duke said, rising to his feet, looking positively giant in her tiny front room. "How lovely you are today."

Chapter Ten

The duke and his arrogant friend were in *her* home, apparently making conversation with Mr. and Mrs. Brown, as though it were perfectly normal and expected for dukes to visit quiet country cottages and chat with the elderly caretakers. Emma was at once aware of the cramped confines of her little home, the looks of sheer panic and awe on the faces of the Browns, and admittedly her own frightful appearance, as she had stopped only once to freshen herself on her journey from London.

If she weren't so livid at the intrusion, she might have been entertained at the oddity of it all. The two men, in their elegantly cut riding clothes and polished boots, were too…large…and certainly too tailored for her tiny cottage.

Poor Mrs. Brown looked frightened to death. Emma went to her and clasped the woman's hands in her own, momentarily ignoring her unexpected guests. "Mrs. Brown, how wonderful it is to be home. I have so missed you and Mr. Brown."

The usually unflappable Mr. Brown was also wide-eyed with uncertainty of just what sort of manners this particular situation required. She shot him a meaningful glance that she hoped conveyed both her apology and gratitude for their forbearance.

"Your Grace," Emma said, finally turning her attention to the duke, "How lovely of you to pay us of a visit." Her smile was tight and insincere. "I see you've acquainted yourself with my good friends, Mr. and Mrs. Brown. May I present as well my dear friend Miss Betancourt? Her father, Mr. Betancourt, is vicar here in Beadwell."

The duke nodded toward Lucy. "How do you do, Miss Betancourt?"

"Very well, thank you, Your Grace," Lucy responded, adding a slight curtsy.

Emma turned at the change she detected in Lucy's voice and saw, despite the strength of her objections just moments before, her friend's complexion was flushed and her hand had traveled upward to confirm the condition of the pale blonde knot at her nape. Emma had known Lucy for so long, she sometimes forgot the stark contrast of their upbringings and the limitations of Lucy's experience, given she'd so rarely been outside the confines of the little village.

"May I introduce to you both my friend Mr. Brydges," the duke said, with a meaningful glance at his friend.

Thus summoned, Mr. Brydges stepped forward. "A pleasure, Lady Emmaline, Miss Betancourt," he said with a polite dip of his chin.

"How kind of you to come, Mr. Brydges." Emma did not reveal their prior acquaintance, though she watched him warily as she greeted him.

He returned her gaze with a challenge of his own, but answered politely as manners dictated. "My pleasure, I assure you."

Emma spotted a tray of tea and biscuits on the table in front of their guests and wondered how long they had been waiting there, conversing with Mr. and Mrs. Brown. She would love to simply send them on their way, but couldn't abruptly do so without scandalizing Lucy and the Browns with her inexcusable manners. If she could manage a moment alone with the duke, however....

"I would offer tea," she said, addressing the duke with the sweetest expression she could muster, "but I can see you've already taken refreshment. In that case, as it is such a lovely day, perhaps you would allow me to show you my garden. It is particularly colorful this time of year."

The duke's expression registered an amused twitch. "An inspired idea."

"I could take a turn in the garden, I suppose," Mr. Brydges offered with a shrug, but he was immediately the recipient of a quelling glance from the duke. "Of course, I might rather have another of Mrs. Brown's excellent biscuits," he amended. "Would you join me, Miss Betancourt?"

* * *

"You have a habit of inserting yourself where your presence is not desired, Your Grace," Emma said as soon as John had drawn the door to the cottage closed behind them. She stared up at him as though demanding an explanation. He had come to recognize the shift in the line of her jaw as a telltale sign of her displeasure—not that her words weren't usually clear enough.

John smiled in spite of himself. He couldn't help it. He had expected that Emma would waste no time on polite exchanges—preferred it actually.

"Ah. There it is," he said.

"There what is?" she demanded.

"Your habit of plain speaking. You are not one to shy away from conflict." He stepped forward from the threshold and lifted his face to the warm afternoon sun. "I was surprised when I learned you left London. Even if you still couldn't accept the betrothal, I would not have expected you to run."

She peered up at him through narrowed eyes. "Is that what you believe? That I've run away from you?" She stared to one side and shook her head, as though commiserating with some unseen third party regarding this revelation. "Of course you never considered the possibility that I left London to manage an entirely unrelated matter."

He paused. He had not. But he looked more closely at her flushed cheeks and her studiously averted gaze and wondered if her claim was only a partial truth anyway. "I am sorry," he said. "I should not have presumed. What matter has brought you racing to Beadwell, may I ask?"

"It is nothing of any account to you," she said, directing him toward a stone-edged path that wound around the side of the little cottage. "And do not mistake that I will view your following me all the way across the countryside as heroic. I find your continued harassment exceedingly frustrating."

He laughed. "Heroic? Of course not. I'd hardly call an hour's ride to call on a neighbor a heroic effort on my part."

Emma paused. "An hour's ride?"

"Hour and one half, then," he said. "No more than that. Don't tell me you've forgotten my estate is so nearby. Mr. and Mrs. Brown and I were just discussing their cousin who is a tenant farmer on my estate."

"How interesting. Surely that information was worth a long and tiring ride from London at a grueling pace."

"Well, it was interesting to me," he said. And it was. John did not yet know his tenants. It was a lack he intended to rectify in the immediate future.

Chasing Emma had certainly proven entertaining, but if the game went on too long, it would be a distraction from other obligations. As they rounded the corner to the back of the cottage, John looked up to share this logic with her. And surely would have, if he hadn't been struck momentarily speechless upon finally taking in his surroundings.

What the devil...

He blinked and looked again. The view didn't change.

Emma's cottage was squarely in the middle of someone's estate gardens. And not just any someone, by the looks of it. John couldn't recall ever seeing a private garden so ornate or extensive. Blooms in a riot of colors and whimsical topiaries carved in geometric shapes were artfully arranged in a design that seemed to radiate out from a central point marked by the statue of an angel with its open hands raised to the sky. Beyond that, there appeared to be satellite gardens, each one different.

It was magnificent.

It was absurd.

Where *were* they?

He stared. Then he stared at her.

"What is this place?" he asked when he had regained his ability to do so.

"Mother's garden," she said matter-of-factly. "Your Grace, do you mean to say you have left London, in the middle of the season, to return to your country home?"

"Yes. I find I have business in the area. Whose property is this?"

"Mine." She did not smile. "For how long should we expect to enjoy your neighborly presence?"

He shrugged. "As long as it takes, I imagine." Then he spun around. "I don't understand." He was surrounded by a garden so elaborate, it rivaled the pleasure gardens of some of the finest estates. "Why is this here?"

"Because my mother decided to put it here." She faced him full on. "Do you honestly expect me to believe that you are not here to chase me?"

"That is precisely why I am here. Isn't that why you ran from London?" he asked. "So I could prove the seriousness of my intent by traipsing across the countryside?"

"I already told you I did not!" The speed and vehemence of her response had him wondering if perhaps it might be genuine. "I am not playing a game with you, and you must have a rather low opinion of me to believe I would."

"My apologies," he said, though he couldn't quite focus on the conversation Emma seemed intent on having. "Whose garden is this and what did your mother have to do with it?"

Her spine straightened in the way he'd come to recognize, and he knew she disliked his question. "The garden is mine." She looked steadily up at him, daring him to object.

"Yours?"

"Yes. It's mine."

Hers. Her garden. Ridiculous. "Is there a manse on the other side of it?"

"No. Just Mr. Crawford's cottage."

John spun, again taking in the sea of flowers and ornamental shrubs divided by wedged sections of hedgerow. Then he gaped at his betrothed. "But...*why?*"

"A large portion of my garden is on property that used to be owned by Mr. Crawford's family. My grandfather purchased it from his father decades ago."

"I don't mean why this Crawford fellow lives on the other side of it, Emma. I meant to ask...just...*why?*"

"You are wondering why my garden is quite so large."

He cast her a baleful glance. "It's a bit grand for a simple cottager in a country village, wouldn't you say?"

She crossed her arms in front of her chest and lifted her chin. "I understand what a folly it seems, my little garden, but it's mine. It's as much my home as this cottage."

"How did it get here?"

"We've been building it and tending it for years. It started out as my mother's hobby when she was a girl. She was lonely. Her mother died young. Her father had the responsibilities of a peer. She befriended the master gardener." Emma shrugged as though the gardener were an expected alternative.

"So she brought him here, to build this?"

Emma shook her head. "No. Sadly, he never saw this. He simply taught my mother his trade." She paused, regarded him a moment. "And she taught me."

He peered at her. "You are responsible for all this?" His hand drew a circle in the air to encompass the garden.

She nodded. "With my mother, of course. And the Browns."

"*This* is the garden you tended with your mother?" He shook his head as though that may clear it.

"Yes, this is my mother's garden."

"So now it is just the three of you—without any other help?"

"I assure you, we can usually manage by ourselves," she told him sharply. "But when we cannot, Simon is happy to take the odd job or two."

John looked out over the grounds again in disbelief. The Browns were getting on in years and Emma, practical as she was, was still a lady. This Simon must be a rather able-bodied sort.

He paused at that thought. "Who is this Simon fellow?"

"He lives in the village. He's the smithy's son." She shook her head. "It matters not. Can you we discuss the matter at hand?"

"Which is?" he asked. Why did he find it so endearing when she was flustered?

"Are we forever to be at odds, Your Grace?"

"There is no requirement that we be so," he stated. "Simply conform to my way of thinking and we need never be at odds again." He grinned at his triumph of logic.

She did not.

John stepped more closely and reached out to take Emma's hand. She did not resist. "I am sorry to have teased you," he said softly, holding her gaze. "Are you truly so opposed to marrying me? I thought we found we can be quite compatible."

Her eyes lowered. Her voice was weak when she responded. "I don't think it very gentlemanly of you to remind us a lapse in good judgment on both our parts."

He reached for the other hand. "I disagree wholeheartedly. I believe kissing you proved that my decision to marry my fiancée has been one of the better applications of good judgment I have made in my life."

Her eyes flew to his and an adorable blush painted her features. "You shouldn't speak so frankly."

He laughed aloud. "Why ever not? You speak plainly. It's one of the things I appreciate most. Why should we be mysterious and leave room for misunderstanding?" He pulled the hands he held captive, drawing her closer. He was firm and unapologetic when he spoke again. "I find I am quite attracted to you, Emma. I heartily enjoyed kissing you. I look forward to where the kissing shall lead once we are married."

Her amber eyes grew large and her blush deepened to crimson. Her lips parted as though some objection would be forthcoming, but none came.

Perhaps to make his point, or perhaps simply because he wanted to, he bent his head to capture those sweetly parted lips with his own. He snaked one arm around her back to pull her into a kiss that should leave her with no doubt as to the passions that could be shared between them, if only she gave up her resistance.

He felt her stiffen, but she did not pull away. Heartened by this, he deepened the kiss, gently urging her lips to part and angling his mouth across hers. She released a sound—a sigh that was swallowed by the kiss and he knew the moment when her resistance yielded entirely. Her rigid posture melted and her hands slid upward across his shoulders until she clung to him as tightly as he held her.

Emma. The force of her willing surrender was nearly more than he could bear, and he was no longer certain which of them was receiving the demonstration. His tongue danced with hers as he clutched her to him, determined to show her the way. His hands roved over her as the urgency built inside him, and he hated every stitch of clothing that separated them. *Damn.*

He tore his lips from hers and held her tightly to his chest, as much to calm his own wild heartbeat as to calm hers. "Dear Emma," he whispered against her hair, "you threaten all my training as a gentleman."

She pushed herself free and stared accusingly up at him. "But you kissed me!" Her gold eyes sparked in indignation, but her complexion was still flushed, and her lips still swollen from their kiss.

"You are right, of course," he said. "I forgot myself. There will come a time for all of that."

She swallowed. When she spoke, it was slow and measured, with just the faintest trace of unsteadiness. "I am very tired, Your Grace, and I have traveled a long way. If you don't mind, I should like to rest."

"Of course you should." He considered asking when he should call upon her again, but changed his mind. "I would like for you to come to dine at Brantmoor. I will be inviting the vicar and his wife and daughter, naturally. Brydges will be there. I assure you, all proprieties will be observed."

She shook her head slightly, then opened her mouth only to close it again, as though not sure how to reply.

"Before you decide your fate," he encouraged, "come dine with me and see my home. Perhaps you'll decide you would like it to be your home as well."

She sighed heavily. "All right. A dinner will be fine. But you must invite the Betancourts, as you promised," she hurried to add.

"Certainly. I shall proceed to the vicarage as soon as we part company." He sincerely hoped he had not miscalculated. This fiancée of his, who preferred cottage life, may not be swayed by the grandeur of Brantmoor. Might he be risking the opposite effect? Would she become even more set against the union?

He looked again at his surroundings. She obviously enjoyed elaborate beauty in certain respects. She was, without doubt, a very surprising woman

* * *

Lucy would always be kind and practical. She would also be loyal and thus willing to take an immediate dislike to anyone, if necessary, on Emma's behalf. Emma knew this and yet recognized the unmistakable flash of wonder and temptation that crossed Lucy's expression when she explained that the vicar and his family—Lucy included—were to be invited to dine at Brantmoor, and that the duke was on his way to the parsonage house this very moment to extend said invitation. "I am invited as well," Emma added.

"Did you accept your invitation?" Lucy asked with an assessing look.

"I did."

Lucy nodded her approval. "I believe that is a wise choice."

"Do you?" Emma asked.

"I do," she answered, without a hint of apology in her tone. "You must be practical, Emma. Your aunt's fears are warranted. What will happen to you once your uncle is gone?"

Lucy's comments were rooted in wisdom and practicality. The cottage was Emma's entirely, as it had been her mother's and was never entailed to her father's, or now her uncle's, title. But the allowance she drew to support herself there, to support the Browns, to clothe herself and travel back and forth…all of that came from the earl. What would happen when her uncle was no longer earl? When a relative she'd never met became earl in her uncle's place, could she rely on this stranger's continued support?

"What if you find yourself in need of a husband five or seven or even a score of years in the future?" Lucy asked. "You would be a bit long in the tooth for a London season then, wouldn't you say? And who would sponsor you?"

A bit direct, even for Lucy, but unfortunately also true.

"Make no mistake," Lucy added. "I would never wish for you to marry an unpleasant person, no matter what sort of wealth or title he possessed. I only preach the wisdom of knowing the duke better before deciding he is unacceptable."

Lucy's practicality was maddeningly sound. Emma was swiftly running out of allies and, aside from the duke's obvious tendencies toward arrogance and highhandedness, running out of practical objections herself.

"You are tired, Emma dear," Lucy said, rising from her seat after a moment of thoughtful silence. "You've had no rest at all since you arrived. And my mother is no doubt beside herself with excitement if the duke has kept his promise."

Emma rose to see her friend to the door. "Wait here a moment and I shall see if Mr. Brown will walk you home."

"Nonsense." Lucy waived her friend's suggestion away. "This is not London. I have walked this lane by myself a thousand times. Rest, my dear, and do not fret. No decisions must be made immediately."

Emma squeezed Lucy's hands, grateful for her friend's innate understanding of exactly the words she needed to hear. With a last wave, Lucy was happily making her way down the cobbled path to the lane.

When Emma closed the door behind her friend, her sigh was heavier than she intended. She turned and saw Mrs. Brown.

"Come rest now, child. If there is another knock on the door this evening, I vow I'll not answer it. You are too tired. Come to the kitchen and have a plate. You must be famished."

"Oh, Mrs. Brown, I may not even eat tonight. I am so tired, I swear I shall take to my bed and may not wake until morning."

"Oh, you poor dear. By all means, take all the rest you need. Your uncle's coachman brought your things earlier and I've got them all arranged for you upstairs."

"You are too good to me, Mrs. Brown."

"Nonsense," she said, though she blushed with the compliment. "You need your rest. It's been a very eventful day."

"That it has, Mrs. Brown," Emma said as she turned to take her leave.

"Lady Emma..."

She turned at the hesitant request from the older woman.

Mrs. Brown stepped forward and wrung her hands. "Mr. Brown and I have had a bit of a talk since his grace left and wondered...since you're acquainted with such an influential lord and, well, since we have this problem with Simon and what with Mr. Crawford knowing the magistrate so well...well, we just thought...perhaps..."

"You are wondering, Mrs. Brown, if I will ask the duke to intervene with the magistrate on Simon's behalf."

"Well, yes, that's it. If you thought he'd be willing. I realize he's a very important man and doesn't have time for our petty concerns."

"Simon's life is hardly petty, Mrs. Brown, and I will certainly ask him. It was an excellent thought."

How had the thought not occurred to her? The duke would be infinitely more powerful with the local magistrate than Mr. Crawford.

And always would be.

In this, or any other mischief Mr. Crawford concocted.

It was significant, that.

Chapter Thirteen

"I have decided to marry the Duke of Worley."

This announcement, given in the carriage the duke had sent for Emma and the Betancourts as their small party rode toward Brantmoor, elicited a variety of responses.

Lucy nodded sagely.

Her mother only stared.

The vicar laughed. "That's a bit ambitious, dear, given we've just been invited for dinner."

Emma felt her cheeks heat.

"The duke has already offered for Emma, Father," Lucy explained. What the explanation lacked in precise accuracy, it was made up in simplicity and brevity.

"Has he now?" Mrs. Betancourt asked breathily, moving forward in her seat to hear more of this tale. "When did this come about?"

"In London," Emma told her. Another slight modification of the complicated truth as Emma's decision had been made in Beadwell, if one were being picky about such things. Realizing he was not only the solution to her present predicament with Mr. Crawford, but would effectively quash all future trouble from that man had been the final weight necessary to tip the scales toward marriage.

"Such momentous news!" Mrs. Betancourt clasped her hands together. "How absolutely wonderful."

"Yes, wonderful news," the vicar echoed. "Your aunt and uncle must be beyond themselves with happiness for you."

The Betancourts were kind and wonderful people who had always cared for Emma and had likely concluded she would never find her way to the altar. Their enthusiasm for her news could not have been greater. Emma saw no reason to explain the extent to which her marriage would be one of convenience. She didn't even want the duke to fully understand. She had decided after a day or so of deliberation that she would not tell the duke of the threats from Mr. Crawford. As his wife, Emma would be able to draw on his power and influence without actually requiring his assistance. And the very important fact was, although marriage to the duke could allow her to protect the cottage from Mr. Crawford, by marrying, she would, in fact, be losing ownership of the cottage to her husband. She intended to gain the duke's assurance that she could keep the cottage, but she did not know him well enough to trust him with the knowledge that there was an interested and enthusiastic potential purchaser right in town.

"I should also tell you," Emma added, "that although I have decided to accept the duke, I have not yet told him. I plan to do so this evening, if an opportunity arises."

Emma watched as the vicar and his wife exchanged glances. She was fairly certain they understood her indirect plea that she be allowed a moment of privacy with the duke for the purpose of accepting his proposal...or, rather, to confirm that she would not be breaking their already existing engagement.

"Have you heard the story of when the vicar and I dined at Brantmoor?" Mrs. Betancourt asked, adjusting herself on the upholstered seat of the richly appointed carriage.

"I have not," Emma said, though she saw in the immediately pained expressions of Lucy and her father that she was in the minority.

Mrs. Betancourt leaned forward to place her hand over Emma's. "The interior of the house is even more beautiful than the exterior. Fit for royalty, I said." She turned to her husband. "Didn't I say that, that day... fit for royalty."

"Yes, I'm sure you did," came his cooperative response.

"The food...oh my...I am convinced still today that the white soup was the richest I've ever tasted. And the roast venison was better even than Mary Finnemore's."

This was high praise indeed, as there was much pride throughout Beadwell for the quality of the food prepared by the innkeeper's wife.

"Ah, yes." Her sigh was wistful. "Well, it was just the one time and it was many, many years ago, before our Lucy was born. The vicar had just been granted the living at Beadwell, so we were invited to dinner at the estate with some of the other local gentry and the parson from Brantmoor Village. Mr. Crawford was there with his wife. She's gone now, of course. So sad."

"Yes." There was not much else for Emma to say in response. Everyone understood there was some measure of mystery and scandal surrounding Mrs. Crawford. *Gone* could mean so many things. Emma and Lucy were too young when the events took place to be privy to details.

"And the duke, naturally," Mrs. Betancourt continued. "Not this duke, but his father. And the duchess. But she died, poor thing, along with her daughter."

Emma looked at Lucy, in whom she'd confided the saga of the duke's sister. Judging by her friend's expression, they both realized the potential for an embarrassing situation during dinner in which these inaccuracies might be repeated. "Mrs. Betancourt, I am told by the duke that the stories generally believed regarding the deaths of his mother and sister are not true. Rather, his mother lived for several more years in Boston and the sister still lives. She will be returning to England forthwith."

"What is this?" the vicar said gruffly. "That can't be true. The old duke observed the mourning and everything. There was a service held."

Mrs. Betancourt reached out and placed a gentle hand on Emma's arm. "That seems a terribly unlikely story, my dear."

Emma sighed at the inarguable truth. "Yes. I understand," Emma conceded, "But as I have had my information directly from the new duke, perhaps it is best this evening if we simply do not refer to it, so as not to introduce an uncomfortable topic of conversation."

"Well thought, my dear," the vicar said, nodding. "Well thought."

Mrs. Betancourt nodded even more vigorously.

Emma wasn't sure what else to say. If she could not convince her dearest friends of the truth of Charlotte's background, convincing all of London seemed a daunting task.

"Well, I, for one, am very much looking forward to dinner," Mrs. Betancourt announced, filling the moment of awkward silence.

"As am I," added her daughter.

Emma smiled encouragingly at all of them, wishing she felt as encouraged.

Then Lucy gasped and the entire party turned.

The long day of summer allowed an unshrouded view of Brantmoor upon their approach. The mansion's opulence exceeded even Emma's expectations, despite her privileged upbringing. Its façade was dominated by a massive, two-story columned portico. This was flanked on either side by large expansions to the main house, both fronted by impressive half-moon towers that rose the full three-story height of the edifice. The ancestral home of the Earls of Ridgely was stately and impressive, but paled in comparison to the intimidating grandeur of the approach to Brantmoor.

"It's magnificent," Lucy whispered, breaking the awe-filled silence.

"As breathtaking as I remember," Mrs. Betancourt added.

The vicar cleared his throat and tugged at the bottom of his waistcoat. "Now then, it's just a house and he's just a man. There's no reason to feel out of place. And if he's to be our Emma's husband, I'm of a mind to like him." He punctuated his speech with a firm nod.

The carriage slowed in front of the house and was greeted by liveried men who aided the ladies as they stepped down. When the small party was ushered into the house, Emma's first thought was that Mrs. Betancourt had been correct in her memory. Everything about the interior of Brantmoor was as grand as its façade. It was not, however, particularly cluttered with decoration, which satisfied Emma's more simple taste.

Emma surveyed the interior with a detailed eye. When one visits the home of a friend or acquaintance, one collects impressions—a home is large, or cozy, or poorly maintained. When one examines for the first time a house that will become one's own home, the details to be catalogued become overwhelming. Who was the subject of the marble bust on the hall table? How long must the staff work to oil the endless length of carved banister on the entry hall staircase? The shorter footman who had nearly stumbled after aiding the ladies down from the carriage—was he nervous? Had he been in the family's employ for long?

Their group was shown into a large drawing room where the duke and Mr. Brydges promptly joined them. As the pleasantries were exchanged, Emma found herself watching John. When finally he stood in front of her and addressed her directly, heat suffused her cheeks. Was he taller and broader than he had been two days before? Surely his hair was sinfully darker and his eyes were more startlingly blue. How strange that this man, this unfamiliar, intimidating lord would be her husband. Emma was mostly quiet as all were seated and conversation circulated around her. Even as she inventoried all that she recognized about him, she was deeply conscious at the same time of all she did not know. She found herself watching him the entire time until they all rose again and were ushered into the grand dining room, with blue damask walls nearly hidden behind massive gilt-framed landscapes and life-sized portraits of notable family members.

When seated with her aunt and uncle, or other familiar company, Emma usually enjoyed the lengthy conversations facilitated by the formal dinner process. Dinner at Brantmoor seemed interminable as Emma became more keenly aware of precisely how difficult it would be to engineer some moments alone with the duke in which to fulfill her purpose.

When the end of the meal arrived, she had no better sense of how she would accomplish such a feat than she did when the meal began.

"Gentlemen," the duke said to their party once all had finished and had their dishes whisked efficiently away, "might I suggest we forgo our port this evening so we do not leave the ladies to withdraw on their own without a hostess? Perhaps we could all partake of cards and conversation together in the music room this evening."

"Of course, of course." Mr. Betancourt nodded.

"So thoughtful of you, Your Grace," his wife added with a beaming smile for the duke. The vicar's wife had had nothing but beatific smiles for the duke all through the meal and Emma wondered if she saw him as the dashing hero simply because of who he was, or because he had heroically offered to marry her. She guessed the latter. She was also certain Mrs. Betancourt particularly enjoyed being in on the secret, knowing the answer the duke was to receive before he received it.

As the group was led from the dining room, Emma again wracked her brain for some excuse to separate herself and the duke, but was left with no plan whatsoever.

"What a magnificent harp, Your Grace!" Mrs. Betancourt exclaimed upon their entry into what appeared to be a large second drawing room that was just as grand and beautifully furnished as the parlor into which they had been shown earlier. Indeed, the large harp at the far end of the room did seem particularly splendid, even among the ornate furnishings in the room, including still more massive, gilt-framed portraits covering the walls. The Brantwood family was apparently very large.

"Why, thank you, Mrs. Betancourt," the duke responded with a gracious nod. "Do you play?"

"Sadly, I do not, but my Lucy plays beautifully. She is quite an accomplished musician."

"Is she?" The duke smiled pleasantly at Lucy. "Can we convince you to play for us, Miss Betancourt?"

"I would be glad to play for everyone, Your Grace. I am complimented by your request."

Emma stared. She'd been certain Lucy would decline—or at least attempt to do so. Lucy always declined invitations to play for an audience.

Lucy rose from the seat she'd just taken and glanced to the settee behind her. "Oh heavens," she said.

"What is it, dear?" her mother asked.

"It seems as though I've forgotten my shawl in the dining room. I shall have to return for it."

Emma noticed then that Lucy was, indeed, without her shawl. "But you've just agreed to play for us, dear." Mrs. Betancourt turned to Emma then with a look of pure, benign innocence. "Perhaps Emma would be so gracious as to retrieve it for you, since she is your very dear friend." She brought a finger to her lips. "I only worry whether she will find her way. Brantmoor is so large and there are so many rooms."

Emma nearly laughed. There were precisely two rooms through which the group had passed between the dining room and the parlor in which they were currently situated, but Emma was in no particular mood to argue the point. Lucy and her mother had clearly been more successful than she in devising a ploy. Emma cast a shrewd look at Lucy. She could not recall Lucy dropping her shawl in the dining room. It was quite clever of her to have managed leaving it behind without it being immediately noticed by one of the staff.

"I will of course accompany Lady Emmaline on her task so as to ensure she is not lost forever in the depths of Brantmoor," the duke declared. His expression was pure sincerity, but his eyes danced with laughter and she knew he guessed the ruse. No matter, really, as long as the task was accomplished.

"Please do not leave the others in suspense, Miss Betancourt," he said. "You mustn't wait for us to begin playing. We will return in no time at all." Then he presented Emma with his arm and a knowing grin. "Shall we, Lady Emmaline?"

Chapter Fourteen

John strolled out of the music room with a wide smile, a spring in his step and his betrothed on his arm. He fully expected to hear more of the same objections she'd been reciting all week, but recalling her reaction to his kisses, he expected to quell those objections in short order.

Emma did not disappoint. Though her posture was rigid and her countenance one of studied serenity, a flush crept from her bodice to her hairline as he met her gaze with a warm smile. As warriors went, she was a delectable example—an ideal choice, really.

"Since we find ourselves with a private moment, I should like to discuss our engagement," she said primly.

Resisting the temptation to simply sweep her into his arms and continue their activities from two days prior, he gave an exaggerated courtly bow. "I am at your service, madam."

Her prim posture fell to one of impatient defeat. "May we *please* have an earnest discussion, Your Grace?"

He could point out the regression to formal addresses, but he thought the better of it, and nodded instead. "Certainly." He was not entirely sorry for baiting her if it had the effect of relaxing the formality of their conversation, but he did very much desire to hear what she had come to say.

"You've been very insensitive to my wishes," she pointed out, partly readopting the scolding expression of a schoolmistress. "The greatest example of that is having the banns read in church despite knowing my intent."

"My intent in having the banns read was not to trap you," he assured her. "The engagement is widely known, banns or no, and will have to be broken if we are not to wed. Calling for the banns simply moves the clock along in the event I can convince you to proceed with the wedding. You will recall, I believe, how anxious I am to have the matter finished." Her eyes surveyed him, her expression unreadable. "A wedding is rarely the *end* of a matter."

He nodded, conceding this point as well.

"I don't entirely believe your claim that calling for the banns was merely a considering of the calendar. I believe you are operating under the misguided assumption that I will be less likely to break the engagement if I am unable to do so quietly and without notice. You should understand," she continued, "I do not appreciate your attempts to lock me into this betrothal through these public spectacles, but it matters not. I am not concerned with my reputation. As I explained before, I have no interest in pushing my way into the *ton* like a mushroom among the flowers."

He laughed and stepped closer. "I can assure you, Emma, I have never likened you to a mushroom."

She cast him a wary glance and took a step back. "As I was saying, I will not be trapped into marriage, but I have decided to consider it."

What was this? He had planned to convince her. He didn't expect her to simply announce a complete reversal.

"May I ask what has caused this change of heart?" From his view, there had only been one event in the past several days that could have made the difference. If his suspicion was correct, he should have kissed her at the Fairhavens' house and saved a great deal of trouble.

"I am only *considering* it," she said, ignoring his question, "under certain conditions."

She had conditions, clever girl. John smiled down at his bride-to-be and marveled again at his great luck. She was formidable and self-possessed. She would make an excellent champion.

"What would these conditions be?" he asked.

"They pertain to my cottage and my garden." She averted her eyes as she answered. "If we are married, I want to keep it. I want it to remain mine."

He shrugged. A simple enough request, really.

"I also want your assurance that I will be allowed to spend time there."

John thought her second condition would go without saying, given the easy distance between Brantmoor and Beadwell. Neither of her conditions appeased his curiosity as to why she had ceased objecting to the marriage. He preferred to assume it was their amorous compatibility, but pragmatism prevented him from adopting the idea as truth.

A deflating thought.

"You still haven't told me *why* you are willing to consider it." He pressed closer, wanting her to look up and meet his eyes so he could judge the honesty in them.

When she finally met his gaze, he saw only the challenge his words inspired. "My reasons are simple. Though I have valid objections, practicality requires that I set those objections aside. It is your desire that we be married. I am now willing to marry you, provided you grant me this one consideration."

"Two considerations, actually." He couldn't resist provoking her.

"*Two* considerations, then." She appeared suitably provoked.

John sighed, tapped his chin with his finger and otherwise made a display of considering her conditions. It was not the conditions that gave him pause, as he had no intention of denying them. Rather, she had not really given a reason other than practicality, which had applied from the outset. Could there be another reason she was unwilling to give? "I'm not sure," he said, deciding to test his theory. "What you ask is not a minor consideration."

Her chin snapped up and her eyes sharpened. "I don't see how it's anything *but* a minor consideration. What possible interest could you have in my cottage?"

"None, of course. Allowing you to spend time there, however, will be in direct conflict with your duties to Charlotte." He cocked his head to one side. "My sister is a lovely girl, but she's wholly unprepared to take on the *ton*. I need a duchess who will dedicate herself to Charlotte's education."

She looked confused by his objection. "Your sister will not require my supervision or instruction every hour of every day. I will not be absent for days at a time."

John released another exaggerated sigh. "Perhaps what you ask is too great and you've been correct all along," he said, watching her closely. "I may have been hasty in my choice."

The annoyance that flashed through her features at this teasing informed him she had now firmly decided that marrying him was wiser than not. Perhaps his dismissed suspicion had been correct after all. Practicality seemed a more convincing argument when paired with growing attraction, was it not?

"Although…" He shifted closer and gently brushed his hand down her forearm. "It seems a shame not to marry when we've only just discovered what a compatible pair we will be."

She looked up, her amber eyes bright with alarm. "The vicar is across the hall."

He smiled wickedly. "I believe I may want to add a condition."

He watched her flush deepen as possible conditions tumbled through her mind.

"But you already have a condition." Her words were hasty and flustered. "You...you want me to help Charlotte."

He shrugged. "Another condition, then." He pressed even closer, using up the remaining inches between them.

When she lifted her amber eyes to his, he took her gaze and held it locked with his own, transmitting all the intensity he'd felt since she'd entered his home, and watched her flush from top to bottom. She'd been feeling the same attraction as he throughout their conversation, and with his stare, he challenged her to admit it.

Her eyes widened, apprehension growing, until she did admit it. She didn't say it, but for a brief, nearly imperceptible moment her gaze dipped to his mouth, betraying her thoughts.

He broke the moment with a triumphant smile.

"I'd like you to ask me."

Her shoulders fell with an exasperated exhale of air. She glared. "You want me to ask you to marry me?"

He nodded. "Sweetly. With a kiss."

"But the vicar is across the hall."

"You've already said that."

"It bears repeating."

He laughed at the reprimand in her tone. She needed kissing—an excessive amount—and he rather looked forward to providing it.

"That is my condition." He made the declaration firmly, but he softened it with a coaxing smile. "Come now, Emma. A chaste kiss shared by an affianced couple won't scandalize the Betancourts or anyone else." In truth, if the vicar understood what John would really like to do with his daughter's dear friend, he should have charged across the hall with a pair of dueling pistols.

Emma swallowed. "Oh, very well." She exhaled and clasped her hands in front of her before looking up at him. "Will you marry me, please?" She darted quickly forward to place a brief kiss in the air near the general location of his cheek.

He shook his head slowly back and forth as she looked defiantly up at him. "That was, frankly, weak in every respect. Surely you're braver than that."

Her eyes narrowed. "My Lord Duke," she began with venom, "would you do me the very great honor of allowing me to become your wife?"

He waited but she failed to follow her words with action. He leaned in. "Now the kiss, dear."

She sent him a look clearly meant to communicate her displeasure before lifting her eyes to the ceiling. Then she set her shoulders and moved toward him with the pursed lips one might use to kiss an elderly relative.

That, he decided, would not do.

As quickly as her lips touched his, his arms stole around her.

The touch of their mouths was brief, but not without impact. When she looked up at him, her amber eyes glowed. "Will you let me go now?" she asked with a voice turned husky.

"I have another condition," he said, his eyes boring into hers.

She pushed at his chest without success. "No more conditions. You're playing with me."

"I want to know the reason—the reason why you changed your mind."

She shook her head. "It doesn't matter."

"It does matter, but I think I know."

She looked wide-eyed up at him. "You do?"

He pulled her fully up against him. "I can think of several reasons."

Her fists balled at his chest but she didn't push him away. He held her gently, easily, as he bent his head to brush his lips near her ear. "Why, your reputation, of course." He nibbled at her earlobe. "You're worried what society will think if you cry off."

He let his breath whisper across her damp earlobe and shared the shiver as it ran down her body.

"I've never cared what society thinks." Her voice came ragged, breathless.

"No?" He trailed his lips from her ear to the base of her neck and felt her fists unfurl on his chest. "It must be Charlotte, then," he murmured.

He dropped his head and touched his lips to her collarbone. "Surely, you haven't forgotten about poor Charlotte, who needs our help."

She shook her head. Whether she meant, "no, she hadn't forgotten," or "no, that wasn't the reason," he had no idea and didn't much care. Her answer to the question his body asked was a resounding yes. She released a soft sigh as the heat of his mouth grazed her nipple through the thin fabric of her dress.

John used one arm to support her as she weakened against him. The other dropped to her hip to tuck her more firmly against him while his lips trailed back upward to her ear. "All of those are good reasons," he whispered between kisses and flicks of his tongue along her neck. "But I suspect another."

He slid the hand from her hip up to cup her breast. It felt full and weighty in his grasp and he longed to free it from its restraint.

She moaned softly, pressing forward into his touch as her arms slid around his neck.

"I think you enjoyed our kisses," he murmured into the crook beneath her jaw. "I think you are as anxious as I am to find out what would have happened if we weren't interrupted that day in the garden." His hand released her breast to stroke slowly down the side of her—over the round of her hip and back up again. "If we had the privacy of a bedchamber and a comfortable bed, I could lay you down and love every inch of you like you were made to be loved." God, what he wouldn't pay for that right now.

Her eyes closed, she shivered at his words. Her fingers clutched the hair at his nape.

He couldn't tease either one of them any longer. He seized her mouth with all the hunger that had been building since she'd arrived—hell, since he'd left her two days ago.

He probed with his tongue until her lips parted to allow him full access and felt more than heard as she moaned into his mouth. *God, Emma.* He could barely restrain the need to lay her back, lift her skirt, and make her his wife in all ways but one, right there on his dining room carpet. What was she doing to him? He could hear the music of the harp coming from across the hall, yet he couldn't peel himself away. He cupped her breast again, even as he promised himself he would end it before they got carried away.

Drawing on his last shred of will, he pulled his lips from hers. Placing his hands upon her waist, he set her away and stepped back to create a buffer of distance.

She looked up at him, lips parted, eyes clouded with passion. Her breath was labored as she recovered herself.

He couldn't stop the satisfied grin that settled onto his mouth to replace her lips. "There is your reason, Emma." His chuckle was weak for want of breath. "We have to marry. Or risk a much greater scandal than anything either of us has done so far."

She brought her hand to her swollen lips as though she might touch what just happened there. Her voice was odd and weak when she spoke. "That wasn't necessary."

John laughed, this time with the full power of his lungs. "Of course it wasn't necessary, Emma. But it was rather enjoyable, don't you think?"

She looked at him with the strangest, almost accusatory expression. "This is a marriage of convenience."

What in heaven's name was she thinking? "True, but just because it's convenient for Charlotte and convenient for society, that doesn't mean it can't be convenient for us as well." He stepped forward, picked up her hand. "You are a very desirable woman, Emma. I anxiously await the day when I have all the rights of a husband and we can finish what we've only just started."

Emma pulled her hand gently from his grasp and clasped it with its mate in front of her. She looked down at them before meeting his eyes again. Her expression was hesitant, uncertain. Where was his clever, snapping Emma?

"I...I have another condition," she said finally.

He stopped. "Another condition?"

She nodded. "If this is to be a true marriage in which we behave as husband and wife, I want you to honor me as a husband."

"Of course, I'll honor you as a husband. Did you think I would mistreat you? You'll have everything you want, Emma. You've only to ask."

"That's not what I mean." She didn't meet his eyes. "I want you to honor your vows as a husband."

"You mean you want me to be faithful to you?"

"Yes. Otherwise, if this is to be truly just a marriage of convenience, let it be a marriage in name only."

"Ridiculous." Was she not in his arms just minutes ago? "Of course, it will not be a marriage in name only," he sputtered. "What of heirs? What of continuation of the line? What of...what just happened, for God's sake?"

"I will give you heirs," she said with quiet resolve, "under the condition that you promise to honor our marriage vows."

He gaped at her. Where in heaven's name was this coming from? He'd only just come to realize his good fortune in marrying a woman whom he found appealing and already she was questioning his fidelity.

He...well, he hadn't thought that far ahead. They weren't even married yet. There was Charlotte, and the estate. He certainly didn't plan to set out as soon as the vows were exchanged and locate a mistress, for God's sake.

"Fine," he said, his tone carrying the extent of his frustration. "I will honor our vows. But no more delays or conditions, Emma. We'll be married in two weeks. Here. There is no time for a society event in London."

She nodded silently.

"We should return to the others. We can tell everyone the happy news," he said more sharply than he had intended.

"The shawl." Her voice was barely louder than a whisper.

"What?"

Emma cleared her throat before she spoke again, this time more firmly. "We came for Lucy's shawl."

The duke strode to the chair in which Lucy had been seated for dinner and spied a blue bit of fabric peeking out from underneath the tablecloth where it hung to the floor. He tugged on it, revealing the missing wrap, and returned to Emma's side. Wordlessly, he handed it to her.

Chapter Fifteen

"Is your father at home?"

Emma stood once again on the doorstep of the Crawford house. Now that her circumstances had changed, she saw no sense in waiting to inform Mr. Crawford. She was looking forward to it.

Juliana Crawford gave her the same unreadable yet haunting gaze that always left Emma wondering if the girl sought rescue, or if she was just as miserable a person as her father. "Is your father at home?" Emma repeated.

Juliana nodded. "He said you would come." She pushed the door wide and turned toward the parlor. Emma followed.

"You are quite proud of yourself, I imagine." Mr. Crawford marched into the room before Emma's weight had even settled into her chair. He stared at her, making no effort to hide his dislike or anger. She nearly recoiled from the malice there.

She stiffened. "I presume you are referring to the fact that I am to be married."

"To the duke." He spoke the words as an accusation.

"Yes. To the duke." She stared steadily back at him. "We have been engaged since before our parents' deaths."

"That's all very convenient for you, isn't it?" he spat out, taking a chair across from hers.

"Do you mean the death of our parents, or the four-year delay in our marriage? I don't find either convenient."

"I mean that my family's land is now going to be the duke's land. Don't think I don't know why you're here with that satisfied smirk."

She was not smirking at all. She was working very hard, in fact, not to scowl at the man. "I am here, Mr. Crawford, because the situation regarding Simon is unresolved, and I wish to resolve it."

She caught his attention with that. He leaned forward in his chair and eyed her shrewdly.

"Do not misunderstand," she clarified. "I am not here to bargain for Simon's innocence. He is innocent. I have only come to seek your confirmation that you understand the same and agree the matter is ended."

"I don't agree with anything of the sort."

"You should. I advise you to consider my change in circumstances. The land in question will only be mine for a short while longer. Once I am married, the cottage and the garden behind it will become the duke's. And Simon will no longer be employed by me, but by His Grace." Emma swallowed. She had understood the truth of this all along, but speaking the words aloud sparked a tumble of discomfort in the pit of her stomach.

Mr. Crawford did not speak. Although she had not believed it possible, his stare became colder, harder. He gripped the worn wooden arms of the chair in which he sat.

"The duke was dismayed to hear of accusations against Simon," Emma lied, feeling only a slight tug of guilt for not informing the duke. Certainly, if she *had* told him, he would have been dismayed. "Especially as I have explained to him what a fine, honest boy Simon has always been." She lifted her chin before revealing her last important news. "His Grace has also assured me he has no intention to sell the cottage or its adjoining parcel of land to you, or to anyone else."

That last bit, at least, was true. The duke had assured her she could keep the cottage. The current offer for purchase of the adjoining land, if one could even call Mr. Crawford's attempt at coercion an offer, was a minor detail at best.

I hate you.

Mr. Crawford did not speak the words, but his snarling expression conveyed the message with eloquence. Then his snarl twisted into a teasing smirk. "Husbands say all sorts of things to brides when they are married," he warned. "But they have more sense in dealing with matters of land and neighbors and finances. Simon may rest easy, but you should not. If I wish to purchase my family's land, you have only a few more days during which you may prevent it. Once you are married, you have no say at all."

Lips tight, eyes hard, Emma's expression yielded nothing, but her heart raced. He was not wrong. Marriage to the duke did not allow Emma to keep her garden. It simply became the duke's property instead of Mr. Crawford's.

If she had sold her mother's garden to Mr. Crawford, it would be lost to her forever. By allowing it to pass to her husband upon their marriage, she had at least hope that he would keep his promise.

"As I said before, Mr. Crawford," she said, with as much confidence as she could muster, "His Grace has most vehemently assured me, the cottage and garden will always be mine, to manage as I please."

Emma wished her words were more persuasive, as she did not trust the calculating gleam in Mr. Crawford's eye, or the niggling doubt in her own heart.

* * *

"There's time enough to arrange another disappearance."

John cast a censuring glance at Brydges as the two rode in his carriage toward the church in Beadwell and, more significantly, toward the fulfillment of John's four-year engagement to Lady Emmaline Shaw.

"The 'call to war' explanation is a bit out of date, but I'm sure there's enough wit between the two of us to devise some believable tale." The man's features betrayed none of the humor his words possessed as he leaned languorously back against the plush seats of the comfortable conveyance and casually suggested his oldest friend abandon his bride-to-be at the altar.

"I've no need for a tale, believable or not," John assured him. "I fully intend to marry Lady Emmaline."

"No temptation whatsoever to flee?"

John sensed the question, though teasing, possessed a thread of sincere inquiry.

"None."

He spoke truthfully. John's resolve to marry had never wavered, but even he was surprised at the peace he felt currently, compared to the dreadful resignation that had enveloped him on his first night in London. Though he had been convinced of his duty to right the injustice done Charlotte, he had dreaded the task of hastily selecting a bride from among the flighty group of debutantes with termagant mothers.

But Emma was not flighty. Her mother was no longer living and her aunt was hardly a termagant. In truth, the whole thing had worked out in a rather convenient way, and he was, for several reasons, glad today was his wedding day.

And his wedding night, he could readily admit.

"The anxious bridegroom, are you?" Brydges asked, coming uncomfortably close to John's actual thoughts. His brow lifted. "Don't say you are enamored of the soon-to-be duchess." John released an inelegant snort. Anxious, yes, but enamored? "Certainly not. When have you known me to be a lovesick fool? That sort of ridiculousness serves no one in a marriage." It was true. Attraction was one thing. Love? That was quite another. Emma was no more caught up in love with him than he with her. But then...she *had* questioned his fidelity, or demanded it rather. Odd to think of Emma as a jealous wife when she'd had to be *persuaded* to marry him. No, whatever had prompted that request was not jealousy. John knew what sort of damage that weakness caused and wouldn't allow that particular emotion from either party to complicate their marriage. All the more reason why Emma was the perfect wife.

Lovesick foolishness, indeed.

Of course, there was a difference between lovesick foolishness and honor. John did not intend to fall madly in love with his wife, but neither did he intend to dishonor her. He had been caught unaware by her question and, admittedly, a bit offended. In his calmer moments, however, he could concede that affairs occurred regularly among the aristocracy. Many men of his circle believed honor demanded discretion rather than faithfulness, but John did not see circumstances in the same light. He hadn't considered the matter before, but now that Emma had made an issue of it, he knew he would honor his promise fidelity. It was simply his way.

John glanced at his friend and for the briefest of moments considered inquiring as to Brydges's opinion regarding the subject, but quickly thought the better of it. Hugh Brydges considered the matrimonial state to be a form of torture reserved for those either destitute of fortune or obligated to produce heirs. Since he was neither, his thoughts on the matter were easy to deduce.

John shook his head and changed the topic. "My sister will be arriving soon." With the ironic timing only the fates can deliver, John had awoken on his wedding day to the awaited letter delivering word of Charlotte's travel arrangements.

"How soon?" asked Brydges.

"Very soon," John replied. "A few days, a week at most. I'll be returning to London shortly to collect her."

As it happened, he and his new wife would have only a brief time during which to acquaint themselves before Charlotte arrived.

His new wife.

He didn't mind that. He had some inclinations as to how they could come to know each other better.

* * *

Emma's wedding day arrived with startling haste. Even simple country weddings took time for planning and arrangements, and the two weeks that had passed since Emma had acquiesced to the inevitability of her engagement had done so in a blur.

Her aunt and uncle had taken up residence at the inn in Beadwell, as the cottage was not large enough to house them all. Aunt Agatha clucked regretfully on several occasions that she'd not been given sufficient time to prepare, but Emma simply waved away her concerns. She chose from among the nicest of her London gowns for the ceremony and insisted all else could be managed after the wedding. There had been one painfully awkward conversation with Aunt Agatha regarding her wedding night that had been vague, uninformative, and peppered with oddly uncharacteristic stuttering on Aunt Agatha's part.

The morning of the day itself was such a rush of activity, she barely had time to think. Her first real opportunity to collect her thoughts came at an unlikely time—during the ceremony. Although she did find it necessary to pay attention at moments in order to provide the required responses, she found during the vicar's sermon she could allow her mind to wander and more closely examine her present situation.

She decided as the duke placed the ring on her finger that the time for questioning her decision had passed. He was to be her husband—if not entirely by choice, then at least by...acceptance. The arrangements had been made for a small wedding breakfast at the inn, after which the couple would depart for Brantmoor, and Emma intended to steer all her energies toward her duties once she became the Duchess of Worley.

Oh.

She looked up at John, who still held her hand after placing the ring.

She supposed she was already the Duchess of Worley.

Or perhaps not. She understood there were still papers to be signed.

Well.

The ceremony was eventually completed—presumably having been carried off with all the necessary steps and words that must be said for a marriage, though she could not say for certain due to the distraction of her thoughts.

As the small group made their way on foot from the church to the inn after the ceremony, it occurred to Emma she was glad the wedding had not been held in London. The spectacle would have been a mad crush. How often, after all, does a near spinster marry a dead man?

Chapter Sixteen

The newlyweds' time alone in the carriage started quietly. As the silence stretched into awkwardness, Emma searched for a topic to inspire some pleasant conversation and distract her from her burgeoning awareness of the man seated across from her, and that man's effect on her physical state. Even the duke's grand carriage was a relatively small space, and she was painfully conscious of her posture, the location of her limbs, the temperature of the air, and the pace of her own heartbeat.

"I received word that Charlotte is due to arrive quite soon," he said, to her great relief. "We probably should have been married in London, I suppose, since we shall have to return there so soon. Though I have to confess, I would not have preferred the fuss associated with a London wedding. I find I tire of London quickly these days." His smile was wan, almost sheepish, with the admission.

Emma smiled, relieved for the benign topic. "I was thinking something similar myself," she admitted. "I try to spend very little time in London and usually do so only to please my aunt."

"Do you not travel back and forth from your uncle's estate as they do? Do you stay in the country even while they have come to town?"

"The country, yes," Emma explained, "but not my uncle's estate. I do visit there, but home for me is my cottage. I am there most of all. I did caution you, did I not, that I was not very duchess-like."

"I recall you did, as a matter of fact, and gave it as one of the strongest reasons we should not marry." He smiled warmly. "Yet I consider that to be one of your more pleasing attributes."

The slow warmth that had been churning at her center developed tendrils and began to creep outward. "Do you?" she asked, averting her gaze to recover her serenity. "But I understood your primary purpose for marrying was to acquire an ally in preparing your sister to meet the *ton*?"

"That is my entire purpose for marrying," he admitted without hesitation, "but the more time I have spent in London, the more I understand how I have been altered by my time away. I find myself feeling a bit…constrained… by everything. There are so many strictures and formalities…" John's brow furrowed with the effort to find the words to express himself. "I am able to enjoy a bit more freedom in the country."

Emma wondered if he even realized that he tugged at his cravat as he spoke.

"Suffice it to say, life in Boston as a clerk was very different than life here as a duke. There are so many things here that must be just so. I've no doubt you can demonstrate for Charlotte what those things are. It's just…"

Emma watched with some wonder as he struggled to land upon the words that would convey his intended meaning. He shook his head as though settling for words that were not quite right. "Are you offended by my admission? That I was a clerk in Boston? I should have told you, I suppose."

She shook her head. "I am not offended." She did not explain that she already knew.

"Well, I appreciate that you might be unoffended or even have a preference for a relaxation of those strictures from time to time, when we are keeping no one's company but our own."

He had managed land upon precisely the reason she preferred life outside London. "Oh, I do have a preference for fewer strictures, Your Grace." With a timid smile, she awkwardly amended her statement, "er…John." She may as well speak his Christian name since she'd been mentally putting his Christian name to use for some number of days.

His brow arched. "Do you?" He leaned toward her, his warmth intensifying.

Emma's eyes widened as she pressed herself back into her seat. What sort of invitation had she inadvertently communicated?

He released a low chuckle. "How difficult we British are to un-train," he teased. "Spend a few years abroad and, I assure you, your training will be threatened."

She exhaled. Was that a stab of disappointment she felt? She chose to ignore it and contemplated his statement instead. How very different life must have been for him in Boston. "You've had a rare gift, haven't you?" she observed. "Not just in experiencing life in a far-off place, but in experiencing life in another sphere. Would you tell me about it?"

"You're a smashing success in abandoning strictures, my dear," he commented with a droll look. "No proper duchess would find interest in the life of a lowly clerk, even if that clerk did inherit a dukedom."

Emma released a laugh and felt the lightness of it. It seemed to carry some of her anxiousness away, this ability to laugh with her new husband. "I'm sure not," she returned. "I suppose I should refer to it only indirectly and with the use of some vague but offensive epitaph such as 'The Folly' or 'Your Unfortunate Period.'"

He grinned. "Come, now, certainly we can be more creative than that. What of 'The Dark Years' or 'The Humiliation?'"

Her laughter bubbled up again. "Oh that does sound bleak. And most assuredly offensive."

He laughed as well. It rumbled low and filled their small space with warmth. "I'll admit 'The Folly' applies best, as my time away was indeed self-inflicted, but I confess to a strong preference for 'The Dark Years.'" He inclined his head. "It's rather mysterious, don't you think?"

"Oh, yes," she assured him in mock sincerity. "I'll make every effort to refer to it as such in the hearing of others...for your sake, of course."

"Of course."

Emma pivoted in her seat and found she was a bit more comfortable leaning against one of the cushions. "But since we are not in the hearing of others presently," she pointed out, "and since I suffer from an unpardonable lack of disapproval for your choice to go to your family's aid, I would like to know more of your time in Boston. Perhaps it would help me to understand Charlotte better."

John's shrugged as though to imply there was not much of interest to tell. "What would you like to know?"

Everything. In truth, Charlotte was not the only person whom Emma wished to know better. As she had resolved to make the best of their marriage of convenience, she found herself impatient to know more about this man to whom she was forever bound and of whom she knew frighteningly little.

Where *does* one begin when one wants to know *everything*?

"How did you travel there?" It was as good a place to start as any.

"Not easily. There were no trading ships going to Boston because of the war with the Americans. I took advantage of a connection of my father's and was able to arrange for passage on a naval ship. I was gone before he was able to prevent it."

"Once you arrived in Boston, how did you find your mother and sister?"

"It wasn't difficult. I had the direction from my mother's letter."

Of course. Silly question. "Well, what did you *do* when you found them?"

He thought a moment before answering that question, as though straining for the exact memory. "I suppose we had a reunion of sorts," he said finally. "I had not seen either of them in some years."

She had forgotten that. Well, not really forgotten as much as hadn't really considered it. She would have crossed the world for her own family, but would she have done so if she had not *known* her family?

"How long did you believe them dead?" she asked.

"Ten or eleven years, I'd say."

"Ten or eleven years," she mused. "So long?"

"Yes. I learned of their existence shortly after I completed my schooling. For several years after that, I sent money when I could, but my desire to aid exceeded my allowance and my debts grew. That is when you became my father's plan to rescue me from my presumed dissolute lifestyle as a gambler and spendthrift."

"Until you learned your mother was ill," she supplied.

"Yes. Until then."

"What was it like, seeing them again after so much time had passed?"

He hesitated before answering.

"Odd," he said finally. "Good."

She sensed his simple answer was probably as articulate as one could be regarding the complicated emotions of those moments of reunion. He'd been a motherless child for so many years and yet he'd determined as a man fully grown that he owed his mother and sister the very care and compassion he'd been denied through no fault of his own. It was, she thought, really quite noble of him. Her eyes roved over him. That nobility was rather appealing. He was rather appealing. She realized then that she had at some point during their conversation scooted forward in her seat and was leaning inward even farther than that.

His eyes caught hers as they had several times as they conversed, but this time her cheeks warmed.

He noticed. He had to have noticed, because the lightness and laughter in his eyes intensified to…something else, something that very eloquently reminded her she was married to this man and the vehicle that carried them was not so much racing toward a place as it was racing through the day toward the night. Her wedding night.

Emma dropped her gaze to her lap. She swallowed, leaned back, and immediately regretted not finding out where the moment could have led. Why should she shy away? They had kissed on more than one occasion and it had been nice. Better than nice. Now they were married. They were allowed to kiss. They were *supposed* to kiss. If only she weren't so nervous.

She sighed. Perhaps it was better that the moment passed. "How old was your sister when she left home?" Emma asked, prodding their conversation forward. "Do you think she has any memory of England?"

She looked up again. The heat had quieted in his gaze, and instead he looked at her with an odd, assessing expression.

"You have not yet asked me about my decision to go to Boston in the first place and whether I had considered the injury my decision would cause you."

Emma couldn't deny the question had crossed her mind. She knew the answer, though, didn't she? She asked it anyway. "Did you consider the injury to me?"

Despite having invited her to ask, he did not answer immediately. He gazed upon her with a pained expression for a long moment then shook his head.

"No," he said. "No, I did not."

Well, then.

He released a heavily burdened sigh before continuing. "Life is complicated in unforeseen ways, it would seem."

"How do you mean?" she asked.

"Well, take my predicament of four years ago," he said. "I harbor no regrets for the choice to alter my life for what was then an uncertain number of years to protect my mother and sister from the consequences of my father's rage and spite." He reached forward and took her hand in his. "But mine was not the only life for whom the course was changed by that decision, was it?"

"No." Still, Emma could not allow him to take responsibility for the full extent of tragedy and upset in her life. "But you could not have predicted my parents' passing," she pointed out. "No one could have. It was a horrible accident."

A horrible, life-altering accident.

"True," he conceded. Then, still with her hand in his, he crossed the small space that separated them and repositioned himself next to her, on the same cushioned seat. "But I should have predicted that you would be marred by scandal due to my actions."

Emma could not deny his reasoning, but chose not to confirm it. At one time her bitterness had been sharp indeed, but now...

"I suppose if the time has come for fairness in perspective, *I* must ask *your* forgiveness as well," she said.

"And what transgressions have you committed to require forgiveness?" he asked, his mouth quirked into a disbelieving half smile.

"I allowed my anger to prevent me from understanding the complexities of your position, Your Grace."

His brow lifted.

"John," she amended. Then she smiled at him with genuine friendship, or the hope of it. Yes, peace and friendship were what she desired.

"I *was* placed in a difficult position," she continued, "and my prospects for marriage were...altered...by the events of that season. But I had never desired marriage in the first place. At least not then—not to anyone in particular. And certainly not to you. I mean no offense, I assure you."

He chuckled. "I assure you, I take none."

"We didn't even know each other," she rushed to explain. "At that time, I only assumed you detested me. I understand now you behaved as you did that day out of disgust for your father, not necessarily for me."

"That day?"

"The day we were introduced."

"I only vaguely recall it," he admitted. "I apologize if I behaved badly, which it seems I did. Was I particularly boorish?"

"I believe you said, 'I will not have her,' or something of that sort," Emma reminded him.

He swallowed. "That was, you'll understand, a rejection of my father's attempt to control me. It was not, as you said, a rejection of you, personally."

Emma must have failed to mask the doubt she felt at his words for he searched her features and spoke again.

"What else did I say that day, Emma?"

She coughed delicately and avoided his direct gaze when she finally answered his query. "You, er, said, 'This owl-faced girl isn't old enough to be out of the school room.' Then you leaned over to me and said, 'but you're old enough to know you want to be a duchess, eh?'" Her shoulders stiffened slightly at the memory.

To his credit, he cringed. "I am so very sorry for that." He squeezed her hand and then lifted his to draw a finger gently down her cheek. "You are strong and utterly lovely, and I was a fool not to have seen it then."

Of all the emotions whirling through Emma just that moment, she didn't think any were aptly described as peaceful. His eyes fell to her lips. She blinked, uncertain what would happen next. Would he kiss her?

Please.

She froze, this time unwilling to break the moment, hoping desperately that he would not.

He leaned toward her and her eyes fluttered closed as his lips fell to hers. They moved gently at first, like a soft caress of his mouth on hers. Then the pressure deepened, his tongue urged her lips apart and met with hers, and the heat inside that she'd worked so hard to constrain broke free.

This was the other part of her bargain, she decided then. Theirs was no great love, but she could have this. She could experience passion, for as long as it lasted. As her palms traveled his back and across his shoulders, she had the satisfying thought that old maids in cottages did not experience passion, did not have kisses from a man like this one. Her lips curled into a smile against his mouth..

Then his hand slid beneath her traveling cloak and closed around one breast, his thumb teasing the nipple that pebbled underneath his touch. A new wave of sensation shot through her, sending the heat to her stomach and lower. She knew what she felt was desire. She desired him in the most basic physical way. She had been warned, as all girls had, to be wary of men's lust. She never understood until just then that a woman could feel the same lust, the same reckless want, for a man.

But she did. She pressed herself boldly against his hand and returned his kiss with every measure of passion he gave.

He groaned and wrenched his mouth from hers, sending her reeling into disappointment, until she realized he had immediately set himself to the task of unfastening her cloak. She waited in silence, anticipation building within her. He cast the cloak aside and gazed down at her chest as it rose and fell. He pushed one side and then the other of her wide neckline down her shoulders then slid his fingers inside the fabric to grasp one breast in his bare hand and pull it free.

Emma's eyes fell shut at the delicious feeling of his warm hand cupping her. Then his mouth closed over the peak and she moaned, her fingers lacing through his hair as she held him there at her breast, reveling in the exquisite new sensations this created.

His lips traced her neck and jaw and captured her mouth again, his hand warming the place his mouth had abandoned. Then he held back again, freed her other breast from its fabric prison and gazed thickly down.

"Beautiful," he whispered.

She blushed, bared openly before him without the distraction of his kisses, but her ardor did not cool.

He pivoted away from her, sitting back, with his knees toward the other seat then motioned to her. "Come here."

She hesitated, her hands fluttering to her bare chest. *Where exactly?*

"We'll be more comfortable this way," he said and patted his hands on his lap.

Emma scooted toward him then awkwardly lifted herself and backed onto his lap, arranging herself like a child might sit.

John laughed, not unkindly. "I meant the other way, Emma. Sit like a man rides a horse, so I can kiss you again."

"Oh," she breathed. She blushed again, suffused with embarrassment. She hadn't realized.

She turned and brought her legs up onto the bench so she was seated sideways on his lap, then realized her mistake as she tried to bring her one leg up over his lap to sit astride him. It was impossibly tangled up in her skirts and she couldn't lift it across without kneeing or kicking him somewhere, and she was painfully aware throughout the entire bungled attempt that her breasts were loose, bare, and bouncing the whole time.

This definitely cooled her ardor.

"I'm sorry," she muttered, trying to arrange herself in some way that wouldn't land her on her bottom on the floor of the carriage.

"Hold on," he said laughingly. He placed his strong hands on her waist and held her up, thus freeing her hands to untangle herself from her skirt, then set her down next to him on the seat. Turning to face her, he gently lifted the fabric of her bodice up over her breasts until she was somewhat covered. "I suppose that was a poorly thought-out plan," he said with a crooked grin.

She stared back at him, fervently wishing she could bury herself under her cloak. How on earth had she completely muddled that? She hadn't realized what he meant and then had managed to ruin everything by nearly strangling herself with her own dress. One moment she'd been congratulating herself on her introduction to passion and the next she had been completely humiliating herself as the inexperienced child that she was.

"We were getting a bit ahead of ourselves anyway, weren't we?" He lowered his head to kiss her and lingered there for a moment before staring intently into her wide eyes. "I look forward to our wedding night with great anticipation."

She smiled hesitantly, thankful for his effort to lessen her embarrassment. She reached down and tugged one shoulder of her dress back into place and then reached up with her other hand to adjust the opposite side.

Silently, John pulled her traveling cloak back around her, leaving it still unfastened at her throat. She thought he would return to the opposite seat but he did not. He pulled her firmly against his side and draped one arm across her shoulders. He took one of her hands and held it in his.

She swallowed and leaned back against her husband, realizing that sitting up against him this way was better than if he sat across from her. Here, he could not see how hotly her face still flamed, and she did not have to meet his gaze, as she was not ready to do so. She sensed he knew her discomfort and was intentionally trying to lessen it. If only her embarrassment were not so all-encompassing in that moment, she would be grateful for his kindness.

Chapter Seventeen

There was no family to greet John and Emma as they arrived at Brantmoor, but the staff turned out en masse to honor their master and new mistress. Emma idly wondered at their thoughts. Surely, when the staff had seen the heir to the dukedom return from the dead, his arrival with a duchess acquired in the normal fashion would not be cause for much curiosity.

Not that she would be aware, of course, even if gossip had risen to a peak below stairs. The staff of Brantmoor was no doubt as well trained as one would expect. Everything about her first evening at the Georgian mansion was precisely as expected—full of ceremony and the structure of ducal life. A staff of at least one hundred, she guessed. Yet there were only two of them in residence. They would be three when Charlotte arrived. It was but a few short miles, yet a world apart from her cottage. When she was shown to her suite of rooms, which connected to the duke's, and introduced to Liese, who had been assigned as her lady's maid, she was very cognizant of her position here at Brantmoor, where daily life would supply ever present reminders of her station and its expectations.

That evening, the newlyweds shared a quiet dinner in the blue parlor, as the main dining room was far too vast for the two of them. Emma was aware of little else through the meal besides John's attention. She must have eaten, but she had no recollection of what was served. They lingered over their last drink of wine, however, and she was glad for the bolster to her courage.

After the remains of the meal had been cleared, John smiled warmly at her and leaned back in his chair. "We have had a very long day. I am anxious to retire."

She swallowed, knowing very well that rest was not his intent. They had no guests to entertain; there was no family to whom they must make excuses. They could simply retire for the night. Their wedding night.

* * *

Emma found Liese in her room, laying out the nicest of her nightdresses and smoothing the linens of an already-made bed.

"Thank you, Liese," Emma said softly, hoping she did not reveal the extent of her trepidation. She faced away from the girl, presenting her back and the long row of tiny buttons that fastened her gown.

Liese made quick work of the buttons and, once Emma's gown was removed, was equally quick at unknotting the laces of her corset. Emma was grateful for the girl's efficiency.

"I will see to myself from here," she said once she was down to her chemise and stockings. She did not need her lady's maid to see the new mistress of Brantmoor shaking with anxiety for her wedding night.

What had she been thinking, asking him to promise fidelity?

She'd just felt so lost that evening, as though she'd ceded control of her mind and her body. She'd grasped for something, anything, to regain a sense of power over herself and her future. Yet she'd only succeeded in making herself more vulnerable. She'd wrenched from him a promise he never intended to make and would like come to resent. He'd looked at her as though she were delusional. Would he question on this night the value of the bargain he'd struck?

"Very well, Your Grace." With a brief curtsy and a flash of conspiratorial smile that proved she had misinterpreted the reason for being rushed away, Liese scurried out of the room.

Emma breathed deeply before discarding her chemise and stockings in exchange for the night rail. She had always seen to herself at the cottage and was fully capable of dressing in her nightclothes and unpinning and braiding her hair without the help of a lady's maid. She was a bit clumsy at the chore this evening however. Her fingers shook as she fastened the short row of buttons on the top panel of her plain night rail. The plait she managed in her long, brown hair was not the tidiest she had ever achieved. Then she looked at her reflection and wondered if she should have left her hair loose. Did it matter? Would he have a preference? Her nightdress and wrapper were not precisely alluring either. They were serviceable. She supposed delicate, prettily embroidered nightclothes were among the things her aunt had wanted for her, but there had been no time.

There was a gentle knock of warning and the adjoining door creaked open. She turned but kept a steadying hand on the bureau.

John walked slowly into the room. He wore a loose, untied white shirt. He still wore breeches. He carried a brown velvet dressing gown draped over one arm. His feet were bare.

Emma's feet were also bare. She knew this, of course, having removed her stockings herself, but somehow noticing *his* bare feet made her more aware of *her* bare feet.

He did not appear to notice her feet. His eyes glowed in the candlelight. They locked with hers, and she remembered his promise to lay her down and love every inch of her. *Every inch.* Surely, every inch of her was alive and aware of him now. Her heart beat like a rabbit's. Her limbs tingled. She was aware of her fingertips, her breasts, the backs of her knees, and the apex of her thighs. Her fingers fumbled as she toyed with the sash at her waist.

He crossed the room to where she stood waiting for him. He leaned forward and gently touched his lips to her cheek. Then he drew back and looked at her again. His lips broke into a wry half smile. He was looking forward to this.

The warm twist in her stomach tightened.

Emma had been alone with John in the interior of the coach all afternoon, and had managed to thoroughly embarrass herself. She was certain of only one thing—she would be a disappointment. She didn't see how she could be anything but, given she didn't have any inkling of what to *do*, really. She had a general sort of knowledge of what would occur, but no details.

Of course, it wasn't as though John would have preferred an experienced wife. Certainly *that* would be a disappointment.

Oh heavens, her mind was rattling.

Oh heavens, he was taking off his clothes.

She froze as she watched him drape the dressing gown over a chair and pull his shirt over his head. He was as lean and strong as she had felt in the brief embraces they'd shared. He reached down to unfasten his buckskin breeches and still she could not look away, though a voice in her head insisted she must or risk appearing immodest. That voice had very little success in dictating to the rest of her.

John's fingers paused at the fall of his breeches. She looked up and met his eyes, mortified to have been caught watching.

He let the laces alone and stepped back to her, the intensity in his eyes only growing. As he grew nearer, she felt closer to panic, wanting to flee.

He leaned forward when he reached her and placed a soft kiss on her forehead. He placed another on her cheek and another at her jaw. He turned her and placed one more electric kiss on the back of her neck before reaching around to untie the sash at the waist of her wrapper.

Well, then. She briefly wondered if he would be willing to delay the consummation of their marriage if she wished it.

Did she wish it?

It would seem not, for although her mind coursed with thoughts of flight or delay, she gave voice to none of it. She remained transfixed as he stood behind her, pushing the fabric of her wrapper over her shoulders and down the length of her arms, revealing the plain white nightdress beneath. His arms wrapped around her shoulders, pulling her back to his chest as he reached to unfasten the buttons she had fastened just a few minutes before. His chest was warm but she shivered from the contact.

With the short row of buttons undone, the neckline of her muslin gown sagged open, leaving the upper portion of her breasts bare. She had ball gowns that were more revealing, but this was different. The muslin was thin and loose. She had felt the warmth of his hands through the fabric as he unbuttoned it. And, most significantly, she knew it would soon be gone.

As though in answer to her thoughts, John gathered handfuls of the fabric at her sides and pulled the garment up over her head in a single motion. She stood there while he bared her completely. She was silent all the while, but her mind was still crowded. She was grateful to be facing away from him. She wondered at her own lack of modesty as she stood bared before him. Mostly she wondered at her own insufficiency and her dread of his inevitable disappointment. The whole thing had seemed very intriguing until she'd gone and wrested that ridiculous promise from him.

He turned her body to face his. She complied without resistance, but she kept her head down, keenly aware of the heat that painted her cheeks.

John set his finger under her chin and tilted it gently upward until her reluctant eyes met his. "What's this? Are you frightened?"

Horribly frightened. "No."

His large, firm hands stroked gently up and down her bare arms. "What's wrong, Emma?"

She had bared her body; she may as well bare her soul. She released a determined sigh and decided she had best come out with it. "I may have made a mistake."

His hands stopped. His expression warned of thunder. "What do you mean a mistake?"

"I fear I may have created an impossible situation for myself."

He shook his head then bent to nuzzle her ear. "You're speaking in riddles, Emma."

Her eyes closed briefly. It felt good, what he was doing just then. Her bared breasts arched involuntarily toward his naked chest. She could just let him continue, but... She pushed back from him. "I trapped you," she blurted. "Into promising fidelity. Now in addition to women you've known in the past, when we...make love...you'll be comparing me to women in the future—the women you might have known." She dropped her head, too humiliated to look him in the eye as she finished. "How can any flesh and blood woman of the present—particularly an inexperienced one—compare with a woman who is naught but a hope or a potential—a promise of better, or even perfect?"

"Oh, Emma." John hugged her to him and the skin-to-skin contact was as deliciously intriguing as she knew it would be, even as she felt his laughter rumble through his warm, broad chest. "Don't you see, you have it wrong? A flesh and blood woman doesn't have to compete with a ghost or a dream."

She let him take her hand and lay it between them, on his bare chest where she could feel his heartbeat through his skin.

"Your flesh against mine and your blood sending heat through your body. That's the only way we can do this."

He slid his hands up to cup her breasts. She leaned into his touch, unable not to.

"Right there." His murmur in her ear was husky. "How does that make you feel?"

"Like I'm falling," she admitted. "Or suspended, but I want to fall the rest of the way."

"Hmmm. Not yet, sweet Emma, but you will, I promise."

He dipped his head to put his lips to hers again. He kissed her softly at first, gently tasting. She parted her lips only a little to start, hesitantly tasting his tongue with her own, but his insistence drew her into the kiss. His tongue teased her lips farther apart and danced freely with hers. She wrapped her arms around his shoulders, burying her fingers into the nape of his neck, pulling herself more tightly into him, crushing her breasts more boldly into his hard chest. He ran his hands up and down the length of her back, and she sighed into his mouth at the loveliness of it. Then his hands slid lower and cupped her bottom as she clung to him, and, God, she like his hands there even better. Her fingers speared into his hair and she moaned. Still he kissed her—deeply, hungrily, until she felt an urgency building inside her. When he finally wrenched his mouth from hers, they both needed deep, panting breaths. He let his forehead fall against hers as they took in needed air.

When he lifted his head and spoke, his blue eyes bore intently into hers. "Lovemaking is not for what might be tomorrow or years from now. It's about losing yourself in this moment, with this person. There has never been anything that is less about the past or the future and more about right now." She looked in his eyes and she believed him. She couldn't imagine herself in any moment other than this one, with his hands moving over her body, sending jolts of sensation to every corner of her being. She let John gently lift her and lay her down across the bed.

He quickly divested himself of the last of his clothing and joined her there. He hovered over her with a knee on each side and lowered his head to her breasts. She nearly rose from the bed as his mouth closed over one nipple. She plunged her fingers into his hair and clutched him to his task. His hand stroked the inside of her leg at her knee and gently teased upward toward the place where her need pulsed the hottest. She twitched and squirmed as he dragged one finger upward at the opening to her very center.

"*John.*" She gripped the bed linen as she called out his name, not certain whether it had been a shout or a whisper.

Emma was acutely aware that she should do something—participate somehow—but she was incapable of anything more than simply reacting to these new sensations and the restlessness building inside her.

His mouth fell onto hers as his hands continued to stroke and knead in places she'd never understood could be so painfully sensitive—so wonderfully, painfully sensitive. She slid her arms around his neck and clung to him, giving all the urgency and passion he was creating inside her back to him in that kiss.

She held on and prayed that the feelings wouldn't stop, even as she begged him to cease his torture.

"John...I need..."

She didn't know precisely what she needed, but she trusted John to know—had no choice but to trust him.

John's breath was labored and short as he hovered above her, watching her. His eyes burned with an intensity that held her focus, warring with the effect his rhythmic touches were causing until she was able to hold no other thought in her mind besides knowing that the hottest part of a flame was not orange or red, but blue. This blue. His blue. *Oh God.* Her back arched. Her eyes fluttered closed. "Please." It was barely a whisper.

"Emma, open your eyes." He said it sharply enough to penetrate her haze, even as his hands and his body worked to keep her fully distracted.

She complied, then gasped, as his fingers plunged inside her.

Her lips stayed parted and he captured them again.

"Look at me, Emma," he said again, once he'd broken the kiss.

Her eyes fluttered open once more and he smiled, wickedly pleased.

Her hips undulated involuntarily against the motion of his hand.

"What did you do yesterday?"

Emma's mind struggled to respond, but the urgency prevented even basic comprehension of his words.

He dipped his fingers inside her again. The low moan she released started in her throat, but reverberated through her body.

"What did you do yesterday, Emma? What did you do this morning?"

Her mouth opened, silently at first. "What...I don't..."

He changed rhythm and her arm flung to the side, clutching at a fistful of bed linens.

John buried his face in her neck. "There is no before or after," he whispered. "Only now."

She quivered at his words.

"I'm going to make love to you now, Emma," he whispered, his lips moving against the skin just below her ear. His voice was low and ragged. "I'll go slow. I don't want to hurt you. I just can't hold out any longer."

His words pierced the veil of Emma's haze. Her eyes opened widely as his fingers slid out of her and his erection probed at her instead. Emma gasped and tensed as John's body slowly invaded hers. There was tightness, she realized, but no pain. He moved rhythmically, first deeper, then shallow, then deeper again, and she relaxed to the pleasure of the sensations his rhythm produced. The rising need for release began building all over again.

She clutched him tightly as it built. She was aware of making sounds, but didn't seem to be in direct control of them. Then the crescendo broke and she clutched him even more tightly. She held him through it as the waves shook her, then felt his body tense. He released a low groan and lowered himself atop her.

He lay there a moment before he spoke.

"I must be heavy. I will move just as soon as I am able."

He was heavy, but she didn't mind the weight. It was...reassuring. She lay there quietly, stretched out underneath him, their bodies in contact in so many places, and tried to simply take it in. This, she decided through a slowly clearing mental fog, was an aspect of marriage she could not have understood beforehand.

John pushed himself up and rolled to his side. He reached down to pull the bed coverings over them both then settled in next to her, with one arm draped across her.

Snugly in this position, Emma was quickly overcome by the exhaustion of the day. She smiled to herself as sleep settled in and granted her own measure of forgiveness to those girls who found themselves tempted into assignations without benefit of the marital blessing. If only she'd understood, she'd have been tempted herself.

Chapter Eighteen

Emma awoke when Liese entered her room. Startled, she turned to see that she was alone in her room. She reached a hand to the spot where her husband had been and felt it still warm. She smiled.

"Good morning, Liese," she said cheerily.

"Good morning, ma'am. His Grace sent me to see if you'll be wanting to dress for breakfast, or have a tray in your room."

"I believe I shall go down to breakfast," she said, anticipating the company of her husband. Emma sent Liese away after she dressed, as she recalled the location of the breakfast room from the previous day's tour and did not require an escort. She wore the nicest of her morning dresses, a pale green she thought complimented her brown hair and eyes. The flutter in her stomach as she went to meet her husband was entirely involuntary.

She shook her head at her own girlishness. There was no need to feel fluttery. He was her husband. They had done what husbands and wives do. She thought for a moment that food may be the cure, but the feeling intensified as she drew nearer to the breakfast room, and she knew that whatever a meal might do to lessen the feeling, the presence of her husband would have the opposite effect.

Goodness. She had better get herself together. She would be mortified to blush and stumble her way through breakfast.

"You found your way, I see." He rose as she entered. "Did you have any difficulty?"

The smile she returned was involuntarily exuberant. "No difficulty, thank you." Heavens. Was she blushing? She walked to the sideboard and busied herself filling a plate with toast, ham, and a boiled egg. She chose the seat at John's right and noticed that no plate sat in front of him. "Have you finished?"

"No, actually, I was waiting for you," he said, and flashed her a charming smile before setting about the task of filling his own plate. "Tell me," he said once he returned to the table, "what has been your impression of Brantmoor, Emma? It has been without a chatelaine for a long while. There may be areas my father neglected."

"None that are evident to me," she commented. "I've not had an opportunity to speak much with Mrs. Dewhurst, but my impression of both the woman and the house is that she must indeed be quite competent." Emma glanced idly at the stoic footman who stood at the ready to see to their needs. She had not noticed any lack, but was also wise enough to realize if she had commented upon anything, that fact would be swiftly reported.

"I am anxious to learn all there is to know about my new home," Emma said.

"There will be time for all of that. We will not be at Brantmoor long, however. We must return to London to meet Charlotte's ship when it arrives."

"Will her ship arrive soon?"

"Very soon. I would like to depart for London tomorrow morning."

Tomorrow? She'd only been duchess for one day. She'd had yet to confirm that Mr. Crawford would indeed be abandoning his claims against Simon. She couldn't return to London until she could be certain Simon was safe. What if Mr. Crawford had changed his mind? "Tomorrow is quite soon for me to travel. I am still unpacking my belongings and moving things from the cottage. I have matters to settle there."

"What is there to settle?" he asked. "It's a tiny cottage and the Browns seem competent."

For the briefest of moments, she considered apprising him of Mr. Crawford's threats to Simon, but she did not. Though her new husband had certainly demonstrated a nobility of character in supporting his mother and rushing to his sister's aid, he had also demonstrated sufficient stubborn will and highhandedness to give her pause. She simply could not be confident, at this early stage, if he would honor his promise regarding the cottage. "Well, there are things to be packed. And I must make sure the Browns and Simon have directions regarding my mother's garden."

He set down his knife and frowned at her. "These matters shall have to wait, I'm afraid, as the arrival of Charlotte's ship will not."

Emma swallowed. "Certainly," she said, "I would never suggest that you not arrive in time to meet your sister. I thought perhaps you would travel to London without me."

"I don't particularly like this idea," he stated, a little more loudly, as though addressing a larger group than just Emma.

She felt a brief tug of guilt for her omissions. Could he be lamenting the lack of her company? She warmed at the thought that he was loathe to leave her behind.

"Your responsibility is to Charlotte, and Charlotte will be in London."

Her guilt faded. He was concerned about her end of the bargain, nothing more. Well, his end of the bargain had been a promise that she could see to the cottage when necessary. "Surely you don't expect Charlotte to begin her education the moment she disembarks," Emma said primly. "She must have time to…absorb England. Besides, she will have missed you, and will want to reacquaint herself. I, on the other hand, am a stranger to her. Perhaps it is better that she and I meet after the two of you have been reunited."

He eyed her unhappily. "I don't understand. You will need to return to London. Charlotte will be there."

"Bring Charlotte to Brantmoor. That is much better, really. You and I have just been married in the country. Everyone will expect us to host our first event as a couple when we return to town. To do so anytime soon would be premature. If Charlotte attends, she would be unprepared. If she does not attend, she will be conspicuously absent."

"Hmmm."

Emma could not determine if her rationale was persuading him, but she continued. "If you bring Charlotte to Brantmoor, we will have some peace and isolation in which to prepare her. We can then return to London in time to attend a few events and host a ball of our own before the season is ended."

John leaned back in his chair and silently contemplated her suggestion. Emma wondered if he was already regretting his choice and wishing he had found a more biddable wife.

Eventually, John relented and agreed to collect Charlotte from London without her, a concession for which Emma should have been glad. But her husband left the room quietly after breakfast and her spirit was unaccountably dampened.

Chapter Nineteen

Despite being the peak of the season, White's was oddly deserted. John would have preferred a bit more action to distract himself that evening. If he and Brydges wanted to sit quietly and consume indecent amounts of liquor in private, they could have done so at Worley House without the trouble of a perfectly tied cravat.

"You are quiet this evening," Brydges noted.

"I am rarely outspoken," John responded, though he knew his friend was correct.

Brydges lounged back in his chair and took a fortifying sip of fine French brandy. "How is *Mrs.* Brantwood settling in these days?"

"Fine, I imagine."

John swirled his own brandy under his nose, breathing deeply. "Ahh, I've missed that."

"So the new duchess is settling in, is she? You're satisfied with your choice?"

"Perfectly," he said, then sniffed his brandy again. "Of course, I don't expect we'll be in each other's company much. She'll have plenty to occupy her time once Charlotte arrives and I've countless areas on the estate requiring my attention."

If Brydges had any questions or had drawn any conclusions as to why the newlyweds had not returned to town together, he did not voice them. Let him judge in silence if he would. John was a bit annoyed by the situation himself. Here he was in his third day of marriage, drinking brandy at his club in London instead of home in bed with his wife. He'd bedded his new wife only once. From his perspective, they'd done a fine job of it, yet she'd been no less stubborn after the event than before. And she'd been more worried about the blasted cottage than accompanying him to fetch Charlotte.

Brydges shook his head. "So the old man left things a mess at Brantmoor, eh?"

John shrugged. "Not entirely, but I think he may have gotten a bit neglectful at the end." He set his snifter on the side table and sat straighter in his chair. "I could use your expertise in evaluating the stables."

Brydges nodded. "I'd be happy to lend it.

"I know you've been busy while I was away," John said, feeling guilt that he had yet to see the successful stud operation Brydges had built during his absence. "I'd like to come out and see what you've built, but there are other demands to my attention at present."

"You may consider it a standing invitation," Brydges assured him. "Are you thinking of expanding the Brantmoor stables?"

"Maybe a bit. Nothing on the scale of what you've got."

"Well, I imagine you'll need a couple of ladies' mounts to start."

John's mouth turned down again at the reminder of his wife. "You're right. The duchess plans to ride a good deal, I understand. Charlotte's never ridden, but she'll have to start."

"Never ridden? But you ride like the animal is an extension of yourself. I can't imagine you having a sister who's never ridden."

"Charlotte's spent her whole life in Boston, not out in the country."

Brydges clucked his tongue. "Never ridden, never spent time in the country. Turning this sister into *Lady* Charlotte Brantwood ought to prove quite a project."

John glared at his friend's comment, but could not dispute it. It was a good reminder, he supposed. Why should he be bothered by his wife not accompanying him to London for a pair of days? They were not meant to be lovesick fools.

"Why don't you let me select a couple of suitable mounts? I'll bring them out to you myself," Brydges suggested.

"I'd appreciate that." It wasn't a half-bad idea. John would need something to entertain himself while the ladies worried about dresses and dances and whatever else they should worry about.

"What's this?" a graveled voice barked at them from across the room and both men turned.

John grimaced. He remembered well enough that Felix Pentwater was not particularly good company sober. He was even worse drunk, especially when one considered the likely damage to one's hearing.

"Didn't expect to see *you* in London so soon after the wedding. Tired of her already, are you?" Pentwater released a hearty laugh at his own humor.

John scowled darkly at him. "Not at all, Pentwater. I'm here out of necessity—to meet a ship."

"Got some precious cargo coming in, have you?"

"I do. My sister's ship will dock in the morning."

That announcement brought Pentwater up short. "What's that? Your sister? I didn't think you had any sisters."

"You were misinformed."

Pentwater's substantial frame swayed precariously with the strain of his thoughts. "Wait…wait… Yes, you did have a sister. The little one who died, right?"

John's jaw tightened. "I have one sister. She is very much alive."

Pentwater's laughter was more of a gurgle as he slapped John on the shoulder. "Well, you'll have to explain that one."

John itched to simply beat Pentwater to a pulp and have him tossed out of the club, but drunk as he was, the man was right. He would have to explain. Hadn't Brydges asked him that afternoon how he planned to explain his sister without completely exposing his father for the bastard that he was?

"There is no explanation. My sister has spent most of her life living abroad with relatives. She's returning home now to live in England."

Pentwater leered at John, swaying as he did, then catching himself. "A bit odd, don't you think, having a sister who shows up out of nowhere? How does anybody know she's really your sister and not some woman you've collected while you've been off doing God knows what for four years?"

Rage settled over John like a cloak, but before he could respond, Brydges stepped between them and threw his arm around the stout man's shoulders.

"Pentwater, you drunken fool, have you been reading ladies' novels again?" Brydges steered the intoxicated ass back toward the room from which he'd come. "Where do you get these outlandish notions? I've known Worley's sister for years. Lovely girl. She'll be the toast of the town, I'd wager."

John took the moment to allow his fists to unclench and his boiling blood to slow to a simmer. "Thank you," he said, when Brydges returned without Pentwater.

Hugh tugged at the bottom of his waistcoat and straightened his jacket. "I left him at the card table. Should be an expensive punishment in his present condition." He recovered his seat and peered at John. "Well, that was poor planning, I'd say."

"Pentwater's a braying ass."

"Of course he's an ass, because he said it to your face. You're a duke, so no one else will, but they will think it behind your back." Brydges recovered his glass and found it empty. He scowled at it and set it back down. "You need a better speech, man—quickly."

"I didn't intend to talk about her yet."

"Then why did you?"

"I don't know. Don't you think keeping her a secret implies there is something to hide? I thought the truth to be the better approach."

Brydges shook his head. "Next time you want to tell the truth, wait until you have a better lie to support it, will you?"

John sighed heavily. "Any story I give will be questioned. They're going to whisper about her no matter what I say."

Brydges didn't dispute it. John knew Charlotte had no idea what she was getting into and she was a scandal before she even arrived.

He wondered if he'd given his new duchess an impossible task.

Chapter Twenty

"Good morning, Emma."

Emma halted in the entryway to the breakfast room, surprised to find her husband already helping himself to a healthy serving of food from the sideboard. She'd had no word in the four days of his absence—no expectation of when he would return.

"Good morning," she said carefully. She continued into the room and slowly began filling a plate, determined to remain unaffected. "Did you arrive in the night?"

"Yes, it was quite late. Charlotte was tired, but I wanted to push through."

She placed a small portion of ham on her plate. "It's dangerous, travelling at such late hours."

"Is that wifely concern, my dear?" His words were teasing, but his tone was absent and he did not look at her.

"Just common sense." She added a boiled egg to her plate and seated herself at the table. She didn't know why she was being so contrary. Why didn't he wake her in the night to tell her he'd returned?

Why would he? They may be husband and wife, and lovers by some definition, but it's not as though they were *in love*, pining away for each other these past several days. She'd been very busy familiarizing herself with the house and the gardens, and arranging her new rooms, as well as seeing Charlotte's room made ready. And dealing with Mr. Crawford, of course. That had been satisfying.

"How is your sister?" she asked, with a new resolve to be amiable.

"Fine. A bit tired, I suppose."

"Yes, I imagine she would be after her journey. May I presume it was uneventful?"

"Yes, that appears to be the case. I arranged for her to travel with a respectable older couple from Boston, and it seems they got on just fine."

"How very overwhelmed she must be." Emma herself had been surprised by the grandeur of Brantmoor. If Charlotte had been awake enough to take in any of it, she would surely have found it intimidating.

"She is perhaps a little out of sorts. I expect she'll do fine, however." He smiled up at her. "She will have an excellent friend and guide in you."

Emma returned his smile with one that was equally pleasant and superficial. Was this the way of marriage, then? Were they to be amiable acquaintances, exchanging polite, meaningless conversation?

"You'll have much to do," John added. "Charlotte has a great deal to learn. Beginning with her riding."

"She does not ride well?"

"She does not ride at all."

Not at all? That circumstance hadn't occurred to Emma. She'd have to arrange riding lessons in addition to the dress fittings, dance lessons, and discussions of general comportment she'd already planned for Charlotte. Poor girl. Emma's heart ached for her. How very frightened and insecure she must feel right now. Even making her way to breakfast in this immense house would be intimidating.

"Did you offer to collect your sister at her room for breakfast?" she thought to ask.

"I had something sent up so she could rest. I expect she'll join us for dinner."

Emma wanted to shout at him to look at her—to meet her eyes. Where was the passionate man from their wedding night? She'd even welcome the debates of their first acquaintance over this indifference.

"Did you plan to introduce us?" She couldn't quite keep the sharp tone from her voice. The result, at least, was a direct look from her husband.

"Of course. I thought this afternoon would be best."

"That would be fine."

"I mentioned Charlotte's need to start riding. My friend Brydges will arrive today with new mounts for both of you."

"That wasn't necessary. The gelding I've been riding is perfectly suitable."

"Nevertheless, you'll have one for yourself. I have complete trust in Brydges's selection. He's a better judge of horseflesh than any man I've ever known."

Emma's brow lifted. "Really? I didn't realize he was so...gifted." Perhaps his judgment of horses would prove more sound than his judgment of people.

John's expression as he studied her was odd, but she was coming to realize she should not attempt to predict his manner toward her, as it could change so dramatically from one moment to the next.

"You may be assured he is," John responded finally. "He's built quite a name for himself with one of the most successful stud operations in England."

Hmmm. She supposed she could tolerate the man's company for an afternoon if he came with a particularly magnificent horse. "Should I instruct Mrs. Dewhurst that there will be four for dinner?" she asked.

"Yes. She should make up a room as well. He's going to remain with us for a time to help me assess the stables."

Splendid. Now she and poor Charlotte would have to contend with an indifferent John *and* the insufferable Mr. Brydges.

They should be a merry party indeed.

* * *

"I've sent Mrs. Dewhurst to bring Charlotte to join us," John announced to Emma and Mr. Brydges when the three were gathered in the rear parlor that afternoon.

"I am eager to make her acquaintance," Mr. Brydges announced.

Emma did rather like her new mount and so endeavored not to be annoyed by his mocking tone.

"Where have you been all day, John? I thought you would come to see me?"

All eyes rose at the intrusion.

A slip of a girl, with hair as dark as her brother's and eyes just as blue, marched into the room without pause or preamble.

"Ah, Charlotte. Welcome." John rose and crossed the room to take his sister's arm. "Did you take the opportunity this afternoon to walk around the house?" he asked solicitously.

Her pretty features bore a dreadful pout. "I've had no choice but to hide in my room all day. Each time I came out, all the servants kept peeping at me as though I'm some sort of ghoulish creature risen from the grave." She put her hands on her hips as she challenged her brother. "When you told them I was coming, did you explain I am a living person and not a ghost?"

John just smiled affectionately. "Come now, Charlotte. They're naturally curious. Most of them were here when you and mother left. They're just trying to match you with their memory of a three-year-old girl."

"Well, can you at least order them to stop staring?"

John only smiled indulgently.

Charlotte turned then, her gaze finally taking in Emma and Mr. Brydges. She glared.

Emma supposed she was staring in as rude a manner as the staff at that moment, but how could she not? She had expected Charlotte to be overwhelmed, intimidated perhaps—certainly grateful. She hadn't expected...this.

"Shall I spin for you as well, so you may examine me? Have you never seen a poor, American relation before?"

"I'll admit *I* never have," Mr. Brydges said from behind Emma. "Are they all this contrary?"

John placed a protective hand on his sister's shoulder. "Let's not argue. Charlotte has been through a harrowing ordeal this past year." He turned to face his sister.

"Charlotte, I want you to meet two very important people. The smug one is my very good friend Mr. Brydges, who has brought you a lovely new horse and will henceforth keep his commentary to himself. And this lovely lady," he said, leading Charlotte to stand in front of Emma, "is the Duchess of Worley. We were married one week past. She is now my wife and your sister."

Charlotte's eyes grew round at her brother's announcement.

Emma cursed John's misjudgment in not informing his sister of his marriage until this moment.

Charlotte faced Emma with narrowed blue daggers that solidly established Emma as a nemesis of the first rank, then turned accusing eyes on her brother. "I cannot believe you would marry without telling me—before I even arrived."

"I am the duke now, Charlotte, and I have responsibilities. Having a wife to act as hostess will make it possible to launch you in society." He took his sister's hands and looked upon her with the indulgence of a parent as she pouted. "Things will be very different for you here. You have much to learn. Emma will help you through it better than I could."

Charlotte looked back at Emma with such warning and distrust, Emma nearly recoiled from the force of it. "If I'm such an inconvenience that I'm to be foisted off upon others, why did you bring me here?"

Emma waited for John's patience to expire, but he seemed to have unlimited stores where Charlotte was concerned.

"You could never be an inconvenience, Charlotte," he declared passionately. "You belong here. This is your home. I only mean that Emma will be able to help you with dresses and the like—those things that are better left to ladies."

From what they'd witnessed so far, Charlotte needed a good deal more than new dresses to become presentable, but Emma kept that opinion to herself. "I hope I can be helpful to you, Charlotte," she said instead. "I know you've been through a difficult time."

"You don't know anything about what I've been through. But I can tell you it's enough to know I don't need your help or anyone else's." She crossed her arms in front of her chest and glared back at the lot of them.

Was that so? Emma turned to her husband and waited, brow raised, for him to respond to this outburst.

He did not.

"Are these the kind of manners commonly displayed in Boston?" she asked then, still wide-eyed at her husband's silence. Was he not even the least bit offended by Charlotte's temper tantrum? Was this to be the kind of behavior he tolerated?

John sighed. "Of course not." He addressed Charlotte again. "Emma is here to help you. There is no reason to feel offended by her presence."

Was he concerned that *Charlotte* had been offended by the conversation?

"I have no reason to be offended by anything you do." Charlotte's blue eyes flashed brightly as she faced Emma with a haughty lift of her chin. "I don't even know you."

"Charlotte." There was finally warning in John's tone, but he said nothing further.

Emma's own chin rose, but she did not respond. She had no possible dignified response to give.

Mr. Brydges, who had returned to lounging askew in his seat, peered at Charlotte. "You're a pretty enough package on the outside. Too bad you're so ugly underneath it."

"How dare you."

"Who are you to reprimand me?" she bit out, struggling against the grasp John held on her arm. "My brother and I are none of your business."

Mr. Brydges rose from his seat. His mocking disdain was replaced with a tight jaw and flashing eyes. "Your brother is my oldest friend and, therefore, very much my business. He's made a great sacrifice for you. The least you could do is demonstrate a little appreciation."

"That's enough, Brydges," John barked, stepping forward.

He loosened his grip on Charlotte as he spoke, and she snatched her arm from his hold. She put her fists on her hips and glared up at Mr. Brydges, as though she were too oblivious or too reckless to care that she was half his size.

"Don't try to tell me what my brother's done for me the past four years. I saw it. I was with him."

"Four years? You think that's all he sacrificed for you." Brydges's laugh was bitter. "Try forty years."

"You're not even making sense. I don't have to listen to you." She flung herself around to present her back to Mr. Brydges.

Charlotte may have been too incensed to understand the subtle barb of the man's comments, but it pricked Emma without any difficulty at all. He referred not to the prior four years, but the next forty married to Emma as John's martyrdom.

John stepped between his sister and Mr. Brydges. "I said that's enough," he thundered. The two men stared in silent challenge before John spoke again, much more quietly. "Tread lightly, Brydges. These ladies are my sister and my wife. We are none of us enemies here."

Charlotte spun around to face them again, her indignant expression turning suspicious. "You're saying John married entirely for my sake?"

Wisely, Mr. Brydges did not confirm Charlotte's belated conclusion. "I still believe you owe an apology to your brother, Lady Charlotte, and his new wife as well."

Emma rather thought Mr. Brydges had a few apologies to be distributed but did not share that. "I do not require any apologies from anyone," Emma declared instead. "Perhaps we are all travel weary and would do better to dine in our rooms this evening." She could not imagine the misery that dinner together would be. "We can all start anew in the morning."

John flashed her a tremulous smile. "Yes. A wise suggestion."

Emma nodded. "I shall inform Mrs. Dewhurst."

"Why would I owe *her* an apology?" Charlotte posed the question to Mr. Brydges, ignoring the discussion regarding dinner.

"Because if you hope to appear anything other than a fool in London," Mr. Brydges said, enunciating purposefully, "you'd do better to make her an ally than an enemy. Acting the spoiled brat and engaging in childish tantrums will get you nowhere."

"Damn it, Brydges," John hollered.

"How dare you speak to me that way?" Charlotte puffed to her full height, which was still considerably below that of Mr. Brydges. "You forget yourself. I am Lady Charlotte Brantwood, daughter of a duke. You, sir, are the just the man who sold me a horse." With that, she turned on her heel and marched from the room.

Chapter Twenty-One

"Are you going after her?"

His wife's question broke his temporary paralysis and John looked up. He experienced an unfamiliar moment of uncertainty regarding just what to do next and realized he quite disliked it.

"I'd say she needs time," he decided finally. "There will be a period of adjustment." Heaven knew he had no particular skill in comforting distraught women.

Brydges stepped up to stand in front of him. "You're my oldest and dearest friend, Worley, so I'll tell you for your own good—your sister should be paddled like the infant she's decided to become."

Heat suffused John. "Old friend or not, you'll watch yourself when speaking of my sister," he warned.

Brydges only ignored the censure. "When is *she* required to watch her speech?"

"Everything in her life as she knows it has changed in a matter of weeks. She is living in a country she does not remember, her mother has died, and she must learn the rules of an entirely different society from that which she has always known. Perhaps you could find some dregs of sympathy in your judgmental heart."

Brydges was unrelenting. "I'm quite capable of sympathizing with her predicament, that does not require that I tolerate her behavior."

Emma released a harangued sigh and glowered at Brydges. "Since I'm to be charged with mentoring Lady Charlotte, if you could find it within your power not to be aggravating to her already unhappy disposition, I would greatly appreciate it."

Brydges only glowered back.

"Charlotte will come around," John said, as much to convince himself as his wife. She didn't verbally object, but he noted the tilt of her head and arch of her brow as she contemplated his claim.

Brydges grunted. "Perhaps she might amend her behavior more quickly if you were to clarify its unacceptability." He shook his head. "I shall leave you to puzzle out this monumental task without me. I fear my contributions on the subject will not be welcome."

John watched Brydges as he strode from the room, then turned to his wife. "She'll come around," he reiterated, much more confident this time. "Charlotte is back in the life she deserves, with a grand house and servants to do her bidding."

"Come around?" Emma's voice had risen to fragile pitch. "Have you *met* Charlotte?"

"She has been through such an ordeal…"

Emma's eyes rolled upward. "Yes, yes, the *ordeal*!" She threw her hands outward. "We have all had our mettle tested in some way, John, but that does not excuse us from returning basic kindness and decency to those who give it. Your sister is abominable."

"That is my sister," he ground out. "Where is your sympathy?"

"*Sympathy*? For that?" She marched toward him and poked her finger into his chest. "You deceived me."

He stared down at her and waited to speak until he was certain he could do so without a string of words that should not be uttered to a lady. "That is a ridiculous claim. You understood from the very first my reasons for marrying."

Her eyes flashed golden fire. "Yes. I understand the bargain I made, but when you spoke to me of your sister, you severely understated the task at hand. You are a liar, your sister is a shrew, and your *dear* friend Mr. Brydges is a pompous fool. Given these circumstances, I can't possibly succeed." She was near to shouting. "If I'm to be general of this crusade of yours, I require *willing* soldiers at the very least!"

He glared down at her as his chest rose and fell with the effort it required to recover his ability to respond without shouting. When he did speak, he did so with deadly calm. "I suggest we end this conversation, madame, before you find yourself turned over my knee for your own tantrum."

In response to his command, Emma followed Charlotte's example and quitted the room. One by one, they had all done so, even Brydges, leaving John to stand alone. What the devil had just happened?

It was an uneasy beginning.

* * *

Emma spent the remainder of the day in her room, as she suspected did several other members of the household. She was not hiding, really. She merely needed the time to collect herself. Charlotte's outburst had been a catalyst, causing the rest of them to lose their tempers and engage in outbursts themselves. *Something* had to be done to divert the course of the day. Isolation seemed as good a plan as any.

She read for a bit, though with poor attention. Thankfully, she'd already read the novel once before. Her dinner tray had come, and she'd eaten a little. She occupied most of her time engaged in a concerted effort *not* to dwell on the present predicament, or more importantly, the future, which currently seemed of interminable duration.

When she was without any further distractions, Emma rose from her chair, resolved to get undressed and retire for the evening. Her intentions were interrupted by a knock on the adjoining door. She wrinkled her nose at it. She was not yet of a mood to continue the arguments of earlier. She hadn't yet decided if she should demand an apology from her husband or provide one. Both seemed the likely answer, but she had expected more time for contemplation before she was required to know for sure.

Sighing, she walked to the door and drew it open. He was there. His shirt was loose and the neck untied. He wore breeches and boots, but no neckcloth. His hair gave her the distinct impression that he'd run his fingers through it more than once. His blue eyes locked into hers, triggering a rush of awareness throughout her body.

She did her best to ignore it and stepped back from the door in invitation. He entered, his eyes traveling the room.

"I've been reading," she said, in answer to his unspoken question. "I've already eaten. Have you?"

He nodded. "I had a bit."

Emma walked over to her bureau and busied herself straightening her book and laying her hair brush atop her hand mirror. He came up behind her and reached out to still her hand then drew the hand toward him, coaxing her to turn. Standing so near him, she was assaulted with memories of their wedding night and how his closeness could feel. Several places on her body remembered very well indeed. The experience had been so much more than she had anticipated—his touch, the words he whispered in his whiskey voice. Now, a simple hand on hers and his presence here in her bedroom was enough to call forth a jolt of desire.

"I am sorry," he said in a voice that was more gravel than whiskey. "I should have prepared you. I knew how resistant Charlotte was to life in England and I should have explained."

"What's done is done."

He shook his head. "I did not anticipate how forcefully that resistance would be displayed and I apologize for her treatment of you."

Emma looked down. She had already received two apologies without demanding any. It was rather deflating to her state of pique. "You do not owe an apology for Charlotte's behavior. We each must be accountable for our own." She laced her fingers together. "Myself included. I am sorry for my harsh words against you, your sister, and your friend."

"No, no. I understand. Your temper was justifiably pricked. Charlotte should never have lashed out as she did. And Brydges…he has never been one to keep quiet when he feels strongly on a subject. He was offended by my sister's behavior, and rightfully so." John placed a finger under Emma's chin to draw her eyes to his. "And his comment regarding you—to imply that by marrying you…"

Emma averted her gaze. She stepped away from John's reach, seeking respite from her rising warmth and quickening pulse. She walked to the bed and traced her finger through the carvings on the ornate wooden post. "There is no need to apologize for Mr. Brydges either. We need not pretend. We married for practicality, not for love."

"A practical marriage does not have to be a prison. We can be friends." He covered the distance between them in two steps and reached for her hands again. "I thought we were becoming friends."

She gazed up at him, unsure how to ask what his friendship entailed, and found blue eyes wide with entreaty.

"I need a friend," he said huskily. "I need you. We are an imperfect coalition with little cause for hope, but the need for our crusade exists nonetheless. Charlotte may be resistant today, but the fact remains, she has no other choice but this one. There is nothing for her in Boston but poverty or worse. My father tore her away from the life she should have had. The life she lived instead with my mother no longer exists." His hands tightened around hers with his fervent speech. "She must make a life here in England now."

Emma could not turn away from the desperate appeal in her husband's soulful eyes. His normally guarded expression had opened, giving her a rare window into tortured depths. Gone was the clipped common sense of every prior conversation regarding John's reasons for marrying. He was pleading, begging, for her help when she had expected matter-of-fact reminders of her obligation. She had the overwhelming sense that, to John, this was not an obligation. It was a quest.

"This is very important to you," she said softly.

"It is not important. It is imperative. I am the duke now. I must restore to Charlotte the life to which she was born."

Had he inherited it, then, this obligation to atone for his father's sins? Did legacies of mistreatment and duty to others pass through generations in the way of land and castles and coin? Emma could not imagine many peers would see it quite this way, but she could not deny the basic nobility of the idea was appealing—idyllic, rather. Yet, how could it be fair or sensible to future generations, the passing of guilt and a burdened conscience?

"Your sister has been through a great ordeal," she said. "I will not withhold my assistance simply because she has not yet accepted the need for it." She watched John's shoulders relax as she spoke. She felt his grip on her hands loosen. "I will grant your sister every ounce of my available patience. You've no need to fear otherwise. She is now my family as well as yours."

"Thank you."

The warmth that shone in her husband's eyes at her assurances sparked a new awareness of his hands holding hers.

He released one hand and drew a single fingertip up the length of her bare arm to her sleeve and down again to her wrist. "I can promise you, marrying you is no sacrifice. We may not have chosen each other, but that is no reason we cannot get on well together." His arm slid around her waist as he spoke, leaving her with no question as to his meaning. If any doubt remained, he cleared it by leaning close to whisper in her ear, "Making love to you far surpassed my expectations and I would very much like to do so again."

His request, more breath than words against her neck, sent trembles through Emma. They were not trembles of fright, but tiny eruptions of delicious anticipation.

Chapter Twenty-Two

John pulsed with desire already. The shot of pure need that coursed through him when his wife lifted amber eyes in silent acquiescence struck him like a blow. He wanted very badly to make love to his wife. More importantly, he wanted very badly for her desire to match his own.

There were places for duty and obligation. This wasn't one of them. He didn't want that here. Emma had yielded to his requests for Charlotte because she was sensible. He wanted her to yield to him now because she was on fire, and he set about causing that very condition. He captured her mouth with his, tantalizing first, then plundering, claiming her lips the way he longed to claim her body. It was a dangerous thought—possession. He shouldn't want her this much. He shouldn't need to *possess* her.

She released a throaty moan and lust charged through him again, scattering any thoughts of what he *shouldn't* feel. He felt. He needed. And, God, it was good. It was very, very good. She kissed him back. She was willing—enthusiastic even—but it was not enough. He would not succumb to his flaring passion until he knew she was insensate with her own. He tore his lips from hers, steeling himself against his reaction to her disappointed sigh. He placed his lips more softly, this time at the gentle curve at the base of her neck, and pressed slow kisses along the length of her throat, punctuating each with a light flick of his tongue. Laying one hand on her breast, he gently squeezed the soft orb, massaging until he felt her press herself farther into his touch. Then he drew his thumb across the sensitive tip, feeling it harden in response beneath the layers of fabric that imprisoned it.

He watched her golden eyes cloud with passion and flutter closed, dark lashes falling onto flushed cheeks. Her lips parted, tantalizing him like a ripe fruit. Using his unoccupied hand to brush aside the tendrils of hair that veiled one tiny, perfect ear, he lowered his mouth and brushed his lips across it. "You are so beautiful like this," he whispered. "From this night on, I will see you just like this." His tongue raked her dainty earlobe and he felt the shiver course through her. "When you come to breakfast in your tidy dress, with your hair in a prim knot, I will look through that and see you as you are now, shivering with passion in my arms, with lips swollen from my kisses and hair falling from pins we'll never find." He teased her earlobe with his tongue again, letting his warm breath blow across her ear. He caught the soft lobe in his teeth then dragged them lightly across it.

She whimpered and he drew back. She stood, fully clothed, eyes closed, gripping the post behind her, as he caressed her breast with his hand. She was a picture of caged passion—alive with it, squirming with it, not yet broken free.

Damn.

He'd fired his own lust as much as hers. It ached. His mouth took hers again, without strategy or intent other than to feed his own hunger. As he ravaged her mouth, he felt her shift. Her hands no longer clutched the bedpost, but were on him, frantically running over his chest and arms and back. Then beautiful feminine hands were boldly tugging at the laces of his breeches. He groaned into her mouth as he kissed her.

As she tugged at his clothes, he pulled at hers. He did not bother with buttons or laces; he yanked up on yards of skirt and petticoat and tore off underthings. He found her warm and wet and waiting for him. She called his name when he touched her and the knowledge that the slick heat between her legs was for him left him mad with wanting. He wanted to make *her* mad with wanting. She wasn't there yet, but he was determined she would be. He tickled and teased her until she squirmed and begged his name again.

Then he turned his attention to the fall of his breeches. He spent only a moment to finish the work she'd started on his laces and lower his breeches to the tops of his boots. Thus freed he took her hand in his own and moved it to him. Damn, but he wanted her to touch him.

As her fingers closed around his flesh, her eyes flew to his. The sweet, hot pain must surely have been his limit, but then her lips quirked into a wicked smile as she held him, and the surge in his heated desire nearly incinerated them both.

Christ.

He may have only thought it. He may have said it aloud. He had no idea. He pulled her hips forward and leaned back, one hand clutching the post. He thrust into her and watched with primal satisfaction as her head fell back and her lips parted again. He gripped the post above her shoulder and slid his other hand around to cup her bottom—supporting her, pulling her to him to meet his thrusts.

And he kissed her. God, he kissed her good, their mouths echoing the mating of their bodies. His urgency climbed with every moan of pure seduction she released into his mouth.

She whimpered his name first, then called it out. She clutched herself to him as he drove into her. She shuddered and moaned, and he felt her body clench around him as it reached its peak. Her release unbound the last of his restraint. He thrust into to her. Once. Twice. He groaned with his own release and held her tightly to him as he came inside her.

God and the devil.

Slowly he withdrew and helped her to finish undressing. He led her limp form to lay across the bed. He lay with her, recovering his breath as she did. Recovering his sanity.

They'd made love half-dressed and frantic, like illicit lovers in darkened corners or secret gardens. It was a heady drug, indeed. Intoxication by that particular drug could only lead to damage. That uncontrolled need was where the danger lurked. His father had succumbed to it, and his obsession for his wife had ruined his family. John would not succumb. He would be stronger than it.

He sighed. She was asleep. He gently rolled her to her side and rose, his languorous body objecting with every inch of movement. He located his cast-aside breeches and pulled them on. He gathered his boots and shirt. It was time for him to retreat to his own chamber, as gentlemen did once they had bedded their wives.

Yet he didn't. Not yet.

He stood over her instead and watched her in repose. She was not a picture of peaceful slumber. Instead, she looked wild in the aftermath of their lovemaking—cheeks still flushed, lips swollen, limbs flung, and hair splayed around her. Persistent tugs in unknown places deep inside urged him to collapse back into the soft mattress and pull her warm, love-weary body up against his.

Tempted though he was, he didn't. He couldn't. How shortsighted he'd been to think attraction to his wife would make this marriage of convenience easier to manage. He hadn't managed his lust at all, nor was he managing this insistent tugging at his soul that urged him to spend the aftermath of their passion with her cradled in his arms. The very strength of his longing built his resolve to go. Lovesick foolishness turned too quickly to obsession and became a path to destruction. He'd witnessed it. He was still unraveling it. He would not become it.

Chapter Twenty-Three

Emma awoke with a catlike stretch. She'd not slept so well since she was a child. She rolled onto her side and sat up on the edge of the bed. The chill was an instant reminder that she was undressed. She grasped a handful of bedding and turned to look behind her.

The bed was empty. He was not there.

How late had she slept? She fetched a wrapper and walked to the window, peering out to take the measure of the day. Her window did not face east to allow her a view of the morning sun and its position, but she could see the early light reflecting on a lawn still wet with dew, still reflecting hues of sunrise gold.

She had not overslept. John had risen earlier still.

Or perhaps—not stayed.

As soon as she gave birth to the question, it set up stubborn residence in her mind. She fretted over the answer as she washed her face with water from the ewer, selected a morning dress, and pinned up her hair.

She could not pinpoint precisely why, but that information—whether her husband had slept the duration of the night in her bed—was suddenly of utmost importance. Yet she could not determine if he had. All his things were gone—boots, clothing—but that was no indication of *when* he had gathered them. Her own place on the mattress was no longer more than barely warm. Had his place cooled for minutes or hours? She could not say.

She paused. She was bent over her bed, running her hand over the mattress, looking for warm spots.

Silliness.

She snatched her hand back. What did it matter anyway? She shook her head to right her senses. Lord, she'd gone daft. Breakfast.

Charlotte. Brantmoor. She had plenty of reasonable subjects on which she could be dwelling.

Emma checked her appearance one more time in her glass before making her way downstairs to the breakfast room. She fervently hoped this day would bring more peaceful relations with Charlotte and the incorrigible Mr. Brydges. If she was able to engage in one polite conversation with her new sister-in-law today, she would consider it a victory. There was much to be accomplished, after all, if the family intended to return to London before the season was out.

Emma walked into the breakfast room and noted, despite the early hour, she was the last to arrive. Three pairs of eyes rose to take in her entrance.

She should have been gratified to enter a peacefully quiet room. She should have been calmed to see that Charlotte had deigned to appear, in what was likely her best dress, and was eating politely in the company of Mr. Brydges. Instead, her eyes, with complete autonomy to her will, traveled to meet John's and, unbidden, the memory of his words from the prior evening assailed her.

I will look through that and see you now, shivering with passion in my arms.

Oh heavens. She was not calm. Heat suffused her from head to toe and surely stained her cheeks with unattractive splotches of the brightest red. Could he tell she remembered? Could they *all* tell?

"Good morning," she said in a clipped, overly bright tone. "You are all early risers, I see."

When one's thoughts were a jumble, as Emma's most certainly were, one did not attempt complex conversation. Verbalizations of the obvious seemed achievement enough.

"Good morning." John's response sounded normal, but Emma caught the heat of his gaze coupled with the slight quirk at the corner of his mouth.

She averted her eyes to focus on her breakfast. If there had been conversation prior to her arrival, it did not continue then. The others ate in silence as Emma filled a plate from the sideboard and seated herself at the table.

"I have decided we shall return to London in three weeks' time," John announced once Emma had begun eating.

Emma swallowed. She sipped tea to wash down the bite upon which she'd nearly choked. "Three weeks?"

John nodded. "We will return to town in three weeks and hold a ball shortly thereafter. We shall all have a great deal to accomplish before then." He turned and looked at Emma, triggering a fresh infusion of awkward heat. "The duchess is quite capable of making the necessary arrangements for such an event." He directed his attention to his sister then. "Charlotte, you will involve yourself as well. You will not only need to ready yourself for London, but it will be beneficial to you to understand how these events are managed. You will likely be planning events such as this for your husband's family one day."

Charlotte cast a suspicious glance at Emma, as though this punishment of a task had been her doing.

"What about you?" Charlotte asked her brother. "What will you be doing?"

Charlotte's question, impertinent though it was, echoed Emma's thoughts. John had seemed to imply he would also be busily engaged and generally unavailable.

"There is a great deal of business with the estate to be addressed following my long absence, including the selection of a new secretary. Brydges has also agreed to stay with us these few weeks to assist me in evaluating and expanding our stables."

Mr. Brydges was the subject of Charlotte's unpleasant gaze this time. He smiled boldly back at her. She pouted.

"Charlotte," Emma said, anxious to interrupt any brewing storm, "I have arranged for a dressmaker to be here this afternoon." Every young girl appreciated new dresses—or at least most young girls. Emma had preferred horses to dresses, but she'd been a rather singular girl. Surely, Charlotte, who'd been raised with very little, would welcome new things.

"I have perfectly serviceable dresses."

"Don't be ridiculous, Charlotte," John said, rising from the table. "Of course you need new dresses. Nothing you have will suffice. Emma knows what you need. Place your trust in her."

Emma was once again the recipient of Charlotte's ire. "I don't want to meet the dressmaker today. I'm still tired from traveling."

Emma exerted a valiant effort not to sigh too loudly. "I'm afraid rescheduling will not be possible." Emma had expended considerable effort in persuading one of the most fashionable modistes in London to leave her shop at the height of the season and travel into the countryside to measure and dress the duke's sister. She had promised an exorbitant expenditure and still several had declined.

"There is no time. It shall be today." John gave the order with finality and quitted the room, as though the thing were done and no possible objection could remain.

Emma recognized the error of that assumption immediately. Charlotte, glaring back at her from across the table with pinched mouth and little blue fires set under slashes of dark, angry brow, was far from cowed.

Chapter Twenty-Four

"I suppose you've come to reprimand me for missing the dressmaker's appointment this afternoon."

Emma sighed. She'd only walked into the front parlor and already Charlotte's hackles were raised. "Where were you, Charlotte?"

Charlotte closed the book in her hands. "I didn't feel well. I stayed in my room. I'm only now feeling a little better, if you care to know."

"I checked your room, as I'm sure you'd expect."

"So I wasn't in my room," she said easily, showing no shame for the prior lie. "Am I to be a prisoner in this house? Do I not have any freedom?"

Emma was exhausted of repeating essentially this same conversation. It was the fourth in the same number of days concerning either the dressmaker or the dance master.

"You are a young, unmarried lady, Charlotte. You cannot go missing for periods of time without putting your reputation at risk. You are also expected to keep appointments that are made on your behalf, particularly those with someone who has gone through a great deal of trouble and traveled all the way from London to meet you. Madame Desmarais refused to return until I reminded her of the sheer volume of garments you require."

Emma stopped. She exhaled. She would *not* lecture Charlotte on her behavior. She'd done enough of that over the past week and she was weary of it. She was weary of so many things and needed a distraction.

"Charlotte," she began again, this time adopting a conciliatory tone. "I don't want to engage in a debate. What's done is done. I think perhaps what we both need is some time out of doors. I thought we could have a ride together."

"A ride?" Charlotte asked, her voice rising. "Do you mean ride horses?" Charlotte stared up at Emma as though she had just suggested they acquire some rope to practice scaling the manor walls in case of fire.

"Yes, I mean ride horses. The mounts Mr. Brydges brought for us are splendid animals. You've never even seen yours, but she's lovely." It was true. Whatever else she found lacking in Mr. Brydges, he clearly had a keen eye for horseflesh.

"I don't want to ride." She crossed her arms in front of her chest. "I don't see why you *people of quality* have such a fascination with horse riding. They are dirty, smelly, ornery animals."

Emma had never met a horse as ornery as her new sister-in-law, but she desperately wanted to go riding and so chose to keep that thought to herself. "Come now, Charlotte. You complain of confinement. Here I am offering you an afternoon of fresh air and freedom."

Emma needed to do something to bring herself joy, or risk becoming overwhelmed with melancholy. So far, the task of preparing Charlotte for the season had proven to be an endless source of frustration. The girl clearly possessed no desire to become prepared and thus chose avoidance or objection instead of cooperation on all possible occasions. Perhaps Emma could have weathered these challenges more happily if she had the benefit of an ally in her husband, but he seemed to have abandoned the entire effort to Emma's management. He seemed to have completely forgotten he had a wife or a sister at all, as he had become so absorbed in the estate he rarely encountered the ladies except at dinner—when he and Mr. Brydges were not so engaged as to miss dinner altogether. John had come to her room precisely twice since returning to Brantmoor—not every night, not even most nights, and she knew now he did not stay. He always returned to his own chamber. She couldn't help but be glad every time he came, but every time he left, she had the sense he saw their coupling as somehow wrong or shameful. She would have asked him about it, but wasn't entirely sure of the question. Besides, she could never locate him anyway. He was always off somewhere with Mr. Brydges.

"If you value fresh air and freedom, then by all means go riding. I'm not going."

"Not going where?" Mr. Brydges asked, entering the room just as Emma was desiring his absence from their midst.

Lovely. In addition to ensuring her husband's constant absence, Mr. Brydges had been a significant contributor to Charlotte's ill disposition. He was the last thing this conversation required for improvement.

"Riding, Mr. Brydges," Charlotte said pointedly. "I am not going riding."

"A worthy skill to possess, riding," Mr. Brydges contributed, predictably taking a contrary position to Charlotte's. Then again, Charlotte was so contrary all the time, it was difficult not to do so.

"I am not particularly interested in that 'worthy skill,'" Charlotte declared, crossing her arms in front of her as she sat erect on the sofa. "If both of you desire a ride, I suggest you take one together and leave me in peace."

Charlotte's eyes narrowed as she spoke and her mouth was set in a firm pout at the conclusion of her speech. Emma could recognize after only a week of the signs of Charlotte's rising temper and did not particularly wish to witness it flaring just then.

"It was only a suggestion, Charlotte. We do not have to ride today," Emma offered.

Mr. Brydges clasped his hands together and brought two pointed fingers to his lips. "Ah, I see," he said dramatically, as though he had solved a puzzle of some complication.

Charlotte's attention snapped to Mr. Brydges. "What do you see?" she sniped.

He placed a hand upon his chest. "If I were a miniature person, I believe I would also be frightened of horses." He addressed Emma next when he said, "Perhaps we can fit a saddle for a small pony or even a large hound for Lady Charlotte to learn to ride."

Emma found herself cursing the timing that had brought Mr. Brydges into the parlor just then. Wasn't he needed somewhere by the duke? Had he no sympathy for Emma, who would be left to deal with Charlotte's foul mood once he'd finished with his game?

Charlotte rose from her seat. "I am not frightened."

"No? Perhaps we should adjourn to the stables now then, so the lesson may begin. I'm a fairly accomplished rider, if I may say so. I'd be happy to tutor you."

"We've no need of your assistance, Mr. Brydges," Emma interjected.

"I've already informed the duchess I've no intention of riding this afternoon," Charlotte said, placing closed fists on either side of a tiny waist.

Mr. Brydges turned to Emma. "You do see it, don't you? She's deathly afraid of the beasts, poor thing. Why I think she's near to tears."

The thought had not occurred to Emma, but now that Mr. Brydges had pointed it out in his usual frank and insensitive manner, she wondered if that weren't the case. If Charlotte had reached the age of eighteen, having never ridden her entire life…well, it was a distinct possibility. Of course, Mr. Brydges could not possibly have made his comment with less sympathy or understanding.

Afraid or not, Charlotte was nowhere near tears. Her blue eyes glittered like shards of brittle glass as she glared at Mr. Brydges. "Do you honestly think I'm so malleable that I could be tricked into riding just to prove I'm not afraid? I've known since we met you are an insensitive lout. As it happens, you are also a fool."

Emma did not believe Charlotte's glare could have become more hateful, more menacing, but it did. She advanced on Mr. Brydges as though stalking him.

"You may as well take your foul-smelling horse back home with you, Mr. Brydges. Because, I assure you, James Madison will swear fealty to the crown before I ever sit atop that animal." She turned her back to them and was, once again, gone.

Emma could have screamed. As it was, she released a huff of air before turning in exasperation to the meddlesome Mr. Brydges. "Are you pleased, now? You've driven her into a corner and she will never ride at all—purely because of her dislike of you." She set her hands at her own hips. "A dislike, I might add, with which I can currently sympathize."

The man shrugged back at with an annoyingly smug expression.

"She's right, isn't she?" Emma demanded. "You were trying to goad her into it. Did you really think that would be effective?"

"Without question. She may have realized the ploy, but it does not necessarily follow that it didn't work. She'll prove me wrong. She'll *have* to prove me wrong."

"You are the blindest seeing man I've ever known. She will never ride that horse. She *cannot* because she has declared she *will* not. That girl, Mr. Brydges, has more stubborn will than Napoleon himself."

Chapter Twenty-Five

The small group in residence at Brantmoor had developed an unspoken synchronicity which saw them all at breakfast together most days. It was odd, in Emma's estimation, as they unfortunately had not seemed to have done so in the interest of seeking each other's company.

In truth, it seemed, they all sought at audience with John. Emma's eyes traveled the room. They were all here—not just at breakfast, but at Brantmoor—because of John. His duchess, his sister, and his friend, all strangers brought together by a single point of connection, she mused.

Only Mr. Brydges seemed to be getting much of the attention from the man in question, though. The two gentlemen dominated conversation at breakfast, but even that observation was true on the greater scale than simply the morning meal. The men were forever off on some estate business or matter to be addressed in the stables.

"You've my undivided attention today," John said to Brydges, as though prompted by Emma's very thoughts. "We can discuss the improvements you are proposing for the stables."

Mr. Brydges nodded his acceptance of this invitation. "Perfect. You will not be at the Glendon farm, after all, then?"

"The Glen*burn* farm," John corrected, "and no I will not. It seems I have forgotten today is market day in Brantmoor Village."

"Market day?" Emma asked, intrigued by this turn in the conversation. "Does Brantmoor Village still have a market?"

"Yes and no," John said. "Brantmoor Village hasn't had a prosperous active market since…well, I suppose I don't know. Market day is probably inaptly named. It's more about revelry than trade, I suppose. It is once yearly, in summer."

"Then it is more of a fair?" Emma asked.

"I understand so, yes".

"Do you mean to say you've never been?" Emma asked.

John seemed taken aback by Emma's question. "The family is generally not in residence for Market Day. We would be in town now if not for Charlotte's arrival," he explained. "There is a fete at harvest time that is sponsored by the family. We are always in attendance for that occasion."

"Well, we are in residence now," Emma pointed out. "There is no reason why we should not attend this year."

Her husband chewed a bite of toast thoughtfully before answering. "Now that I think of it, you are right. Frankly, I regret not arriving at this conclusion myself. Everyone is well aware we are in residence. We should absolutely attend."

Emma smiled at him. "Lovely," she said, with a nod. "An outing shall do us all some good." And she truly believed it would. It would certainly do *her* some good. Hopefully, it would be beneficial to Charlotte's disposition as well.

"That sounds a brilliant idea," Mr. Brydges declared.

Immediately Emma turned to Charlotte, concerned this effusive approval from Mr. Brydges would threaten Charlotte's view of the day's plan.

Charlotte's pout validated her concerns. She turned to Emma with a saucy tilt of her head. "Now that I am such an elevated personage, what am I expected to don for such an outing?"

"Naturally, you should wear your most elegant evening wear," Mr. Brydges offered up before Emma could answer. "How else will the simple townsfolk recognize their betters?"

Charlotte glared.

Emma did as well.

"Sheath your sword, Brydges," John said, his own expression conveying his disapproval of the man's heckling. "What has gotten into you?"

Mr. Brydges only frowned.

Emma sighed and turned her attention back to her disgruntled protégé. "Which of your day dresses have been completed?"

"The pale blue and the lemon-colored one with the white flowers," Charlotte replied, somewhat mollified by her brother's defense.

"You should wear the plain blue," Emma told her.

"You don't have to wear a plain dress to spite Brydges," John said with an emphasizing glare for the other man.

"The blue will be better," Emma stated more firmly.

Charlotte gave a rare obedient nod. "I don't remember the village," she said. "How far shall we have to walk?"

"The walk could be a bit far," John cautioned.

Charlotte's eyes had already begun to expand like blue blooms in spring.

"The ladies shall take the comfort of the carriage," Emma quickly announced. "The gentlemen can ride," she added. Though she did not wish to encounter Charlotte's response if the entire party had planned to proceed on horseback, neither did she yearn to spend even a few minutes enclosed in a carriage with both Charlotte and Mr. Brydges.

John caught Emma's eye and smiled. She sensed he approved of her suggestion, whether the outing or the means of conveyance, she couldn't be sure. Regardless, she was quite pleased, in spite of herself, at his approval and at the prospect of a day in the company of her husband.

* * *

Brantmoor Village was situated immediately adjacent to the eastern border of the Brantmoor lands. It was not as near as one might expect, however, given the vastness of the estate. The ladies traversed the distance in the carriage as Emma had suggested, but John was happy to ride.

It was a distinctly pleasant day. Beyond that, he took a measure of pride in riding through the verdant hills dotted with livestock. This was the land to which he belonged. He belonged to the land more than it belonged to him; that fact had been impressed upon him these past few weeks—more so than he'd ever understood before his time away.

Perhaps he'd been too young before to comprehend the responsibility of it, or perhaps his father had never taken the time to impress upon him the philosophy of stewardship. Regardless, John understood now in a way he couldn't before.

In Boston, John had spent hours on a hard wooden chair at a cramped desk in the corner of a dimly lit room making tidy rows of entries into ledgers as the ships came and went. He made entries until his knuckles ached and swelled, then he collected his wage and prized it all the more both for what he'd paid of himself in exchange for it and how badly he had needed it. His hard work alone did not guarantee his wage, however. In a much larger, richer office two floors above his own, the merchant had reigned over his shipping enterprise. If the enterprise failed, his position would disappear and the wages with it.

The tenant farmers on the Brantmoor estate were no different. They worked hard to till the land and harvest the crops, and they valued the spoils of their labor, but their future and security depended upon much more than their individual efforts. Their livelihoods and their hopes for their children and grandchildren depended upon the prosperity of the entire estate—upon the diligent stewardship of its master.

The village is no different, John thought, reining in his horse as it came into view.

He and Brydges had ridden ahead of the ladies, willing to remain confined to neither the carriage's path nor its pace. They dismounted just outside the village and waited for the carriage to arrive. It was not far behind and the ladies were soon handed down from its interior.

The group turned down the single thoroughfare that traversed Brantmoor Village and boasted the requirements of rural life—a parish church, a pub, a smithy, a school, and a post office. The usually sleepy village was teeming with activity. People, animals, and assorted carts filled the span from the small inn and public house all the way to the miller's cottage at the far end of the lane. As the foursome stood in front of the inn, taking in the scene before them, John watched both women with curiosity, eager to assess their reactions.

Any concerns he might have had on either score were unfounded, as both women gazed upon the revelry with enthusiasm. John even spied his wife's toe tapping in time to the music when the breeze shifted her skirts.

The innkeeper, if that was fair title for a man who presided over two available rooms above a small public house, had a weathered trestle table set up in front of the pub from which he filled cups from pitchers of ale while his wife bustled in and out of the timber frame building in an effort to keep him supplied with freshly filled replacements.

"Good day, Mr. Cluett," John called pleasantly, leading his party toward the man and his ale.

"Good day, Your Grace," the man called cheerily back, managing both a beaming smile and an abbreviated bow without an interruption in cup-filling.

John turned back to his entourage. "Our esteemed publican, Mr. Cluett," he said to the group. "Mr. Cluett, may I present the Duchess of Worley, my sister Lady Charlotte, and my friend Mr. Brydges."

Charlotte and Brydges nodded politely in acknowledgement, but Emma stepped quickly forward. "Mr. Cluett and I have met," she said with a wide, warm smile for the ruddy-faced man. "He and his wife were my saviors when I was out riding last week and caught by the rain. How lovely to see you again. Has your son's ankle healed?"

"Oh, it's on the mend to be sure, Your Grace," he said with a vigorous nod and a deeper reddening of his complexion. "And always pleased to be at your service."

John thought they could all do with a cup of ale, but noticed then that the convenience of serving in the open meant villagers could drink as they wandered, but it also meant each had brought their own cup. Certainly Mr. Cluett was not so well-off as to allow his tankards and mugs to go wandering off down the lane.

"Mr. Cluett, I must apologize," John told him. "We are without cups, sir."

"Nothing of it. Nothing of it," he said, with a flustered wave toward a young boy who rushed forward with four dented but serviceable mugs. John noted the hint of a limp in the boy's gait.

"How were you injured, Samuel?" John asked.

Samuel cast a questioning look toward his father who answered with an affirmative nod. Eyes cast downward, his fingers fidgeted as he explained. "I was foolish and took a dare, Your Grace. Will Gibbon said I couldn't get across the creek in a single leap. I caught a tree root on the far side and turned my ankle." He looked up then with a mischievous glint shining from brown eyes nearly covered by shaggy hair of the same color. "I made it full across, though."

"Well done," John said with a respectful nod. "I remember the first time I made it full across, and I can assure you it was not my first attempt."

The words won him an admiring look from both his wife and the boy, the former being unexpected, but pleasant all the same.

Once Mr. Cluett had distributed a full mug to each and John had laid the appropriate coin atop the wooden table, their party wandered slowly onward to see what else Market Day had to offer. As John had understood, the purpose of the day was not for the regular trade of merchants, but rather for the farmers and villagers to become merchants for the day, offering for sale the handicrafts and homespun goods they made as hobby or necessity.

Emma enthusiastically greeted the vicar's wife, to whom he'd introduced her at Sunday services. The graying but still handsome woman returned the greeting happily, without hint of anxiety or intimidation. She gave a slight curtsy in deference to the rank, but that was all. John had noticed his wife had a way of making others comfortable, diminishing the difference in status, while many in her position would have done the opposite.

"What a great pleasure for us that you are able to be here," Mrs. Sharpe said, taking in the entire party with her comment, though her curious gaze lingered on Charlotte for a bit longer than the others. "Everyone has brought out their best for Market Day. I've just purchased a pendant from

Mrs. Hawkins." To illustrate her words, she lifted a small pendant that hung from her neck for better viewing.

His wife had stepped forward to peer closely at it. "Is that made of wood?" she asked.

"It is," Mrs. Sharpe confirmed with a nod.

Emma's eyes brightened at the confirmation. "How clever! Charlotte, just look at this lovely pendant."

Charlotte did indeed step forward and with some genuine curiosity, John was happy to note. "It is very well done," Charlotte commented once she had inspected the item.

"Did you say Mrs. Hawkins made it?" Emma asked.

"Yes," Mrs. Sharpe said, taking Emma by the arm and beckoning to Charlotte. "Come and see what else she has made."

The ladies of Brantmoor followed the vicar's wife a bit farther down the lane to where the smithy's wife flitted to and fro around a small cart she had draped with a cloth. John watched as the women leaned over it in some excitement, perusing the items displayed there with interest.

"I do believe even your sister may be enjoying this outing," Brydges said, sidling up to John as he watched the ladies and sipped his ale.

She did not, for once, seem determined to wear the pout that had become as customary for Charlotte as epaulettes on regimentals. "I daresay you may be right."

"She ought to smile a bit more. If she's to distract the *ton* from their questions regarding her past, I would expect she'll have better success with charm than unpleasantness."

John eyed his friend. "Do not think I don't notice how you seem to enjoy provoking that unpleasantness. You might exercise more charm yourself and have some sympathy for her predicament."

"She'll find London society far more provoking, I assure you." Brydges drank from his own mug and walked alongside John as they followed in the wake of the ladies, who had continued down the lane.

"I expect she will," John said, eyeing his friend carefully. "Just as I expect you will be helpful to her cause in London, rather than antagonistic."

Brydges nodded affably. "You can rely on my full support. I only mean that our behavior will not matter a whit if Lady Charlotte does not amend her disposition."

"Her disposition will amend itself as soon as she feels more comfortable with her surroundings," John said. "Shall we see what the ladies have found?"

They found Emma, Charlotte, and the vicar's wife hovering near a cart full of flowers and presided over by a girl whom John did not recognize, but judged to be a few years younger than Charlotte. He had made a diligent effort to recall all the people of the estate and village over the past weeks, but he could not yet name their children.

He watched as his wife selected a large yellow bloom, which she immediately affixed to her bonnet, and another bright pink one which she applied to Charlotte's. Mrs. Sharpe nodded her approval of these additions. Emma plucked another bloom from the cart and held it up in the sun admiringly.

"I have never seen a rose this shade," she told the girl, exclaiming over the bloom.

John didn't see anything particularly notable about the shade, which he would have described somewhere in the space between orange and brown, but in truth, he'd never paid particular attention. And if one could trust anyone's gardening expertise, he was inclined to trust his wife's.

The girl blushed under the admiration of the duchess. "I don't know as it's a rare color or not, ma'am, Your Grace. These roses have grown behind the mill for all of my life."

Emma waved the flower slowly beneath her nose, as though taking in the scent while she spoke. "Behind the mill? Are you the miller's daughter, then?"

"Yes, ma'am, Your Grace," she said, adding a little curtsy for good measure. "They grow quite well there. The yellow ones grow a bit farther down the hill. I've taken to tending them a bit, but I can't seem to coax as many blooms from the yellow as I do these."

"Well, what a lovely discovery," Emma said, smiling as though thoroughly enchanted by both the flower and the girl. "I should so love to come and see them sometime. Would that be all right?"

The girl's blush deepened. "Oh, of course, ma'am, Your Grace. I'll show you any time you'd like."

"Splendid," Emma pronounced, reaching into her coin purse to pay the girl for the flowers she'd selected. "I shall call upon you soon, my dear, and we can discuss roses. I am quite looking forward to it."

Their party continued onward, leaving the beaming young girl behind.

Hours later, they had left countless joyous expressions in their wake. The Duchess of Worley had managed to charm an entire village in an afternoon by the application of genuine interest and artless compliments. She accumulated numerous purchases, still more admirers, and had personally returned their borrowed cups to Mr. Cluett with expressions of sincere gratitude for the consideration.

She had been perfectly simple, and thus entirely magnificent.

John watched his wife and his sister as they were once again handed down from the carriage after their brief return journey to the house, noting the transformation in the appearance of both ladies. Their eyes were bright and their complexions heightened by the sun and the day's enjoyment, but most striking were the adornments. The plain dresses and bonnets in which they had departed that morning were now resplendent with flowers, handmade jewelry, ribbons of various colors, and even a shawl fringed with carved wooden beads.

The women swept into the house with Brydges behind them. John followed more sedately, his chest swelling with a lightness that belied the crunch of gravel underneath the weight of his boots.

His wife would have been ridiculous in any London drawing room in her present garb, but what a pity that London society should not ever see her thus. She was utterly delightful.

And breathtakingly beautiful.

He was impatient to tell her so—impatient for his turn to stand in the warm light she cast all around her.

He stopped.

Panic suffused him.

It was not only in his mind, where he'd always assumed panic must reside, but throughout his entire form. His sturdy legs weakened. His breath constricted. Bile rose in his throat.

He placed one hand on the thick stone of the entryway, drawing on its solidity when he had none. How could he have been so weak? Why hadn't he recognized what was happening?

He was thoroughly infatuated with his wife.

He shook his head.

It was a foolish mistake, nothing more, brought on by the proximity of the day. He knew too well the damage caused by sinking into a mad obsession with one's own wife.

John stood, again relying upon his own sturdiness to hold himself upright. He would not fall prey to weakness again.

Chapter Twenty-Six

John lay back in exhaustion and marveled at the extent to which he enjoyed making love to his wife. It had been damned difficult, trying to keep up his indifference to Emma all week when they shared such powerful moments at night and she crept into his thoughts throughout the day. Avoiding her company had made his affliction worse, not better. He looked down at her then, curled naked under the bedclothes, eyes still hazy from their lovemaking, and knew tomorrow was going to be harder still.

He rose, donned his dressing gown, and leaned to place a kiss on Emma's forehead, as had become his habit before leaving her for the night—but not every night. He could not let himself go to her every night.

"Wait."

The request, spoken in a soft, husky voice, halted him.

"Will you stay?"

Would he stay? God, if only she knew how much he wanted to stay. If he knew the words to make her understand, he would explain. He was protecting her, for God's sake. The more enchanted by her he became, the more he was in peril of repeating his father's sins. He'd not thought it possible, rational man that he was, that he could repeat the destructive and irreversible acts to which his father's obsession had driven him, but neither had he believed he could be so inexorably drawn to this woman he'd known for mere weeks.

"Not tonight," he said gruffly.

Not ever, but he didn't say it. He didn't want her to see the miserably black mood that came over him each time he made that cruelly short walk back to his own bedchamber. He wore it each night whether he'd lain with her or not—a dressing gown intricately woven of want and frustration and fear and sheer exhaustion. He'd been so desperate to avoid her, he'd run himself ragged, working sunup to sundown to learn the workings of the estate and tenants and see to every pent-up need that had been waiting during his father's illness and his long absence. He'd been desperate to keep Brydges at Brantmoor, so reliant he was on the distraction. John had even gone so far as to imply to Brydges that he, too, may be considering beginning a stud operation.

"Can you at least wait to go?" she asked.

He turned to look at her.

She sat up in the bed with pulled-up knees. She held the bed covers over her bare breasts, but the graceful curve of her back was still uncovered—and wickedly lovely.

"I need to talk with you about Charlotte," she said. Amber eyes fell then lifted again, wide and pleading. "It's just that you are so busy during the days, and I can barely ever find you, much less speak to you."

"How are things proceeding with Charlotte?" The question was admittedly days late, and he felt a stab of guilt for the sharpness in his tone.

She heard it too, because he saw her bristle and tug the covers higher. "They are not."

"What do you mean, they are not?" he asked. "We've only two weeks left before we are to return to London."

Emma sighed. She tossed the covers back and rose from the bed, immodest in her nudity. She walked, unhurried to the chair over which her night rail and wrapper were slung. She pulled the night rail over her head and smoothed it down her body before answering his question. "She has failed to appear for two appointments with dressmakers who traveled all the way from London. The first refused to make the trip again. I have promised a ridiculously large expenditure to the second. Charlotte has also stormed out of all but one of her dancing lessons." She picked up the wrapper and slid one arm then the other through the sleeves.

"Well, so things are improving, if she stayed for the last one."

Emma turned and leveled him with an unamused glare for his sarcasm. "There was no need for her to storm out after she *injured* the dance master. He will not be returning." She tied the sash at the wrapper's waist and jerked it tight.

He nearly flinched with it, that final tug, as though it were the click of a lock that closed her treasures away for the night.

"I may need you to stand in for a lesson," she continued. "A dance master seems a waste at this stage regardless. Charlotte lacks even a rudimentary knowledge of the dances. She's intelligent enough to learn quickly, but she absolutely refuses to try." She stepped forward, her features softening.

"Perhaps if you were to stand in as her partner, she'd be more willing to take some basic instruction. You're the only one who can influence her."

"I'm certain that's not true," John replied, with an involuntary step back.

She cast him a dubious glance but otherwise ignored his comment. "Beyond that, your friend Mr. Brydges has successfully goaded Charlotte into declaring that she will never, under any circumstance, learn to ride a horse. Frankly, given what little we've accomplished and how few days we have left, I can't imagine riding lessons should matter anyway. We will be lucky if she is dressed and able to curtsy to the queen by the time we are back in town." John sighed heavily. This news of Charlotte's progress—or lack thereof—made no sense. The two seemed to get on well in the village market. "How is it she has been missing appointments?" he asked. "Hasn't she been with you?"

Emma's lips pressed tightly and her arms crossed in front of her chest. "I am doing the best I can to help a person who does not want my help. She is a grown woman and is not in my keeping every moment of the day."

He'd only asked the question to gain some understanding, not to blame Emma, but she'd pricked up nonetheless. He kept his voice carefully matter-of-fact as he explained, "I did not mean her behavior is your fault. I only wonder, if she fails to appear, why don't you simply go get her?"

"Yes, that would be simple," Emma bit back, "if she were not regularly missing."

"What do you mean, missing?"

"I mean in a location which I am unable to divine."

Had John not paused before he spoke, his response would have been much more unpleasant. Her rising temper was unproductive and, to his mind, disproportionate. He was only attempting to understand and apply some common sense to the situation. "I don't require your wit, only the answer," he told her.

Brown eyes that had so recently glowed amber with passion now flashed with anger. "I do not know where she goes. You should ask her. She will not share it with me."

This should not be so difficult. Why couldn't these two women get along and manage to order a few dresses and learn a few dances without requiring his presence? He could not spend his days with Charlotte if it meant spending his days with Emma.

He released another burdened sigh. "I will talk with Charlotte."

"Thank you. When?"

"When?"

"When will you talk with Charlotte?"

He stared at her. "Soon."

"Will you talk with her tomorrow?"

His jaw tightened. "Tomorrow," he agreed.

She nodded tightly. "Fine. Tomorrow. And the dancing lesson?"

He shifted his eyes. He did not want to become Charlotte's new dance master and spend his days in Emma's company. Any benefit he could provide to Charlotte was far outweighed by the consequences of his infatuation with Emma. He could not conduct a dance lesson tomorrow. He would spend the day away from his wife—all day, and the evening too. "We will see to it," he agreed, retreating toward the adjoining door, "but not tomorrow. I will be otherwise engaged. It will have to be another day."

"Fine," she said again. "Since there are no appointments tomorrow and there will be no dance lesson, I will spend the day at my cottage." She turned then and sat at her dressing table.

He stopped and faced her again. "That's ridiculous. You can't spend the day in Beadwell."

She picked up her hairbrush and ran it through her unbound hair in one long continuous stroke. "Why ever not?" she asked, watching her own reflection rather than looking at him.

"Because you just explained how little progress you've made with Charlotte and how much there is to be done in the time remaining. It makes no sense to leave. You have committed to Charlotte."

Her brush landed forcefully on the dressing table and her eyes met his in the mirror. When she spoke it was slow and deliberate. "And you have committed to allowing me time at my cottage. If you have need of me tomorrow, you will find me there."

* * *

Emma awoke to sun streaming through a gap in her curtains. She sighed and rose from the bed to retrieve a thin, lace-trimmed wrap from its place draped across the back of a delicately carved chair. She donned the wrap and walked to the window, where she pushed back the curtain gazed out on the room's unobstructed view of the west lawn and the crescent-shaped pond that bordered it. Beyond the pond, the landscape rose into a forested hill. She recalled being told of riding trails through the forest.

She would like to ride those trails, but not today. Today she would ride all the way to Beadwell.

She could take the carriage, as surely the duke assumed she would, but she wanted the ride. She would take a groomsman to accompany her, since her husband did not have time for such things and her sister-in-law objected so fiercely.

A ride would help her to gather herself again. Emma had begun to feel less like a rudder-steered boat on a well-mapped course and more like driftwood bouncing about on the ocean's whim. No more. She resolved to remember she was the Duchess of Worley, for better or worse. Too much of her frustration the prior evening had nothing to do with Charlotte and everything to do with her growing resentment over the fact that her husband not only ignored Charlotte, but *her* as well. Mooning over a man who did not care was a thoughtless use of her time and heartache. She'd struck a bargain with her husband. Passion, at least on occasion, was a part of that bargain.

More was not.

That point had been eloquently made to her last evening.

She was a member of the family now—the matriarch of it, rather—and helping Charlotte was not merely a debt she owed John, but a familial responsibility. She should focus her attentions on that task.

After her ride to Beadwell, of course. She fully intended to take this day for herself. For just this day, John, Charlotte, and Mr. Brydges could all go to the devil.

Emma stepped away from the window and pondered what, precisely, she would do with her day at the cottage. There would certainly be work in the garden, but she would visit the parsonage as well. Her mood lifted even as she said it. She knew sharing her frustrations with Lucy would make them more manageable, and Lucy's advice would always be practical.

Lucy would probably manage the entire situation better than Emma ever could. She almost never lost her temper and everyone loved her. Even Charlotte would probably love her.

Even Charlotte *would* probably love Lucy…

A thought found purchase in Emma's mind. Charlotte didn't want to ride. She needed something else to fill her time and round out her accomplishments. What of the pianoforte? She wouldn't get far in two weeks, but she could begin now and continue when the season was ended.

Lucy played beautifully and had the patience of a saint! Emma could trust Lucy not to tell tales about any lapses in behavior she witnessed from Charlotte. She could also trust Lucy not to be provoking. Why, she positively exuded sunshine and happiness.

Emma was resolved. She would not just visit Lucy in Beadwell. She would invite her to Brantmoor. Charlotte needed a music teacher, but even more…Emma desperately needed a friend and ally.

Chapter Twenty-Seven

"There is a visitor, Your Grace."

This unwelcome announcement brought forth only a grunt of response from John. His head was bent over papers, reviewing sums and evaluating reports prepared by his father's secretary. He'd let the man go, as he was not capable of continuing the employ of a secretary complicit in denying aid to a dying woman. Now he found himself acting as his own secretary until the replacement he hired arrived at Brantmoor.

"Shall I send him away, sir?"

John finally looked up. "Whom did you say it was?"

The man coughed. John could not for the life of him remember this man's name. There had been too many employees and too few weeks to learn them all. "I did not say, Your Grace, but he has given his name as Pritchard—of the Boston Pritchards."

Damn. John closed the ledger. There was no one from Boston whose visit would bode well, particularly not a visitor with the last name of Pritchard. "I will see Mr. Pritchard here, in my study."

The man gave a slight bow. "As you wish, Your Grace."

Mr. Pritchard of Boston walked into the private study of the Duke of Worley with his head held high and enough swagger to fill a gentleman's club in London. He appeared in worn boots with an untidy shave and clothing that looked as though it had made the entire journey from Boston on the man's form. He should have had the good sense to understand where he was and with whom he was dealing. He should have been dignified—or at least respectable. Or at the very least, sober. He was none of these things. Therefore, he was on John's nerves before he had even spoken.

"Mr. Pritchard," John said, rising reluctantly from his seat and walking round his desk to stand in front of it. Standing was better. He did not want this Pritchard fellow to feel welcome to stay.

"My Lord Duke," he said with an awkward bow that pitched slightly to the left, "I have come to inquire after the welfare of your sister, Charlotte."

"You have come a long way just to inquire, Mr. Pritchard. A letter would have been a less troublesome manner of inquiry."

"Certainly." The man brought a hand to the breast of his rumpled coat. "But I do not think I could have satisfied myself with only a letter. I feel—responsible—for Lottie."

John bristled. He'd always hated that particular familiarity—Lottie. He and his mother did not use it. The Pritchards did. John had never met the Pritchard family while he was in Boston, which evidently was for the best. He didn't like this man. And he didn't like him claiming responsibility for Charlotte.

"You have made a long journey for naught, Mr. Pritchard. I am responsible for Lady Charlotte." He stressed the title. "Her welfare, were it any concern of yours, is not in jeopardy."

"Please understand," the American said, stepping closer to John, "I never saw Lottie as just our kitchen girl. I always thought we had a special friendship."

John glared and took a heavy step toward Pritchard. His voice was low and quiet when he responded, but he pronounced each word with careful intent. "Unless you've traveled across the sea with a pair of dueling pistols, Mr. Pritchard, do not suggest again that you have enjoyed any manner of friendship with my sister."

Our kitchen girl. John sneered at the thought. The Pritchard standing in his study lacked the age and the consequence to be the Pritchard in whose kitchen Charlotte had found employment when Mother turned ill. He was the son perhaps. How disappointed the father must be.

"I meant no insult to be sure. I am only concerned for your family. How hard this must be, trying to explain how your sister was plucked out of a Boston kitchen and dropped into the ballrooms of London."

John felt a small tic begin in his right temple. It seemed connected to his right fist, for that pulsed as well—tightening and releasing on a steady beat.

The man kept talking, unaware of the increasing threat to his person. "It would be much easier for all concerned if instead, you presented a sister who has returned to England after her marriage to the son of a respectable Boston family."

John's voice was barely more than a growl when he asked, "And you propose to be that man?"

"Yes." He nodded gravely as though this offer were a brave self-sacrifice.

The Pritchards, from what John knew of his sister's employers during her brief tenure as a kitchen maid, were a fine Boston family. This man, Pritchard or not, did not appear even close to John's expectation of respectable. His bold manner, his loose speech, and his ruddy color were confirmation enough that the man had stopped off for a pint—or more likely several—before imposing himself upon John's productive afternoon.

"Perhaps Lottie has mentioned me, Your Grace," he said with a proud grin.

John was finished with this man and this conversation. "She has not. That part of Charlotte's life is done and left behind in Boston. Your concern is appreciated. My man will show you out."

For the first time since the American arrived, his bravado faltered. His mouth opened and shut without sound before opening again to squawk, "I've come a very long way."

"And you have a long journey home. There is no sense in delaying."

"But I haven't even seen your sister yet."

"Nor will you."

Pritchard's eyes narrowed again. Did the man refuse to understand he'd been instructed to go? John was dangerously close to physically removing the man from his home.

"I don't think you've really considered the situation. Think of how uncomfortable everyone will be when they realize this year's newest debutante is nothing but a kitchen maid."

Pritchard's threats were no longer veiled, so John's directions ceased to be subtle. "Get out," he commanded.

The bastard still didn't move. John strode forward, fists clenched.

Finally, reality registered with the American. His eyes grew round and he leapt to attention.

John glared, towering several inches above him, his face no more than a foot from the other man's when he bellowed for a footman. He did not yield his position, even when the footman arrived.

"Yes, Your Grace?"

"Remove this man." He said it with quiet finality, and the American did not balk this time. He quit the room, with the footman behind him.

"See to it that man leaves the grounds," John barked. "And summon my sister."

John fumed. Did that drunkard actually think he would make his fortune by blackmailing his way into marrying a duke's sister? He was lucky to be allowed to leave unscathed. He needed to be soundly beaten and dragged onto the next departing ship, regardless of its destination. If he wasn't far enough away by nightfall, he may yet get just that.

John forced himself to sit at his desk and take a deep settling breath, but he felt no calmer than he'd been a moment before. What sort of lion's den had his sister been forced to work within? Fresh rage for his father ran through him that his sister was made to be subservient to a man like Pritchard, who was no better than vermin

There was a tentative rap on the study's heavy oak door.

"Yes."

The door creaked open and Charlotte walked in.

Little Charlotte.

John and a few long-standing servants at Brantmoor were probably the last few living in England with any memory of Charlotte as an infant. She'd been all smiles and gurgles then, with everyone cooing over her. A mere boy himself, John had been disgusted by her. Now, smiles were scarce and she wanted no help from anyone, much less cooing. She was not always contrary, though that might surprise Emma or Brydges. Even after long days of laboring, she could have a sunny disposition, when she chose to have one.

From her mulish expression and wary eyes, he divined she had not chosen so today. She wore a simple, worn dress and her hair in a plain, plaited bun. John recognized the dress because he was tired of seeing it. She'd arrived from Boston in it and, with the exception of the new dress debuted on Market day, she'd worn this and one other even older garment every day since.

"Are there no new dresses yet?" he asked.

"The duchess ordered all sorts, but they've yet to be fitted."

"Hmmm." He crossed his arms and leaned his hips back against the generations-old desk that had served all the Dukes of Worley before him. "That bit is difficult if you do not attend fittings."

Charlotte looked down and tucked a stray tendril of dark hair behind her ear. "I thought the duchess was away today."

"She is. I am referring to fittings on other days," he said flatly. "Don't you want new dresses?"

"I have perfectly fine dresses." Her declaration lacked vehemence.

"You're being objectionable for no reason. Why on earth would you refuse new clothing?"

Charlotte shrugged, still not meeting his eyes. "I don't like to be poked all over with pins by clumsy seamstresses."

"Don't be ridiculous. You have to meet them first to know if they're clumsy. And if you are pricked, it's likely because you are behaving as a brat and the seamstress chooses to prick you."

Her head snapped up and she smiled. "I am not a brat."

"You are and it will not continue." He pointed at her present attire. "You have precisely one week before this dress and its partner will be taken from your room while you sleep and burned on my orders. You will cooperate in fittings or catch a chill."

Charlotte laughed. It was a light, easy laugh. John was happy to hear the sound. If others could see her smiling and laughing as she was now, perhaps they would not judge her so harshly.

"Fine," she said. "I will order a thousand dresses and it will cost you a fortune."

"I'm sure you would."

Her smiles were so rare these days he was loath to chase one away, but he must. "I had a visitor just now."

Still laughing, Charlotte leaned dramatically to one side, drawing the fingertips of one hand to her chest and extending the other as though holding an imaginary train. She lifted her chin in exaggerated importance. "Was it the queen? I am a very highborn lady, you know."

"It was a Mr. Pritchard."

The laughter died quickly. She pulled her outstretched hand back and clasped her two hands together in front of her. Her shoulders slouched. "Mr. Pritchard? In England. Why would he come here?" she asked, her voice low and fragile.

Did she realize she was doing that? He'd merely spoken the name Pritchard and she'd suddenly taken on the meek, deferential posture of a servant—a kitchen girl. John liked this demeanor even less than the prickly contrarian they'd seen all week.

"What could Mr. Pritchard want of me?" she asked.

"Our visitor was the younger Mr. Pritchard."

She looked up slowly. Gone was her submissive stance. Her lips curled in a sneer as she asked, "The son? Mr. *Randall* Pritchard?"

"He was the son, yes. Are there more than one?"

"No," she bit out. "One is quite enough."

"You were not friends, then?"

"Friends?" Her laugh this time was barely more than a bitter exhale of air. Young innocents did not yet possess this sort of laugh. It was reserved for those whose illusions had been dismantled by the realities of their lives.

John hated that his pretty young sister possessed such a laugh.

"Randall Pritchard and I were never friends. I was the lowly kitchen girl. He was the drunken sod who shamed his parents and menaced every member of the household staff."

John's heart began to thud more heavily in his chest. It seemed to be reverberating in his ears. His jaw tightened. His chin lowered. His voice lowered. "And you?"

"What of me?" she asked.

He stared hard at her because her response to his next question was of pivotal importance. "In what way, exactly, was he menacing to you?"

She paused and bit her lip. "He did nothing I wasn't capable of handling on my own."

She had paused. That was answer enough. The man had better be on a boat by morning, or he'd be dead by the afternoon.

"What did he do to you?" John growled.

Charlotte lifted her chin. "He didn't *do* anything. He *tried* to kiss me. Kitchens have knives—large, sharp knives." Her eyes glinted with ferocity that belied her size. "They also have small, pointy knives—the kind you can hide in the fold of your skirt, so no one knows it's there until it's needed."

John's rage unfurled. If this bastard Pritchard was the sort to prey on household servants, he wasn't going to make the trip all the way to England and be content to go home empty-handed.

Which meant he would be lurking about.

Which meant he would not be far enough gone to escape John's wrath.

"You won't have need for a knife here," John said. He'd have a man following Pritchard within the hour. "I will take care of Pritchard."

"What did he want?" Charlotte asked shrewdly. "If he followed me all the way here, he wanted something."

"He wanted to elevate his station in life," John said, "by marrying the daughter of a duke."

Charlotte gasped. "He knows I hate him. What could he possibly believe would induce me to consider marriage to him?"

"Blackmail."

"Blackmail? What sort of blackmail?"

"He suggested we might prefer presenting you to society as my sister who married into a respectable Boston family, as opposed to my sister, the former kitchen maid."

It was not an idle threat. Duke's sister or not, if society knew Charlotte had actually been a kitchen maid, she would not survive the social ruin.

Charlotte swallowed. "But…I was a kitchen maid," she said, her voice losing much of the force her ire had given it.

"Yes, but we are not going to share that information. There are many here who would deem you beneath them simply because your circumstances required you to earn a wage upon which to live. Those people could make your entrance into society difficult. We will explain you are my sister. We will explain you were raised in Boston. We need not provide all the unnecessary details. I won't have people looking down their noses at you."

"What about the duchess?" she asked. "Does the duchess know?"

"The duchess knows you lived modestly in Boston. She does not care."

"But does she know I was a servant?"

John looked steadily at his sister. "She does not."

Charlotte pressed her lips together. She nodded her head slowly in acceptance of this admission.

It was not possible to make her understand. He had not intentionally hidden it from Emma. He simply hadn't seen a need to share it.

"Will you tell her?" Charlotte asked.

"I believe I must. With Pritchard lurking about, she should know."

"I thought you were handling Mr. Pritchard. You said I needn't worry. Why should the duchess be in danger if I am not?"

"She will not be in danger. I will have my man following Pritchard every moment. He won't be allowed to come near either of you."

"Then she doesn't need to know."

John looked at Charlotte. "There is no reason to keep it from her." He said it, but he could not have sworn to it. Emma's frustration with Charlotte was high. Her frustration with him was higher still. Did he believe knowing Charlotte's occupation as a servant would matter one whit to Emma?

No.

"I don't want her to know," Charlotte said. "Please."

John considered his sister's request. Charlotte needed Emma's help. Emma was perilously close to denying that help already, due to Charlotte's poor behavior. Perhaps he could satisfy both women in one exchange.

"All right," he said. "I will agree to keep Mr. Pritchard and your past between us. But you must agree there will be no more missed appointments. You will cooperate with everything the duchess requests and be an apt pupil."

Charlotte released the frustrated sigh of one who has been outmaneuvered. "Agreed."

"You will attend all of it, Charlotte. I will know if you do not."

"Yes. All of it," she said, crossing her arms with a huff. "But not until tomorrow. The duchess is gone today."

"Tomorrow, then. You may go back to whatever you were doing." He, on the other hand, would not be returning to his ledgers. He had an American to hunt down.

Charlotte turned to go, but stopped when she reached the door. She turned back. "I'm sorry," she said. "I'm sorry that he's followed me here and for the trouble that's caused." Her eyes were bright.

"No, Charlotte, I am sorry. You should never have suffered through so many of the trials you've experienced. I will make it right, I promise you."

Chapter Twenty-Eight

There were no knocks on Emma's adjoining door for the next two nights. The day she rode to Beadwell, she returned in time for dinner, but John and Mr. Brydges were caught up in estate business. The ladies ate separately in their rooms. The following evening, John and Mr. Brydges did appear for dinner. John was pleasant, solicitous even, as though their row had never occurred. He also announced at dinner, to Emma's great relief, that he would participate in a dance lesson the following day.

He'd been so pleasant that evening, Emma found herself waiting for him to come that evening, but he did not come. She fell asleep wondering if he would. Wondering if she wanted him to come.

Knowing very well that she did.

Still, she was encouraged when she awoke. He had committed to the dance lesson that day, and it was the day of Lucy's arrival. She was grateful for both.

Charlotte was alone in the empty ballroom when Emma appeared a few minutes prior to the agreed upon time, followed closely by the housekeeper's daughter, Eliza, who'd been recruited to provide music for this and the previous lessons.

Charlotte was standing in the center of the room with her back to the entryway, looking to the far wall of arched windows. She was so still and seemingly unaware of Emma's arrival that Emma wondered what had captured her thoughts.

"Good morning, Charlotte," she offered in the pleasant, but carefully unenthusiastic voice she applied during the young girl's calmer moments. She chose not to remark on Charlotte's early arrival, when she'd been either late or missing for all prior appointments.

Charlotte turned quickly. "I thought my brother was to be here."

"He will have remembered our appointment," Emma assured her. "I assume he will join us momentarily." She waved for Eliza to take a seat at the pianoforte and the girl did so, limbering her fingers with a few chords before they began.

As though summoned by Emma's words, John strode into the ballroom. "Ladies." He barely spared her a glance, though he did give a small nod in her direction.

Emma did not bother gracing him with the warm smile she would have had for him, if only he would reciprocate.

Then Mr. Brydges sauntered into the room.

Emma groaned inwardly. She'd been hoping for a productive session.

"Why is he here?" Charlotte demanded.

Mr. Brydges graced the ladies with a wide, tooth-filled grin. "News of Miss Brantwood's great skill as a dancer has reached even me, and I have come to witness it firsthand."

"That's Lady Charlotte to you," Charlotte said, predictably rising to his bait.

Emma sighed. Didn't the man have a horse farm to run? "Shall we begin, everyone?" she suggested in an attempt to head off the inevitable skirmish.

"Yes, let's begin," John concurred. "Brydges, you will behave yourself or you will be removed. Find a seat and endeavor to be civil, will you?"

"But of course," Mr. Brydges replied in a mocking tone that threatened to rile even Emma's temper. He swept himself dramatically toward the window alcove on the far side of the room in which a small grouping of chairs remained arranged, and perched himself upon one of them.

Disregarding these theatrics, Emma gave instruction to Eliza regarding the piece of music to be played. John had joined Charlotte in the center of the room and both took the opening position for the simple dance that had been the subject of Charlotte's lessons thus far.

Eliza began playing with enthusiasm, but it became apparent only a few bars into the tune that Charlotte had failed to retain any memory of the steps from her previous lessons. She was quite obviously watching her brother's movements for direction, under the misguided presumption that the lady's steps would always mirror the gentleman's.

Emma held her hand up to Eliza to halt her playing.

"It appears we will require some review of the steps before proceeding," she said, approaching the pair who had abruptly stopped when the music was silenced. "Charlotte, if you will step back a few paces, I will demonstrate the steps with your brother—a few at a time—and you can step in again to practice them. Will that be all right?"

Charlotte shrugged.

Aware she would receive no stronger confirmation than that, Emma proceeded with her suggestion. She stepped up, nodded at Eliza, and turned to smile at her husband.

Unexpectedly, he smiled back.

It was pleasant and warm, and Emma nearly missed her first step when the music began. She righted herself, thankfully, and followed the simple steps of the dance, speaking them aloud as she moved, for Charlotte's benefit.

Her attention, however, was on John. The dance did not require that they touch at all, but his attention was on her and hers on him. It was a rare moment of intimacy despite the others present. He felt it too. She knew he did. She hated to break the connection, but the lesson had to continue.

"Let's stop there," she said, "so you can take my place, Charlotte."

Charlotte stepped up as instructed and Emma once again nodded to their musician. This time, as Charlotte attempted the steps from memory, Emma stood more closely and gave spoken directions as the pair danced.

Charlotte was doing well. Quite well. She recalled nearly all of it. Just as Emma had hoped, John's presence had inspired a greater effort on Charlotte's part.

Emma instructed Charlotte through the first set of steps a second time then positioned herself across from her husband again to demonstrate the next steps. They began and she watched him move through the dance, His steps were perfectly made and perfectly timed, but lacked the flourish some would no doubt find artistic, but he would view as superfluous.

She agreed. His manner was more...male.

Perhaps she was affected by the unanswered anticipation of waiting up for her husband to visit her the prior evening, but it seemed to Emma just then that everything about him was more masculine than other men. Her eyes roved over him with both a woman's interest and the benefit of her wifely knowledge. His lean muscular legs. His trim waist. His strong shoulders that were nearly too broad to be fashionable. Her inventory brought her to his strong features and ended inevitably at his deep blue eyes.

Deep blue eyes that stared hotly back at hers.

Oh my.

She'd been ogling her husband like a bit of forbidden candy, and he was clearly aware of her having done so.

He smiled knowingly at her and she was certain her temperature gained several degrees.

"Shall we allow Charlotte a turn through the set we've demonstrated?" he suggested, his eyes still locked with hers.

"Yes." She sincerely hoped no one else of their number noted the slight croak to her response. In an attempt to recover the moment, she granted John what she hoped was a placid smile before yielding her place to Charlotte.

Though Emma's mind had wandered through the previous set, Charlotte had clearly been well focused. She moved unerringly through the steps a first and second time, and in no time at all, Emma was once again readying herself to partner with John for a demonstration of the third and final portion of the dance.

"I beg your pardon, ladies," John spoke before Emma reached him. "But I fear my new steward cannot yet be expected to work very long without requiring my guidance on some matter or another. I should not neglect him." John turned to where Mr. Brydges had been sitting quietly in the alcove. "Brydges, you'll take my place."

Emma was weak enough in that moment to feel truly stung. She would have sworn on everything important to her that *she* had not been the only one aware of the significance of the moments they'd shared while dancing.

Yet he was avoiding her. He'd been closeted with Mr. Brydges and this new steward for days. Surely the man could manage another half an hour on his own.

"But why must you leave now, when we are almost finished?" Charlotte asked, echoing Emma's thoughts. Charlotte's expression looked as deflated as Emma felt.

"I'm afraid my responsibilities call. Brydges will be obliging enough to complete the lesson." He turned again to where his friend still sat. "Be a sport, won't you, Brydges?" He did not stay to hear his friend's response.

Mr. Brydges rose. He strode regally across the room to stand in front of Emma and gave an exaggerated bow.

Emma wanted to roll her eyes, but resisted. She allowed him to lead her through the steps just once then moved back and motioned to Charlotte to take her place. "I'm sure you've got the idea now."

He leered comically at Charlotte. "Do recall this lesson is for dancing, my dear, and not pugilism. I understand your last dance master may have been the victim of confusion over that very issue."

"I'm not going to dance with that…that…jackanapes." Her flush deepened to crimson as she turned to Emma. "If learning to dance with boorish oafs is necessary to the education of an English lady, I'm proud to say I'm not one." She punctuated her speech as she did all tantrums, by pivoting about and stomping toward the wide double doors that stood open at the ballroom's entry.

Honestly, Emma had seen more of the girl's back than of her face, but she didn't get far this time. Mr. Brydges followed her with long strides and caught her before she reached the threshold. From behind her, he placed his hands on either side of her slip of a frame and, with seemingly little effort, lifted her from the ground.

"Let me go!" Charlotte's feet continued moving but no longer propelled her forward.

Mr. Brydges calmly turned and carried her back into the room.

Ignored by her captor, Charlotte hollered more loudly, swinging her fists blindly behind her. "Put me down, you...you...bastard."

Having the advantage of arm span, Mr. Brydges merely held Charlotte farther away from his body so that her fists caught only air.

"I hate you," she spat.

"And I you, my dear," he assured her sweetly.

Emma watched in awe and horror. She should, of course, step in immediately and object to such gross mistreatment of a lady. The trouble was, she'd wanted to do much the same thing herself many times over the past several weeks—and would have done if only she possessed the physical strength to do so.

Charlotte was back on her feet but still red-faced and shouting when the footman entered and addressed the duchess with a perfectly unaffected demeanor.

"You have a visitor arrived, Your Grace. A Miss Lucy Betancourt."

Lucy's arrival was the best possible diversion she could imagine. "We are clearly done with the dancing lesson for today," she announced.

Charlotte crossed her arms and glared threateningly at Mr. Brydges. "I'll be in my room."

He met her gaze with equal menace. "You should go greet your guest."

"She's not *my* guest."

"It's good practice."

For heaven's sake. If the two of them wanted to bicker like children, Emma was happy to leave them to it for once. She hurried into the hall to meet her friend.

"Lucy!"

Her pale hair was no more golden than it had been just days before and her familiar smile no more beaming, but to Emma at that moment, Lucy appeared more angelic than she had ever been. The sight of her so warmed Emma's heart, she had to measure her steps for fear she would set off into a run most inappropriate for a duchess.

Lucy's eyes widened just as Emma reached her, and Emma turned, cringing, to see Mr. Brydges following behind her—again holding Charlotte by the waist so that her toes hovered inches above the floor.

Emma turned back to a shocked Lucy and desperately gripped her friend's hands.

"Oh, Lucy. Thank God you've come."

Chapter Twenty-Nine

It seemed to Emma that Lucy's presence brought an immediate improvement in the disposition of all the residents of Brantmoor. With the addition of a stranger, both Charlotte and Mr. Brydges seemed less overt in their bickering, and John seemed less determined to avoid the ladies at all but mealtimes. He made no effort to excuse himself when the entire group—less Charlotte—set off for a ride through the estate the following afternoon. The ride had been Mr. Brydges's idea—no doubt inspired by the desire to prick Charlotte, who did indeed seem irritated.

Emma was, for once, not at all irritated by his suggestion. She had no regular companion for riding. To do so with the company of her husband and her newly arrived friend was a rare treat, and she intended to take full advantage.

The greater surprise had come after the ride, however. Once the party had returned, the gentleman had retreated back into their estate business, but Charlotte had appeared in her riding habit of all things and declared herself ready for a lesson. Unable to see the wisdom in allowing the opportunity to pass, Emma had refastened her hat and returned to the stable, musing that Mr. Brydges's manipulation—mean-spirited or not—had unarguably produced results.

In truth, as she sat in the drawing room with Lucy and Charlotte the afternoon following the somewhat questionable riding lesson, Emma's perspective was more hopeful than it had been in the weeks since she'd come to Brantmoor.

"Ah, there you ladies are."

As though in proof of Emma's hope, John sauntered into the room with an easy smile, and greeted the ladies one by one. As always, he was followed closely by Mr. Brydges.

"Duchess," he said with a nod in her direction. "You look in particularly fine spirits today."

"I am, thank you."

He smiled warmly at Lucy. "Miss Betancourt. A lovely addition to our party, if I may say."

When Mr. Brydges turned to Charlotte, he did so with a twinkle in his eye, and Emma had an awful premonition that her peaceful harmony was about to be broken.

"Ah, Lady Charlotte. I see you're wearing a new dress. Has the duchess finally found a modiste able to fit a dress for a woman she's never seen?"

Emma cringed, waiting for Charlotte's reaction. Notwithstanding the man's inexcusably rude manners, his comment had been dangerously close to the truth. Though Charlotte had finally consented to a dress fitting, Emma had very nearly resorted to stealing one of the girl's worn dresses and suggesting the dressmaker use it as a pattern to measure a dress for her sister-in-law.

True to form, Charlotte snapped back at Mr. Brydges. "You cross the line, Mr. Brydges. I expect men of greater consequence than you to be noticing things such as my gowns."

"Well done, Lady Charlotte," Mr. Brydges said with a deferential nod, but a teasing tone. "Or should I call you Lady Godiva? I understand you've taken up riding of late."

Charlotte's face took on an immediate flush.

"My, how news travels," Emma cut in, hoping to avoid an escalation. "We did begin riding lessons yesterday afternoon, so we must thank you again for our lovely mounts, Mr. Brydges."

She was not certain how Mr. Brydges had become aware of Charlotte's riding lesson—if it could be referred to as a lesson—but she certainly didn't want it to become the topic of discussion. The full extent of progress they'd achieved in nearly an hour's time had resulted in Charlotte sitting atop the horse, petrified in fear, as the stable hand held the animal's bridle and Emma held Charlotte's hand. It had convinced Emma she might be wise to encourage Charlotte away from accepting the suit of any enthusiastic equestrians once they returned to London.

"I did begin my riding lessons," Charlotte finally responded, with a haughty lift of her chin. "I thoroughly enjoyed it, though I'm sure that will disappoint you to hear, Mr. Brydges."

His expression became more cunning and Emma knew he was somehow fully aware of Charlotte's bald-faced lie.

"Now, now," John interjected. "The two of you bicker like siblings."

Siblings? Bitter enemies would be more accurate. Emma's suspicions were true. John was completely ignorant of all matters concerning Charlotte.

Charlotte looked appalled at her brother's comment. "Please. If Mr. Brydges behaves as a sibling, it is as a child of no more than five or six, I assure you."

"I've still the advantage of age on you, my dear," he returned. "As your tantrums are better suited for an infant."

Red-faced, Charlotte glared back.

Emma sighed. The calming effect of Lucy's presence as an outsider had clearly expired after only a few glorious days. In truth, they were both behaving as infants, but to say so would only inflame them. She had no choice but to side with Charlotte as her charge. In this instance, and indeed in many instances, Charlotte's lack of decorum was instigated first by some rude comment from Mr. Brydges.

"You may disagree with Charlotte's behavior, Mr. Brydges," Emma spoke up before Charlotte could spew the venom she'd been building. "But I can say in her defense that our manners are foreign to her in many ways and that she is allowing herself to be mentored in those areas that will no doubt improve her manners." She leveled him with a steady gaze. "How, pray tell, do you explain your lack, Mr. Brydges, when you have been an English gentleman all your life?"

He did not answer, so in the hope of restoring peace, Emma reminded them of Lucy's presence. "What must our guest think?"

"Oh, it's fine, really," Lucy demurred. "I imagine most close families engage in a bit of good-natured bickering."

Since Emma had been thorough in updating her friend on the state of things with Charlotte, she recognized the lie Lucy told.

Charlotte was quick to correct her. "Mr. Brydges is neither family nor close friend, and he has never been good-natured."

"I am extremely good-natured," Mr. Brydges declared. "I have remained so despite interacting with an ungrateful viper each day."

"Brydges." John's tone was a warning. "You'd better mind how harshly you speak of my sister."

Mr. Brydges reacted to his friend's censure with an immediate reversal of demeanor. "My sincerest apologies," he said to John, rather than Charlotte. He then turned to Lucy. "Particularly to you, Miss Betancourt, as I did not take into consideration your discomfort when I so brutally attacked

Lady Charlotte. I am sure a lady as sweet-natured as you can find it in your heart to forgive me."

John seemed satisfied with his friend's theatrical apology, but Emma knew better. He'd not actually apologized to Charlotte. Rather, his particular note of Lucy's sweet nature was meant to be another veiled poke at his nemesis. And the jab found its mark, judging by the way Charlotte's face pinched as Hugh gushed over Lucy.

Emma desperately wanted to change the subject, and racked her brain to think of even one topic toward which to steer the conversation that Mr. Brydges could not somehow use to ridicule Charlotte.

John interrupted before she could settle on one. "I understand you play the pianoforte as well as the harp, Miss Betancourt—perhaps you would grace us with a performance while you are here?"

"I am far from a master, Your Grace, but my playing is reasonably tolerated by my family and friends."

"Nonsense. Lucy plays beautifully," Emma offered.

As soon as she spoke the words, Emma realized she had delivered to Mr. Brydges another ideal opportunity to highlight Charlotte's failings as compared with Lucy.

"I am impressed, Miss Betancourt. We learned just yesterday that you are an accomplished horsewoman, we've already had a demonstration of your excellent skill at the harp, and we now learn you are an accomplished pianist as well. I believe if we brought you to London, you should be the talk of the town."

Rather than the simpering pleasure of a young impressionable girl, Lucy's smile was patronizing at best. "I thank you for your flattery, Mr. Brydges, but I sincerely doubt a vicar's daughter with no connections or fortune will ever be much to talk of in London. Unless of course she manages to disgrace herself."

"Lucy has offered to tutor you on the pianoforte, Charlotte. She would be an excellent teacher."

Lucy addressed Charlotte. "My proficiency at either instrument falls below the expectations of these two exaggerators, but I am reasonably tolerable. I would be very happy to aid in your musical instruction until you have need of a more accomplished teacher."

Hoping for the best in Charlotte's response to this kind offer, Emma turned to the young woman and saw immediately she would instead be disappointed. Charlotte's rising pique was evident in the deepening flush that started in her cheeks and had already crept down to the neckline of her gown.

"As you said," Charlotte began, narrowing her eyes into catlike meanness, "you are only a vicar's daughter and have probably never even been to London. I don't imagine I can learn anything from you that will prepare me for the high society I'm expected to become."

"Charlotte!" John gaped at his sister, yet he said nothing further.

Emma was incredulous. Lucy was her closest and dearest friend, and Charlotte's comment was nothing short of hateful. Well, John could choose silence, but *she* certainly would not.

"You will not speak to Miss Betancourt that way. She is a dear friend of mine and she has done *you* a great favor by agreeing to share her skill at the pianoforte. She seeks only to provide you with every advantage in your debut, as do we all." Emma rose from her chair and turned the full measure of her indignation onto Charlotte. "You may be a duke's daughter, while her father is merely a clergyman, but she is worthy of your respect. Horses, carriages, and dresses are fine indeed, and *they* are the entitlement of your birth, as is deference to your rank. But true respect, Charlotte, is something you must earn. You earn it in the way you treat others—all others."

Emma wasn't certain what sort of response she had expected from Charlotte after that, but she received none—at least not one in spoken words.

Charlotte simply rose from her seat and ran from the room, as she always did. Flight, it seemed, was her primary line of defense.

Chapter Thirty

The following afternoon, Emma was seated at the writing desk in the corner of the drawing room when her husband and Mr. Brydges found her.

"Are you alone, Emma?" John asked.

She lay down her pen and lifted her gaze to her husband. She so wished her mood didn't improve by his presence, but it did and there seemed to be nothing she could do to prevent it.

"Yes. I am alone. Lucy took a book to her room and I am writing a letter to my aunt."

John looked around the room. "But where is Charlotte?"

Emma smiled. "I've no idea."

"What do you mean, you've no idea?" Mr. Brydges asked sharply.

"I mean simply that. I've no inkling as to her whereabouts."

John frowned. "What did you have planned for today? Has she run off again? I thought the two of you smoothed things over."

"We did. All is fine between us," she reassured him. When Emma had finally caught up with Charlotte, they had talked, but John had never inquired as to how things had been resolved, and that had irked Emma ever since.

"When did you last speak to her?"

"At breakfast this morning."

"But it's half four," Mr. Brydges said, eyes widened in alarm.

"Is it?" Emma checked the mantle clock. "Why I suppose it is."

John's expression was quizzical. "Do you mean to say you've not spoken to Charlotte *all day*?"

"No. I did speak with her today. At breakfast, as I just said."

Let them expire from frustration, Emma thought. If John harbored so much concern for his sister, perhaps he should have involved himself before now.

"*Since* breakfast, then," John asked. "You've not spoken with her since breakfast?"

"No, I have not."

Mr. Brydges threw up his hands. "Well, why ever not? You're supposed to be looking out for her, aren't you? She's in your charge."

"She's not an infant, Mr. Brydges."

"Well, she's not exactly sensible either," the man blurted.

Emma ignored Mr. Brydges and looked placidly up at her husband, squaring her shoulders against any disapproval that may be forthcoming. "I have given Charlotte a reprieve."

"A reprieve from what? Her lessons?"

"A reprieve from everything. All of it. The lessons, the strictures. She's not behaved well, I'll be the first to tell you, but she's not been treated well either. In trying to help her learn our ways, we've made her feel as though she were broken somehow and needed to be fixed. I have given Charlotte some time to do as she pleases. I believe that should improve her disposition when we continue preparations in a few days." When Emma had finally caught up with Charlotte, she'd found her crying. These were the terms of their truce.

"But we are returning to London in less than two weeks," John hastily reminded her.

"And we shall accomplish nothing in that time if Charlotte is not in the correct frame of mind." Since John had abdicated responsibility for Charlotte's preparations to Emma, she did not really think it fair of him to question her approach.

Emma steeled herself for further recriminations, but they did not come. Instead, John pulled the nearest chair closer and sat. A number of expressions crossed his face as he digested what she'd told him. He ended with concern. "Do you really believe she's been made to feel broken? That was never my intention."

He was concerned for his sister and her feelings, rather than his grand plans. Emma supposed his loyalty and deep concern for his sister was one of the reasons she admired him so, despite his avoidance of her company. He was a good man—protective and loyal. Selfishly, she felt a stab of envy. She wondered whether John would someday feel the same protective loyalty for his wife, then immediately pushed the silly, romantic notion out of her head.

"I know it was not your intention, nor was it mine, but I do believe that's how she feels. She was very insecure coming here. She already felt out of place. By immediately throwing her into dance lessons and riding lessons and dress fittings, we only confirmed her feelings. We should have given her some time for adjustment."

"You say you've given her complete freedom?" Mr. Brydges interjected. "You've not spoken with her for hours and you have no idea where she could be?"

"That is correct, Mr. Brydges. She is a grown woman, not a child."

"She could be anywhere," he insisted, "getting into to God knows what mischief."

Emma was not surprised by his absolute certainty in Charlotte's irresponsibility. She was taken aback, however, by the force of his concern for it. "She cannot be far, Mr. Brydges, given that she's terrified to mount a horse."

He looked unconvinced. "Excuse me," he said, and left them.

"What does he think she'll do?" Emma asked, gaping at the doorway through which Mr. Brydges had disappeared. "Set fire to the manor?"

John shook his head. "I'm afraid Brydges does not have a very high opinion of my sister."

"I believe you are correct."

"He's a good man and normally a sound judge of character. I don't know why he fails to see the good in Charlotte."

Emma had a few thoughts as to why that might be the case, but she kept them to herself. "What about you, John?" she asked. "Do you have a high opinion of your sister?"

His attention shot to her. "What do you mean? Naturally I have a high opinion of her. She's my sister."

"Perhaps you could make sure she knows that."

John searched her face in genuine confusion. "I've gone to great lengths for Charlotte. She should have no doubt of it."

Emma's voice softened to calm the rising alarm in her husband's. "No one could deny the effort and sacrifice you have made for Charlotte, but you've barely seen her. She feels as though she's only an obligation—one that's been foisted off on the wife you acquired to be her governess in disguise."

"Well…that's not even…" John sputtered in an attempt to respond. Then he stopped. He took a deep breath and met her gaze with clear, direct honesty. "I never considered she would see it that way. Charlotte is my sister. My goal has always been for her to feel as though she belonged here, and I didn't want her unorthodox upbringing to be a barrier to that sense of belonging." He paused and released another breath. "I've done the opposite, haven't I? By insisting she change so many things, I've made certain she feels out-of-place."

Emma's heart sunk. She was heartened by John's concern for his sister, but he had not disputed that she was, in fact, a governess in disguise. She tamped those feeling down and tried to concentrate on the girl in her charge. "I am just as complicit in the lack of consideration we have shown Charlotte," she told John. "She has been extremely difficult, but we've been a bit merciless in our expectations. I think, more than an English lady, Charlotte would like to feel that she is a member of the family. You are the one person who is familiar to her and she has spent very little time with you."

We all have spent very little time with you. The thought proved she had not buried her own selfish concerns as deeply as she thought. Though she knew better, Emma yearned to campaign for her own feelings of neglect. Charlotte was John's blood sister. He had crossed the sea to rescue her, lived as a pauper for four years to protect her, and then married a stranger to secure her future. Emma was simply the stranger. She'd understood the arrangement perfectly. In truth, to realize she had an amicable marriage to a man for whom she felt respect and affection was better than she could have hoped. To expect him to return that affection with anything resembling passion or love...was a discredit to her good sense.

She could use a dose of practical, good sense just then, she realized.

She patted John's hand one more time. "I think I will go find Lucy and see if she would like to take a short walk through the garden before dinner."

She rose and so did he, with the crestfallen look of a boy who'd lost a game he didn't understand.

"Just make time for Charlotte," Emma implored him. "I truly believe that is all she needs." Then she swept from the room to seek out Lucy, thinking a walk might be just the thing.

* * *

Hugh shook his head as he hurried along the corridor.

A reprieve. Ridiculous.

He could see a break from lessons and the like. But no supervision whatsoever? That was pure foolishness. Who knew what sort of trouble that headstrong girl could find? She was likely in danger already, horse or no.

He checked the library first, as it was the nearest place to check, but did not expect to find her there. He wandered to the east parlor next, thinking it might be a good place to hide in the afternoon, since it was usually only used in the morning. She was not in either place, nor in any of the rooms he checked on the way, so he quickly climbed the steps in the hope that she was simply sulking in her bedchamber.

He found her bedchamber door closed. He rapped quickly and waited only a moment for a response before rapping again.

Still nothing.

He opened the door and was greeted with an empty room. He walked into it and spun around. He considered peeking under the bed, but decided against it. She was not *that* juvenile, and she was too ornery to hide.

He thought of the duchess's offhand comment about Charlotte being terrified of horses.

She wouldn't have...

No. He'd had a report from the stable master that her lesson had been a dismal failure.

Still...she'd been compliant enough to endure a lesson in the first place.

Hugh strode out of the bedchamber, pausing only to pull the door closed behind him, and saw a flash of movement in his peripheral vision.

He quickly stepped into a shadow. One of the maids? Who else would be hurrying toward the back stair? This particular maid, however, was unusually petite with raven hair. Or was his mind playing tricks on him?

He peeked out from the doorway. No maid he'd ever seen at Brantmoor looked quite so much like Charlotte Brantwood. Had she stolen a dress from the household staff?

No, the rag of a dress fit too well to be borrowed.

As he had on more than one occasion, Hugh marveled at how Charlotte's childish temper could be contained in a package so womanly for its small size. In the rare moments when she was not scowling at him, she was lovely to look upon.

As he watched, she disappeared down the back stair that led to the kitchen. Did she expect to sneak out of the manor without notice simply because she'd worn an old dress and exited through the kitchen? She may be small, but with her ebony hair and sapphire eyes, she was a striking woman and would be noticed anywhere, particularly in this house.

Once she was no longer in sight, Hugh cleared the distance to the steps in three long strides and followed her down the spiral staircase. He was careful to maintain a discreet distance.

He stopped before rounding the last curve of the staircase, keeping out of view. He listened, waiting to hear the commotion among the kitchen staff when a lady of the house walked into their midst—dressed as a ragamuffin.

"Well, here she is, ladies," barked a voice from the kitchen. It carried not even a hint of the scandalized shock Hugh had expected. "What is it today, my dear? Another dress fitting?"

Charlotte released a light, easy laugh.

A laugh?

"Nothing of the sort," she answered. "I've been given a reprieve and told I may do as I please."

The other woman clucked. "I doubt Her Grace meant to send you to the kitchens when she told you to do as you please."

"Of course she didn't." Charlotte's voice was...different. It lacked its usual bite. "She wouldn't approve of my coming here.." She laughed again. "Of course, I've not heard any complaints of the food either."

Laughter from several women trickled up to Hugh as he hid.

Unable to resist the temptation, Hugh bent forward to peek around the corner. He was stunned to find Lady Charlotte Brantwood, wrapped in an apron even more worn than her dress, wandering expertly around the kitchen gathering implements and ingredients in a large wooden bowl.

A stout woman with sleeves rolled up to her elbows walked over to Charlotte. "What's it to be today, Lottie?"

Lottie?

"What are you serving us?" Charlotte asked.

"It's squab for tonight."

"Hmmm." Her back to the staircase, Charlotte rested the large bowl on her hip as she considered the question. "Do you have mace and nutmeg?" she asked.

"Always."

"Could you get me a small glass of brandy?"

"I think we can manage that."

"Perfect. I'll make tavern biscuits—American biscuits. They're delicious. Fit for a king."

"Are they fit for a duke?" the cook asked.

"They were fit enough for him when he was a lowly clerk in Boston." The ladies shared another laugh.

Hugh receded into the shadow and out of view.

Of all the possibilities for mischief, his thoughts had never landed upon this one. How long had this been going on?

He slowly turned and began quietly climbing the steps.

Lottie?

He smiled to himself.

The stair tread creaked loudly under his step.

He stopped, waiting.

"You!"

Hugh turned just as Charlotte appeared at the base of the narrow staircase.

She crossed her arms and leveled him with an accusing glare. "What are you doing here?"

He'd been caught. He could do nothing else but grin. "I might ask the same of you, *Lottie*."

She gasped, then glared again. She charged up the stairs until she stood one step below him. "You've been spying on me."

Hugh could not deny it. "Guilty, I suppose. Though in my defense, the mischief I imagined you getting into was something altogether different."

"What did you think I would do? Steal away for a tryst in the stables? You've a rather low opinion of me, haven't you?"

In all honesty, the vision that assaulted Hugh at her mention of a tryst in the stables left him with a rather low opinion of *himself.*

He looked down into her defiant blue eyes and pout-pinched lips and was struck with a veritable chain of inappropriate thoughts.

He moved from the step above her to the step below and tried not to think of kissing the pout right off her lips. "What are you doing here, Charlotte?"

"If you've been spying, you already know."

"I can see that you are cooking, but why?"

Her chin jutted forward. "Because I like to cook and I'm good at it."

He lifted a brow at her boast.

"You've eaten plenty of my cooking and seemed to enjoy it." She put her fists at her hips and dared him to deny it.

As he had no idea which food she might have prepared, he couldn't very well say. "I gather you prepared meals in Boston?"

"Yes. There is nothing wrong with that."

Hugh shook his head. "Sheath your weapon, would you? I never said there was anything wrong about it. Why must you be so contrary all the time? I'd be more offended if you told me you sat around and tried to act like a lady while your mother and brother worked hard to support you."

"Well. Fine then."

"Fine."

Charlotte's eyes fell, then rose again with less defiance. "You're going to tell them, aren't you? What I've been doing."

"You don't want me to?"

She pulled her bottom lip between her teeth and trapped it there—held his gaze trapped there—before she answered. "I'd be grateful if you wouldn't. He'd put a stop to my coming if he knew. Or *she* would."

Her tone wasn't precisely submissive, but her request was delivered with more civility than he'd ever received from her before.

"You don't mean to stop cooking, do you?" he asked.

"No. I like it. I know what I'm doing."

That was the second time she'd told him not only that she liked working in the kitchen, but that she was skilled at it. Maybe the duchess was right. Perhaps Charlotte *had* been made to feel inferior.

Of course, if sneaking off to the kitchen was that important to her, and he held the power to prevent it in his hands...

He smiled wickedly.

Her eyes narrowed.

"I would like to help you, Lady Charlotte. Truly, I would. But you see, we boorish oafs are rather selfish. I look at our present predicament and wonder if there isn't something in it for me."

"Do you really intend to blackmail me over a bit of cooking, Mr. Brydges?"

"Oh, you really should start calling me Hugh, now that we're sharing secrets, don't you agree?"

When she didn't immediately agree, he waited.

"All right, *Hugh*," she ground out. Her eyes narrowed. "Are you trying to blackmail me over a batch of biscuits?"

He stepped up this time, filling the space next to where she stood and creating a tight fit in the narrow stairwell. "Put that way, it does seem rather trivial I suppose. I can't demand too high a price, but perhaps a small one."

"What is your price, Mr. Brydges—*Hugh*—since you lack the integrity to honor the request of a lady?" Her expression remained defiant, but she had lost a bit of her confidence. Uncertainty crept into her gaze.

Hugh leaned toward her until their bodies were nearly touching. "I believe I would like to see you atop my horse."

"I beg your pardon?"

He laughed. Her expression was so delightfully scandalized. "If I recall, Charlotte, you told me James Madison would swear fealty to the crown before you sat atop my horse. If you want me to keep your kitchen escapades a secret, you will agree to a riding lesson given by me—on the horse I delivered especially for you."

She leaned away from him, but the wall prevented her from gaining much distance. "But I'm on a reprieve. I'm to have no lessons. The duchess promised."

"The duchess won't give the lesson. I will."

She glared at him. "You swear if I agree to this lesson—one lesson—you will tell no one about this? Ever?"

"I swear."

She thought a moment, then nodded. "Agreed. One lesson. Now go away before someone comes looking for you and finds me. I have work to do." She turned and flounced down the steps.

"Charlotte?" He couldn't help calling her back.

She stopped and turned. "What is it?"

"You didn't by any chance make the pear tart with lemon custard that was served Saturday last, did you?"

"I did, actually," she said, watching him with a bemused expression.

"Do you suppose that could find its way onto the menu again some evening soon?"

Her smile was hesitant, then beaming.

"I imagine it could." She turned and was around the corner and gone.

Hugh stood arrested, watching the spot from which she'd smiled brilliantly up at him. It was the first time he'd been the recipient of such an expression from Charlotte Brantwood. She was a beautiful woman when her eyes flashed with the blue heat of anger, but when she smiled—that brilliant, artless smile—she was incomparable.

Chapter Thirty-One

Emma knocked and entered Lucy's room to find her, not reading as she'd predicted, but standing at the window, staring out. "You seem troubled, Lucy, and I must apologize for that," Emma said, walking to where her friend stood. "I was only thinking of my own comfort when I brought you into our uneasy situation here. I am very sorry."

Lucy turned from the window and took Emma's hand in hers. "How can you owe an apology for calling upon your dearest friend when you are in need, and how could I demand one, when I am glad to be the person you would call upon?"

Emma's lips turned up at the corners. She should have expected Lucy would find a way to make an apology seem not only superfluous but an offense if given.

"I am not troubled," Lucy continued, "but I have been thinking of the challenges facing your family. They are more than they should be, it seems, for just the few of you."

"Indeed." They were a family of but three.

Lucy sat on the high poster bed and patted the place next to her. "Why don't you sit? We can talk about these troubles, and even if we aren't able to solve them, perhaps we can make them feel a bit smaller for a time."

Emma welled up with gratitude at the simple comfort her friend offered. "That is why I so love you, Lucy. I had come to suggest a walk, but this is better. You always seem to know just what I need to hear. How do you manage to know every time?"

It was true. How many times as young girls had they draped themselves across either Emma or Lucy's bed while Lucy dispensed wisdom that belied her years to apply to the dilemma of the day.

"Why don't you begin," Lucy suggested.

"No, you. Go ahead, please."

Neither woman spoke.

Then both laughed.

Lucy pulled her legs up onto the bed. "When did we become so polite?"

Emma sat beside her. "We can't help it, I suppose." She faced her friend with a comically severe expression. "I *am* a duchess, you know."

"Good heavens, you are. You know I feel very guilty that I'm not intimidated by you. I've tried very hard to be."

Emma patted her friend's hand. "I'm sure you have and I am grateful for your efforts." She sighed. "Since you insist, I suppose I will begin. I wanted to talk to you about Charlotte and the scene we all caused in the drawing room yesterday and…well, just everything. You must believe they are all mad and I've gone mad right along with them."

Lucy's laugh was bright and natural. "Of course you haven't gone mad, any of you. You've all just been thrust into an impossible situation. Charlotte is young. Her mother has only been gone a short while and everything is different here. She will settle in, I'm sure of it." Lucy set her hand gently on Emma's arm. "And so will you. I know you never wanted to be a duchess, but you are. You will be a grand one, I know it."

Emma's look was dubious. "How would you know that?"

"Because you will snub all of society thus leaving them all vying for your favor. Nothing is so desirable as that which is withheld, wouldn't you agree?"

Emma laughed. "Lucy, my dear, you are very wise. I believe *you* would make an excellent duchess."

"Don't be silly. You are the perfect duchess."

Laugh as she might, Emma knew she was not the perfect duchess. She had so far made negligible progress in preparing Charlotte and had failed entirely in all ways but one of becoming a wife to her husband.

She was determined, however, not to fail in her friendship to Lucy. "We should speak of Mr. Brydges."

"What of Mr. Brydges?" Lucy asked. "He seems an incorrigible sort, but he and the duke are clearly very thick. They've been friends a long time, I presume?"

"Yes. I believe so," Emma answered, "but I am more concerned with the man's attention to you. Have you noticed, when he is critical of Charlotte, it is most commonly now as a comparison to you? He is always very complimentary and attentive to you, I have noticed. I simply thought to caution you, in case you might be developing a preference for him. I'm not certain I trust Mr. Brydges, entirely."

Lucy's laugh was light and unconcerned. "Emma, dear, Mr. Brydges is handsome, clever, and comfortably situated. He has, through his great skill and effort, built a successful horse farm. He also appears to be a rather loyal friend to your husband. Have you failed to notice the inaccuracy of your early opinion of him?"

"So you do prefer him?"

Lucy's smile in response held a secret. It sent warning bells pealing through Emma's brain.

"I would be fortunate to have the affection of Mr. Brydges, but I would not waste my time hoping for it. His interest is directed elsewhere."

"Elsewhere?"

"Must I take your hand and lead you to it? Mr. Brydges is completely taken with Charlotte."

"Charlotte? You can't be serious!"

"My dear, I am gravely serious."

"But he criticizes her mercilessly."

"One must be watching very closely to notice the detailed imperfections Mr. Brydges seems to notice in Charlotte, wouldn't you agree?" Lucy asked.

Impossible. They detested each other. Emma couldn't countenance what it would mean if they did not. Or at least if *he* did not. "Even if he did have some interest in Charlotte, it could not be serious," she observed. "Mr. Brydges does not seem the sort to have serious intentions toward anyone."

"Are you so certain? Mr. Brydges has no pressure to marry. He has no title to perpetuate or need for financial rescue. But that does not mean he will not marry for love, when he is struck by it."

Emma shook her head. "I don't believe it. I cannot believe it. I am sorry for doubting you when you are usually so wise, but there it is. I cannot believe Mr. Brydges is lovesick for Charlotte."

Lucy's eyes danced with laughter. "Wait and see, and we will know if I am correct."

"I suppose," Emma conceded.

Lucy shifted her legs underneath her and the laughter in her expression fell away. "And last to speak of is the duke."

There was too much knowing behind Lucy's concerned gaze. Emma's cheeks flamed. "There are no troubles with the duke," she demurred. "I asked him just this afternoon to pay more attention to Charlotte and he has promised he will."

"What of you?" Lucy asked. "When will he begin paying more attention to you?"

"I…well…I have not *asked* him to pay more attention to me. There is no need."

"You are not happy."

"I worry. I have much to do. Once things have calmed down with Charlotte, I will be content."

"Only content?"

Emma sighed. There really was no way to hide her feelings from Lucy. In truth, she wasn't sure she wanted to hide them.

"My marriage was built upon a bargain, not a romantic dream."

"Does it have to follow, then, that you cannot be happy in your marriage? Are there no marriages of convenience that become *more* than just convenient?"

"I cannot claim that I am *not* happy in my marriage. My husband is kind and honorable. I respect his desire to restore his sister to her rightful place. My resistance to marrying him was, in hindsight, obstinate and foolish," she admitted. "He is a good man."

"I believe the primary reason for your objection was the fact the matter had been decided for you," Lucy offered wisely. "But wisdom prevailed, didn't it?"

"Marriage to the duke was, as you say, a wise choice. I am fortuitously near to Beadwell, my husband is exceedingly kind, and I cannot in good conscience complain of the fact that nearly all of my conceivable desires are addressed with immediacy by a perfectly trained staff of a number I could not begin to count."

"But not *all* of your desires," Lucy suggested softly, her eyes searching.

Emma tried to ensure her responding smile was in no way self-pitying. Perhaps she even succeeded.

Lucy took Emma's hand in hers. "I knew there was more."

Perhaps she did not succeed after all.

She exhaled and met her friend's gaze directly. "The unfortunate truth, Lucy, is that I have made the grave mistake of falling in love with my husband."

Lucy released an incredulous laugh. "Was that so difficult to admit? I suspected as much," she insisted. "But why must that be a grave mistake? You have said yourself, he is kind and honorable."

"And honest. His reasons for marrying were made very clear. He has been a responsible and kind husband and duke. He is…attentive," she said, struggling for the word, "to his husbandly duties." The heat rose in Emma's cheeks. "But he has many responsibilities. We do not spend much time in each other's company. We are not a love match, nor will we become one."

"Are you so certain?" Lucy asked.

"I am a grown woman. I may not possess as much wisdom and practicality as you do, dear, but I have enough good sense not to be mooning around composing sonnets about unrequited love."

"What good would a sonnet do?" Lucy asked sharply. "If you want to see what can be made of your marriage, you don't hide in your room writing poetry. You seek out your husband and spend time in his company."

Emma laughed this time. "I cannot very well chase the duke around the estate all day, as though he is the fox in a hunt. He may, in fact, find that unsettling."

Lucy's expression remained one of concern. "I am in earnest, Emma. Affection cannot grow between you while you are apart. If he has not yet become thoroughly enchanted by the woman he has taken to wife, I am convinced it is due to a lack of time in your presence, not any lack in the woman herself."

"So speaks my most fiercely loyal friend."

"Dismiss if you will, but I am unwavering in this belief. What harm can it cause to test my hypothesis?"

"Perhaps." Emma's response was intentionally noncommittal. She was tempted to follow Lucy's advice. But *why* was she tempted? Did it appeal to her for its practicality, or because, out of weakness, she was grasping at a seemingly rational excuse to chase down her husband and claim some of his time and attention for herself?

Lucy knew her too well. "Do not deny I am correct, Emma. The consequences of *not* testing my theory may be greater. In the end, inaction constitutes acceptance."

Emma considered this. Was she ready to accept? She had accepted these circumstances when she agreed to marry John, but her feelings and wishes had changed. She was *not* ready. She did want more. "Very well, Lucy," she said with a decisive nod. "I shall test your theory. I shall endeavor to seek out my husband's company and see what may come of it."

* * *

Dressed for dinner, Emma walked into the drawing room, pleased to discover only her husband. He stood on the far side of the room, gazing out the window at the estate cast in the last light of evening. She wondered if she saw it at all. His gaze appeared unfocused, as though he was more attentive to his thoughts than the picture before him.

He was dressed for dinner as well, his tall, broad-shouldered frame trimmed in perfectly tailored clothes. He looked entirely ducal from head to toe—from the rich cloth of his jacket to the perfectly clipped dark locks at the nape of his neck to his unyielding posture. She liked how he looked just then—dignified, authoritative, regal almost.

Her teeth tugged at her lower lip as she recalled she also very much liked the way he looked with mussed hair and a wolfish grin. She was, sadly, thoroughly enamored with her husband. Emma had come to terms with her sister-in-law this week. She was not ready to come to terms with her husband—not these terms anyway. She *was* going to follow Lucy's advice, and though she had no skill, or even an inkling of how to begin, she was going to seek to capture her husband's attention.

She released a quiet sigh.

The slight sound prompted him to turn.

"Emma." The smile she received allowed her to believe he was genuinely happy to see her. He crossed the room in a few long strides and took her hands. "You are a vision this evening. I do not recognize this dress."

"It's new," she confirmed, girlishly pleased that he should notice. She had ordered several new dresses along with those for Charlotte. This dress was her favorite among them. Her conversation with Lucy had inspired her to take extra care with her appearance that evening.

"A lovely color," he added. "Brighter than I've seen you wear, but you are beautiful in it."

The dress had been a bold choice for her. She possessed rust-colored dresses that were nearer to brown and felt they were a fair complement to her coloring. This dress, however, could not bear a name so drab as rust. It was the red-orange of flame, with not a hint of brown to mute the tone.

"I'm pleased you like it," she told her husband. "I was just thinking as I saw you what a dashing picture you make yourself this evening."

He grinned. "Pity that we are such a handsome couple but have only Brydges, Charlotte, and Miss Betancourt to see us. I fear they have known us too long and too well to be impressed with our finery."

Emma barely recognized the sparkling laughter as her own. If only this could always be the way between them. She smiled up at her husband with open affection, being for once completely unguarded.

Her efforts were rewarded as he gazed back at her with equal warmth. His hand still held hers and he squeezed it, tugging her gently toward him. The heat in his blue eyes intensified and held hers.

She stood, arrested by her own desire for him, until he lowered his mouth to slowly brush his lips against hers. The kiss was not long, his touch barely a whisper, yet she shivered.

At the sound of voices in the hall, he stepped back a respectable distance, but continued to hold her gaze with a look that promised of a moment delayed rather than a moment ended.

"Good evening, Lucy, Mr. Brydges." She turned and greeted their guests with a bit more exuberance than intended.

"Good evening to you," Lucy responded with an amused grin and an elevated brow. "You are looking especially lovely."

"Why thank you. As are you."

"That color is striking," Mr. Brydges observed, in a rare compliment to Emma.

"Thank you." She nodded graciously. She was not of a mood in that moment to be annoyed with any of their party.

She was not even annoyed with Charlotte, who arrived considerably later than the rest of them, leaving the group to wait before dinner.

Once they were seated for the evening meal, the conversation began easily enough. John remarked upon the cooling weather and Mr. Brydges insisted he preferred the brisk temperatures for riding. Emma concurred with his sentiment.

They were well into the meal before John turned to his sister and commented, "I understand you've been granted a furlough from lessons, Charlotte. I hope you'll find something to occupy your time."

Charlotte's smile was cryptic. "I am looking forward to some rest and time to myself."

John set his utensils aside and regarded her more intently. "For my part, I apologize if we have asked too much of you too quickly. I want you to be comfortable here. This is your home, Charlotte."

Charlotte seemed taken aback by her brother's forthright manner, but Emma was glad for it. It was well past time for John to pay his sister some well-needed attention.

"I...I know this is my home now." Charlotte glanced around the table. "I am becoming accustomed to things here."

Whether or not Charlotte was becoming accustomed to life at Brantmoor, she certainly seemed more subdued, to Emma's great relief.

"Are these tavern biscuits?" John asked. He broke one open and tasted it. "They are. Charlotte, did you give Cook your recipe for my favorite biscuits?"

Charlotte's face reddened and she glanced around the room before answering. "I, um, yes. I told Cook they were your favorite."

John turned to Emma. "Charlotte used to make these for me in Boston."

Emma smiled, keenly aware that Charlotte must be anxious to know their reactions. It was exactly the kind of thing for which Charlotte would be judged by others, but Emma saw nothing shameful. "I did not realize you were so skilled in the kitchen, Charlotte. You must have been a great help to your mother."

"They are delicious." Lucy announced it to the table at large.

"I do believe she makes them nearly as well as you do, Charlotte," John declared.

Charlotte smiled and glanced at...

Mr. Brydges?

Emma watched in surprise as the two shared an unspoken exchange before Mr. Brydges broke the contact and reached for another biscuit.

"My first was a bit dry, actually. I think I'll have to try another."

"They aren't at all dry," Charlotte insisted. "I believe Cook has outdone herself."

Had Lucy witnessed this? Emma turned to her friend.

Judging by Lucy's triumphant expression, she had indeed.

Could Lucy be correct? It still seemed so unlikely. Conversation at the table moved from an evaluation of the biscuits to discussion of the other food, and the general consensus was reached that Brantmoor's cook was without equal. Emma, however, was still pondering the possibility that Mr. Brydges may have developed an interest in Charlotte.

It was her concern, after all, given that Charlotte's debut season and chaperonage were really in her hands.

Chapter Thirty-Two

Undressed for the night and exhausted from the day's activities, John dismissed his valet but did not climb into his bed. He stared at it instead. He had begun to hate the thing. It was a luxuriously large and soft chamber of tortures. It was the cold, empty scene of sleepless nights and unsatisfied lust. His wife's similarly soft, significantly more interesting bed was just steps away. Besides, he reasoned, enjoying the benefits of his marital status was not only a right but a duty for a duke such as himself. How did one go about producing heirs if one did not bed one's wife?

It was a lot of bollocks, that. John didn't give a damn about an heir at that moment. He wasn't even with Emma and he was already fully aroused. Denying himself had been a wasted effort. He certainly hadn't prevented distraction. He was more randy now than he could ever remember being in his damned life. And at every ridiculously inappropriate moment. She'd been delectable in that red dress, and he'd been dangerously close to taking her right there in the drawing room where anyone could have seen them.

That was it. He swung a dressing gown over his shoulders and charged toward the door that led to his wife's chamber.

Emma was not alone. She was still in her own dressing room, on the far side of the chamber, seated at her dressing table. Her long hair was unbound and her maid stood behind her, brushing through the chestnut tresses with long, steady strokes.

Though her back was to him, Emma met his eyes in the mirror as he approached and smiled warmly. He smiled languorously back at her reflection and, taking the brush from the maid's hands, sent the girl from the room.

John continued the task himself, pulling the brush through the full length of his wife's thick fall of hair. He followed the brush with the palm of his hand, smoothing the silken locks after each stroke. He watched Emma's face in the mirror as he continued, watched her eyelids flutter closed and her head fall farther back in surrender to his ministrations. Her lips parted with a faint sigh, and he felt the stab of lust as sharply as though her hot hands had closed around him.

He wanted her hands there...wanted to put his hands on her, but he continued brushing and smoothing her hair with long, deliberate motions. He had no need to rush. He intended to do the opposite, in fact. He had plans to slowly revisit all the places on his wife's body that warranted attention, and he could think of several. As he inventoried them in his mind, he watched the rhythm of her breathing change, her chest rising and falling as though his every thought had been whispered aloud to her and heightened her arousal.

When his need to touch her became too great, he gently lay the brush on the table and brought both hands to her shoulders, kneading with his thumb along her neck and driving his fingers into her mass of hair.

She released a ragged sigh and leaned back against him in full surrender. He reached forward with one hand and untied the tidy bow at the neckline of her nightgown. The collar thus freed, he pushed the garment down, baring her shoulders, and moved his massage outward. He kneaded her shoulders and upper arms, pushing the gown lower as he went until it was barely draped across the upturned, tightened peaks of her breasts.

Unable to resist any longer, he slid his hands forward to cup both, while leaning in to trace his lips across her collarbone and along her neck. He kneaded and teased and watched in the mirror as her lips parted farther and her breath became more labored. When she opened her eyes, he was gratified to see the cloud of desire that reflected back at him.

Their eyes held for a moment while he touched her then she rose and turned to face him. As she did, he pushed the thin nightgown all the way to her waist, leaving her top bare. She reached for the tie to his dressing gown, pulled it undone, and slid her hands inside, pressing herself against him so her bare breasts teased his chest. He could feel her heat against his arousal, despite the thin fabric barrier that remained.

She lifted her face to his and he captured her mouth. He probed with his tongue while she clung to him and slid his hand down her backside until the nightgown finally fell away, then he cupped her buttocks and pressed her tightly against his arousal, this time flesh to flesh.

She groaned. At least he thought it was her. He couldn't be certain, because it was so good, this hot desire that rippled between them as his hands slid and grabbed with a will of their own, and his mouth plundered hers with bruising kisses. With one arm around her back, he slid his other hand between them to tease her sex. He slid one finger inside her and felt her quiver, felt her lean more heavily on his supporting arm. Eyes closed, her head lolled backward, lips open, and John thought nothing could be more arousing than watching his wife surrender to the ecstasy of his touch.

Then she lifted her head, opened her eyes, and locked her gaze on his just as her warm hand reached forward and closed around his erection, forcing John to amend his prior judgment.

No longer able to trust himself on his own two feet, John interrupted their exploration to lead his wife to her bed and lay her sideways across it. With complete lack of inhibition, she opened herself to him. He could bury himself inside her right then, but no. He had given in to his baser need, thrown all his fears and better judgment away. He was going to take his time and make every moment of this worth the wait and the self-sacrifice he had forced them both to endure.

Hovering over her, he trailed a single finger upward along the pale satin skin of her inner thigh, brushing ever so lightly past the apex between her legs and watching her tense and quiver as he approached. Then he trailed the finger just as slowly down the other side. Cupping her mound with one hand, he bent his head and traced his lips along the line his finger had drawn. When he had finished teasing her with both his hands and his lips, he used his fingers to spread her folds and lowered his mouth to kiss her.

She lifted her head. "John…I don't…is that…"

"Shhh." He reassuringly massaged the inside of one creamy thigh. "Trust me." He bent his head again and licked her, eliciting a shiver that seemed to course through them both. She was beautiful and she was his and he was going to savor every last part of her. He'd been wanting to do just this for so damned long. "Trust me," he repeated, then set himself to the task of making love to her with his lips and his tongue.

She tensed at first, then relaxed, clutching the bed linens at her side as he brought her to the brink this way she'd never experienced. Then he slid a finger inside her and she strained against him—against his mouth.

"Holy God." She barely whispered it.

He felt her muscles contract around his finger, felt her body succumb to climax. He kissed her through it. He placed a soft, slow kiss on her inside of her thigh as she fell from the precipice.

"John," she said hesitantly, "I didn't know…"

"Now you know," he said, rising to sit back on his heels. "I should have shown you sooner."

She looked at him through passion-clouded eyes. "But you haven't..." He eyes dipped meaningfully.

"Not yet."

"But we can still..."

He smiled wickedly at her. "Most definitely."

She eyed his nakedness with unabashed curiosity. "Could I... do that...to you?"

Her hesitantly eager question was nearly his undoing. Bloody hell, he wasn't sure if he could survive it if she did. He knew for certain he didn't have the strength of will to decline the offer. He nodded gruffly. "Are you sure?"

She nodded and rose to her knees, directing him to lie down in her place. She hovered over him, unsure and timid, strands of chestnut silk draping over his midsection. He could not have imagined there was a more alluring seductress in all the world. She licked her lips, then lowered her head. She kissed the tip of him first and he groaned. Then she tasted him and he shivered. She closed her hand and then her mouth over him, and his hips rose off the bed of their own accord. He only survived a few moments of the delicious torture before he lifted her from him and reversed their positions, tucking her underneath him and burying himself deep inside her. He groaned aloud and thrust with an urgency that had been building for what seemed a lifetime. She met each one, shuddering and calling his name just a moment before he clutched her tightly and met his release with one final thrust.

Some while later, as Emma lay peacefully tucked against his side because he was, frankly, still too weak to consider returning to his own bed, John realized neither one of them had spoken since their lovemaking had ended. There'd been no need. This night had been unlike anything he'd ever experienced, even in his previous nights with Emma, and he knew it had been because of her...because she'd met his passion with a need that was just as great.

He'd always thought of sex as good—sometimes very good—but essentially as a physical release, the satisfaction of a need. This night had been more than that. It had been an elevating experience. It was unexpected. She was unexpected. So much more than willing and interested, she'd been...combustible.

She lay peacefully alongside him, and he suspected she was already asleep, understandably spent. He would be asleep soon too, and needed to remove himself to his own chamber, but he didn't move yet. He considered his wife. Had she spent the day, as he had, anticipating their coupling? Did ladies do that as men did? He thought of Emma at the breakfast table, or discussing the week's menu with Mrs. Dewhurst, all the while assailed with visions of what they'd just done, and quite liked the idea. He would endeavor to remind her at some point tomorrow, just to see what sort of blushes he could inspire.

He lay back. He wasn't going anywhere. She was warm. He was comfortable. There need be no greater significance than that. He was finished with pointless self-denial. He could not lose his soul or his sanity to this woman, but neither would he allow his father's legacy to rob him of the basic joys of his marriage.

Chapter Thirty-Three

Mr. Brydges—Hugh, as he'd instructed her to call him—had kept his promise. Despite teasing her a little during dinner, he hadn't revealed Charlotte's activities to anyone in the family. Thus Charlotte was honor bound to keep her own promise as well, and the following afternoon, found herself in her riding habit for a second time in one week, walking to the stables for a riding lesson. This time, accompanied by Mr. Brydges.

She could smell the stable before they reached it. It smelled of dirty horses and sweaty leather. She was frightened. She'd made virtually no progress in her first lesson with Emma, a circumstance which was, admittedly, her own fault. She was deathly afraid of the ridiculously large animals. Whoever first saw a horse and thought to himself, *I must climb atop that animal*, she had no earthly idea. She'd done it, though, in her first lesson...climbed atop the horse. That had been about the extent of it, thankfully. She had been so frozen with fear just mounting the horse that the duchess hadn't pushed for more. She had simply used a tether to lead the horse around the stable yard while Charlotte sat in the saddle, willing herself not to fall.

As a kindness, the duchess had sent the stable hands away, and led the horse around the yard herself, so others would not bear witness to Charlotte's very severe fright and embarrassment. It would be revealed for certain this afternoon, however.

"You are very quiet," Mr. Brydges observed. "Are you very nervous?" He appeared to ask the question out of genuine concern. Still, she disliked him knowing that she found this a considerable challenge when most everyone else in this country seemed to have no hesitation in hopping onto the backs of oversized animals within months of their birth.

"I shall be fine, Mr. Brydges. You have kept your promise and I shall keep mine."

Charlotte did not look to take in his expression, but she could feel him looking down at her as they walked. She stiffened her shoulders and willed herself to be brave in front of him.

When they reached the stable, they were met by one of the stable hands, an earnest looking boy with unkempt hair who looked younger than Charlotte and probably rode better than she ever would.

"She's all ready for you, Mr. Brydges," the boy said, indicating a large horse of dappled gray who snorted and shook its mane at the two of them.

Where was the docile horse she had ridden with Emma? This horse was larger and seemed...unruly.

Mr. Brydges walked directly to the horse and stroked his hand down its mane. "Why don't you come here and meet Comtessa, Charlotte? She is a magnificent animal."

Charlotte took one step forward but made no farther motion toward the beast. It was lowering to reveal the extent of her fear to anyone, but here was a man who made his living from horses—spent all day with them. He would think her an absolute ninny if he understood how violently she quaked inside.

"I..." She failed to concoct a reasonable excuse for cancellation of their plans. "What about the horse I rode the other day?" She turned to the stable hand. "The...smaller one."

"Mr. Brydges hand selected this mount especially for you, my lady." The stable hand was beaming. "She just arrived three days ago."

Three days ago? She'd only agreed to the riding lesson yesterday. She looked up accusingly.

"I see," she answered. She looked uncertainly at the horse.

"Thank you for your help," Mr. Brydges said to the stable hand. "I think I can help Lady Charlotte from here."

The stable boy nodded and disappeared inside the stable, leaving them alone.

"Why don't you come closer and get to know Comtessa first?" Mr. Brydges suggested. He walked to Charlotte and, tucking her arm into his, walked her slowly toward the horse.

By the time they reached the animal, Charlotte was certain she was shaking strongly enough for Mr. Brydges to feel. They stood closely enough to the horse that Charlotte could feel its warmth.

"Come now," Mr. Brydges whispered as his head bent toward hers. "I thought you already had a lesson with the duchess."

Charlotte shot him what she hoped was a baleful glance, but feared it was more likely a pitiful plea for rescue.

His brows knitted together in concern. "Let's start slowly," he said, with an unusual softness in his voice. His hand slid down her arm until he held her hand in his. He gently removed her glove then pulled her bare hand forward to lay her trembling fingers onto the soft hide of the horse. It was warm and tight. The horse blew, but remained still.

"Comtessa," Charlotte said, as though by saying the name she might know the animal better.

Mr. Brydges pushed in closer behind her and she stiffened. She swallowed.

"You have nothing to be afraid of," he whispered, laying his gloved hand fully over her bare one.

She felt she rather did, though she was no longer sure the threat originated with the animal in front of her. "I'm not afraid," she whispered, lying on both counts. She turned her head to the side and would have tried her best to look defiant, but the gentleness of his expression halted her. Something about him felt safe in a way that prompted her to admit softly, "I am terrified."

He smiled crookedly at her and whispered, "I have never encountered another person with more pluck than you, my dear. You can ride this horse. We shall go slowly."

"What if I fall?" she asked, turning back to the animal in front of her.

"You won't fall," he said.

Charlotte looked up at the saddle, the seat of which was higher than the top of her head. "How will you prevent it?" she asked.

"We could have the sidesaddle changed. You could ride with me."

She pivoted to face him. She didn't want to ride that animal by herself, but she didn't want to ride with him holding her either.

"It wouldn't be much use in teaching you to ride on your own," he said, his voice soft and cajoling, "but if it would help you to relax your fear, it's a good start."

She looked up at him. She swallowed. Why was he looking at her that way—as though he could devour her like a treat? She couldn't think when he did that.

He stepped forward.

She stepped backward...into the solid bulk of the horse. It shied and blew. She was trapped between him and the horse. Tears stung in her eyes and she blinked, hating that they were there.

His hand closed around her upper arm. "Shh," he said softly. "Calm down."

His head bent toward hers. She froze. She couldn't shriek and push him away without being trampled by the horse. Contrary to every instinct, she accepted his kiss without resistance. She stood, still as a stone, until it was over.

He lifted his head as quickly as he had lowered it, and she stared up at him, wanting to ask why, waiting for the smug arrogance to settle into his features.

Only it wasn't there. He looked...confused.

He closed his eyes and exhaled. When he opened them again, he said, "My apologies. That was...wrong of me."

"I—I think we should be finished with the lesson for today," she said.

"Perhaps so." Mr. Brydges stepped back. "You should return to the house. I will see to the horse."

* * *

By the time Charlotte had nearly reached the house, she decided she should forget everything that had happened in her very brief riding lesson. She could not make sense of Mr. Brydges. It didn't seem as though he was teasing her again, but surely he wouldn't be attracted to her. Was he trying to comfort her? Was it pity? She hated that thought. Pity was *worse* than teasing.

"Hello, Lottie."

Charlotte froze. Feline alertness suffused her. She recognized the voice. She hated that voice.

Slowly, she pivoted on her heal. "Mr. Pritchard. You are a long way from home."

"I could say the same for you." He looked unkempt, with a days-grown beard and rumpled clothes. She suspected he might be intoxicated, as in her experience, he often was.

She gave a silent, unladylike curse. Where was the man her brother had sent to keep Mr. Pritchard away? She hastily looked around. When she had confirmed no one had seen them, she grabbed the man by his sleeve and dragged him into the relative privacy of one of the arched stone alcoves on the manor's ground level.

She glared at him and crossed her arms in front of her chest. "This *is* my home. And you are not welcome in it."

"Yes it is, isn't it?" he drawled, choosing to ignore the latter portion of her statement. He stepped in for a closer inspection. "Look at you now, Lottie, in such fine clothing and such grand circumstances. You won't be grand for long, I don't think."

She stiffened. She didn't answer to his family anymore. She didn't have to listen to him. "Why have you come, Mr. Pritchard? What do you want?"

"I've come for you," he told her with a head cocked to one side and a smirk that threatened to release alcohol-laden breath. .

"What could you possibly want from me?" she asked, though she already knew the answer

"Why, marriage of course." He swayed slightly but righted himself, grinning all the while.

"No."

"You will marry me. You may look dressed up and dignified now, but who will want you when they know you were nothing but my kitchen maid?"

"I was never *your* maid. I was employed by your father and mother. They, at least, are good, decent people."

"Good people or no, you were a common laborer." He leaned against the arch, posing as the lord of the manor. His grin widened. "There was even some suspicion you may have engaged in an inappropriate relationship with the young man of the house."

"That's a lie and if you try anything again, you'll feel the blade of a knife just the same as before."

"Threaten all you want, Lottie, but you'll be a laughingstock." He shook his head in mock consternation. "Think of the shame you'll bring on your family. Wouldn't it be so much better to have your brother introduce you as the sister who went abroad and married the son of a respectable Boston family?"

"You have never been respectable no matter who your family is," she spat.

His expression quickly transitioned from a taunting smirk to one of grave warning. "I'm sure the duke and duchess will see the merits of this solution if you do not. I've spoken to your brother already." The smirk returned. "I think he's warming to the idea. I'm sure he and his new wife will want to avoid a scandal at all costs."

She glared at him. "They would never let me marry you. You will leave England, or they will chase you out." Even as she vowed it to him, a fist seemed to clench around her insides. Everyone was so fixated on her reputation and acceptance into high society.

He pushed himself forward. No longer supported by the solid stones of the archway, he stumbled, gained his footing, then smiled up at her. "Don't be so certain, my pet. Besides," he said, lifting a hand to touch her, "I think you and I could get on very well together."

She slapped his hand away. "Don't you touch me."

His look became foul. Violence threatened in his eyes and she wished for a knife, riding crop, anything she could use to fend him off without shouting and bringing the entire household out to witness her shame. She was mentally assessing whether his drunkenness would be more harm or help, when a shadow dimmed the alcove.

"I would apologize for interrupting," Mr. Brydges said aridly, "but I'm not at all sorry."

Shame chased quickly behind the relief that had coursed through Charlotte upon hearing his voice. Unsure what he had assumed, but unwilling to stammer explanations, Charlotte looked up at him, but he did not see her. His eyes were daggers that should have flayed Mr. Pritchard where he stood.

Mr. Pritchard was too drunk or too foolhardy to be cowed by the presence of a man who was angry, sober, and substantially larger than he was. He leered toward Charlotte. "We'll have to finish our talk later, sweetheart."

At the word "sweetheart," Mr. Pritchard was summarily yanked from the alcove by Mr. Brydges. He yelped as his backside landed hard on the crushed stone.

Charlotte had no time to take pleasure in his indignity, as she was pulled from the alcove next. She was not allowed to fall, however, as Mr. Brydges large hand remained firmly closed around her arm.

"I will be accompanying the lady to the house. I will send men to search for you. If you have enough sense to run now, you may escape their worst." He walked away, dragging Charlotte with him, before Mr. Pritchard could even respond.

As they rounded the corner, Charlotte glared back over her shoulder for good measure, but Mr. Pritchard did not see her. He was occupied levering himself up from the ground and inspecting the scrapes on the palms of this hands.

Struggling to keep up with Mr. Brydges's purposeful strides, Charlotte hurried along beside him. "How much of that did you hear?" she asked.

"Enough to know you were reckless for even speaking with him. You should have run to the house the moment he appeared."

"Will you tell anyone?" she asked.

He stopped abruptly and spun her. She nearly pitched forward into him from the force of it. "You will tell them. I will not be staying for conversation." He glanced toward the corner around which they had just come. "Part of me hopes he has taken his time."

He began walking again, still dragging Charlotte with him. He didn't release her until they had reached the main entryway.

She stopped on the threshold and looked back at him as he stood, like a guard, waiting to see her safely inside. "Thank you," she said softly.

He nodded and she hurried inside.

Chapter Thirty-Four

Emma and Lucy were sitting in the drawing room, finishing a tea tray, when Charlotte walked in, flushed, out of breath, and still in her riding habit.

"Charlotte! Did you...were you...riding?" Emma asked.

"I...um...visited a horse," Charlotte said. She looked down and picked something from her sleeve, though Emma could not see that anything had been there.

Emma glanced at Lucy and saw her own confusion reflected in her friend's expression.

"I see." In fact, Emma did not see at all. *Visited a horse*? The answer was odd, to say the least. Though the girl did have a riding habit on, and Emma knew she could not possibly have gone riding, so...perhaps a visit *was* what had occurred.

"I have an urgent matter to discuss. Privately," she added, with a glance at Lucy.

Emma and Lucy exchanged curious looks.

Lucy rose and smoothed the front of her dress. "I was just commenting that I should see to packing my things. I've had a lovely visit, but I will be returning to Beadwell in the morning."

Emma and Charlotte waited in expectant silence for Lucy to retire from the room, then Emma turned to a flushed and anxious Charlotte. "Sit down, dear. What is your urgent matter? If something is troubling you, I'm certain we can address it."

Charlotte did not sit. She remained standing, wringing her hands, in the center of the room. "Why did you marry my brother?" she blurted.

Emma stilled. "That is your urgent matter?"

"No. Well—sort of." Charlotte paced. "It's not really, but I'd like to know the answer before we continue."

Emma watched Charlotte continue to pace and fidget. What on earth had prompted her question? "Charlotte, why don't you sit?"

Charlotte did as Emma asked, looking up at her with wide, expectant eyes.

Emma swallowed. "I will tell you," Emma began, "that your question is rather impertinent and I would be entirely justified in refusing to answer it."

Annoyance flashed through Charlotte's deep blue eyes. John's eyes. They were an uncanny match.

"I will answer you the best I am able, though. Our lives have been thrust together, so we may as well know each other better."

Charlotte nodded, thus signaling the point in the conversation in which Emma should supply the promised answer. She tapped her fingers on the upholstered arm of the sofa. "Yes. Well, then," she said. *The answer. Yes. Hmmm.* She sighed. "I suppose I agreed to marry your brother because it was the sensible thing to do. Women must be practical. Marrying your brother provided me with security for my future and, besides, he needed my help."

"For me."

"For you, yes."

Charlotte considered this response, which Emma sensed did not resolve whatever burning question the girl desired to have answered. "In my experience," Charlotte said, after a lengthy pause, "whenever anyone says they chose something because it was sensible, usually that means there was another, less sensible choice they would have preferred. Did you want to marry someone else?" She asked the question very plainly, her expression void of accusation.

Emma coughed. She smiled. "No. I was not hoping to marry someone other than your brother, but your judgment is correct. I had hoped to do something less sensible. I had hoped to not marry at all. I had thought I could happily live out my days as an old maid in my tiny cottage in Beadwell, tending my mother's garden."

"You would have chosen to be an old maid in a cottage over becoming a duchess?" Charlotte asked, disbelief heavy in her watchful expression.

Emma laughed. "Yes. Impractical through it was, I hadn't any particular aspiration to be a duchess. I just happened to be engaged to a duke."

Charlotte nodded thoughtfully.

This last revelation seemed to hold the answer Charlotte sought. She nodded, puzzled a moment, then nodded again. "I need your help," she said finally.

"What is the matter?" Emma asked. Alarm coursed through her.

"I'm not a lady. I'm a kitchen girl." Charlotte blurted the words in a loud rush.

Emma's alarm dissipated. She patted Charlotte's hand. "Of course you are a lady, Charlotte. You are a lady by birth. What do you mean by kitchen girl?"

"I mean I had to take a position—in the kitchen—for a family in Boston named Pritchard. I was their kitchen girl. I had to do something when my mother fell ill. I worked for them and they were nice people, but their son was horrid, and he's followed me here and is demanding I marry him or he'll tell everyone." The words spilled out of Charlotte in a frantic rush. Her color rose as she spoke and her gestures became more animated.

"Stop." Emma held up a staying hand. "This horrid son, you say he followed you? He has traveled from Boston to England?"

Charlotte nodded. "Yes."

"Now. Explain again, perhaps more slowly this time, the part about him wanting to marry you."

Charlotte blew out an anxious breath. "He is here. He was just here—at Brantmoor. He says he'll tell everyone I am nothing but a kitchen girl and I will be an outcast. But if I agree to marry him, you can present me as the sister who married the son of a respectable Boston family and there will be no scandal at all."

"Where is he now?" Emma asked, glancing involuntarily at the window.

"Mr. Brydges is chasing him off."

"Good." Emma nodded then and clutched Charlotte's hands in hers. "Charlotte, dear, you listen to me. You won't be marrying anyone who believes he can force you with threats. That I assure you."

"But I *was* a kitchen maid," Charlotte insisted. "It's not a story. It's the truth." She delivered it as a dare and waited for Emma's response.

"And your brother was a clerk. Anyone who is shallow enough to be offended by either fact is not worthy of our concern." Of course, it would have been beneficial to know of Charlotte's employment beforehand. She was certain John had not mentioned it. She would not have forgotten.

"You are not offended that I was a kitchen maid?" Charlotte asked.

"Certainly not. That's a ridiculous suggestion." Hadn't she been the one to lecture Charlotte about earning respect through one's conduct, not through one's birth? "My concern is not for your past employment, Charlotte, but for your present safety. You say this man followed you to Brantmoor. If he is persistent enough to travel to England and threaten blackmail, then he is persistent enough to cause you harm."

"You are not worried about the scandal?" Charlotte asked again.

"Only if it is hurtful to you, Charlotte. There will be gossip regardless and we shall overcome it."

"But you and my brother are so intent on my becoming a lady," she said.

Emma shook her head. "Oh, Charlotte, we only want to prepare you—to help you know what to expect for your own benefit. Your brother's desire was to spare you the hurt that rejection and gossip would cause. I'm afraid he would see it as a failure on his part, Charlotte, if you were not accepted. He feels compelled to atone for your father's sins. He must restore to you every advantage, every connection, every opportunity of which you've been deprived." She looked at the uneasy young girl who sat across from her and wanted so much to take away her anxiety. "He loves you, Charlotte. He seeks your happiness and security above all else." Emma had no doubt of it. In truth, she loved him for it.

She loved him.

She loved his tortured, well-meaning soul. And by extension, she loved Charlotte as well. She squeezed Charlotte's hand again. "That is why we must go to your brother, Charlotte. This man could be dangerous. Your brother will know how to protect you." He would. Emma had complete faith that John would spring into immediate action once he knew of this new threat.

"But he already had his man following Mr. Pritchard," Charlotte said. "And Mr. Pritchard must have gotten away from him,."

Emma let go of Charlotte's hands and pressed fingers to her temples in an attempt to sort in her mind this jumble of new information. "Your brother had a man following Mr. Pritchard?"

"Yes," Charlotte said, her voice rising, "but not a very competent man, it seems."

"Your brother knows this man is in England?"

"Yes. John is the one who told me. He said he would have him followed and not let him near us, but then he was outside today making his threats again. I had to know for sure that you would not make me marry him." She took Emma's hand this time. "I believe you. I believe you will not make me marry him."

Emma gulped. Anger and heartbreak roared through her. "How long has your brother known about Mr. Pritchard?"

"Since the day you went to your cottage. Before Miss Betancourt came to visit. Please don't be angry with him. I asked him not to tell you about Mr. Pritchard because I didn't want you to know I was a maid. I was worried about what you would think of me."

A heavy lump sat in Emma's stomach and seemed to grow there, becoming heavier and more difficult to ignore. "Fear not, Charlotte," she said, struggling to project the confidence the girl needed. "You were right to come to me. I will talk with your brother."

Chapter Thirty-Five

Emma sat quietly as Liese brushed and plaited her hair that evening. Emma had always performed the task for herself, but Liese seemed disappointed when Emma sent her way, so she'd begun allowing the girl to do it as part of her nightly routine. She had even begun to enjoy the pampering, but she was too distracted to enjoy it this night.

She gazed at her reflection in the mirror. She was not a great beauty, but she was not without handsome attributes. Her hair was only brown—not richly dark, like Charlotte's, or angelic blonde, like Lucy's, but it was thick and soft and fell in nice waves when Liese brushed it out and left it loose, as she sometimes did. Her eyes were also simple brown, but her nose and ears were delicately sized. She was not a person who had ever been particularly preoccupied with her outward appearance—until now. She sighed.

"Are you tired, Your Grace?"

"I suppose I am, Liese."

"Well, you've been very busy, if you don't mind my saying so. Maybe you would be more rested if you weren't such an early riser in the mornings. I don't mean to be presumptuous, Your Grace, but a little more rest might serve you well."

"Thank you for your suggestion, Liese, and for your concern."

She looked at her reflection again. "Perhaps you are right, Liese," she said with a wistful smile. "I will try to get some extra rest tomorrow. If you can bring me a breakfast tray in the morning, I will linger a little longer in my bed."

"Of course, Your Grace." Liese preened at such attention being paid to her advice. The girl tidied a few last things and bade Emma a quick, "Goodnight, Your Grace," as she ducked out of the room.

With impossibly perfect timing, the rap on the adjoining door sounded just as the door to the hall closed. John's knock was more a notice than a request, as he did not wait for a response before opening the door and entering. His dressing gown was knotted loosely at his waist, allowing for a gap that displayed a wide expanse of lightly furred chest. He smiled knowingly at her. "Good evening, sweet Emma."

She tried to smile encouragingly, but her efforts were weak, for his smile faltered just a bit in response. Once they had their necessary conversation, his mood of happy anticipation would be dashed entirely.

He walked to where she still sat at her dressing table. He placed his hands on her shoulders, kneading there, then sliding up to soothe the tightness in her neck. She very nearly sighed and leaned into his ministrations.

"I'm sorry for my absence at dinner this evening," he said. "I was visiting the western farms with Mr. Marshall."

"That's fine," Emma said. "We had an eventful afternoon and took trays in our rooms this evening."

"Has there been more difficulty with Charlotte?"

Has there been more difficulty with Charlotte? She might ask the question of him. What else did she not know of her little protégé? She leaned away from his touch and stood. "There has been a development with Charlotte, but it seems I am the last to know." She had tried to keep the bitterness from her tone, but he recoiled as though bitten. He eyed her warily, but did not attempt to guess her meaning. She saw no purpose in guessing games anyway. "Charlotte came to me today because she received a threat, in person, from a Mr. Pritchard. I understand this is not his first visit to Brantmoor."

John's eyes flew to hers. "Here? Today? Why didn't she come to me? How was he able to get anywhere close to Charlotte? I'm paying richly to have him watched round the clock!" John's fists clenched as his voice rose. "Someone will answer for this; I will be certain."

Emma watched him placidly. He was overcome with concern for his sister, as well he should be. His protection had failed. Perhaps he did not consider the significance of this revelation for Emma. Or, even worse, perhaps he did and did not consider it a betrayal. Emma waited silently as John tugged on the sash of his dressing gown, strode to the door, and summoned the nearest footman. "Awaken Mr. Marshall. I shall meet him in my study shortly."

He shut the door and returned to Emma. "How long ago did this occur?"

"Charlotte came to me this afternoon, before dinner."

His brow furrowed. "That was hours ago. Why was I not told immediately?"

Emma stared at him. A coldness had settled over her as he spoke. "I can understand your frustration at the delay," she said steadily, intentionally contrasting the urgency of his demeanor. "Perhaps if I had been made aware of this threat to Charlotte's safety, I would have been more alert in keeping watch and more prepared to act quickly when the circumstance arose."

He stopped, realization of her meaning settling onto his countenance. "Emma," he began, palm raised in supplication, "I will concede, it was a mistake to keep this from you, but you cannot possibly compare my informing you of some details of Charlotte's past to a failure to immediately alert me of a threat delivered to her personally at our home. It is my responsibility to protect this family, and I cannot do so when I am not aware of threats which require my protection."

She could not have worded the case more eloquently herself. "How can *I* protect Charlotte from threats to her reputation if *I* am not made aware of the threats?" she snapped. "By the time Charlotte came to me, Mr. Brydges had already seen to his removal." She arched one brow and crossed her arms. "What I cannot understand is why you felt it necessary to keep these details from me in the first place."

John looked away. Much of the bluster was lost from his voice when he answered. "Charlotte asked that I not tell you about Mr. Pritchard. She wasn't sure of your reaction. There was no way to discuss him without revealing that she worked in the kitchens. She didn't want you to know."

"Naturally, you assured her that her fears were unfounded." She knew he had not. She would have known even if his expression just then had not confirmed it.

She had never in her life felt more like scenery or decoration. If he could not find in her actions enough illustration of her character to know she would not judge Charlotte's employment, then he had given her no more notice than he gave the statues in the entry hall. If he had applied any effort, shown any interest in knowing her, he would have been certain of her lack of prejudice. But, in the end, he had not. He had doubted.

John only shook his head at her question. "I must dress and find Brydges. We must locate Pritchard immediately."

She watched him as he left.

John had sailed across the ocean to rush to his sister's aid, lived as a poor clerk for four long years, then married a stranger to give his sister the best possible launch into society. Yet he suspected Emma might find cause to judge in knowing Charlotte had been forced, through no fault of her own, to support herself through her own labors.

He did not love her. If he believed her capable of such judgments, he did not even know her, despite their time together and the moments they had shared. Their marriage was truly nothing more than the mercenary bargain they had made.

Emma wept. Even as she chided herself for her girlish foolishness, she grieved for the loss of a thing she had never had.

Chapter Thirty-Six

John rose late, as he had been awake long into the night, awaiting confirmation that Pritchard had been located and that two men, instead of one, held vigil at the inn in Beadwell to monitor his movements. He'd already come to the decision he would not be idly waiting to see what Pritchard planned next. He would be riding to that particular inn himself to see to the conclusion of this episode with the American.

He passed Emma's lady's maid in the hall upon leaving his room for the morning. "Has my wife been down to breakfast?"

"No, Your Grace. She took a tray in her room this morning. Her Grace was wanting extra time to rest."

"I see. Thank you."

"Certainly, Your Grace." The girl gave a quick bob of a curtsy and scurried off.

He had a fence to mend there, he knew. She should have immediately informed him of the threat from Pritchard. That was not in question. But she had a right to be bothered by his omissions in explaining Charlotte's past and the man lurking about Brantmoor. He'd been too mired in his concerns upon hearing of Pritchard's visit to recognize the need to atone for that mistake last evening. Now that Pritchard was in hand, he could explain himself. In his defense, it *had* been Charlotte's request to keep the information from Emma, but if he truly believed his defense, he wouldn't feel the twinge of guilt that plucked at him as he made his way to find some food. After all, he'd only assented to Charlotte's wishes because he'd gained her agreement to attend dress fittings and dance lessons in exchange. In the end, it had been for the greater good.

It truly had.

He simply needed to explain this to Emma.

Once John found his way to the empty breakfast room, he discovered he was too preoccupied to linger long. He consumed just enough to stave off any immediate hunger pangs and retreated to his study where he found his secretary, Marshall, waiting for him.

"I've had a report on Pritchard, Your Grace. He will not be returning to Brantmoor today, as he is currently en route to London. He bought a place on the stage that passed through this morning."

"To London, you say?" It was too much to hope the man was giving up and seeking a ship to return to Boston. "There is a great deal of trouble the man could cause in London."

"He's not likely to gain entrée with any of your circle, Your Grace."

"Hmmm." Pritchard would not gain acceptance into any respectable home or exclusive club, but that did not mean he could not find a sympathetic ear were he bent on locating one. There were certain gaming hells or other establishments of vice where a man of the any station could encounter the occasional titled gentleman. Men were just as wont to repeat gossip as women, John well knew.

"Your men are following the stage. Once he arrives in London, they will determine his destination and report back."

John sighed heavily. "If Pritchard goes to London, I go to London. We do not know what this man may do."

Marshall nodded and left John to his burdens. How naïve he had been. He had genuinely believed once he was able to bring Charlotte to England, he should have every aspect of her future well in hand.

* * *

Given his recent lapses in judgment in sharing details with the duchess, John proceeded to her bedchamber to inform her immediately of the latest developments regarding Pritchard. The bedchamber, however, was empty. He inquired of four members of the staff, who did not know her whereabouts, and located her lady's maid again, who insisted she had not seen the duchess since delivering her tray early that morning.

"Well, go and find Miss Betancourt, then," he barked at the maid. "I'm sure the duchess is with her."

The girl stepped back from his blustered command. "I...I'm sorry, Your Grace," she stammered. "Miss Betancourt is gone. She left this morning to return home."

"Are you sure?"

"Yes, Your Grace. I believe the carriage has already returned."

Of course. Beadwell. Emma was upset and she had retreated to her blessed cottage and her mother's garden. Pritchard or no, it seemed John was destined to make the journey to Beadwell this morning.

* * *

John arrived at the cottage a mere forty minutes later, having forgone the comfort of the coach for the speed of his mount. He rapped on the door and heard the flutter of hurried footsteps before it was answered by Mrs. Brown.

"I've come to see my wife."

"Oh." Mrs. Brown looked past the duke and around him in confusion. "I'm so sorry, Your Grace. She's not here. Should she be? Is something amiss?"

John shook his head. "Do not fear, Mrs. Brown. I'm sure the duchess is quite well and I am guilty of misunderstanding. She must be at the parsonage house with Miss Betancourt today. I'm sure I will find her there."

Only Emma was not at the parsonage house. Lucy was as alarmed as Mrs. Brown.

John was becoming so as well.

Where did the woman go? If she was not in Beadwell, why wasn't she at home? John cursed himself for not inquiring more thoroughly at the stables before rushing away. He didn't even know if her horse was gone. What if she had taken a morning ride to clear her head and met with some mishap? Would they have the sense at Brantmoor to search for her, even though he'd run impulsively off to Beadwell, certain of finding her here?

John felt a slow thickening in his gut that significantly impeded his ability to develop rational alternatives for where she may safely be. All sorts of torturous possibilities assaulted him. Most involved serious injury for which she was unable to gain help. One particularly disturbing possibility was Pritchard. The American had evaded his surveillance before. A drunk and desperate man was capable of anything. If he could not reach Charlotte, would he harm Emma?

John could not account for the depth of his fear other than to accept how greatly he had come to care for his wife. He needed her. He needed her back, safe and sound. Not because Charlotte's debut was coming and he knew nothing of dress fittings or dance lessons. Not because he needed an heir to the dukedom. Not because he was *supposed* to marry. He wanted her back for himself. Even if they shut themselves up in Brantmoor and never entered polite society again, he wanted his Emma back—his sharp-tongued, brilliantly beautiful, perfectly sensual Emma. If he could have that, he would hold her to him and beg forgiveness for his stupidity, his lack of faith and any other transgression he may have committed.

If Emma were lying hurt somewhere, he was wasting precious moments here in Beadwell. He should be combing the forest around the estate. Still, he could not quite let go of the image of a drunken Pritchard somehow getting his hands on her. After talking with Lucy, he did not turn in the direction of home. He turned toward the inn.

* * *

It was midday, but the inn was mostly empty, as the stage had come and gone. John ducked his head through the low doorway into the shadowed public room that remained dark despite the bits of cloudless sunshine that were allowed to leak in through still-shuttered windows. John called for the innkeeper.

"Your Grace!" The man rushed in, red faced and perspiring, and wiping his hands on a dirty apron knotted around his waist. "Welcome, welcome. Would you like a meal, Your Grace? My wife has venison stew today. I'll have to warm it, but it won't take a moment."

"I do not seek a meal. I am seeking information."

"Anything you need, Your Grace. How can I help?"

"I need information on this man Pritchard who stayed here. The American."

The innkeeper's red face twisted at the mention of Pritchard's name. "That man stayed here all right, but he'll not be staying again until he's settled with me for the lodging and the drink he's already got."

"I understand he bought a place on the London stage this morning."

"Aye. He did. Snuck off before I had a chance to claim my due."

John peered at the man. "So you did not actually see him depart on the stage?"

"I did, Your Grace, but not until it was too late to stop him. That stage doesn't stop for anyone, once it goes. If you're a few minutes late, or wanting to collect a fare. No mercy. They just keep right on going." He sliced his hand through the air to illustrate the forward trajectory of the stage in question.

"Are you absolutely certain that Pritchard boarded the stage?"

"As certain as my own name, Your Grace, not that it does me any good. He's hours down the road by now and I'll never collect."

"Could he have gotten off the stage outside of town?"

The innkeeper considered this a moment, then shook his head—slowly at first, but with increasing certainty. "I said before, the stage won't stop for anybody. And even if the American did get off, he's got no horse. Where would he go?"

The lump in the pit of John's stomach dissipated just a bit. Where would the man go without a horse? He'd likely used the services of the livery when he came to Brantmoor before, but if he leapt off the coach on the London road, he'd not find an available livery for miles.

"How long until the next stop?"

"Won't stop for half the day, Your Grace. Not until Peckingham."

John released a breath he hadn't even realized had been caught up. If Pritchard was trapped on the stage until Peckingham, he could not possibly have harmed Emma. He had nowhere else to look but to return home. Perhaps she had already returned. God, he hoped she had. If she had, he would kiss her silly then lay into her for worrying him so damned much.

"You've been most helpful," John told the innkeeper, sliding a smooth coin into his hand.

The man palmed it for a moment, then changed his mind and held the coin back out to John. "Happy to be of help, Your Grace, but I couldn't rightly take a payment from you. Consider it the paying of a debt. All of us here are grateful for what you done for Simon, Your Grace."

John paused. "For Simon?"

"The duchess...well, she weren't the duchess, then, but she was worried sick for Simon, I know. We all were, what with Crawford's accusations. We all knew them to be lies, especially the duchess." The innkeeper smiled and shook his head. "She's got a real tender heart for Simon, that one."

John stiffened. A tender heart? He searched the depths of his memory and seemed to have some faint recollection of a Simon. Then he landed on it. Her gardener. She had mentioned him once or twice.

"Yes, well, I don't recall being of any assistance to Simon."

"Mrs. Brown told us all about it—what we didn't already know from Crawford's caterwauling—how you agreed to vouch for young Simon on account of him being such a good friend of your betrothed, so Crawford couldn't take his foul accusations to the magistrate. We all breathed a sigh of relief for that, Your Grace."

"Did you? I am happy to have been of assistance. And thank you for the information. Please consider your debt repaid."

John walked out of the inn. He was no longer certain he felt compelled to rush to his wife's aid. A tender heart for Simon, her gardener. *Such good friends.* My, but she was full of secrets, wasn't she? She'd been no less mercenary than he in pursuing their marriage. She'd done it to save her precious Simon. And to think, she'd demanded a promise of fidelity from him. *From him.*

John mounted his horse and turned toward Brantmoor. He'd come on a fool's errand. He'd raced across the countryside to find her. When he'd not found her in the village, he'd immediately feared the worst and bargained with the devil himself for her safe return.

The devil had taken the bargain. His wife was no doubt safe and sound. When she wanted to be found, she would be. That was the way with women who held secrets, and unexplainable attachments to gardens, and tender hearts for strong, able-bodied gardeners.

Chapter Thirty-Seven

Upon hearing word that her guests had arrived, Emma hurried to the parlor of Worley House. They were assembled. Her comrades. They were not great in number, but they were mighty in faith—an aging army in muslin and lace that would be her salvation. As any good general would, Emma greeted her troops with warm compliments, an affectionate squeeze of their hands, and an invitation to sit.

"Ladies, I have called you here to beg your help. You have been supportive of me and great friends to both my dear Aunt Agatha"—she smiled warmly at Lady Ridgely—"and my departed mother. I know I can count on your support and discretion now." She *did* know it. It was why she'd come to London when she could no longer stay at Brantmoor.

Lady Blythe lay a gentle hand on Emma's arm. "You've only to ask, dear, and we shall help however we can."

"Always be assured of our friendship and support," Lady Markwood added.

Emma looked among her comrades-in-arms—three faces of sincerity and fierce loyalty—and was near to tears. They could not know how much their heartfelt friendship meant at just this moment. She had been in London for less than a day when she sent out the missives and her friends had come. She swallowed a very large lump of emotion and forced a confident smile. "Very well then."

And then she explained. She told them absolutely everything she knew about Charlotte. The truth of her upbringing, the death of her mother, her time as a kitchen maid, and the threats of Mr. Pritchard. All the ladies listened without disapproval or judgment—at least not for Charlotte.

Lady Blythe shook her head. "I never had much interaction with the old Worley, but I always thought he seemed surly and unpleasant."

"Such a shame for Charlotte and her mother," Aunt Agatha added, "to endure such difficult circumstances, struggling to make their way, when all the while, the duke had the means to provide for their ease."

Lady Markwood nodded. "My thoughts precisely. Even if he chose to be unyielding and would not restore them to their places in the family, he should have seen to their welfare. It was a duty of both honor and matrimony."

"Sadly," Emma said, "we cannot undo it. Charlotte's upbringing has been…quite unconventional." She sighed, but it did not expel the heaviness from her heart. "Charlotte's knowledge of England is not favorable. She spent her entire life knowing her *English* father would allow her to starve or worse because he would not accept her. Now that she has arrived in England, she has been told she must change herself entirely, or the rest of society may not accept her either." Emma looked from one lady to the next. She had to make them understand. "Charlotte does not play the harp or the pianoforte. She does not know the steps to any dance but one. She is still very unsure of the orders of rank, and as you may understand, she does not much care. But she is a good girl. She deserves to have some happiness and acceptance restored to her."

"She is already accepted." Aunt Agatha took Emma's hand in a firm grip. "There may still be many to win over, but she will not begin without family or friends."

"Thank you—all of you," Emma said softly. She hoped Charlotte would be grateful for this show of support. How could she not? It wrapped around Emma like a comforting blanket on a frigid night, and it would comfort Charlotte too, if she would receive it.

"Ladies," Lady Markwood said, setting aside her teacup. "I am sorry to disrupt all of this positivity with a reminder of bad news, but rumors are already building about this mysterious sister of Worley's. Lady Charlotte will require more than the smiling attendance of a few well-meaning friends if we want to assure her acceptance. She will require those friends to have a plan."

Lady Markwood was not wrong. Too much about Charlotte was shrouded in mystery. Her connection to a duke who mysteriously withdrew from society would only fuel speculation. The sponsorship of a social failure, duchess or not, and her three aging friends hardly constituted a promising launch for a new debutante.

"You are right of course," Emma said. "As I have not been in London since Charlotte arrived, I'll need detailed accounts of the rumors currently circulating." When none of the ladies responded, Emma smiled gently. "I'm well aware of the sort of rumors likely being discussed about my family. I will not be offended to have you repeat them to me. You are not the authors. This is absolutely necessary."

Lady Markwood offered first. "I heard the family had hidden her away in an asylum because she was unwell in the head."

Once the dam was broken, the news rushed forth.

"I heard she ran away as a child and was raised by gypsies," Lady Blythe contributed.

Gypsies? "But that makes no sense," Emma said. "Charlotte was only three when she disappeared. How could she have run away on her own?"

Lady Markwood's shoulders lifted and fell. "Logic is rarely a prerequisite for rumor, I have found."

Lady Blythe patted her friend's hand. "Very true, my dear."

Aunt Agatha cleared her throat. "Your uncle heard at the club that Lady Charlotte is not Worley's sister at all, but a mistress he collected during his years away and he has declared her his long-lost sister in order to bring her into his household under the new duchess's very nose." Aunt Agatha's cheeks flamed.

"Yes. Well. I have heard that one too," Lady Markwood admitted. "Only I heard specifically that they met in Spain—that the girl is Spanish."

Lady Blythe nodded. "Yes. Yes, I've heard that as well. There is also the rumor that Lady Charlotte is a complete impostor—that she heard of the duke's reappearance and has popped up to claim a connection because the duke is not in his right mind."

Well, they were getting into the spirit now, weren't they, Emma thought. "And why, pray tell, is the duke not in his right mind?"

"He was injured in the war and has become an excessive opium eater."

"Oh my." Emma blinked. She tapped her finger to her lips. "I think we shall have to start writing these out." She rose and crossed to the writing desk. Gypsies? Opium eaters? The stories were even more outlandish than she'd expected. She sat at the desk and found a sheath of paper and pen. Quill poised, she turned to the other women. "All right, you shall have to repeat everything. Then I will take down any others if there are more. Are there more?"

The three ladies exchanged glances.

Clearly, there was a great deal more.

* * *

"Are you not at all worried for the duchess?" Charlotte asked, as the ducal coach drew to a halt in front of John's London residence.

Blast. He wanted the silence back. He was only partially guilt-stricken for the harshness of his conversation for the first part of their journey from Brantmoor, because it had gained him the silence. "I am not." It was even mostly true. "She is a resourceful woman." That bit was definitely true.

"I still do not understand," Charlotte said plaintively. "Where would she have gone?"

"I do not know. For the moment it is not my primary concern. We shall proceed as planned. You will ready yourself for your debut and I will locate and handle Pritchard."

Charlotte stared as though he were daft. "How am I to ready myself?"

"Do you not know the name of your dressmaker?"

"Madame Desmarais."

"Perfect. We will be able to locate her shop without difficulty, I am certain."

"*You* are taking me?"

John wanted out of this carriage. He needed a drink, but first he had a man to find. "You can't be wandering the streets of London with only a maid for your chaperone while Pritchard is running loose planning God knows what."

Charlotte quieted, but her mouth drew into a scowl. He paused and softened his tone. "We must be cautious for your safety, Charlotte."

"What of everything else?" she asked. "The dances and the horse riding?"

"We won't be riding any horses this week, Charlotte, and we shall sort everything else out. If the duchess does not return in time."

The door to the seating compartment was opened and a hand offered to aid Charlotte down. John followed her, gratified to be out of the damned box. Dances and riding lessons didn't matter if there was danger of harm befalling Charlotte. "There will be no preparations today, Charlotte," he told her. "I will be otherwise occupied. I suggest you take the time to settle yourself into your room and become acquainted with the house."

She nodded.

"Do not leave the house," he commanded, as they entered the main hall, his boots echoing on the black-and-white marbled floor. "Do not allow visitors in."

Charlotte began to nod, but halted as a chorus of ladies' laughter filtered to them. She froze and looked to John.

John's jaw set. With booted footsteps thudding, he tramped up the stairs to the main parlor and swung open the door. A cluster of matrons, giggling like schoolgirls, stood gathered around the writing desk.

He cleared his throat. When that went unnoticed, he cleared his throat again. Loudly.

The laughter ceased and the cluster broke apart, revealing the duchess seated in the small chair, pen in hand, as though happily writing a letter. Here he'd been tearing across the countryside looking for her, and she was managing her correspondence.

She lay the pen down and pivoted in her chair to face him, chin raised. "Your Grace," she said.

"You're here."

"I am."

"Good."

He turned and shut the door on them all, manners be damned. Let them go back to cackling over whatever it was that so entertained them. He stomped back to the main hall where Charlotte stood waiting, still in her bonnet and shawl.

"The duchess has arrived," he announced. "She will see to whatever is left to be done. The housekeeper will show you to a room."

He found his study and shut himself up in it. He would have his manhunt, but first he would have a drink.

* * *

Four ladies stared at the recently slammed parlor door, then glanced at each other in awkward uncertainty.

"Well," Emma said, rising from her seat, "We have made good progress. We should reconvene in a few days."

"Yes. Of course," Aunt Agatha said, already reaching for her shawl.

"We shall leave you to your family, now that they have arrived," Lady Markwood said.

Emma smiled at them. *We shall leave you to your scowling duke, more like.* She didn't blame any of them for fleeing. She didn't really want to speak to him herself. "Thank you, truly, for your help," she said, squeezing each woman's hand in turn. "Your support is a great comfort to me."

She accompanied them to the front hall and wished them good day again. "Don't forget," she reminded them as they departed, "if you have any new stories, please jot them down."

Then they were gone and there was nothing left to do but see him. She considered a walk to clear her head, but knew she was only unnecessarily delaying the conversation. She'd been impulsive to run off. He was rightfully angry with her. Once she had reached London and thought to send a letter, it was too late. The family had intended to leave for London in the next few days anyway. By the time she was able to get a letter to Brantmoor, explaining that she'd gone ahead early, they would be traveling themselves.

Emma rapped lightly on the study door.

"Come."

She hesitated before pushing the door open, but immediately chided herself for her timidity. What was there to fear? That he would not love her? That was already the case. She turned the knob and walked into the study.

He was seated at his desk, with his chair turned to the side, facing the window rather than the desktop. He had no papers in front of him, no quills at the ready. He only stared out the window. He continued to do so for a very long, quiet moment then he turned to look at her over his shoulder. The look was so cold, she felt the chill from it run through the length of her spine. Angry, perhaps, had been an underestimation on her part.

"Why are you here?" he demanded.

"This is my home."

His glare tightened and Emma chose not to test his limits. She revised her response.

"I came to begin preparations for Charlotte's come out. There is much to be done."

"You left without word. What need was there to run off in secret?" His words were not the plaintive request of a loved one, but the harsh accusation of a prejudiced inquisitor.

"I apologize for my impulsive departure. It was inconsiderate of me."

One eyebrow rose. "Inconsiderate?" He rose and bore down on her with more malice than she'd ever seen possess him. "My wife was missing. The entire household was concerned for your safety," he bit out. "It was a great deal more than inconsiderate."

He stared at her, waiting for an explanation. She could see he wanted to know why. How could she tell him? How could she explain she'd run away from her broken heart? How could she explain that she couldn't forget how he'd found a way to sail to Boston in the middle of a war. How he'd sacrificed his comforts and the only life he'd known to rush to his sister's aid. How could she explain that she was weakly and sinfully jealous of the love and protectiveness he gave to Charlotte, because she wanted those things for herself?

She could not, so she told him, "It was wrong of me. I regret causing needless worry for any member of the household. And I *am* very sorry."

He stared, unyielding, down into her face as she gave her apology. Then he stepped away and turned his back to her as he spoke. "Imagine my dismay," he said, his voice menacingly low, "upon realizing my wife had not been seen all morning, racing to Beadwell to find you, and fearing the worst when you were not there."

Racing to Beadwell? He *raced* to Beadwell? For her? Emma's heart lifted, despite his scowling expression. The ride from Brantmoor to Beadwell was not so long—hardly a voyage across the sea—but still, it warmed Emma's heart. He had sprung into action for her. Because he feared she was in danger.

Because he cared.

"Imagine my dismay," he repeated, "when I learned the truth."

"The truth?" she asked. "What truth?"

"Oh yes. Let's discuss some of that, shall we?" His cruel tone bit through her. She stepped back in response, but he continued without even looking at her. "When I was questioning the innkeeper about Pritchard, for fear that you had met with some foul play, he made certain to thank me for vouching for your gardener, thus saving him from facing charges with the magistrate. I was confused, considering I know no gardeners and have not been asked to vouch for the good character of anyone in years."

Relief bubbled through Emma. "Oh, he meant Simon," she hastened to explain.

"Yes, I gathered," John drawled. "It was convenient, how quickly you acquiesced to our engagement after this Simon was accused."

Emma bit her lip. It did sound rather mercenary, didn't it? Of course it was no more so than *his* purpose for marrying. "What does it matter? Your reasons for agreeing to the marriage were no less practical than mine."

He turned, eyes flashing with anger. His fist slammed onto the desk. "It matters if my duchess is consorting with the village gardener so openly that the innkeeper would comment to me regarding your 'tender heart' for the man!"

Emma stared. Consorting? "Wait, John, you misunderstand."

His expression became frighteningly calm and cold. "I'm sure you have some perfectly plausible explanation that I am entirely uninterested in hearing."

"But I do!" She nearly laughed aloud. God, was it true? Was he jealous—for her?

"Let's have it then," he snapped.

She did laugh then. She must appear maniacal. Her husband was berating her—accusing her of infidelity—yet the relief and hope she felt far surpassed any affront she might take with his surly demeanor or even offense at his lack of trust.

He cared.

"It is quite good," she assured him, when her laughter had only brought a darker scowl to his face. "I *do* have a tender heart for Simon, because he is a boy. He is only thirteen. He is the smithy's son and his mother died years ago. Mrs. Brown and I—we take care of him, and when I have need of him, he works in my garden."

"Thirteen?" John asked sharply. He stepped directly in front of her.

"Yes."

"A mere boy?"

Relief bubbled through her. "Yes," she said. "Yes." He cared a great deal. He cared enough to be possessive and—jealous. Oh God, was it wicked that she *wanted* this man to feel possessive of her, even more than she wanted him to feel worried or protective? Anything was better than the indifference of which she had been so certain.

"A boy." He spat it. He speared fingers through his hair, sending tidy locks into dishevel. "A damned boy."

"Yes." She lay a hand on his arm and beamed up at him. "It was all a misunderstanding."

He pulled his arm away from her touch as though she had struck him. Why was he acting this way? This was *good*. His suspicions were wrong. And he cared.

More than cared.

He *possessed*. Her.

Emma's heart soared. Hope bloomed within her and sent dancing light to all her limbs.

"I'm so sorry I worried you," she said, unable to prevent the joyful smile as she gazed up at him. "I never realized you would be frightened for me. I am so dreadfully sorry."

He stepped away to the desk. He placed his hand upon it and looked down at the hand. "Charlotte is upstairs. I'm sure you two have much to accomplish. I must contact my men regarding Pritchard. I will keep you apprised of all developments regarding Charlotte henceforth."

Emma didn't move. She should go. She had, after all, been summarily dismissed. But why? Didn't he understand? She waited a moment in silence. Surely, he had something more to say.

Only he did not. He said nothing, and it was clear to her she was the one who did not understand.

Chapter Thirty-Eight

Emma and Charlotte had a herculean feat to accomplish in just five days' time. This distraction made it easier for Emma to bear her husband's avoidance. She tried not to think of it, instead declaring that their limited time dictated abandonment of all but the most imperative training for Charlotte's debut ball—dancing, dresses, and basic comportment. Their days consisted of dance lessons each morning followed by outings in the afternoon, for Charlotte needed not only dresses, but undergarments, hats, gloves, and a complete wardrobe of shoes. Emma spent each evening closeted with the housekeeper and butler of Worley House, planning every last detail of the event, while Charlotte was given time to herself.

Two days before Charlotte's debut ball the ladies attended a final gown fitting at the shop of Madame Desmarais. The dressmaker had proven most graciously willing to forgive Charlotte's prior poor behavior in light of the liberty with which the duchess accumulated purchases and the haste with which the duke's steward settled the charges on her account.

On this particular afternoon, the ladies were ushered to a private room where Charlotte donned the nearly completed creation.

"Oh, Madame Desmarais, you were so very wise," Aunt Agatha gasped when she saw Charlotte in the gown. Most of the other fabrics the ladies had chosen for Charlotte were shades of blue or lavender that brought out her stunning eyes. On their first visit, Madame Desmarais had looked at Charlotte's mass of raven hair and sapphire eyes and announced she had the perfect vision.

She had proceeded to show the ladies a bolt of rich satin in such a muted dusty rose, that nearly blended with the skin. All three ladies had attempted to tactfully suggest to Madame Desmarais that perhaps the color was too drab. The countess pointed out that most women would not find their complexion flattered by the shade they'd been shown. But Madame Desmarais had been insistent.

And she had clearly been correct. Emma could not believe how effectively the dress transformed Charlotte from a lovely young girl into an elegant, exotic-looking woman. While Emma's brown hair and golden brown eyes would have been washed out by the bare rose color, Charlotte's rich, dark locks and sparklingly blue eyes were strikingly bold in contrast to the pale fabric.

In her creative genius, the dressmaker had not accented the dress with any color that would have lessened the effect, but rather heightened the contrast between the pale dress and Charlotte's dark coloring by trimming it with handmade Venetian lace dyed midnight black. The lace began at the lower left corner of gown's raised waistline and spread like a creeping, tentacled vine across her chest and over her right shoulder. The lace angled across Charlotte's back in meandering scrolls and wound its way down the left side of the long skirt.

"It is absolutely stunning," Emma announced. "You look sophisticated and mysterious in this gown. You will be declared an incomparable."

Charlotte was completely engaged in spinning in front of the mirror and admiring her reflection in the dress. "I *do* look mysterious, don't I?"

Emma laughed, pleased with Charlotte's growing enthusiasm. "You certainly do."

One of the shop girls bustled into the room and whispered to Madame Desmarais, who smiled at the ladies. "I must see to another matter. I will leave you to admire the beautiful Lady Charlotte for a little while longer and return in just a moment."

"Of course," Emma responded. Charlotte seemed perfectly content gazing at the reflection of her new self.

The seamstress left and soon her loud greeting of another customer filtered to them in their privacy. Emma's face pinched as she recognized the voice that responded. Lady Wolfe. Emma caught her aunt's eye and they both looked at Charlotte, who remained enraptured with her appearance and none the wiser that the Queen of Gossips had just entered their midst.

"Ah the lovely Georgiana," they heard Madame Desmarais gush. "I do love to dress such a beautiful young lady."

"She is not as young as when you first dressed her," came Lady Wolfe's curt reply. "I will not have her in a third season without a serious suitor. Her dresses must get her noticed."

"*Certainement.*" The dressmaker's lilting voice sailed past the awkwardness of Lady Wolfe's harsh comment. "No one will fail to notice you in my next creation, darling. You may be sure of it."

"I...I don't think I would be comfortable in anything too bold," Georgiana's soft voice declared.

"Of course you wouldn't," snapped her mother. "If you were willing to be bold, you'd be married to the Duke of Worley now, instead of that ridiculous upstart he rejected years ago."

That comment drew Charlotte's attention. Her eyes shot to Emma's in the mirror.

Emma went to Charlotte's side. "It's no matter," she said quietly. "There will always be unkind people. Why don't we get you out of this dress?"

Emma began unfastening Charlotte's new dress. She could only imagine the depth of poor Georgiana's embarrassment. She hoped for the girl's sake the shop was otherwise empty.

"It's for the best anyway, I say," Lady Wolfe continued eventually, completely contradicting her prior criticism. "I wouldn't want a respectable daughter of mine charged with launching Charlotte Brantwood into society. I have heard from a reliable source that she isn't even his sister. She is his Spanish mistress and he has brought her to England right under his new duchess's nose. Scandalous."

Charlotte's eyes widened at this latest slander. The flush rose quickly from her chest to her hairline and her eyes narrowed. "Who is that woman?" she hissed.

"Lady Wolfe. She is a ridiculous gossip," Emma said quietly, aiding Charlotte in stepping out of the dress. "Those who prefer to be unkind will repeat the things she says, but most among the *ton* know she is considerably more mean spirited than she is well informed."

"My, well..." The dressmaker's voice faltered. "I certainly know nothing about all of that, but I *do* know dresses, and we shall have you in lovelier gowns than you could possibly have imagined. Why don't you come with me into my private office?" she suggested conspiratorially. "I have drawings there of some new designs I've been working on. I think we can find something entirely original for Georgiana."

The offer to have her daughter at the cutting edge of fashion was enough to tempt Lady Wolfe into the shop's back office. When Madame Desmarais returned to the private dressing room in which Emma and her family waited, the dressmaker looked positively stricken. "Your Grace, I do so sincerely apologize..."

"There is no need," Emma said, with a dismissive wave. "You are not responsible for the poor behavior of your customers, Madame. We are overwhelmingly pleased with all you've prepared for us, particularly this latest gown for Lady Charlotte. I have decided she must have it for her debut ball. Will it be ready in time?"

Madame Desmarais clasped her hands together. "*Absolument*! Oh, I am so glad. She will be stunning," the seamstress said, with a beaming smile toward Charlotte. "*Très belle*."

The seamstress shuffled off again and Charlotte gazed mournfully down at the dress, now lying draped across the shop's table. "Emma," she said uncertainly.

Emma stilled. It was the first time Charlotte had ever called her by name. "Yes, Charlotte?"

Charlotte's playful joy was gone. "Are you certain this is the right dress for my debut?" She ran one hand over the trail of black lace down the gown's side. "This dress is beautiful, but I look so different in it. We all agreed. Given what I'll be facing, I think we should choose one of the other gowns. One of the plainer gowns that would never be described as exotic or mysterious."

"Oh, Charlotte, you are wrong. This dress is exactly what you need. Tomorrow afternoon Aunt Agatha will bring her friends for tea and we shall discuss the whole thing. I'm not the least concerned about Lady Wolfe. She will be more help than harm. Just wait."

* * *

Emma found an opportunity to address one of the final, more important details of Charlotte's debut when she shared a few moments with Mr. Brydges in the drawing room while awaiting John and Charlotte for dinner.

"We are just a few short days away. Such an important day for us all," Emma commented to open the conversation as she seated herself on the sofa. "I am so proud of Charlotte's progress. She has a lovely way about her when she dances. She will draw attention, I am certain."

"She will draw attention if she stands in the corner," was his droll reply. "Given the stories that are circulating."

"Charlotte should have no trouble finding a bevy of suitors," Emma continued, ignoring his reference to the gossips. "I believe Mr. Greystoke is still in need of a wife," she offered casually.

Mr. Brydges charged forward in his seat. "That's preposterous. He's ancient."

Emma feigned indignation at the voracity of his response. "I don't see how it's so preposterous. He was, after all, considered a perfectly acceptable suitor for me. I should think he would be so for Charlotte as well."

"He's not good enough. She's…she's the daughter of a duke, for one thing."

Emma's expression remained placid as she digested the voracity of his response. "I am the daughter of an earl. Besides, even though she is the daughter of a duke, you must allow her background is not entirely conventional. She was raised in America, after all."

"In Boston, for God's sake, not by a pack of wolves."

She continued without regard to his darkening expression. "And as we've discussed, there are the inevitable rumors of her legitimacy."

"Lies, all of it. If any of that tripe ever reaches her ears…"

The implied violence of his incomplete thought had Emma softening her tone. "You can't protect her from it."

"Like hell, I can't."

Emma smiled. Satisfied she had her answer, she straightened her shoulders. "Good," she clipped. "Then I may count on you to be in attendance at Charlotte's come out and at more than your normal number of events for the remainder of the season? If we are to put the strongest foot forward on her behalf, we'll require a show of solidarity."

Hugh grunted. "Greystoke. Preposterous."

Emma wasn't fooled by his noncommittal response. "I've come to care about Charlotte a great deal. I'm sure she is greatly comforted to know she can rely upon your friendship through this daunting experience."

"She does not require friends who are intent on steering her into marriages to ancient men."

Once again ignoring his comment, she reached out to place a hand on his arm and smiled warmly up at him. "Just as I have come to consider you a friend."

He raised a questioning brow. "A friend, Your Grace? Are you sure it's wise to become friends with an insufferable oaf such as me?"

Emma laughed. He was teasing her with her own words, but this time he meant it kindly. He loved Charlotte and so she could love him, particularly if he would protect Charlotte with the ferocity she'd glimpsed that afternoon. Charlotte was not in need of suitors. She, at least, would have a love match. He had her blessing, did he understand that? There was no way for her to explain while he was not ready to admit his feelings, but she would have liked to be able to tell him.

"Yes," she said, with her hand still on his arm, "I think I shall be very glad of your friendship."

* * *

Emma spoke little as Liese arranged her hair for the evening's event. Her mind, however, was not quiet as she stared at the elaborate jade-and-pearl evening gown she would don when her hair was finished. The event was not only Charlotte's debut. It was Emma's debut as well—her first society appearance as Duchess of Worley.

Most importantly, though, it was the fulfillment of her bargain. Her marriage was built upon this night. All that her husband had asked of her would be measured by the conduct of one girl and the reactions of a hundred others. Yet the question that occupied her mind was not one of success or failure.

Was she satisfied with the bargain she had struck?

She looked at her dress again. It was without doubt the most extravagant garment she'd ever owned. She had not married John for fine dresses or any of the other trappings of life as a duchess. She had bargained for her mother's garden and a boy's life, and she had received those things, but she was not satisfied. She now wanted something entirely different for her side of the trade. Even mercenary dealings allowed for renegotiations, did they not? She had already given more to the bargain that she had ever intended. Could she ask for more in return?

There was a knock on her chamber door and, with a fleeting and futile hope that her husband had come, she sent Liese to answer it. Liese went quickly to the door, spoke a moment, and returned, her eyes wide with concern.

"It seems you're needed, Your Grace. There's a man downstairs to see you."

A man. Not a guest. *A man.* Carriages bearing their arriving guests were expected to begin appearing any moment, but if this man were a guest, the staff would have known what to do.

"Were you given a name, Liese?"

"Pritchard, Your Grace."

Pritchard? "Where is my husband? Inform him of the visitor at once."

"His Grace is not in. That's why I'm to send you. The gentleman asked for the duke first."

Emma's chin fell. She briefly closed her eyes and allowed herself one slow, deep breath. She could hear Lucy's voice in her mind, urging her to be practical. If she intended to ask for more from her husband, then she must be all that he expected of her as well. Tonight she would prove her mettle. Charlotte's success would be her success and then, just perhaps, she could recapture her husband's attention.

She opened her eyes and instructed Liese calmly. "Tell them to put Pritchard in His Grace's study. I will speak with him there. Also, if my uncle or Mr. Brydges have arrived, they should be informed as well and join us in the study." She exhaled. "Then hurry back, as I'll require your assistance to get into this dress as quickly as possible."

* * *

John cursed as he felt the carriage come to a stop yet again. He and his men had spent an entire wasted day tracking Pritchard, only to have him evade them again. He had remained steadfast in his determination to search for the man until the last possible moment at which he must return home. John was barely arriving back at the town house in time to don his evening finery and appear at his family's side to greet their guests.

He rapped on the carriage. "What is the hold up?" he called.

"Can't get through," his coachman called back. "There's a line o' carriages in front of the house, takin' up the square."

John moved to the small window and peeked out. "Take me around to the mews," he called. He would have to enter the house through the kitchen. He couldn't very well arrive along with the guests.

Chapter Thirty-Nine

Emma walked into her husband's study to find an unfamiliar man lounging comfortably in one of the high-backed chairs in the center of the room.

"Mr. Pritchard, I presume."

He started and jumped to his feet. His balance faltered, but he regained it. He grinned. "A pleasure, Your Grace."

Her smile was tight. It was most certainly not a pleasure. She studied him, finally able to satisfy her curiosity of the man. He was young. Tall. He was also dirty and most decidedly drunk. Hopefully not so much that he was incapable of being persuaded.

"From the looks of it, I'd say I've come at an inconvenient time," he said, though his smirk implied he was rather pleased with the timing.

"As you are well aware, we have guests arriving, Mr. Pritchard. Perhaps you should address your purpose quickly, so that I may see to them."

He placed his hand dramatically upon his heart. "I've already spoken my purpose to your husband, Your Grace. I'm told he's not available, but I'm content to wait here until he returns."

"I'm well aware of your prior discussion with my husband and see no reason to delay. He has already communicated to you that Charlotte has no interest in your proposal and kindly declines."

"I'm very sorry to hear that, Your Grace, as I am afraid for Charlotte's reputation. With all these guests arriving, it would be an awful time for a rumor to take hold. Some rumors may be very difficult to disprove."

Intoxicated or not, Mr. Pritchard was proving sharper of wit than she had first assessed. Still, she was unconcerned about his rumor. She was only concerned about his presence.

"Nevertheless, Mr. Pritchard, Charlotte has decided to decline your kind offer and we must ask that you accept her decision as final."

His eyes hardened. "I don't think that's a very wise decision."

Emma had not really expected him to be reasonable. She stepped forward and smiled sweetly. "We are both people who simply seek an opportunity, wouldn't you say, Mr. Pritchard? I've known Charlotte only a short while, but I find I feel rather protective of her and would not take kindly to the spreading of damaging rumors. You, on the other hand, have traveled a long way. You have another long and costly voyage to return home. Perhaps what we have now is an opportunity, Mr. Pritchard, for each of us to have what we want."

Emma untied a small bag of gold pieces from her waist and held it in her hand, testing the weight so Mr. Pritchard could see. "How do you suppose we find a compromise?"

He eyed the bag and grinned.

The door to the study flung open.

"What in blasted hell is going on in here?"

Ah, the cavalry. Her husband, dressed in his evening finery, stalked into the room, followed closely by Mr. Brydges and Lord Ridgely.

Mr. Pritchard's grin faltered. His eyes darted to the pouch of coins and back to the three men who glared menacingly at him.

Emma ignored the shift in her pulse that her husband's entrance caused. She was certain she still had Mr. Pritchard's attention with her previous offer.

"There is no cause for alarm," she announced loudly to the latecomers, her eyes still narrowed at the American. "Mr. Pritchard and I were having a discussion, but I believe we see eye to eye, do we not, Mr. Pritchard?" She juggled the coins in her hand.

He stared at it and nodded slowly. "I believe we do."

She turned to the men and smiled sweetly. "So you see, everything is taken care of. Mr. Pritchard was just taking his leave." She held the pouch out as she spoke and he snatched it quickly.

John stepped toward him. "If he intends to take his leave, we shall make certain of it."

Emma walked to him, steeling herself against the feelings his proximity elicited. "As our guests are arriving, perhaps Mr. Brydges should see him out."

Mr. Brydges stepped forward. "That I would be happy to do," he said with decided unhappiness.

John reached out to halt his friend. "My two men are probably still in the mews. Have them take Pritchard to the harbor and detain him until morning."

John turned at the outcry from Mr. Pritchard. "Consider yourself fortunate, Pritchard. You have been given a gift. Take it. Take those coins and return to Boston on the first available ship. If you have further contact with my family, or come anywhere near us again, we will not be so kind."

John faced the door and held his arm for Emma to take. She stepped forward and, with one final glare for the American, left the room on her husband's arm.

Chapter Forty

Worley House glowed with what must have been a thousand candles. John couldn't begin to imagine where so many came from. Everything caught the light: golden urns, silver candelabra, gilt-framed paintings, bejeweled ladies, and glassy-eyed gentleman. Smiles and laughter reigned as the duke and duchess greeted their guests and graciously received well wishes for their nuptials. Lady Charlotte, by their side, was the recipient of effusive compliments on her appearance, most specifically her striking gown.

It was all very necessary, but by the time the last guest arrived, John had exchanged enough polite greetings to last the remainder of his life. He was hot already, as the number of people and candles had considerably increased the temperature in the room. He was also exhausted from the strain of standing for nearly an hour next to his wife in her ravishing gown, all the while reminding himself that he needed to take firm rein of his wits and not sink into the quicksand of besotted idiocy.

She smiled, laughed, and exchanged compliments with seemingly no awareness at all of the effect she was having on his sanity. How had she found the exact shade of green that at once made her eyes glow with golden light and her lips appear as honeyed apricots waiting to be tasted? Though he'd glared pointedly at more than one gentleman who'd cast a greedy glance toward the duchess's ample décolletage, only *he* truly understood the treasures offered there and the way she responded when he lavished attention to her sweet, creamy breasts.

Lord, he needed air.

"I'll return in a moment," he said.

"Don't be too long," Emma told him, with a distracted smile in his general direction. "We have to open the dances." She quickly returned to her conversation with Charlotte and two other ladies who had been calling regularly at the house that week—Ladies Blythe and Marcus, or something.

John had woven himself approximately halfway through the throng in his ballroom when he changed his mind regarding his destination and, instead of the outside air, sought a generous pour of scotch in the quiet of his study.

What sort of man required fortification to dance with his own wife?

* * *

The opening set was miserable. Why matrons were so scandalized by the waltz, he would never again understand. The traditional dances were so much more torturous for a wanting partner. Stepping tantalizingly close, only to be required to step away—yet unable to look away. John was aware of so many eyes and so many restrictions when he longed to simply take his wife in his arms and sink all of himself into all of her—her mouth, her bosom, her sex. Every single place on her body tempted him. It drove a man nearly to the brink, this teasing dance.

He was contemplating another scotch after the dance. The matter was decided when Brydges caught him by the arm.

"I must speak with you privately."

Brydges's grave expression alarmed him. Brydges was never grave.

"That room is full of vicious liars," he shouted the instant the heavy oak door was shut behind him.

"Explain."

"No one has spent a single moment since they've arrived talking about any subject other than your sister."

"What are they saying?" John asked, feeling the anger rising already. There should be talk about Charlotte—it was her debut, after all—but not the sort of talk that would have Brydges so riled.

"What are they *not* saying! There is not a decent person here!" Brydges shouted. He pointed an accusing finger toward the closed oak door. "There are at least fifty men out there who should be called out for the vicious slander they've repeated."

John's jaw set. "You repeat it. To me."

"The most vicious is that Charlotte your mistress from wherever you've been the past four years, and you're so brazen, you've got her living in the same house as your wife by claiming she's your sister." Brydges looked back at him with brows arched in expectation, as though daring him *not* to be offended by that one.

No dare was necessary..

"And?" John asked.

"Every ridiculous story imaginable," Brydges spat. "Gypsies, kitchen maids, opium eaters, troupes of traveling players. Some stories claim she is a stranger who has duped you into believing she is your long-lost sister, because your mother and father are not alive to dispute it."

John breathed deeply. He waited for the rage to fully consume him, expecting it to settle into his limbs and send him charging into action. He waited. Then he felt something entirely unexpected. Defeat. He could not call out fifty men. He could not disprove fifty lies, when he had no truth to share that would not be equally damaging to Charlotte's reputation.

"We have failed her," he said, tipping the decanter to fill two glasses with amber liquid. "I have failed her." John lifted both glasses and held one out to Brydges.

His friend only stared at it. "Are you daft? Failed her? You are done, then? Not two hours into your sister's debut and you are finished? You would toss her to the wolves and let them have their way?"

He glared at Brydges. "I will not let them have their way. I will not force her to remain among the jackals. I intend to remove her immediately."

"Ridiculous. Do something, man. That is your sister!"

"What is your brilliant plan, Brydges? One against fifty at dawn? Should we use pistols or swords? Are you to be my second?" He nearly laughed at the futility of it. He had failed Charlotte. His noble intentions were nothing more than a lone, tattered sail in the maelstrom of his father's obsessive hatred.

"You can't let them ruin her. Every single one of those stories is pure shite. I won't stand by while you let them spread these lies."

"I don't intend to allow her to be ruined. This night is a loss. We shall have to evaluate our next steps carefully, but I won't force her to stand in a room full of idiots who have decided to judge and shun her." John slammed his own glass on the desk, causing a splash of undrunk spirits to slosh onto his hand. He shook it, glared one last time at Brydges, and marched out of the room.

* * *

John found Emma watching the dance with her aunt. "My apologies, Lady Ridgely," he said tightly, "but I must claim my wife for a moment."

The lady nodded. "Certainly." She smiled pleasantly as John led his wife away to a secluded corner.

"I've just spoken with Brydges. This night is a disaster. It is worse than I thought possible."

Earnest concern filled her gaze. "What is it?" she asked.

"There are rumors circulating everywhere—horrendous, damaging rumors."

He would have sworn she smiled. Smiled?

"I don't know about that," she said.

"Of course you are not hearing the rumors," he pointed out. "No one would be so careless as to repeat them to you or me or Charlotte, but nearly everyone else is talking openly. I've had a full account from Brydges."

She lay a hand on his arm. "I'm sorry for my lack of clarity. I knew about the rumors. I meant the damage. Charlotte will have to dance every set to satisfy the requests she's received. The musicians have been instructed to only play dances for which she has learned the steps, and she has performed beautifully."

"Not damaging?" he ground out, conscious of their lack of privacy. "Think of her reputation. Brydges even heard a rumor about her being a kitchen maid. How the devil would anyone know that? We took care of Pritchard."

"For the time being," Emma said. "He may pop up again after today. I needed to make certain his threats wouldn't matter."

"What are you saying?"

Emma smiled brightly at two ladies who passed and gave a slight nod. John only scowled at them. They were likely as caught up as everyone else in all the gossiping.

"I am saying," Emma said after the ladies had passed, "I have resolved the matter. If anyone hears Mr. Pritchard's version of Charlotte's past, it will not be a new revelation. It will instead be just another bit of woefully out-of-date and disappointing gossip."

John gaped at his wife. He could have her committed. What had she done? "Do you mean to tell me that *you* have started the rumor that Charlotte was a kitchen maid?"

"Certainly not."

He was lost. Well and truly lost. What the devil was going on here?

"No one will gossip to me about Charlotte," Emma continued matter-of-factly. "How could I start a rumor? I believe Lady Markwood started that one." She scowled in thought. "Or was it Lady Blythe? I'm not sure. Only I know for certain it was not Aunt Agatha. Aunt Agatha was assigned the raised-by-gypsies story. And a new one—daughter of a Drury Lane actress."

He could only stare, his heart growing heavy in his chest. "Dear God, Emma, what have you done?" What had he *allowed* her to do?

She ignored him, tapping one finger on her chin. "No, I was right, the kitchen maid story was definitely assigned to Lady Markwood. Lady Blythe had the story about escaping from an Australian-bound convict ship." She beamed proudly up at him. "That one was particularly brilliant in its outlandishness."

"Why?" he asked. "Why would you do this to Charlotte? After all the trust she's placed in you—that I have placed in you—why would you sabotage her in this way?"

Emma shook her head. "We are not sabotaging Charlotte's debut. We are saving it."

"I should have you committed for lunacy."

"Listen," Emma coaxed. "There were already rumors—awful rumors— circulating about Charlotte before we arrived in town. Any of them, if believed, would have been damaging to her reputation. The only way to directly discredit each rumor would be to provide the truth."

That reasoning was at least sound. John had just given the same explanation to Brydges. "Go on," he said.

"Since the truth is just as damaging to Charlotte's reputation as any of the rumors, we concluded we could not discredit any one rumor, but could discredit the whole lot by making it into a bunch of ridiculous nonsense— the more ridiculous the better."

John peered at her. He no longer could say if she required commitment for lunacy or a knighthood for brilliance. "Do you mean to tell me, you and your cohort of ladies have been circling the room, intentionally spreading rumors about Charlotte all evening?"

"Not quite. Not me, as I've already explained. And not all evening. Each lady was assigned just one or two stories, and she was only to tell her story to one other, carefully selected, gossip. And she did not tell her story directly to the most notorious gossips, but to a known intimate friend of the most notorious gossips. That way, by the time the stories really began circulating, they were several steps removed from their source, and no one really knew where they originated."

John said nothing. He had no bloody idea what to say. The music stopped. The dance had ended. Should he still collect Charlotte as he planned?

"Have faith, John," Emma said in whisper soft tones. "I have accomplished what you asked of me. I would have told you *how* I intended to accomplish it, if you had been able to spare a moment of your time over this past week, but now it is done. If just one story, no matter how false, had been allowed to take hold of everyone's imagination, we could never have overcome it. Instead, the stories will be so great in number and so absurdly outrageous that every sensible person will eventually discount all of them as patently false. What else could they conclude? There will always be some mystery surrounding Charlotte, but she is a success."

"How can you be so sure there are enough 'sensible' people to conclude the stories are all bollocks?"

She grinned at him. "That is second part of our plan."

He nearly smiled back. "You are disturbingly strategic, madam."

Her grin widened. "Each lady was to launch a story or two at the beginning of the evening to add to those that would already be circulating. Once the stories have made the full rounds of the room, each lady is to separately plant the seed that the entire nonsense is an affront to sensible people. Gypsies, really?" Emma said in feigned, superior tones. "Sheer stupidity, if you ask me."

John looked around the room. He sighted the ladies in question, all in different corners of the ballroom, all engaging in animated conversations with groups of tittering ladies. He did not, however, see Charlotte. "You may have miscalculated one factor in your stratagem," he told her.

"What is that?" she asked.

"Charlotte."

"How so?"

"What if Charlotte happens to hear one of these horrible rumors? Worse yet, what if she hears the truth?"

"Oh, Charlotte is fully aware of the game," Emma said. "She held an important role."

John was afraid to ask what sort of role Charlotte had played in this game. "Do not tell me, you had Charlotte attempting to spread her own rumors?"

"No, nothing like that," Emma assured him. A smile tugged at the corners of her mouth. "Not directly, anyway."

"How would Charlotte *indirectly* start rumors?"

"Charlotte was tasked with saying one vague, mysterious thing to each of her dance partners, but never the same thing twice, leaving them all guessing as to what sort of clue it may be to her true background. A Spanish word here. A reference to a storybook childhood there. She's been having such fun. She really is creative, that one."

The strains of the next piece of music reached them and John looked to the dancers to observe his sister in this unlikely task. "Where is she?" he asked.

Emma looked as well. "I don't see her. That's odd. This set was spoken for. She should be dancing."

Chapter Forty-One

Hugh charged into the ballroom and strode directly toward Charlotte. John Brantwood was a damned fool. What on earth was the bloody idiot thinking? Charlotte was his sister for God's sake.

He cleared his throat quite loudly once he reached her. "Lady Charlotte, you will need to come with me for a moment." When she only stared, he added, "Your brother has sent me to fetch you."

"But I am promised for the next set," Charlotte said. She turned to look at her present partner, but the young pup had managed to disappear into the assembled revelers.

He was probably intimidated. Possibly due to the frightening scowl Hugh had sent in his direction for just that purpose.

"You should come with me," he told her.

"Whatever for?"

God, she was lovely. Whoever had created that dress she wore was a cruel, cruel woman.

"Do not argue, Charlotte. Come with me. Do not make a scene of it. Just take my arm and I will lead you to your brother."

He led her to her brother's study, shut the door, and stood in front of it, barring any attempt to exit.

"Where is my brother?"

"I lied to you, Charlotte. Your brother is not here. I have brought you here because I will not allow you to return to that room full of jackals."

"Are you mad? You will not allow me to return to my own debut ball? You're ridiculous." She marched forward to stand in front of him and stared upward, considerably less intimidated by his scowls than the schoolboy she'd been dancing with. "Allow me to pass, immediately."

"You cannot go out there."

"Why not?"

"Your reputation is at stake."

One dubious eyebrow rose to register her disbelief in that statement. "I may not be an expert as yet with the rules of English high society, but I'm quite certain it is far more damaging to a young girl's reputation to be alone behind a closed door with a rakish gentleman than to be dancing in the middle of a ballroom with a hundred pairs of eyes watching."

God, she had no idea. His eyes raked over her. "It may be more dangerous to your virtue, love, but in this circumstance your reputation is far safer here."

Charlotte's confident expression faltered. She stepped back. "Why?"

He stepped forward. She would not cooperate unless he told her why, but he did not want to tell her. He wanted her to be daring and furious and alive with fire, as she usually was. He did not want her to see her meek, unsure, and saddened by the rejection of an entire society. "There is untrue gossip circulating about you. A lot of it. It is all quite damning to your reputation. I won't allow you to blindly move about in an entire room full of people who are so cruelly abusing you."

"Why do you care? You have been cruelly abusing me for weeks?"

His tone softened. "I won't let them hurt you, Charlotte. I will protect you."

Accusation flared in her sapphire eyes. "Don't look at me that way. Don't give me that pitying look." She crossed her arms tightly in front of her chest and cocked her head to one side. "I know what falsehoods are circulating about me. I also know which rumor is true, scandal or not. I worked in a kitchen. It's not as though I sold myself."

Hugh advanced slowly into the room, never taking his eyes from her. "A lady doesn't speak that way."

"You know I have never been and never will be a lady."

She said it as if it didn't matter, as though a lady were the last thing she'd ever aspire to be, but it was a lie. He'd have known that even if her eyes weren't glassy with unshed tears.

He stepped to her, took her fisted hands, opened them, and kept them captive as he beheld her. "You are a better lady than any of them will ever have a chance to be."

Charlotte sneered and tugged to free her hands, but he did not yield them. "It's a game," she said, her voice rising. "It's all a game the duchess devised. There were already too many rumors to start, so instead of attempting to quash them, we are adding to them, until there are so many and they are so ridiculous that no one could possibly believe them."

Hugh stared. "A game?"

"Why do they want so badly to find a scandal where there doesn't need to be one? Why am I working so hard to become one of those hateful people?"

Hugh stared down into the blue pools of pure misery and failed to find the words to relieve her distress. With no other way of giving her comfort, he released her hands and crushed her to him instead, cradling her head against his chest.

He waited for her to pull away, but she didn't. She released a small, muffled sob and clutched him tightly.

In that moment, he vowed revenge on every person who had ever dared to breathe a single disparaging word about this spirited, resilient, nymph-sized girl who'd never done anything to harm any one of them. He longed to lower his face to hers and kiss away every salty tear. He would take her into his arms the way he wanted and show her just how desirable she was, if only she wouldn't hate him for it.

Charlotte released a sigh. She lifted a hand to wipe at her tears.

Hugh reached down to place his hand beneath her chin and tilt her face to his. He meant to say something clever—something teasing that would raise her ire and pull her out of tear-soaked misery. He meant to be the hero.

Instead, he was the villain. He made the terrible mistake of crushing his lips to hers and pouring every bit of fierce protectiveness into bruising kisses as though the strength of his passion could somehow overcome any weakness to which she had succumbed.

To his wonderment, she did not resist. Her arms stole around his neck, and Charlotte—his Charlotte—returned his kisses as urgently as he gave them. Unable to turn away what she gave so sweetly, his hands slid down her back to where he could lift her bottom and hold her firmly against him.

For this moment, just this moment, he would believe he nobly provided what Charlotte so desperately needed, and not that he had taken callous advantage.

Chapter Forty-Two

"What the *bloody* hell?"

Emma had trailed John out of the ballroom, so she heard the curse before she saw its cause. She picked up her skirts and hurried after him.

She stopped short as soon as she passed through the door. Mr. Brydges stood in the middle of John's study, trying to push Charlotte behind him in an attempt to position himself between Charlotte and John. John stood just a few paces away from Emma and glared menacingly toward them both.

Emma's shoulders slumped Perhaps she should have alerted John to her suspicions regarding Mr. Brydges and Charlotte. She sighed. Discussions with her husband would have required time spent in his presence and she had not been allotted that this past week. "John, wait."

"I'll not wait," he roared, pointing frantically in the couple's direction. "I've just discovered my oldest friend accosting my sister! Have you no scruples, man? Take your hands off her."

Cringing at the volume of her husband's bellow, Emma rushed to close the door. Rumors were one thing; a scene with witnesses would be an entirely different matter.

Charlotte pushed herself out from behind Mr. Brydges. "John, stop. No one was accosted."

"Then you were a willing participant," he bellowed. "That is no better! Your family has been working to protect *your* reputation, and you sneak out in the middle of your debut to behave like a harlot!"

Mr. Brydges pushed Charlotte behind him again. He stepped forward and stared at John with cold, hard eyes. When he spoke, his words were slow and deliberate. "Old friend or no, you had better mind your manners in speaking of Charlotte."

John advanced on him. "Take your hands off her."

"Not while you're attacking her." His chin and chest rose. "You can accuse me of whatever you like, but you may accuse Charlotte of nothing. She was cast aside by her family as a child, forced to live like a pauper, and lost her mother only to be uprooted from everything she knows and dragged across the ocean so you could make her into an English lady then abandon her when she needed you most." His eyes flashed as he advanced another step. "Maybe I've mistreated her because I had no right to love her, but you've given up on her and you are supposed to love her."

John halted. He stared. "You love her." It was more revelation than question.

"You're damned right I love her."

"Well, you'd better bloody well marry her now," John thundered as he advanced on the two of them.

"Of course I plan to bloody well marry her," Mr. Brydges shouted back.

Charlotte stepped forward with hands on her hips and shouted at both of them. "Don't you think someone ought to bloody well ask *me*?"

Mr. Brydges turned his thunderous expression on Charlotte. "Well, are you going to marry me or aren't you?"

There was a pause. Charlotte gaped up at him as though she hadn't really expected him to do it. Then her arms flew around his neck and she peppered his face with laughing kisses. "Yes. Yes. Of course, yes."

John's stared mutely at the two of them. Then he turned to Emma, his complexion mottled with anger even while his eyes clouded with confusion. "Did you know about this?"

She stiffened. "I did."

He shook his head as though the jumbled thoughts might somehow fall in line, then his hands closed into fists in front of him. "How is it," he said through a clenched jaw, "that I have no bloody idea what the devil is going on in my own house!" His volume rose over the course of his question and culminated when he slammed the side of his fist against the bookcase.

Charlotte only gaped.

Brydges glared.

Emma hoped it hurt. She hoped it smarted for days. What did he want? She had given him what he asked. They had *all* given him what he professed to want. Charlotte's reputation was spared. Moreover, she was happy. *Happy?* She was delirious. She was clutching the arm of a man who had just vowed his fierce protection and declared his great love and desire to marry her.

But how could John understand that any woman might want that? A cage of bitterness clamped around her ridiculous hope of proving her worth to her blind, uncaring husband. The cage closed and tightened until she had nothing left but exasperation.

When she spoke into the silence, her voice was low and unfamiliar. "Clearly you didn't know. You have no idea what love looks like. How could you possibly recognize it under your very nose?" She spun on her heel and walked out. She was still the duchess. And she still had a ballroom full of people and rumors to quell.

Chapter Forty-Three

John paced. His head ached because he'd drunk too much scotch the night before. He should close his eyes to drown the dim light of his study. He should ring the bell and have someone bring him a cold damp cloth for his pounding skull.

But he paced. And became angry at himself for being contrary. To himself. *Damn.*

What reason had he to feel so disgruntled? It was done. He had done his part. Everyone had done their God damned part. Emma, in particular, had been brilliantly clever. Why didn't he feel relieved? Why was he plagued with restlessness?

There was a rap on the door.

"Come," he bade. He would ask for the damn cloth after all.

The door swung wide and slammed the wall opposite with a merciless thud. It reverberated through his throbbing head.

"There you are," Charlotte chirped at an excessively loud volume.

"Here I am," he confirmed unnecessarily. "I know why I am here. Why are you here?"

Charlotte ignored the question and approached, undaunted, sharp eyes peering at him. "You are worse than I thought."

He flashed her an annoyed look for her impertinence and retreated to the seat behind his desk. "I am fine, Charlotte," he said, making what he considered a noble attempt to keep the edge from his tone. "I am tired and my head aches. I need nothing more than the absence of company."

He chided himself as soon as the words were out. His foul mood was not due to Charlotte. It wasn't due to *anything* that he could discern.

Charlotte was too thick-skinned to be put off by his cantankerous mood or thinly veiled request for solitude. "I don't think you have any idea what you need," she said, calmly settling into a chair opposite his desk.

"Whatever does that mean?"

She smiled. "Let us begin another way," she suggested lightly, her mood impervious to the blackening influence of his own. "I've come to convey my gratitude. You've turned your entire life on its end for me. I may not have shown the proper gratitude all of the time, but I wish to show it now. I am beyond fortunate to have you as my brother. And as I am currently rather pleased with my situation, which I owe in no small part to you. I thank you."

That made him feel churlish. Now he was grumpy with himself for behaving like an ass. "You're welcome," he said gruffly. "I am sorry for my rudeness. It is only the ache in my head."

Her lip pursed and drew to one side in an expression of patent disbelief.

She exhaled, rearranged her shoulders, and lay clasped hands in her lap. "Very well, then. Now it is your turn."

She waited.

"Turn for what?" he asked.

"Your turn to thank me."

He stared. His head was addled. "For what, precisely, am I to extend my gratitude?"

"Just as you have rearranged my life in a way I find satisfactory to me, I have rearranged yours in a way that should be satisfactory to you."

"Have you now?" he asked. He was certain he would feel quite satisfied as soon as his headache dissipated, but he could hardly credit Charlotte with such an event.

Charlotte rose. Her pert expression tempered to one of pleading as she circled the desk to stand at his side as he sat and place one hand on his shoulder. "You're my brother and I love you. I am the only family you have left, so I believe the task falls upon me to inform you that you are an ass."

He turned and half-rose in his chair. "What?"

She released a beleaguered sigh. "You have the lucky fortune of accidentally marrying your love match. Please don't follow in father's footsteps," she pleaded.

He slammed palms on the desk and rose all the way this time. "I assure you, I have no intention of following in father's footsteps."

"Good," she said with a firm nod. She returned to the other side of the desk, leaving him standing there.

How could she even think he would become like their father? It cut deep that she thought it even worthy to point out.

Her expression held nothing but pure sincerity as she paused at the door to his study. "Father had a love match and he squandered it. He pushed her away. All the way to Boston. I do hope you don't squander yours, John. Don't repeat his mistake."

Charlotte pulled the heavy door shut behind her as she quit the room.

John stared at the door as though it might open and provide some greater clarity with which to evaluate her parting sentiments.

He pushed her away. Don't repeat his mistake.

* * *

Emma wasn't entirely sure what to do with herself. She wasn't lacking things to do, precisely, just the inclination to do them. Her growing pile of notes and invitations would be a reasonable place to start, but she wasn't in a mood for correspondence.

She made a face at the pile.

Nothing that occurred to her as an outlet for her attention seemed likely to succeed in calming the tumult in her heart and her mind, despite her desperate need for it. Peace and calm. The particular brand of peace she sought today was resignation and acceptance. Her part was finished. All had been well at Charlotte's debut. It had been entirely as scripted. Just as the rumors had enveloped the room early in the evening, so had the attitude, hours later, that so many ridiculous stories were just imaginative nonsense. Charlotte danced each dance—smiling, beautiful, and mysterious.

The last dance had been reserved for Mr. Brydges. No formal announcement had been made that evening, but the fact that both were spoken-for could not have been clearer upon their faces.

It had all gone exactly as it should have gone for Charlotte, and Emma was truly glad for her sister-in-law. She should be content, yet she had spent all morning chasing the elusive serenity in the small park at the center of the square over which Worley House presided. It was not quite a garden. It was certainly not *her* garden, but living things grew there and she had thought the surroundings might calm her emotions.

She had wandered at first, circling the space to investigate the few trees that populated it. Then she had found a small metal bench and simply contemplated.

Therein had been the trouble. She had found contemplation, rather than distraction, and thus no peace at all. She had returned to the house for a light luncheon, learned the duke had gone out, and spent much of the afternoon staring blindly at the pages of a novel she had located in the library.

She disliked this feeling—as though she were hungry for something in particular, but could not name the food and so could only go unsatisfied. No distraction seemed worthwhile.

She rose from her seat at the writing desk, letters still untouched and moved half-heartedly to the sofa. Perhaps, she thought, if the duke was still out, she should just take her supper in her room and retire for the evening. In the morning, she would be more ambitious in arranging for distraction. Perhaps she and Charlotte could call upon Aunt Agatha.

She had just decided that, yes, she would definitely call upon Aunt Agatha in the morning when she heard voices in the hall.

"Is the duchess in the library?" she heard her husband ask.

"In the front sitting room, Your Grace," came the reply.

Emma rose, anticipating his entry, and felt a moment of frustration for the quickening of her pulse.

He walked into the room and caught her eyes with a look of determined purpose that seemed a warning. He strode to her and reached out to take her hands. His eyes caught hers and she was struck by the passion she saw there before he lowered his mouth to kiss her.

He kissed her thoroughly. He let go of her hands and placed his upon her waist, pulling her more firmly against him. She yielded to his passion completely, slipping her hands around him and returning his ardor, measure for measure. He released her mouth and dropped his lips to her throat and then to the swell of her décolletage. When he captured her mouth again, he placed his hand where his lips had been, teasing and cupping one breast through her gown until her nipple pebbled beneath his touch.

When she was absolutely certain she cared not one whit for peace or serenity or the possibility of someone walking into the parlor to find them, he pulled away, leaving her breathless and brain-addled. He stood one pace away and stared at her hungrily, as though at a signal from her, it would begin again.

She placed a hand over her chest as it rose and fell and felt her pulse pounding there. "I...were you...was there something you needed, then?" Her voice was weak for lack of breath.

He shook his head. "I will muddle the words, Emma. Before I did, I wanted to make my point more eloquently."

"I'm not sure I understand."

His lips turned upward. "I could explain again."

She held up a staying hand. "Let us try the words this time."

He reached forward and took her hand. He didn't use it to pull her into his embrace as before, but held it as he gazed warmly down at her. "I owe you an apology."

"I've been so determined not to succumb to foolishness that I've been an even greater fool than I'd feared."

It seemed a riddle she couldn't solve. "Foolish, how?" she asked.

He backed away and raised a single finger. "Wait here."

He darted from the room and returned moments later with a small copper pot. Rising from the pot was a white flower on a tall stem. He held it out to her.

"What is this?" she asked.

"It is my apology," he said, still extending the pot toward her.

She gazed at the unfamiliar flower. It was a single, tall green stem with one large, dark green leaf and the most graceful white flower she had ever seen. It was a single, fluted petal around a thick yellow stamen. Only the petal was longer on one side, as though if she held it upside down, it would resemble a skirt with a train.

"Where did it come from?" she asked, finally accepting the pot from him. She set it on the side table and seated herself next to it, to examine it more closely.

"From the botanist at Kew Gardens. He assures me it's quite exotic. It's an Ethiopian Calla."

A calla lily. She'd heard of them. How lovely and graceful it was.

She looked up at her husband. "Thank you," she said humbly. "It's truly lovely."

"It's not an entire garden and I know a piece of your heart will always reside there, but perhaps this can be the place where a piece of your heart begins to reside too," he said, lowering himself next to her on the sofa.

"I have been a prize fool," he said, taking her hands in his. "My father's jealousy and possessiveness toward my mother destroyed this family. I was convinced the only way to keep from repeating his mistake was to make certain I did not fall insensibly in love with my wife."

Emma's eyes and heart fell in unison. "I see."

John set his finger below her chin and forced her eyes to meet his again. "In the end, my choice of wife could not have been more perfect for championing Charlotte. For keeping my indifference, however, it seems I have made a poor choice."

Emma's breath caught. "Have you?" she asked, her voice barely more than a whisper.

John stepped closer and slipped his arms around her waist. "I have worked very diligently to remain detached from you, Emma, but have failed in every respect. The more I have avoided your company, the more I have longed for it." He held her eyes captive with a gaze that nearly melted her with its heat and intensity. "I realized today—with Charlotte's help—that I had it all reversed."

"Reversed?" she asked, barely able to voice the word.

"When I have been angry with you, you have been calm. When I have been irrational, you have been my reason. When I was defeated, you were victorious. You are not my folly, Emma. You are my balance. You are my sanity. You are precisely what I need, whenever I need it, and I don't want to waste another moment not believing it. I love you, Emma." He placed a gentle kiss on her forehead.

She leaned into it. Eyes closed, his lips still pressed to her skin, she murmured, "Oh, John, I thought I was the foolish one—to hope that I might ever hear those words." She smiled. "They are just as wonderful as I thought they would be."

"I love you," he said again.

She clutched his strong hands in hers and kissed each one of them. "I love you too."

"Of course you don't," he said, pulling back to gaze at her again. He grinned sheepishly. "I am foolishly, insensibly, ridiculously in love with a woman who only married me out of pity for my sister and the convenience of my proximity to her cottage."

Emma laughed, even as tears of love and joy pooled in her eyes. "And the title," she reminded him as his mouth descended toward hers. "Do not forget the title."

**Keep reading for a sneak peek
at Lucy's upcoming adventure in**

THE OFFER

Coming soon from

Lyrical Books

Lucy left Emma's room and walked to the drawing room to recover both the book and shawl she had abandoned there prior to Emma's sudden malady. As she walked, she lamented the loss of the opportunity to apply for the position of governess to the Ashby girls. She had never met Lord or Lady Ashby, but if Emma considered them friends, they were surely good, decent people. Though Lucy was reconciled to taking a position, she most definitely wished to avoid one in which she would be ill treated.

Several days had passed since Lady Ashby had mentioned to Emma her intent to employ a governess. She may well have already begun assessing potential candidates. If Emma insisted upon waiting much longer to aid Lucy in finding a position, this particular post was sure to be already taken.

Lucy sighed loudly as she turned the handle and pushed open one of the painted paneled doors that led to the drawing room, noting the household staff had efficiently whisked away the remnants of tea and closed up the room after she and Emma had fled so suddenly earlier. She crossed the room to retrieve the shawl and book and, as she did so, walked through a slanted column of light caused by the late afternoon sun shining through the windows. Each of the three tall windows opposite the door created such a column, giving the room odd, striped bands of shadow and light.

Lucy had not seen the room in such a state before. Sunlight saturated the room at midday, when it was commonly used, and by dinnertime lit tapers in the sconces would provide a weaker but equally warm source of light.

The household staff saw it this way. They saw it striped in fading afternoon sun, or fully engulfed in darkness before the sun rose or fires were lit. The tentacles of this thought took an odd, fixating hold on her. Was Emma right to caution her so sharply? Was she entering an entirely new realm? Lucy had never lived a life of privilege or luxury, but neither had she ever been a servant. Modest living and domestic service were two very different things.

It was only common sense to understand the lives of some occupants in this house would be unrecognizably different to the others depending on their station. Same house. Entirely different worlds.

She shook her head at the silly thought. She was already in a different world. She was a simple vicar's daughter. She was no duchess, nor the daughter of a peer. Her life would not be unrecognizable because she came into a household like this one at a lesser station. Life at the parsonage house had never been so segmented. She was both family *and* domestic there, as were her mother and father.

As she picked up the book and shawl, she looked down and noted how the line between light and dark slashed across the front of her dress.

Where had all this fanciful thinking come from? Emma, well-intentioned though she may be, was wrong—Lucy was perfectly suited to a position as a governess. Yet, after one pleading conversation, here she stood, dancing in shadows, questioning her entire future.

My goodness. She shook her head. She was too practical for that.

She stared unseeingly at the shadow-striped floor and tapped her fingers on the cracked spine of her book. Emma would come around. She always eventually came around to Lucy's sensible view of things. It was one of Emma's best attributes, really. But would it be too late? Here—this evening—was a very good opportunity with a very good family.

Hmmm. She shifted her weight between her feet and continued the rhythmic tap of her fingers along the book in her hands. Perhaps all was not lost and she could at least build some sort of a start. She could not very well introduce the topic of needing a position at dinner, of course, but perhaps she could offer to play—exhibit her qualifications in pianoforte. Then the evening would not be a total loss.

"Are you lost?"

Good heavens.

Lucy spun about to discover she was not alone in the drawing room. She blinked. A man rose from a chair in the shadow-shrouded corner of the room and took several steps toward her. She could not make out all the details of his features, but he was tall and finely dressed.

She blinked again and looked back at the doorway through which she had come. Had he been there the entire time and she'd not even noticed him?

A heavy weight began to congeal inside her. She'd been staring at shadows and daydreaming like a ninny and had made a perfect idiot of herself in front of none other than Lord Ashby.

"I beg your pardon, my lord," she said in her most sensible tone, rushing to repair his impression that she must be a half-wit. "I was just retrieving my things. I had not realized the dinner hour was so nearly upon us."

"Oh, I don't believe it is upon us quite yet," he said. "Worley summoned me early so that we might meet before dinner."

His response was not unkindly given, and the tightness that had bunched around Lucy's neck and shoulders upon his greeting unwound a bit—though not entirely. Of course he had come early to meet with the duke. They were political allies, were they not? They must meet regularly. Where was her head? If Lord Ashby had arrived only for dinner, he would be accompanied by his wife.

"It appears His Grace is a bit delayed, however," he said, stepping forward into the slash of light.

"I apologize for disturbing you," she said, nodding politely and gathering her book and shawl more tightly to her. She was conscious of wanting to make a positive impression with Lord Ashby, but how precisely did one going about doing such a thing after he had caught her woolgathering?

"I have the sense it is I who has disturbed your private thoughts, rather than you disturbing mine."

Lucy groaned inwardly and felt the flush rising in her cheeks. "I do beg your pardon, my lord. It seems I was preoccupied."

"No apology is necessary."

He smiled at her. It was not a dismissal. It was...kind. Perhaps she *hadn't* disturbed him. Perhaps he had waited some time and was happy for the distraction, however insignificant. He stepped back slightly and, even in the dim light, Lucy could see it was to allow his eyes to drop all the way to her feet before returning to her face as he took in her full measure. She squared her shoulders and did her best to appear both pleasant and deferential, as she presumed one should when being evaluated by a prospective employer.

"Are you always such a daydreamer?" he asked finally.

"I am not," she assured him firmly. "I am usually quite sensible, as a matter of fact. I have always been reliable, I assure you. My mother has relied upon me from a very young age in aiding her in her work with parishioners in my village. I was never wayward or flighty as a child."

A smile tilted the corners of his mouth. "No?"

"No, my lord, not at all."

His only response was a mildly dubious lift of one brow. How was it that lords always managed to seem so...lordly? Lucy had simply stopped gaining height at the age of thirteen. She had felt small compared to nearly every person she had ever met, but compared to this broad-shouldered man who towered over her in heavy boots and dark coat, she felt positively elfin. How did one project competence and sensibility under these conditions?

"You are probably wondering who I am," she said. "My name is Lucy Betancourt. I am..." She paused. She had begun to say she was a friend of the duchess, but amended her words. "I am at Worley House as companion to the duchess during her confinement." Better that he see her as an employee, rather than a friend of the family.

"I am sure she is quite grateful for your companionship."

"Thank you, my lord." Perhaps because he seemed so kind, or perhaps because his expectant look demanded some continuation of the conversation, she added, "I am sorry to have intruded upon your wait, my lord, but perhaps it is fortuitous that I have done so." Lucy smiled brightly at him, then faltered. Would Lord and Lady Ashby would prefer a stern governess?

She amended her expression to a more neutral, less happy one. It would not do to appear overeager, after all.

She thought idly as she stood, not quite smiling, not quite scowling at the man, that Lady Ashby must be a particularly lovely woman. He was handsome enough to have set thousands of lashes fluttering across London before he was married, and with his title to match, he would have had his pick of any lady. His eyes were the dark gray of smoldering coals.

Those eyes, she realized, were staring at her in patent confusion. "Fortuitous in what manner?" he inquired.

She immediately regretted her choice to speak boldly, though the quirk of his brow did appear more amused than annoyed. There was no help for it now.

In for a penny, as they say...

"I am so terribly sorry to be presumptuous, my lord. I mean only that I am...that is, circumstances are such that I find I must..." Her flush deepened. Lucy looked up at the imposingly tall man with dark eyes and hair too perfectly unstudied to be accidental and knew without question that she was making an absolute fool of herself.

She had to get through it now that she had begun. Pleasant, but not eager, she reminded herself. Serious, but not stern. "As a matter of fact, I had hoped for an introduction as...well, you see, once I am no longer needed here, I will be in need of another position."

She felt the heat in her cheeks rising and concentrating into burning splotches. Even as she knew she appeared more foolish with every word, she continued speaking, somehow unable to stop. "My Lord," she said, stepping forward, "I apologize. It was very unconventional and impulsive for me to approach you in this manner, and I am sorry for it. It was poorly done of me, but I assure you I am not usually impulsive. I had hoped to make a positive impression when first we met." She smiled bravely up at him, wishing fervently that he would somehow at least see the good intention behind her error.

Again, the eyebrow danced. This time his dark eyes danced as well. "Did you, now?" he asked, seeming more curious now that she'd explained.

She relaxed just a bit. At least he could see the humor in it. She considered it a boon that she had not been summarily dismissed. "Of course, my lord. I'm sure you can understand my desire to gain your favorable opinion."

"You desire *my* favorable opinion?"

"Certainly." She tilted her head to the side and peered up at him. "On what other basis would you select me, my lord?"

* * *

Select her?

Bex Brantwood peered down at the pixie-sized person who stared back up at him with wide frost-blue eyes that matched her frock and decided he must have misheard the girl. "Select you?" he asked.

She bit her lip, drawing his gaze to her mouth, which was just as sweetly pink as her cheeks at that very moment. She looked like a fairy sprite—an odd, nonsensical fairy sprite who had wandered distractedly into the room and then calmly requested that he *select* her.

Select her for what?

"You seem to know considerably more of me than I know of you," he observed.

"Oh, of course, my lord," she gushed, clasping her hands in front of her. "How thoughtless of me." She ran her hands down the front of her frock and took a deep inhale of air before beginning. "I am the only daughter of the vicar in the village of Beadwell. I am a longtime acquaintance of the Duchess of Worley. I play both the pianoforte and harp and am widely read. At four and twenty, I have recently concluded that it is well past time I cease to be a burden to my parents and make some arrangement for my future, so you can understand how fortuitous it was to learn that your visit to the duke and duchess would be coinciding with my own."

She exhaled. Good lord, how did she have breath left after that soliloquy?

He said nothing. So that was it. The poor vicar's daughter from the local village had decided to arrange for her future and was importuning *him* to become that arrangement. So much boldness for such a little thing. At least she was honest. That was a bit braver than most girls who might have tried to lure him into a situation that compromised her and forced his hand.

Honesty or not, she had chosen the wrong mark. Security was the last thing he had to offer anyone. All attempts at marital arrangements concerning Bexley Brantwood had come to a definitive halt the previous year when his cousin, the true duke, had returned to claim the title. Clearly this poor girl was too naïve to realize Bex's only remaining friends were gamblers, ladies of the night, and unscrupulous money lenders.

"I applaud you, dear, for your sensibility in addressing your future. You are young and pretty. Marriage to some amiable and stable young gentleman is, of course, what you should consider. For precisely that reason, I am unable to be of any assistance to you. I do wish you success in your pursuit." With the briefest of smiles meant to punctuate the end of their conversation, Bex stepped aside so that she might be allowed to exit the room.

She remained standing in place, her eyes growing large as she comprehended his response. "Oh, no, my lord. I understand you might have concerns about taking me on if you believed I intended to marry, but I am much more…practical…than that." Her cheeks flushed again and her smile took on a self-deprecating asymmetry. "I am well aware that without any family connections or dowry my marriage prospects are dismal indeed. When added to the fact that I am limited to my small village with no gentleman of marriageable age and the lack of funds for even a local season…I…well, I am resigned to my circumstances, sir." She averted her eyes, but he could see the way her cheeks flamed to be laying bare these truths of her situation. "I understand I must be practical about my future and pursue other arrangements."

Other arrangements? *Christ.* What had he stumbled into? Was this angelic sprite of a vicar's daughter actually offering herself up to him as his mistress? Bex had received such offers in the past, but they were veiled invitations from the jaded London set, not blushing, flustered proposals from the daughters of country gentlemen.

She was very becoming in the way that a china doll is becoming—all pale porcelain and disastrously fragile. Her frost-blue eyes were anything but cold, however. They were quick. They darted everywhere and expressed everything. They had none of the veiled mystery she would need if she truly expected to spend her prettiest years moving from one protector to the next based upon their pocketbook rather than their likeability.

He tilted his head to one side. "So you've given up entirely on the prospect of marriage, have you?"

She nodded vehemently. "I have, my lord, and I assure you, I am quite enthusiastic about this next endeavor."

Bex couldn't help it. He threw his head back and laughed aloud. This was becoming absurd. If he were a good man—a truly, good man—he would pat her on the head, send her on her way, and perhaps even have a good talk with her father once he'd done so.

Frankly, whatever she thought she knew of his reputation was inflated and he couldn't afford her anyway, but still his conscience could not find any objection to at least humoring the girl for a few more minutes just to see what else she might say. She'd told him about her skill at the harp, for God's sake. Who gave a fig whether their mistress could play the damned harp?

"You're a bold bit of cake, aren't you?"

She managed to look genuinely confused at his question. She took a small step backward. "I…I apologize," she said. "I realize it was unforgivably impertinent of me to approach you."

Don't back away now, you little minx, he thought. *Not now that you've put the proposal to me and I've not yet answered.* She bit her lower lip and the action caught his attention. She was lovely. He had never been particularly drawn to the sweet and innocent, but never had it been offered up to him so audaciously. He regretted that he could not afford her in that moment, watching how her pink lower lip slid temptingly from the hold of white teeth. If he could, he would be quite tempted to accept.

Of course, she may not be as innocent as she appeared. It was very likely, he reasoned, that she was ruined already. That would certainly make a respectable marriage unlikely, wouldn't it? He looked at her again, hints of her dainty shape visible beneath her prim pastel gown. He wondered whether her boldness would manifest itself in the bedroom, then the unexpected thought captured his imagination.

His body heated at the visions that assailed him and he stepped toward her. "I respect your self-sufficiency and…shall we say, ingenuity… Miss Betancourt. I cannot in good conscience deny you without a fair trial," he coaxed.

She eyed him warily. "A fair trial?" she asked. "I'm not sure what you mean?"

"A sample of your skills, perhaps?" he said, warming more and more to the idea.

"My skills?" she asked, her eyes wide with uncertainty. "I…I could play for you, I suppose."

His grin widened. "I do not require a musical audition." The more wolfish he felt, the more visibly apprehensive she became. She had approached him, had she not?

"There are more applicable skills to consider," he said, and catching her around her doll-sized waist with one arm, he dropped his mouth to hers in a searing kiss.

ABOUT THE AUTHOR

Sara Portman is an award-winning author of historical and contemporary romance. Her debut historical romance, *The Reunion*, was named the 2015 winner in the Historical Category of the Romance Writers of America Golden Heart contest. A daughter of the Midwest, Sara was born in Illinois, grew up in Michigan, and currently lives in Ohio. In addition to her writing endeavors, Sara is a wife and mother in a large, blended family. When not reading or dreaming up romantic fiction, Sara works in corporate finance by day. As part of her academic experience, Sara spent a semester studying in London, England. Her anglophile tendencies continue today. Visit her at www.saraportman.com.

CPSIA information can be obtained
at www.ICGtesting.com
Printed in the USA
LVOW12s0256210917
549508LV00001B/76/P